# GHO

Autocannon fire blasted into the heathen nightmares, sustained heavy fire from an angle nearby. Gaunt turned, and saw the boy, the piper with the fish tattoo. He was laying down an arc of covering fire from the portico of the silo bay with a sentry's autocannon that he had rested across the stonework. 'Get in! The last cutter's waiting for you!' cried the boy.

Gaunt threw himself through the bay doors into the fierce whirlwind of the cutter's engine backwash. The side hatch was just closing and he scrambled through, losing the tails of his coat to the biting hinge.

Enemy weapons fire resounded off the hull.

'Open the door again!' Gaunt yelled. 'Open it again!'

None of them moved to do so. Gaunt hauled himself up and heaved on the hatch lever. The door thumped open and the boy scrambled inside.

Gaunt dragged him clear of the hatch and yanked it shut. 'Now!' he bellowed down the cabin to the pilot's bay. 'Go now if you're going!'

The cutter rose from the tower bay hard and fast, lifter jets screaming as they were jammed into overdrive. Left to die, the forests burned.

A WARHAMMER 40,000 NOVEL

## Gaunt's Ghosts

# GHOSTMAKER

## Dan Abnett

*For Craig, who was there with Nova, long ago.*

**A BLACK LIBRARY PUBLICATION**

First published in Great Britain in 2000.

This edition published in 2004 by
BL Publishing,
Games Workshop Ltd.,
Willow Road, Nottingham,
NG7 2WS, UK.

10 9 8 7 6 5 4 3 2 1

Cover illustration by Adrian Smith.

A CIP record for this book is available from the British Library.

ISBN 1 84416 165 X

Distributed in the US by Simon & Schuster
1230 Avenue of the Americas, New York, NY 10020, US.

Printed and bound in Great Britain by
Cox & Wyman Ltd, Reading, Berkshire, UK.

See the Black Library on the Internet at
**www.blacklibrary.com**

Find out more about Games Workshop
and the world of Warhammer 40,000 at
**www.games-workshop.com**

IT IS THE 41st millennium. For more than a hundred centuries the Emperor has sat immobile on the Golden Throne of Earth. He is the master of mankind by the will of the gods, and master of a million worlds by the might of his inexhaustible armies. He is a rotting carcass writhing invisibly with power from the Dark Age of Technology. He is the Carrion Lord of the Imperium for whom a thousand souls are sacrificed every day, so that he may never truly die.

YET EVEN IN his deathless state, the Emperor continues his eternal vigilance. Mighty battlefleets cross the daemon-infested miasma of the warp, the only route between distant stars, their way lit by the Astronomican, the psychic manifestation of the Emperor's will. Vast armies give battle in his name on uncounted worlds. Greatest amongst his soldiers are the Adeptus Astartes, the Space Marines, bio-engineered super-warriors. Their comrades in arms are legion: the Imperial Guard and countless planetary defence forces, the ever-vigilant Inquisition and the tech-priests of the Adeptus Mechanicus to name only a few. But for all their multitudes, they are barely enough to hold off the ever-present threat from aliens, heretics, mutants – and worse.

TO BE A man in such times is to be one amongst untold billions. It is to live in the cruellest and most bloody regime imaginable. These are the tales of those times. Forget the power of technology and science, for so much has been forgotten, never to be re-learned. Forget the promise of progress and understanding, for in the grim dark future there is only war. There is no peace amongst the stars, only an eternity of carnage and slaughter, and the laughter of thirsting gods.

I NHERITING COMMAND *of the Sabbat Worlds Crusade force from the late and lauded Warmaster Slaydo, Warmaster Macaroth renewed the Imperial offensive to liberate the Sabbat Worlds, a cluster of nearly one hundred inhabited systems along the edge of the Segmentum Pacificus.*

*'Many legendary actions distinguished that twenty year campaign, and many legends were made: the last stand of the Latarii Gundogs at Lamicia, the Iron Snakes' victories at Presarius, Ambold Eleven and Fornax Aleph, and the dogged prosecution of the enemy by the so-called Ghosts of Tanith on Canemara, Spurtis Elipse, Menezoid Epsilon and Monthax. Of these, perhaps Monthax presents the most intriguing question for Imperial historians. Ostensibly a head-on confrontation with the forces of Chaos, this action is clouded in mystery and the details are still sequestered in the archives of Imperial High Command. Only speculation remains as to what truly occurred on the tangled shores of that hideous battle site.'*

— from *A History of the Later Imperial Crusades*

IT WAS SUMMER here, apparently.

Intermittent but heavy rain sluiced the Imperium lines from a sky wrinkled with grey cloud cover. Barbed, twisted root-plants with florid, heavy leaves groped their way out of every inch of muddy land and poked from the shimmering waterbeds too. As land went, most of it had gone. Lagoons and long pools of sheened water forked through the groves of undergrowth, home to billowing micro-flies and unseen, chirruping insects.

There was a smell in the air, a smell like rank sweat. The smell didn't surprise Colonel-Commissar Ibram Gaunt. What did surprise him was that it wasn't coming from his men. It was exuding from the water, the plants, the mud. Monthax reeked of corruption and rot.

There was no digging-in on Monthax. Trenches were raised abutments of imported flak-board and locally cut timber. Levees and sand-bagged walls had been dug out and raised by the Ghosts. For three days, since the drop-ships landed them, there had been no other sound except the squelch of entrenching tools as work parties filled plastic sacks. No other sound except the chirrup of a billion insects.

Seeping sweat into his freshly-donned tunic from the moment he had it on, Gaunt emerged from his command shed, a three chamber modular habitat staked up on girder poles out of the soupy water. He put his commissar's cap squarely on his head, knowing full well that it would make sweat run into his eyes. He wore high boots, breeches and a tunic shirt, carrying his weatherproof overcoat over his shoulders. It was too hot to wear it, too wet to go without.

Ibram Gaunt stepped down off the shed steps and his feet settled in satin-skinned water twenty centimetres deep. He paused. The oily ripples ebbed away and he looked down at himself. A reflected Gaunt lay horizontal in the rank water at his feet. Tall, lean, with a sculpted, high-cheeked face that ironically mocked his name.

He looked away, up, through the fleshy leaves of the thickets and the coiled low cover of the plant growth. On the horizon, partly screened by sweating mist, firepower roared back and forth as Imperial gunnery duelled with the heavy artillery of Chaos.

He strode forward through the slushy water, up through the dry land of an islet thick with tendrils and overhanging flowers, and along a duck-board walkway towards the lines.

Behind a long, meandering, S-shaped embankment levee three kilometres long, the Tanith First-and-Only stood ready. They had raised this dyke themselves, armouring it with rapidly decaying planks of flak-board. Artificial mounds had been dug behind the defence to keep ammo piles out of the water. His men stood ready in fire-teams, fifteen hundred strong, dressed in the black capes and dull body-armour uniform that was their signature. Some stood at eyeholes in the dyke, guns fixed. Others manned heavy weapon nests. Others stood and smoked and chatted and speculated. All stood in at least fifteen centimetres of murky slime.

The bivouacs, also raised on girder legs out of the swamp, were set back from the dyke line by about thirty metres. Little sanctuaries of dryness lifted out of the ooze.

Gaunt wandered along the dyke to the first group of men, who were digging up a footstep by the dyke wall from mud spaded out of the waterline.

Whooping birds swung overhead, large-winged and stark-white with folded, gangly pink legs. The insects chirruped.

Sweat made half moons in the underarms of his tunic in less than a dozen paces. Flies stung him. All thoughts of future glory, of the bitter action to come, left Ibram Gaunt's mind. Instead, the echoes came. The memories.

Gaunt cursed quietly, wiped his brow. It was days like this, in the slow, loaded hours while they waited for combat, that the memories flooded back at their most intense. Of the past, of lost comrades and missed friends, of glories and defeats long gone, of ends.

And of beginnings…

# ONE
# GHOSTMAKER

FIRE, LIKE A FLOWER. *Blossoming. Pale, greenish fire, scuttling like it was alive. Eating the world, the whole world…*

Opening his eyes, Ibram Gaunt, Imperial commissar, gazed into his own lean, pale face.

Trees, as dark green as an ocean at night, rushed past behind his eyes.

'We're making the final approach now, sir.'

Gaunt looked round, away from his reflection in the small, thick port of the orbital cutter, and saw his adjutant, Sym. Sym was an efficient man of middle years, his slightly puffy flesh marked across the throat and cheek by a livid, ancient burn.

'I said, we're making the final approach,' Sym repeated.

'I heard you,' Gaunt nodded gently. 'Remind me again of the schedule.'

Sym sat back in his padded leather G-chair and perused a data-slate. 'Official greeting ceremony. Formal introductions to the Elector of Tanith and the government assembly. Review of the Founding regiments. And a formal dinner tonight.'

Gaunt's gaze drifted back to the vast forests that flew by under the window. He hated the trappings of pomp and protocol, and Sym knew it.

'Tomorrow, sir, the transfer shifts begin. We'll have all the regiments aboard and ready to embark before the end of the week,' the man said, trying to put a more positive spin on things.

Gaunt didn't look round but said, 'See if you can get the transfers to begin directly after the review. Why waste the rest of today and tonight?'

Sym nodded, thoughtful. 'That should be possible.'

A soft chime signalled imminent landfall, and they both felt the sudden pull of deceleration g-forces. The other passengers in the craft's long cabin: an astropath, silent in his robes, and officials of the Adeptus Ministorum and the Departmento Munitorium, began to buckle their harnesses and settle back for landing. Sym found himself looking out of the port, watching the endless forests that so intrigued Gaunt.

'Strange place this, this Tanith. So they say.' He rubbed his chin. 'They say the forests move. Change. The trees apparently… uhm… shift. According to the pilot, you can get lost in the woods in a matter of minutes.'

Sym's voice dropped to a whisper. 'They say it's a touch of Chaos! Can you believe that? They say Tanith has a touch of Chaos, being this close to the Edge, you see.'

Gaunt did not reply.

THE SPIRES AND towers of Tanith Magna rose to meet the small barbed shape of the cutter. The city, set here amid the endless oceans of evergreen trees, looked from the air like a complex circle of standing stones, dark grey slabs raised in a clearing in defiance of the forest around. Banners and brazier smoke fluttered from the higher fortress walls, and outside the city perimeter, Gaunt could see a vast plain cut from the forest. Row upon row of tents stood there, thousands of them, each with its own cookfire. The Founding Fields.

Beyond the tent-town, the huge black shadows of the bulk transports, whale-mouths and belly ramps open, squatting in fire-blackened craters of earth, ready to eat up the men and the machines of the new regiments of Tanith. His regiments, he reminded himself, the first Imperial Guard regiments to be founded on this enigmatic, sparsely populated frontier world.

For eight years, Gaunt had served as political officer with the Hyrkan 8th, a brave regiment that he had been with from its founding on the windy hills of Hyrkan to the ferocious victory of Balhaut. But so many had fallen, and another founding would fill familiar uniforms with unfamiliar faces. It was time to move on, and Gaunt had felt grateful to be reassigned. His seniority, his experience… his very notoriety made him an ideal choice to whip the virgin units of Tanith into shape. Part of him, a young, eager but small part deep inside, relished the prospect of building a fresh name for the Guard's roll of honour. But the rest of him was dull, set rigid, empty. More than anything, he felt he was simply going through the motions.

He had felt that way since Slaydo's death. The old commander would have wanted him here, wanted him to carry on to glory… after all, wasn't that why he'd made his gift? Promoting him there, on the firefields of Balhaut, to colonel-commissar… making him one of the few political officers in the Guard capable of commanding a regiment. Such trust, such faith. But Gaunt was so tired. It didn't seem much like a reward now.

The cutter dipped. Great brass shutters atop one of the city's largest towers hinged open like an orchid's petals to receive it.

ON THE FOUNDING Fields, the men looked up as the approaching cutter purred overhead, banked against the slow cloud and settled like a beetle over the city wall towards the landing tower.

'Someone important,' noted Larkin, squinting up at the sky. He spat on the wirecloth in his hand and resumed polishing his webbing buckles.

'Just more traffic. More pompous off-worlders.' Rawne lay back and turned his face to the sun.

Corbec, stood by his tent, shielded his eyes against the glare and nodded. 'I think Larkin's right. Someone important. There was a big Guard crest on the flank of that flier. Someone come for the Founding Review. Maybe this colonel-commissar himself.'

He dropped his gaze and looked about. On either side of him, the rows of three-man tents stretched away in ordered files, and guardsmen in brand new uniforms sat around, cleaning kit, stripping guns, eating, dicing, smoking, sleeping.

Six thousand men, all told, mostly infantry but some artillery and armoured crews, three whole regiments and men of Tanith all.

Corbec sat down by his own cook stove and rubbed his hands. His new, black-cloth uniform chafed at the edges of his big frame. It would be the very devil to wear in. He looked across at his tent-mates, Larkin and Rawne. Larkin was a slender, whipcord man with a dagger face. Like all the Tanith, he was pale-skinned and black-haired. Larkin had dangerous eyes like blue fire, a left ear studded with three silver hoops, and a blue spiral-wyrm tattoo on his right cheek. Corbec had known him for a good while: they had served together in the same unit of the Tanith Magna militia before the Founding. He knew Larkin's strengths – a marksman's eyes and a brave heart – and his weaknesses – an unstable character, easily rattled.

Rawne he did not know as well. Rawne was a handsome devil, his clean, sleek features decorated by a tattoo starburst over one eye. He had been a junior officer in the militia of Tanith Attica, or one of the other southern cities, but he didn't talk about it much. Corbec had a bad feeling there was a murderous, ruthless streak under Rawne's oily charm.

Bragg – huge, hulking, genial Bragg – shuffled over from his tent, a flask of hot sacra in his hands. 'Need warming up?' he asked and Corbec nodded a smile to the giant man. Bragg poured four cups, and passed one to Larkin, who barely looked up but muttered thanks, and one to Rawne, who said nothing as he knocked it back.

'You reckon that was our commissar, then?' Bragg said at last, asking the question Corbec knew he had been dying to get out since overhearing Corbec's remark.

Corbec sipped and nodded. 'Gaunt? Yeah, most like.'

'I heard stuff, from the Munitorium blokes at the transports. They say he's hard as nails. Got medals too. A real killer, they say.'

Rawne sniffed. 'Why can't we be led by our own, is what I want to know. A good militia commander's all we need.'

'I could offer,' Corbec joked softly.

'He said a good one, dog!' Larkin snapped, returning to his obsessive polishing.

Corbec winked across at Bragg and they sipped some more.

'It seems funny to be going though, dunnit?' Bragg said after a spell. 'I mean, for good. Might never be coming back.'

'Most like,' Corbec said. 'That's the job. To serve the Emperor in his wars, over the stars and far away. Best get used to the idea.'

'Eyes up!' Forgal called from a tent nearby. 'Here comes big Garth with a face on!'

They looked around. Major Garth, their unit commander, was thumping down the tent line issuing quick orders left and right. Garth was a barrel-chested buttress of a man, whose sloping bulk and heavy, lined features seemed to suggest that gravity pulled on him harder than most. He drew up to them.

'Pack it up, boys. Time to ship,' he said.

Corbec raised an eyebrow. 'I thought that was tomorrow?' he began.

'So did I, so did Colonel Torth, so did the Departmento Munitorium, but it looks like our new colonel-commissar is an impatient man, so he wants us to start lifting to the troop-ships right after the Review.'

Garth passed on, shouting more instructions.

'Well,' Colm Corbec said to no one in particular, 'I guess this is where it all starts.'

* * *

GAUNT'S HEAD ACHED. He wasn't sure if it was the interminable introductions to Tanith dignitaries and politicos, the endless small talk, the achingly slow review of the troops out on the marshalling yard in front of the Tanith Assembly, or simply the bloody pipe music that seemed to be playing in every damn chamber, street and courtyard of the city that he walked into.

And the troops hadn't been that impressive either. Pale, dark-haired, undernourished-looking somehow, haggard in plain black fatigues, each with a piebald camo-cloak swept over the shoulder opposite the one to which their lasgun was slung. Not to mention the damn earstuds and hoops, the facial tattoos, the unkempt hair, the lilting, sing-song accents.

The 'glorious 1st, 2nd and 3rd of Tanith', the new regiments; a scrawny, scruffy mob of soft-voiced woodsmen indeed, and nothing to write home about.

The Elector of Tanith, the local planetary lord, himself sporting a cheek tattoo of a snake, had assured Gaunt of the fighting mettle of the Tanith militia.

'They are resolute and cunning,' the Elector had said as they stood on the terrace overlooking the massed ranks. 'Tanith breeds indefatigable men. And our particular strengths are in scouting and stealth. As you might expect on a world whose moving forests blur the topography with bewildering speed, the Tanith have an unerring sense of place and direction. They do not get lost. They perceive what others miss.'

'In the main, I need fighters, not guides,' Gaunt had said, trying not to sound too snide.

The Elector had merely smiled. 'Oh, we fight too. And now for the first time we are honoured to be adding our fighting spirit to that of the Imperium. The regiments of Tanith will serve you well, colonel-commissar.'

Gaunt had nodded politely.

Now Gaunt sat in private in an anteroom of the Assembly. He'd slung his greatcoat and his cap on a hardwood chest nearby and Sym had laid out his dress jacket for the dinner that would commence in thirty minutes. If only he could rid

himself of his headache and of the bad taste in his throat
that he had landed a weak command.

And the music! The damn pipe music, invading his head
even here in the private rooms!

He got to his feet and strode to the sloping windows. Out
beyond the cityscape and the Founding Fields, orange fire
thumped into the twilight as the heavy transports departed
and returned, ferrying the regimental components to the
vast troop carriers in high orbit.

That music still!

Gaunt walked to a set of dark green velvet drapes and
swept them aside. The music stopped.

The boy with the small set of pipes looked at his raging
eyes in astonishment.

'What are you doing?' Gaunt asked, as threatening as a
drawn knife.

'Playing, sir,' the boy said. He was about seventeen, not yet
a man, but tall and well-made. His face, a blue fish tattoo
over the left eye, was strong and handsome. His be-ringed
fingers clutched a Tanith pipe, a spidery clutch of reeds
attached to a small bellows bag that was rhythmically
squeezed under the arm.

'Was this your idea?' Gaunt asked.

The boy shook his head. 'It's tradition. For every visitor,
the pipes of Tanith will play, wherever they go, to lead them
back through the forest safely.'

'I'm not in the forest, so shut up!' Gaunt paused. He
turned back to the boy. 'I respect the traditions and customs
of the Tanith, but I… I have a headache.'

'I'll stop then,' the boy said. 'I– I'll wait outside. The Elector told me to attend on you and pipe you while you were
here. I'll be outside if you need me.'

Gaunt nodded. On his way out of the door, the boy collided with Sym, who was on the way in.

'I know, I know…' Gaunt began. 'If I don't hurry, I'll be
late for the dinner and– What? Sym? What is it?'

The look on Sym's face immediately told Gaunt that
something was very, very wrong.

* * *

GAUNT GATHERED HIS senior staff in a small, wood-panelled lobby off the main banqueting hall. Most were dressed for the formal function, stiff in gilt collars and cuffs. Junior Munitorium staff watched the doors, politely barring the entry of any Tanith dignitaries.

'I don't understand!' said a senior Departmento Munitorium staffer. 'The nearest edge of the warzone is meant to be eighty days from here! How can this be?'

Gaunt was pacing, reviewing a data-slate with fierce intensity. 'We broke them at Balhaut, but they splintered. Deep intelligence and the scout squadrons suggested they were running scared, but it was always possible that some of their larger components would scatter inwards, looping towards us, rather than running for the back end of the Sabbat Worlds and away.'

Gaunt wheeled on them and cursed out loud. 'In the name of Solan! On his damn deathbed, Slaydo was quite precise about this! Picket fleets were meant to guard all the warpgates towards territories like Tanith, particularly when we're still at founding and vulnerable like this! What does Macaroth think he's playing at?'

Sym looked up from a flatplan-chart he had unfurled on a desk. 'The lord high militant commander has deployed most of the Crusade Forces in the liberation push. It is clear he is intent on pressing the advantage won by his predecessor.'

'Balhaut was a significant win...' began one of the Ecclesiarchy.

'It will only stay a victory if we police the won territories correctly. Macaroth has broken the new front by racing to pursue the foe. And that's let the foe through, in behind our main army. It's textbook stupidity! The enemy may even have lured us on!'

'It leaves us wide open,' another Ecclesiarch agreed flatly.

Gaunt nodded. 'An hour ago, our ships in orbit detected a massive enemy armada coming in-system. It is no exaggeration to say that Tanith has just hours of life left to it.'

'We could fight–' someone ventured bravely.

'We have just three regiments. Untried, unproven. We have no defensive position and no prepared emplacements. Half of our force is already stowed in the troop carriers upstairs and the other half is penned in transit. We couldn't turn them around and get them unlimbered and dug in in under two full days. Either way, they are cannon fodder.'

'What do we do?' Sym asked. Some of the others nodded as if urging the same question.

'Our astropaths must send word immediately to the main crusade command, to Macaroth, and tell him of the insurgency. If nothing else, they need to turn and guard their flank and back. The rest of you: the carrier ships will leave orbit in one hour or at the point of attack, whichever comes first. Get as much of the remaining disembarked men and equipment aboard as you can before then. Whatever's left gets left behind.'

'We're abandoning Tanith?' a Munitorium aide said, disbelief in his thin voice.

'Tanith is already dead. We can die with it, or we can salvage as many fighting men as we can and re-deploy them somewhere they will actually do some good. In the Emperor's name.'

They all looked at him, incredulous, the enormity of his decision sinking in.

'DO IT!' he bawled.


THE NIGHT SKY above Tanith Magna caught fire and fell on the world. The orbital bombardment blew white-hot holes out of the ancient forests, melted the high walls, splintered the towers, and shattered the paved yards.

Dark shapes moved through the smoke-choked corridors of the Assembly, dark shapes that gibbered and hissed, clutching chattering, whining implements of death in their stinking paws.

With a brutal cry, Gaunt kicked his way through a burning set of doors and fired his bolt pistol.

He was a tall, powerful shape in the swirling smoke, a striding figure with a long coat sweeping like a cloak from his broad shoulders. His bright eyes tightened in his lean, grim face and he wheeled and fired again into the gloom. In the smoke-shadows nearby, red-eyed shapes shrieked and burst, spraying fluid across the stonework.

Las fire cut the air near him. He turned and fired, and then took the staircase at a run, vaulting over the bodies of the fallen. There was a struggling group up ahead, on the main landing. Two bloodied fighting men of the Tanith militia, wrestling with Sym at the doors to the launch silos.

'Let us through, you bastard!' Gaunt could hear one of them crying, 'You'd leave us here to die! Let us through!'

Gaunt saw the autopistol in the hand of the other too late. It fired the moment before he ploughed into them.

Raging, he broke one's jaw with the butt of his bolter, knocking the man backwards to the head of the stairs. He picked up the other and threw him over the stair rail into the smoke below.

Sym lay in a pool of blood.

'I– I've signalled... the carrier fleet, as you ordered... for the final withdrawal... Leave me and get aboard the cutter or–' Sym began.

'Shut up!' Gaunt snapped, trying to lift him, his hand slick with the man's blood. 'We're both going!'

'T-there's no time, not for me... just for you! Go, sir!' Sym rasped, his voice high with pain. From the bay beyond, Gaunt heard the scream of the cutter's thrusters rising to take-off readiness.

'Damn it, Sym!' Gaunt said. The aide seemed to reach for him, clawing at his tunic. For a second, Gaunt though Sym was trying to pull himself up so that Gaunt could carry him.

Then Sym's torso exploded in a red mist and Gaunt was thrown back off his feet.

At the head of the stairs, the grotesque shock troops of Chaos bayed and advanced. Sym had seen them over Gaunt's shoulder, had pulled himself up and round to shield Gaunt with his own body.

Gaunt got to his feet. His first shot burst the horned skull of the nearest beast. His second and third tore apart the body of another. His fourth, fifth and sixth gutted two more and sent them spinning back into their comrades behind on the steps.

His seventh was a dull clack of dry metal.

Hurling the spent bolter aside, Gaunt backed away towards the silo bay doors. He could smell the rancid scents of Chaos over the smoke now, and hear the buzz of the maggot-flies. In a second they would be on him.

Autocannon fire blasted into the heathen nightmares, sustained heavy fire from an angle nearby. Gaunt turned, and saw the boy, the piper with the fish tattoo. He was laying down an arc of covering fire from the portico of the silo bay with a sentry's autocannon that he had rested across the stonework. 'Get in! The last cutter's waiting for you!' cried the boy.

Gaunt threw himself through the bay doors into the fierce whirlwind of the cutter's engine backwash. The side hatch was just closing and he scrambled through, losing the tails of his coat to the biting hinge.

Enemy weapons fire resounded off the hull.

Gaunt was face down on the cabin floor, drenched in blood, looking up at the terrified faces of the Munitorium officials who made up this last evacuation flight to the fleet.

'Open the door again!' he yelled. 'Open it again!'

None of them moved to do so. Gaunt hauled himself up and heaved on the hatch lever. The door thumped open and the boy scrambled inside.

Gaunt dragged him clear of the hatch and yanked it shut. 'Now!' he bellowed down the cabin to the pilot's bay. 'Go now if you're going!'

The cutter rose from the tower bay hard and fast, lifter jets screaming as they were jammed into overdrive. Aerial laser fire exploded the brass orchid-shutters around them and clipped a landing stanchion. Hovering, the cutter wobbled. Below it, Tanith Magna was a blazing inferno.

Forgetting fuel tolerances, flight discipline, even his own mother's name, the pilot hammered the main thrusters to maximum and the cutter fired itself up through the black smoke like a bullet.

Left to die, the forests burned.

Gaunt fell against a bulkhead and clawed his way to a porthole. Just like in his dreams – fire, like a flower. Blossoming. Pale, greenish fire, scuttling like it was alive. Eating the world, the whole world.

Ibram Gaunt gazed into his reflection, his own lean, pale, bloody face. Trees, blazing like the heart of a star, rushed past behind his eyes.

HIGH OVER THE cold, mauve, marbled world of Nameth, Gaunt's ships hung like creatures of the deep marine places. Three great troop carriers, their ash-grey, crenellated hulls vaulted like monstrous cathedrals, and the long, muscular escort frigate *Navarre*, spined and blistered with lance weapons and turrets, hooked and angular like a woodwasp, two kilometres long.

In his stateroom on the *Navarre*, Gaunt reviewed the latest survey intelligence. Tanith was lost, part of a conquered wedge of six planet systems that fell to the Chaos armada pincer which Macaroth had allowed to slip behind his over-eager warfront. Now Crusade forces were doubling back and re-engaging the surprise enemy. Sporadic reports had come in of a thirty-six hour deep-space engagement of capital ships near the Circudus. The Imperial Crusaders now faced a war on two fronts.

Gaunt's ruthless retreat had salvaged three and a half thousand fighting men, just over half of the Tanith regiments, and most of their equipment. The cruellest, most cynical view could call it a victory of sorts.

Gaunt slid a data-slate out from under a pile of other documents on his desk and eyed it. It was the transcript of the communiqué from Macaroth himself, applauding Gaunt's survival instinct and his great feat in salvaging for the crusade a significant force of men. Macaroth had not seen fit to mention the loss of a planet and its population. He spoke of 'Colonel-Commissar Gaunt's correct choice, and frank evaluation of an impossible situation', and ordered him to a holding position at Nameth to await deployment.

It made Gaunt queasy. He tossed the slate aside.

The shutter opened and Kreff entered. Kreff was the frigate's executive officer, a hard-faced, shaven-headed man in the emerald, tailored uniform of the Segmentum Pacificus Fleet. He saluted, a pointless over-formality given that he had been covering as Gaunt's adjutant in Sym's place, and had been in and out of the room ten times an hour since Gaunt came aboard.

'Anything?' Gaunt asked.

'The astropaths tell us that something may be coming soon. Perhaps our orders. There is a current, a feeling. And also, uhm…' Kreff was obviously uncomfortable. He didn't know Gaunt and vice versa. It had taken Sym four years to get used to the commissar.

*Sym…*

'What is it?' Gaunt asked.

'I wondered if you would care to discuss our more immediate concern? The morale of the men.'

Gaunt got up. 'Okay, Kreff. Speak your mind.'

Kreff hesitated. 'I didn't mean with me. There is a deputation from the troop-ships–'

Gaunt turned hard at this. 'A what?'

'A deputation of Tanith. They want to speak to you. They came aboard thirty minutes ago.'

Gaunt took his bolt pistol out of the holster slung over his chair back and checked the magazine. 'Is this your discreet way of announcing a mutiny, Kreff?'

Kreff shook his head and laughed humourlessly. He seemed relieved when Gaunt reholstered his weapon.

'How many?'

'Fifteen. Mostly enlisted men. Few of the officers came out alive.'

'Send three of them in. Just three. They can choose who.'

Gaunt sat down behind his desk again. He thought about putting his cap on, his jacket. He looked across the cabin and saw his own reflection in the vast bay port. Two metres twenty of solid bone and sinew, the narrow, dangerous face that so well matched his name, the cropped blond hair. He wore his high-waisted dress breeches with their leather braces, a sleeveless undershirt and jack boots. His jacket and cap gave him command and authority. Bare-armed, he gave himself physical power.

The shutter clanked and three men entered. Gaunt viewed them without comment. One was tall, taller and older than Gaunt and built heavily, if a little paunchy. His arms were like hams and were decorated with blue spirals. His beard was shaggy, and his eyes might once have twinkled. The second was slim and dark, with sinister good looks that were almost reptilian. He had a blue star tattooed across his right eye. The third was the boy, the piper.

'Let's know you,' Gaunt said simply.

'I'm Corbec,' said the big man. 'This is Rawne.'

The snake nodded.

'And you know the boy,' Corbec said.

'Not his name.'

'Milo,' the boy said clearly. 'Brin Milo.'

'I imagine you're here to tell me that the men of Tanith want me dead,' said Gaunt simply.

'Perfectly true,' Rawne said. Gaunt was impressed. None of them even bothered to acknowledge his rank and seniority. Not a 'sir', not a 'commissar'.

'Do you know why I did what I did?' Gaunt asked. 'Do you know why I ordered the regiments off Tanith and left it to die? Do you know why I refused all your pleas to let you turn and fight?'

'It was our right—' Rawne began.

'Our world died, Colonel-Commissar Gaunt,' Corbec said, the title bringing Gaunt's head up sharp. 'We saw it flame out from the windows of our transports. You should have let us stand and fight. We would have died for Tanith.'

'You still can, just somewhere else.' Gaunt got to his feet. 'You're not men of Tanith any more. You weren't when you were camped out on the Founding Fields. You're Imperial Guard, servants of the Emperor first and nothing else second.'

He turned to face the window port, his back to them. 'I mourn the loss of any world, any life. I did not want to see Tanith die, nor did I want to abandon it. But my duty is to the Emperor, and the Sabbat Worlds Crusade must be fought and won for the good of the entire Imperium. The only thing you could have done if I had left you on Tanith was die. If that's what you want, I can provide you with many opportunities. What I need is soldiers, not corpses.'

Gaunt gazed out into space. 'Use your loss, don't be crippled by it. Put the pain into your fighting spirit. Think hard! Most men who join the Guard never see their homes again. You are no different.'

'But most have a home to return to!' Corbec spat.

'Most can look forward to living through a campaign and mustering to settle on some world their leader has conquered and won. Slaydo made me a gift after Balhaut. He gave me the military rank of colonel and granted me settlement rights to the first planet I win. Help me by doing your job, and I'll help you by sharing that with you.'

'Is that a bribe?' Rawne asked.

Gaunt shook his head. 'Just a promise. We need each other. I need an able, motivated army, you need something to take the pain away, something to fight for, something to look forward to.'

Gaunt saw something in the reflection on the glass. He didn't turn his head. 'Is that a laspistol, Rawne? Would you have come here and murdered me?'

Rawne grinned. 'What makes you put that in the past tense, commissar?'

Gaunt turned. 'What do I have here then? A regiment or a mutiny?'

Corbec met his gaze. 'The men will need convincing. You've made ghosts of them, hollow echoes. We'll take word back to the troop-ships of why you did what you did and what the future might hold. Then it's up to them.'

'They need to rally around their officers.'

Rawne laughed. 'There are none! Our command staff were all on the Founding Fields trying to embark the men when the bombardment started. None of them made it off Tanith alive.'

Gaunt nodded. 'But the men elected you to lead the deputation? You're leaders.'

'Or simply bold and dumb enough to be the ones to front you,' Corbec said.

'It's the same thing,' Gaunt said. 'Colonel Corbec. Major Rawne. You can appoint your own juniors and unit chiefs and report back to me in six hours with an assessment of morale. I should have our deployment by then.'

They glanced at each other, taken aback.

'Dismissed,' prompted Gaunt.

The trio turned away confused.

'Milo? Wait, please,' Gaunt said. The boy stopped as the shutter closed after the two men.

'I owe you,' Gaunt told him baldly.

'And you paid me back. I'm not militia or Guard. I only got off Tanith alive because you brought me.'

'Because of your service to me.'

Milo paused. 'The Elector himself ordered me to stay with you, to see to your needs. I was just doing my duty.'

'Those two brought you along because they thought the sight of you might mollify me, didn't they?'

'They're not stupid,' noted Milo.

Gaunt sat back at his desk. 'Neither are you. I have need of an adjutant, a personal aide. It's dogsbody, gopher work mostly, and the harder stuff you can learn. It would help me to have a Tanith in the post if my working relationship with them is going to continue.'

Before Milo could answer, the shutter slammed open again and Kreff entered, a slate in his hand. He saluted again. 'We've got our orders, sir,' he said.

DISTANT, RUMBLING explosions seemed a constant feature of the deadzone on Blackshard. The persistent crump of heavy gunnery drummed the low, leaden sky over the ridgeline. An earthwork had been built up along the ridge's spine and, under hardened bunkers, a detachment of Imperial Guard – six units of the 10th Royal Sloka – were readying to mobilise.

Colonel Thoren walked the line. The men looked like world-killers in their ornate battledress: crested, enamelled scarlet and silver warsuits built by the artisans of Sloka to inspire terror in the enemy.

But perhaps not this enemy. General Hadrak's orders had been precise, but Thoren's heart was heavy. He had no relish for the approaching push. He had no doubt at all it would cost him dearly.

To push blind, unsupported, into treacherous unknown territory in the hope of finding a wormhole into the enemy positions that might not even be there. The prospect made him feel sick.

Thoren's subaltern drew his attention suddenly to the double file of sixty men moving down the covered transit trench towards them. Scrawny ruffians, dressed in black, camo-cloaks draped over them, plastered to their bodies by the rain.

'Who in the name of Balor's blood…?' Thorne began.

Halting his column, the leader, a huge blackguard with a mess of tangled beard and a tattoo – a tattoo! – marched up to Thoren and saluted.

'Colonel Corbec, 1st Tanith. First-and-Only. General Hadrak has ordered us forward to assist you.'

'Tanith? Where the hell is that?' asked Thoren.

'It isn't,' replied the big man genially. 'The general said you were set to advance on the enemy positions over the dead-zone. Suggested you might need a covert scouting force seeing as how your boys' scarlet armour stands out like a baboon's arse.'

Thoren felt his face flush. 'Now listen to me, you piece–'

A shadow fell across them. 'Colonel Thoren, I presume?'

Gaunt dropped down into the dugout from the trench boarding. 'My regiment arrived here on Blackshard yesterday night, with orders to reinforce General Hadrak's efforts to seize the Chaos stronghold. That presupposes co-operative efforts between our units.'

Thoren nodded. This was Gaunt, the upstart colonel-commissar, it had to be. He'd heard stories.

'Appraise me, please,' said Gaunt.

Thoren waved up an aide who flipped up a map-projector, and displayed a fuzzy image of the deadzone. 'The foe are dug in deep in the old citadel ruins. The citadel had a size-able standing defence force, so they're well equipped. Chaos cultists, mostly, about seventeen thousand able fighting men. We also…' he paused.

Gaunt raised a questioning eyebrow.

'We believe there may be other abominations in there. Chaos spawn.' Thoren breathed heavily. 'Most of the main fighting is contained in this area here, while artillery duels blight the other fronts.'

Gaunt nodded. 'Most of my strength is deployed along the front line. But General Hadrak also directed us to this second front.'

Thoren indicated the map again. 'The foe are up to more than simply holding us out. They know sooner or later we'll break through, so they must be up to something – trying to complete something, perhaps. Recon showed that this flank of the city might be vulnerable to a smaller force. There are channels and ducts leading in under the old walls, a rat-maze, really.'

'My boys specialise in rat-mazes,' Gaunt said.

'You want to go in first?' Thoren asked.

'It's mud and tunnels. The Tanith are light infantry, you're armoured and heavy. Let us lead through and then follow us in support when we've secured a beachhead. Bring up some support weapons.'

Thoren nodded. 'Very well, colonel-commissar.'

Gaunt and Corbec withdrew to their men.

'This will be the first blooding for this regiment, for the Tanith First-and-Only,' began Gaunt.

'For Gaunt's Ghosts,' someone murmured. Mad Larkin, Corbec was sure.

Gaunt smiled. 'Gaunt's Ghosts. Don't disappoint me.'

They needed no other instructions. At Corbec's gesture, they hurried forward in pairs, slipping their camo-cloaks down as shrouds around them, lasguns held loose and ready. The hybrid weave of the hooded cloaks blurred to match the dark grey mud of the ridgeway, and each man stooped to smear his cheeks and brow with wet mud before slipping over the earthwork.

Thoren watched the last one disappear and then span the trench macro-periscope around. He looked out, but of the

sixty plus men who had just passed his position, there was
no sign.

'Where in the name of Solan did they go?' he breathed.

GAUNT WAS AMAZED. He'd seen them practise and train in the
belly holds of the big carrier ships, but now here, in the wild
of a real deadzone, their skills startled him. They were all but
invisible in the stinking mire, just tiny blurs of movement
edging between stacks of debris and over mounds of wreckage towards the slumped but massive curtain walls of the
citadel.

He pulled his own Tanith camo-cloak around him. It had
been part of his deal with Corbec: he insisted on leading
them in to assure loyalty, they insisted he didn't give their
position away.

The micro-bead in his ear tickled. It was Corbec. 'First
units at the tunnels now. Move up close in pairs.'

Gaunt touched his throat mike. 'Hostiles?' he asked.

'A little light knife work,' crackled the reply.

A few moment later he was entering the dripping, dark
mouth of the rubble tunnel. Five Chaos-bred warriors in the
orange robes of their cult lay dead. Before him, the Tanith
were forming up. Corbec was wiping blood from the blade
of his long, silver knife.

'Let's go,' said Gaunt.

THE ELECTOR OF Tanith, may his soul rest, had not lied
about anything, Gaunt decided. The Ghosts had proved
their cunning stealth crossing the open waste of the deadzone, and he had no clue as to how they threaded their way
through the crazy lightless warren of the tunnels so surely.
'They do not get lost,' the Elector had boasted, and it was
true. Gaunt suspected that the foe had assumed nothing
bigger than a cockroach would ever find its way through
those half-collapsed, death-trap tunnels.

But Corbec's men had, effortlessly, in scant minutes. Rising from the tunnels' ends inside the curtain wall of the city,
and taking long, silver Tanith knives to pallid, blotchy
throats, they had burned their way in through the enemy's

hindquarters. Now the Tanith First-and-Only were proving they could fight. Just like the Elector had said.

From behind a shattered pillar, Gaunt blasted with his bolter, blowing two cultists apart and destroying a doorway. Around him, the advancing Tanith lacerated the air with precise shots from five dozen lasguns.

Near to Gaunt, a sharp-faced, older Tanith Gaunt had heard the men call Larkin was sniping cultists off the top of the nearest balconies. His eye was tremendous. A little further on, a huge man, a gentle giant called Bragg, was shouldering the heavy bolter and taking down walls and columns. The big weapon had originally been pintle-mounted on a sled, but Bragg had torn it off its mount and slung it up like a rifle. Gaunt had never seen a heavy bolter carried by an unarmoured man before. The Tanith called Bragg 'Try Again' Bragg. He was a terrible shot, admittedly, but with firepower like that he could afford to be sloppy.

Just ahead, a six man fire-team led by Corbec gained the entrance to a temple building complex, grenaded the doorway and went in with lasguns, paired off to give bounding cover.

'Heavy fire in my section!' Corbec radioed to Gaunt. 'Some kind of church or temple. Could be a primary target.'

Gaunt acknowledged. He would move more teams up.

CREEPING DOWN THE aisle of the massive temple, Corbec edged through rubble and heavy crossfire. He nodded a pair past him – Rawne and Suth – and then the next. His own cover partner, Forgal, bellied up close in the mica dust of the temple floor and unslung his lasgun.

'Down there,' he hissed, his eyes as sharp as ever. 'There's a lower storey down behind the altar. They've got a lot of defence around that doorway. The big arch under the stained-glass.'

It was true.

'You smell that?' Rawne asked over the radio.

Corbec did. Decay, stale sweat, dead blood. Rank and harsh, oozing from the crypt.

Forgal began to crawl forward. A lucky shot vaporised the top of his head.

'Sacred Feth!' Corbec howled and opened up in rage, bringing the entire stained glass window down in a sheet onto the altar.

Rawne and Suth took advantage of the confusion to grab a few more metres. Rawne unwrapped a tube-charge and hurled it over-arm into the archway.

The blast was deafening.

GAUNT HEARD CORBEC'S call in his ear-piece. 'Get in here!' He scrambled into the smoky interior of the temple. At the door, he paused. 'Larkin! Bragg! Orcha! Varl! With me! You three, cordon the door! Cluggan, take two teams down the flank of the building and scout!'

Gaunt entered the chapel, mashing broken glass under foot. He could smell the stink.

Corbec and Rawne were waiting for him, their other men stood around, watching with lasguns ready.

'Something down here,' Rawne said and led Gaunt on down the littered steps. Gaunt slammed fresh rounds home into his boltgun, then holstered it and picked up Forgal's fallen lasgun.

Beneath the chapel was an undercroft. Dead cultists were strewn like rag dolls around the smouldering floor. In the centre of the chamber stood a rusty, metallic box, two metres square, its lid etched with twisted sigils of Chaos.

Gaunt reached out. The metal was warm. It pulsed.

He snatched his hand back.

'What is it?' asked Corbec.

'I don't think any of us want to know,' Gaunt said. 'Some relic of the enemy, some unholy object, an icon... Whatever, it's something valuable to these monsters, something they're defending to the last.'

'That Sloka colonel was sure there was a reason they were holding on,' Corbec said. 'Maybe they're hoping support will arrive in time to save this.'

'Let's spoil those chances. I want a systematic withdrawal from this point, back out under the wall. Each man is to leave his tube-charges here. Rawne, collect them and rig them – you seem to be good with explosives.'

Within minutes, the Ghosts had withdrawn. Rawne crouched and connected the firing pins of the small but potent anti-personnel charges. Gaunt watched him and the door.

'Pick it up, Rawne. We haven't much time. The enemy aren't going to leave this area open for long.'

'Nearly done,' Rawne said. 'Check the door again, sir. I thought I heard something.'

The 'sir' should have warned him. As Gaunt turned, Rawne rose and clubbed him around the back of the head with his fist. Gaunt dropped, stunned, and Rawne rolled him over next to the charges.

'A fitting place for scum like you to die, ghost maker!' he murmured. 'Down here amongst the vermin and the filth. It's so tragic that the brave commissar didn't make it out, but the cultists were all over us.' Rawne drew his laspistol and lowered it towards Gaunt's head.

Gaunt kicked out and brought Rawne down. He rolled and slammed into him, punching him once, twice. Blood marked Rawne's mouth.

He tried to hit again but Gaunt was so much bigger. He struck Rawne so hard he was afraid he'd broken his neck. The Tanith lolled in the dust.

Gaunt got up, and eyed the timer setting. It was just dropping under two minutes. Time to leave.

Gaunt turned. But in the doorway of the room, the warriors of Chaos moved towards him.

THE BLAST SENT a column of dirt and fire up into the sky that could be seen from the Guard trenches across the deadzone. Six minutes later, the defenders' big guns stopped and fell silent. Then all firing ceased completely from the enemy lines.

Guard units moved in, cautiously at first. They found the cultists dead at their positions. Each one had, in unison, taken his own life, as if in response to some great loss. In the conclusion of his report on the victory at Blackshard,

General Hadrak surmised that the destruction of the Chaos relic, which had given meaning to the cult defence, robbed them of the will or need to continue. Hadrak also noted the significant role in the victory played by the newly founded Tanith 1st, which had supplemented his own forces. Though as C-in-C of the Blackshard action, he took overall credit for the victory, he was magnanimous in acknowledging the work of 'Gaunt's Ghosts', and particularly recommended their stealth and scouting abilities.

Colonel-Commissar Gaunt, wounded in the stomach and shoulder, emerged alive from the deadzone twenty minutes after the blast and was treated by medical teams before returning to his frigate. He might have made his way out of the enemy lines faster, had he not carried the unconscious body of one of his officers, a Major Rawne, back to safety.

STIFF WITH drug-dulled pain, Gaunt walked down the companion way of the troop carrier and into the holding bay. Nearly nine hundred of the Tanith were billeted here. They looked up from their weapons drills and Gaunt felt the silence on him.

'First blood to you,' he said to them. 'First blood to Tanith. The first wound of vengeance. Savour it.'

By his side, Corbec began to clap. The men picked it up, more and more, until the hold shook with applause.

Gaunt eyed the crowd. Maybe there was a future here, after all. A regiment worth the leading, a prize worth chasing all the way to glory.

His eyes found Major Rawne in the crowd. Their eyes fixed. Rawne was not applauding.

That made Gaunt laugh. He turned to Milo and gestured to the Tanith pipes cradled in his aide's hands.

'*Now* you can play something,' he told him.

GAUNT WALKED THE line through the early morning, the stink of the Monthax jungle swards filling and sickening his senses. Tanith, working stripped to the waists, digging the wet ooze with entrenching tools to fill sacking, paused to nod at his greetings, exchange a few words with him, or ask cautious questions about the fight to come.

Gaunt answered as best he could. As a commissar, a political officer, charged with morale and propaganda, he could turn a good, pompous phrase. But as a colonel, he felt a duty of truth to his men.

And the truth was, he knew little of what to expect. It would be bitter, he knew that much, though the commissar part of him spared the men that thought. Gaunt spoke of courage and glory in general, uplifting terms, talking softly and firmly as his mentor, Commissar-General Oktar, had taught him all those years ago when he was just a raw cadet with the Hyrkans. 'Save the yelling and screaming for battle, Ibram. Before that comes, build their morale with gentle encouragement. Make it look like you haven't a care in the world.'

Gaunt prided himself on knowing not only the names of all his men, but a little about each of them too. A private joke here, a common interest there. Oktar's way, tried and tested, Emperor rest his soul these long years. Gaunt tried to memorise each muddy, smiling face as he passed along. He knew his soul would be damned the day he was told Trooper so-and-so had fallen and he couldn't bring the man's face to mind. 'The dead will always haunt you,' Oktar had told him, 'so make certain the ghosts are friendly.' If only Oktar had known the literal truth of that advice.

Gaunt paused at the edge of a dispersal gully and smiled to himself at the memory. Beyond, some troopers were kicking a balled sack of mud around in an impromptu off-watch game. The 'ball' came his way, and he hoisted it back to them on the point of his boot. Let them have their fun while it lasts. How many would be alive to play the game again tomorrow?

How many indeed? There were losses and losses. Some worthy, some dreadful, and some plain unnecessary. Still the memories dogged his mind in these crawling hours of waiting. Praise be the Emperor that Gaunt's losses of brave, common troopers would never be as great, as wholesale or as senseless as that day on Voltemand, a year before...

# TWO
# A BLOODING

THEY WERE A good two hours into the dark, black-trunked forests of the Voltemand Mirewoods, tracks churning the filthy ooze and the roar of their engines resonating from the sickly canopy of leaves above, when Colonel Ortiz saw death.

It wore red, and stood in the trees to the right of the track, in plain sight, unmoving, watching his column of Basilisks as they passed along the trackway. It was the lack of movement that chilled Ortiz. He did a double take, first seeing the figure as they passed it before realising what it was.

Almost twice a man's height, frighteningly broad, armour the colour of rusty blood, crested by recurve brass antlers. The face was a graven death's head. Daemon. Chaos Warrior. *World Eater.*

Ortiz snapped his gaze back to it and felt his blood drain away. He fumbled for his radio link.

'Alarm! Alarm! Ambush to the right!' he yelled into the set. Gears slammed and whined, and hundreds of tons of mechanised steel shuddered, foundered and slithered on the muddy track, penned, trapped, too cumbersome to react quickly.

By then the Chaos Space Marine had begun to move. So had its six comrades, each emerging from the woods around them.

Panic seized Ortiz's convoy cluster: the ten-vehicle forward portion of a heavy column of eighty flame-and-feather painted Basilisk tanks of the 'Serpents', the Ketzok 17th Armoured Regiment, sent in to support the frontal push of the Royal Volpone 50th, the so-called 'Bluebloods'. The Ketzok had the firepower to flatten a city, but caught on a strangled trackway, in a thick woodland, with no room to turn or traverse, and with monstrous enemies at close quarters, far too close to bring the main guns to bear, they were all but helpless. Panic alarms spread backwards down the straggled column, from convoy portion to portion. Ortiz heard tree trunks shatter as some commanders tried to haul their machines off the track.

The World Eaters started baying as they advanced, wrenching out of their augmented throats deep, inhuman calls that whooped across the trackway and shivered the metal of the tank armour. They howled the name of the bloody abomination they worshipped.

'Small arms!' Ortiz ordered. 'Use the pintle mounts!' As he spoke, he cranked round the autocannon mounted on his vehicle's rear and angled it at the nearest monster.

The killing started. The rasping belch of flamers reached his ears and he heard the screams of men cooking inside their superheated tank hulls. The Chaos Marine he had first spotted reached the Basilisk ahead of his and began to chop its shell like firewood with a chain-axe. Sparks blew up from punctured metal. Sparks, flames, metal shards, meat.

Screaming, Ortiz trained his mounted gun on the World Eater and fired. He shot long at first, but corrected before the monster could turn. The creature didn't seem to feel the first hits. Ortiz clenched the trigger and streamed the heavy tracer fire at the red spectre. At last the figure shuddered, convulsed and then blew apart.

Ortiz cursed. The World Eaters soaked up the sort of punishment that would kill a Leman Russ. He realised his ammo drum was almost empty. He was snapping it free and shouting to his bombardier for a fresh one when the shadow fell on him.

Ortiz turned.

Another Chaos Marine stood on the rear of the Basilisk behind him, a giant blocking out the pale sunlight. It stooped, and howled its victory shout into his face, assaulting him with concussive sonic force and wretched odour. Ortiz recoiled as if he had been hit by a macro shell. He could not move. The World Eater chuckled, a macabre, deep growl from behind the visor, a seismic rumble. The chainsword in its fist whined and swung up...

The blow didn't fall. The monster rocked, two or three times, swayed for a moment. And exploded.

Smeared with grease and ichor, Ortiz scrambled up out of his hatch. He was suddenly aware of a whole new layer of gunfire – sustained lasgun blasts, the chatter of support weapons, the crump of grenades. Another force was moving out of the woods, crushing the Chaos Marine ambush hard against the steel flanks of his artillery machines.

As Ortiz watched, the remaining World Eaters died. One was punctured dozens of times by lasgun fire and fell face down into the mire. Another was flamed repeatedly as he ripped apart the wreck of a Basilisk with his steel hands. The flames touched off the tank's magazine and the marine was incinerated with his victims. His hideous roar lingered long after the white-hot flames had consumed him.

The column's saviours emerged from the forest around them. Imperial Guards: tall, dark-haired, pale-skinned men in black fatigues, a scruffy, straggle-haired mob almost invisible in their patterned camo-cloaks. Ortiz heard strange, disturbing pipe music strike up a banshee wail in the close forest, and a victory yelp erupted from the men. It was met by cheers and whoops from his own crews.

Ortiz leapt down into the mud and approached the Imperial Guardsmen through the drifting smoke.

'I'm Colonel Ortiz. You boys have my earnest thanks.' he said. 'Who are you?'

The nearest man, a giant with unruly black hair, a tangled, braided beard and thick, bare arms decorated with

blue spiral tattoos, smiled jauntily and saluted, bringing up
his lasgun. 'Colonel Corbec, Tanith First-and-Only. Our
pleasure, I'm sure.'

Ortiz nodded back. He found he was still shaking. He
could barely bring himself to look down at the dead Chaos
Marine, sprawled in the mud nearby. 'Takes discipline to
ambush an ambush. Your men certainly know stealth. Why
is–'

He got no further. The bearded giant, Corbec, suddenly
froze, a look of dismay on his face. Then he was leaping forward with a cry, tackling Ortiz down into the blue-black
mud.

The 'dead' World Eater lifted his horned skull out of the
muck and half-raised his bolter. But that was all. Then a
shrieking chainsword decapitated him.

The heavy, dead parts flopped back into the mud. One of
them rolled.

Ibram Gaunt brandished with his keening chain sword
like a duellist and then thumbed it to 'idle'. He turned to
Corbec and Ortiz as they got up, caked in black filth. Ortiz
stared at the tall, powerful man in the long dark coat and
cap of an Imperial Commissar. His face was blade thin, his
eyes as dark as space. He looked like he could rip a world
asunder with his hands.

'Meet the boss,' Corbec chuckled at Ortiz's side. 'Colonel-
Commissar Gaunt.'

Ortiz nodded, wiping his face. 'So, you're Gaunt's Ghosts.'

MAJOR GILBEAR POURED himself a brandy from the decanter
on the teak stand. 'Just who the hell are these awful barbarian scum?' he asked, sipping from the huge crystal balloon.

At his desk, General Noches Sturm put down his pen and
sat back. 'Oh, please, help yourself to my brandy, Gilbear,' he
muttered, though the sarcasm was lost on his massive aide.

Gilbear reclined on a chaise beside the flickering amber
displays of the message-caster, and gazed at his commander.
'Ghosts? That's what they call them, isn't it?'

Sturm nodded, observing his senior adjutant. Gilbear –
Gizhaum Danver De Banzi Haight Gilbear, to give him his

full name – was the second son of the Haight Gilbears of Solenhofen, the royal house of Volpone. He was nearly two and a half metres tall and arrogantly powerful, with the big, blunt, bland features and languid, hooded eyes of the aristocracy. Gilbear wore the grey and gold uniform of the Royal Volpone 50th, the so-called Bluebloods, who believed they were the noblest regiment in the Imperial Guard.

Sturm sat back in his chair. 'They are indeed called Ghosts. Gaunt's Ghosts. And they're here because I requested them.'

Gilbear cocked a disdainful eyebrow. 'You requested them?'

'We've had nigh on six weeks, and we can't shake the enemy from Voltis City. They command everything west of the Bokore Valley. Warmaster Macaroth is not pleased. All the while they hold Voltemand, they have a road into the heart of the Sabbat Worlds. So you see I need a lever. I need to introduce a new element to break our deadlock.'

'That rabble?' Gilbear sneered. 'I watched them as they mustered after the drop-ships landed them. Hairy, illiterate primitives, with tattoos and nose rings.'

Sturm lifted a data-slate from his desktop and shook it at Gilbear. 'Have you read the reports General Hadrak filed after the Sloka took Blackshard? He credits Gaunt's mob with the decisive incursion. It seems they excel at stealth raids.'

Sturm got to his feet and adjusted the sit of his resplendent Blueblood staff uniform. The study was bathed in yellow sunlight that streamed in through the conservatory doors at the end, softened by net drapes. He rested his hand on the antique globe of Voltemand in its mahogany stand by the desk and span it idly, gazing out across the grounds of Vortimor House. This place had been the country seat of one of Voltemand's most honoured noble families, a vast, grey manse, fringed with mauve climbing plants, situated in ornamental parkland thirty kilometres south of Voltis City. It had been an ideal location to establish his Supreme Headquarters.

Outside, on the lawn, a squad of Blueblood elite in full battle dress were executing a precision synchronised drill with chainswords. Metal flashed and whirled, perfect and poised. Beyond them, a garden of trellises and arbours led down to a boating lake, calm and smoky in the afternoon light. Navigation lights flashed slowly on the barbed masts of the communications array in the herbarium. Somewhere in the stable block, strutting gaudcocks whooped and called.

You wouldn't think there was a war on, mused Sturm. He wondered where the previous owners of the manse were now. Did they make it off-world before the first assault? Are they huddled and starving in the belly hold of a refugee ship, reduced overnight to a level with their former vassals? Or are they bone-ash in the ruins of Kosdorf, or on the burning Metis Road? Or did they die screaming and melting at the orbital port when the legions of Chaos first fell on their world, vaporised with the very ships they struggled to escape in?

Who cares? thought Sturm. The war is all that matters. The glory, the crusade, the Emperor. He would only care for the fallen when the bloody head of Chanthar, demagogue of the Chaos army that held Voltis Citadel, was served up to him on a carving dish. And even then, he wouldn't care much.

Gilbear was on his feet, refilling his glass. 'This Gaunt, he's quite a fellow, isn't he? Wasn't he with the Hyrkan 8th?'

Sturm cleared his throat. 'Led them to victory at Balhaut. One of old Slaydo's chosen favourites. Made him a colonel-commissar, no less. It was decided he had the prestige to hammer a new regiment or two into shape, so they sent him to the planet Tanith to supervise the Founding there. A Chaos space fleet hit the world that very night, and he got out with just a few thousand men.'

Gilbear nodded. 'That's what I heard. Skin of his teeth. But that's his career in tatters, stuck with an under-strength rabble like that. Macaroth won't transfer him, will he?'

Sturm managed a small smile. 'Our beloved overlord does not look kindly on the favourites of his predecessor. Especially as Slaydo granted Gaunt and a handful of others the settlement rights of the first world they conquered. He and his Tanith rabble are an embarrassment to the new regime.

But that serves us well. They will fight hard because they have everything to prove, and everything to win.'

'I say,' said Gilbear suddenly, lowering his glass. 'What if they do win? I mean, if they're as useful as you say?'

'They will facilitate our victory,' Sturm said, pouring himself a drink. 'They will not achieve anything else. We will serve Lord Macaroth twofold, by taking this world for him, and ridding him of Gaunt and his damn Ghosts.'

'YOU WERE EXPECTING us?' Gaunt asked, riding on the top of Ortiz's Basilisk as the convoy moved on.

Colonel Ortiz nodded, leaning back against the raised top-hatch cover. 'We were ordered up the line last night to dig in at the north end of the Bokore Valley and pound the enemy fortifications on the western side. Soften them up, I suppose. En route, I got coded orders sent, telling us to meet your regiment at Pavis Crossroads and transport you as we advanced.'

Gaunt removed his cap and ran a hand through his short fair hair. 'We were ordered across country to the crossroads, all right,' he responded. 'Told to meet transport there for the next leg. But my scouts picked up the World Eaters' stench, so we doubled back and met you early.'

Ortiz shuddered. 'Good thing for us.'

Gaunt gazed along the line of the convoy as they moved on, taking in the massive bulk of the Basilisks as they ground up the snaking mud-track through the sickly, dim forest. His men were riding on the flanks of the great war machines, a dozen or more per vehicle, joking with the Serpent crews, exchanging drinks and smokes, some cleaning weapons or even snoozing as the lurch of the metal beasts allowed.

'So Sturm's sending you in?' Ortiz asked presently.

'Right down the river's floodplain to the gates of Voltis. He thinks we can take the city where fifty thousand of his Bluebloods have failed.'

'Can you?'

'We'll see,' Gaunt said, without the flicker of a smile. 'The Ghosts are new, unproven but for a skirmish on Blackshard.

But they have certain... strengths.' He fell silent, and seemed to be admiring the gold and turquoise lines of the feather serpent design painted on the barrel of the Basilisk's main weapon. Its open beak was the muzzle. All the Ketzok machines were rich with similar decorations.

Ortiz whistled low to himself. 'Down the Bokore Valley into the mouth of hell. I don't envy you.'

Now Gaunt smiled. 'Just you keep pounding the western hills and keep them busy. In fact, blow them all away to kingdom come before we get there.'

'Deal,' laughed Ortiz.

'And don't drop your damn aim!' Gaunt added with a threatening chuckle. 'Remember you have friends in the valley!'

TWO VEHICLES BACK, Corbec nodded his thanks as he took the dark thin cigar his Basilisk commander offered.

'Doranz,' the Serpent said, introducing himself.

'Charmed,' Corbec said. The cigar tasted of licorice, but he smoked it anyway.

Lower down the hull of the tank, by Corbec's sprawled feet, the boy Milo was cleaning out the chanters of his Tanith pipe. It wheezed and squealed hoarsely.

Doranz blanched. 'I'll tell you this: when I heard that boy's piping today, that hell-note, it almost scared me more than the damn blood cries of the enemy.'

Corbec chuckled. 'The pipe has its uses. It rallies us, it spooks the foe. Back home, the forests move and change. The pipes were a way to follow and not get lost.'

'Where is home?' Doranz asked.

'Nowhere now,' Corbec said and returned to his smoke.

ON THE BACK armour of another Basilisk, hulking Bragg, the biggest of the Ghosts, and small, wiry Larkin, were dicing with two of the tank's gun crew.

Larkin had already won a gold signet ring set with a turquoise skull. Bragg had lost all his smokes, and two bottles of sacra. Every now and then, the lurch of the tank beneath them would flip the dice, or slide them under an exhaust baffle, prompting groans and accusations of fixing and cheating.

Up by the top hatch with the vehicle's commander, Major Rawne watched the game without amusement. The Basilisk commander felt uneasy about his passenger. Rawne was slender, dark and somehow dangerous. A starburst tattoo covered one eye. He was not… likeable or open like the other Ghosts seemed to be.

'So, major… what's your commissar like?' the commander began, by way of easing the silence.

'Gaunt?' Rawne asked, turning slowly to face the Serpent. 'He's a despicable bastard who left my world to die and one day I will slay him with my own hands.'

'Oh,' said the commander and found something rather more important to do down below.

ORTIZ PASSED GAUNT his flask. The afternoon was going and they were losing the light. Ortiz consulted a map-slate, angling it to show Gaunt. 'Navigation puts us about two kilometres or so short of Pavis Crossroads. We've made good time. We'll be on it before dark. I'm glad, I didn't want to have to turn on the floods and running lights to continue.'

'What do we know about Pavis?' Gaunt asked.

'Last reports were it was held by a battalion of Bluebloods. That was at oh-five-hundred this morning.'

'Wouldn't hurt to check,' Gaunt mused. 'There are worse things than rolling into an ambush position at twilight, but not many. Cluggan!'

He called down the hull to a big, grey-haired Ghost sat with others playing cards.

'Sir!' Cluggan said, scrambling back up the rocking Basilisk.

'Sergeant, take six men, jump down and scout ahead of the column. We're two kilometres short of this crossroads,' Gaunt showed Cluggan the map. 'Should be clear, but after our tangle with the damn World Eaters we'd best be sure.'

Cluggan saluted and slid back to his men. In a few moments they had gathered up their kits and weapons and swung down off the skirt armour onto the track. A moment more and they had vanished like smoke into the woods.

'That is impressive,' Ortiz said.

AT PAVIS CROSSROADS, the serpents spoke. Stretching their great painted beaks towards the night sky, they began their vast barrage.

Brin Milo cowered in the shadow of a medical Chimera, pressing his hands to his ears. He'd seen two battles up close: the fall of Tanith Magna and the storming of the citadel on Blackshard, but this was the first time he had ever encountered the sheer numbing wrath of armoured artillery.

The Ketzok Basilisks were dug in along the ridge in a straggled line about half a kilometre long. They were hull-down into the grey earth, main weapons swung high, hurling death at the western hills across the valley nine kilometres away. They were firing at will, a sustained barrage that could, Corbec had assured him, go on all night. Every second at least one gun was sounding, lighting the darkness with its fierce muzzle flash, shaking the ground with its firing and recoil.

Pavis Crossroads was a stone obelisk marking the junction of the Metis Road that ran up the valley from Voltis City, and the Mirewood track that carried on towards the east. The Serpents' armour had rolled in at nightfall, ousting the encamped Bluebloods who held the junction, and deploying around the ridge-line, looking west. As the first stars began to shine, Ortiz's men began their onslaught.

Milo kept his eyes sharp for the commissar, and when he saw Gaunt striding towards a tented dugout beside the orbital communication stack, accompanied by his senior officers, Milo ran to join them.

'My scope!' requested Gaunt over the barrage. Milo pulled the commissar's brass-capped nightscope from his pack and Gaunt stepped up onto the parapet, scanning out of the dugout.

Corbec leaned up close by him, a thin black tube protruding from his beard.

Gaunt glanced round. 'What is that thing?' he asked.

Corbec took it out and displayed it proudly. 'Cigar. Liquorice, no less. Won a box off my gun-crate's C.O. and I think I'm getting a taste for them.

'See much?' he added.

'I can see the lights of Voltis. Watch fires and shrine-lights mostly. Not so inviting.'

Gaunt flipped his scope shut and jumped down from the parapet, handing the device back to Milo. The boy had already set up the field-map, a glass plate in a metal frame mounted like an easel on a brass tripod. Gaunt cranked the knurled lever on the side and the glass slowly lit with bluish light. He dropped in a ceramic slide engraved with the local geography and then angled the screen to show the assembled men: Corbec, Rawne, Cluggan, Orcha and the other officers.

'Bokore Valley,' Gaunt said, tapping the glass viewer with the tip of his long, silver Tanith war-knife. As if for emphasis, the nearest Basilisk outside fired and the dugout shook. The field map wobbled and soil trickled in from the roof.

'Four kilometres wide, twelve long, flanked to the west by steep hills where the enemy is well established. At the far end, Voltis City, the old Capital of Voltemand. Thirty-metre curtain walls of basalt. Built as a fortress three hundred years ago, when they knew the art. The invading Chaos Host from off-planet seized it at day one as their main stronghold. The Volpone 50th have spent six weeks trying to crack it, but the bastards we met today show the kind of force they've been up against. We'll have a go tonight.'

He looked up, oblivious to the constant thunder outside. 'Major Rawne?'

Rawne stepped forward, almost reluctant to be anywhere near Gaunt. No one knew what had passed between them when they had been alone together on Blackshard, but everyone had seen Gaunt carry Rawne to safety on his shoulder, despite his own injuries. Surely that sort of action bonded men, not deepened their enmity?

Rawne adjusted a dial on the field-map's edge so that the plate displayed a different section of the chart-slide. 'The approach is straightforward. The Bokore River runs along the wide valley floor. It is broad and slow-moving, especially at this time of year. Most of the way is choked with bulrushes and waterweed. We can move down the river channel undetected.'

'You've scouted this?' Gaunt asked.

'My squad returned not half an hour ago,' Rawne said smoothly. 'The Bluebloods had tried it a number of times, but they are semi-armoured and the mud was too great an impediment. We are lighter – and we are good.'

Gaunt nodded. 'Corbec?'

The big man sucked on his cigar. His genial eyes twinkled and it made Milo smile. 'We move by dark, of course. In the next half-hour. Staggered squads of thirty men to spread out our traces.' He tapped the map-screen at another place. 'Primary point of entry is the old city watergate. Heavily defended of course. Secondary squads under Sergeant Cluggan will attempt to storm the wall at the western sanitation outfalls. I won't pretend either way will be a picnic.'

'Objective,' Gaunt said, 'get inside and open the city. We'll move in squads. One man in every ten will be carrying as much high explosive as he can. Squad leaders should select any man with demol experience. We provide cover for these demolition specialists to allow them to set charges that will take out sections of wall or gates. Anything that splits the city open.

'I've spoken to the Blueblood colonel. He has seven thousand men in motorised units ready to advance and take advantage of any opening we can make. They will be monitoring on channel eighty. The signal will be "Thunderhead".'

There was silence, silence except for the relentless hammering of the Basilisk guns.

'Form up and move out,' Gaunt said.

Outside, Ortiz stood talking to several of his senior officers, one of them Doranz. They saw the Ghost officers emerge from the dugout and orders being given.

Across the emplacement, Ortiz caught Gaunt's eye. It was too loud for words, so he clenched his fist and rapped it twice against his heart, an old gesture for luck.

Gaunt nodded.

'Scary men,' Doranz said. 'I almost feel sorry for the enemy.'

Ortiz glanced round at him.

'I'm joking, of course,' Doranz added, but Ortiz wasn't sure he was.

MIDNIGHT HAD SEEN them waist deep in the stinking black water of the Bokore River reed beds, assailed by clouds of biting flies. Three hours' hard trudge through the oily shallows of the old river, and now the sheer walls of Voltis rose before them, lit by cressets and braziers high up. Behind them, like a distant argument, the Basilisks spat death up into the heavens, a distant, rolling roar and a series of orange flashes on the skyline.

Gaunt adjusted his nightscope and panned it round, seeing features in the darkness as a green negative. The watergate was thirty metres across and forty tall, the mouth of a great chute and adjoining system that returned water to the Bokore once it had driven the mills inside the city. Gaunt knew that somewhere sluices must have been lowered, and the flow staunched, closing off the chute's operation. Sandbagged emplacements could be made out up in the shadows behind the gate's breastwork.

He adjusted his micro-bead link. 'Corbec?'

Colm Corbec heard his commander in the darkness and acknowledged. He waded forward through the reeds to Bragg, who had hunkered down behind a rotting jetty.

'When you're ready…' Corbec invited.

Bragg grinned, teeth bright in the starlight. He dragged the canvas cover off one of the two huge weapons he had lugged on his shoulders from Pavis Crossroads. The polished metal of the missile launcher had been dulled down with smears of Mirewood mud.

'Try Again' Bragg was a spectacularly lousy shot. But the watergate was a big target, and the missile rack held four melta-missiles.

The night exploded. Three missiles went straight up the throat of the chute. The force of the heat-blast sent stone debris, metal shards, water vapour and body parts out in a radius of fifty metres. The fourth vaporised a chunk of wall, and brought down a small avalanche of basalt chunks. For a moment the heat was so intense that Gaunt's nightscope read nothing but emerald glare. Then it showed him the chiselled mouth of the watergate had become a bubbling, blazing wound in the huge wall, a ragged, slumping incision in the sheer basalt. He could hear agonised screaming from within the chute. Beyond the city wall, alarm bells and sirens rose in pandemonium.

The Ghosts charged the watergate. Orcha led the first squad up the sloping drain-away under the molten arch of ruptured stone. He and three of his men swung flamers in wide arcs, scorching and scouring up into the darkness of the echoing chute.

Behind them, Corbec brought in fire teams with lasguns who darted down into the side passages and cisterns of the watergate, butchering the cultists who had limped or crawled into cover after the first attack.

The third wave went in, under Major Rawne. In the front rank was Bragg, his empty launcher discarded in favour of the heavy bolter that he had liberated from its mounting back on Blackshard and now lugged around like a smaller man might heft a heavy rifle.

Gaunt leapt forward too, bolt pistol in one hand, chainsword in the other. He bellowed after his attacking men, all of them racing silhouettes backlit against the glittering water by fire.

Milo sprang up, fumbling with the Tanith pipes under his arm.

'Now would be a good time, Brin,' Gaunt said.

Milo found the mouthpiece, inflated the bag and began to keen an old battle lament of Tanith, 'The Dark Path of the Forest'.

UP IN THE CHUTE, Orcha and his squad heard the shrill wail of the pipes outside. Damp darkness was before them.

'Close up,' Orcha snapped into his micro-bead.

'Aye.'

'To your left,' Brith yelled suddenly.

An assault cannon raged out of the darkness of a side chute. Brith, Orcha and two others disintegrated instantly into red mist and flesh pulp.

Troopers Gades and Caffran ducked back behind the buttress work of the huge vault.

'Enemy fire!' Caffran yelled into his bead. 'They have the chute covered in a killing sweep.'

Corbec cursed. He might have expected this.

'Stay down!' he ordered the young Ghost over the mike as he beckoned his first two squads up the lower chute, black water swilling around their knees.

'Hell of a foul place for a firefight,' mourned Mad Larkin, scoping with his lasgun.

'Stow it, Larks,' Corbec growled. Ahead they heard the nightmare chatter of the cannon, and the added rhythm of drums and guttural chants. Corbec knew Larkin was right. A tight, confined, unyielding stone tunnel was no place for a serious fight. This was a two-way massacre in the making.

'They're just trying to psyche us out,' he told his Ghosts smoothly as they edged forward.

'What d'you know? It's working!' Varl said.

The drums and chanting got louder, but suddenly the cannon shut off.

'It's stopped,' Caffran reported over the link.

Corbec looked round into Larkin's crazed eyes. 'What do you think? A trick to lure us out?'

Larkin sniffed the thick air. 'Smell that? Burning ceramite. I'd wager they've got an overheat jam.'

Corbec didn't answer. He cinched his bayonet onto his lasgun and charged up the slope of the chute, screaming louder and shriller than Milo's pipes. In uproar, the Ghost squads followed him.

Caffran and Gades joined the charge, bellowing, weapons held low as they splashed out from behind the buttress into the main vault.

Corbec leapt clear a sandbag line damming one gully and disembowelled the two cultists who were struggling to unjam the assault cannon.

Larkin dropped down on one knee in the brackish soup and popped the cover on his lasgun's darkscope. Carefully selecting his expert long shots, he blasted four cultists further down the chute.

Las and bolt fire slammed back at the Ghosts, dropping several of them. The charging Guardsmen met the cultist force head on in a tight, tall sub-chute, no wider than two men abreast. Bodies exploded, blasted at close range. Bayonets and blades sliced and jabbed. Corbec was in the thick of it. Already a chainsword had gashed his left hand and cost him a finger, and blood blurted from a slash to his shoulder. He speared a man, but lost his gun when the corpse's weight on the bayonet tore it out of his hands. He ripped out his fallback weapons, a laspistol and his Tanith knife of sheer silver. Around him in the frenzy, men killed or died in a confined press that was packed in close like a busy work transit, crowded at rush hour. Already the water level was rising because of the depth of bodies and body parts in the gully.

Corbec shot a cultist through the head as he was charged, and then lashed sideways with the silver blade, opening a throat.

'For Tanith! First and Last and Only!' he screamed.

ADVANCING UP THE tunnel fifty paces back, Gaunt could hear the sheer tumult of the nightmarish close-quarters fight in the chute. He looked down and saw that the trickle of Bokore River water that ran down over his boots was thick and red.

Ten metres further, he found Trooper Gades, part of Orcha's original squad. The boy had lost his legs to a chainsword and the water had carried his twitching form back down the smooth slope of the channel.

'Medic! Dorden! To me!' Gaunt bellow, cradling the coughing, gagging Gades in his arms.

Gades looked up at his commissar. 'A real close fight, so it is,' he said with remarkable clarity, 'packed in like fish in a can. The Ghosts will make ghosts tonight.'

Then he coughed again. Bloody matter vomited from his mouth and he was gone.

Gaunt stood.

Milo had faltered, looking down at Gades's stricken, miserable death.

'Play up!' urged Gaunt, and turned to shout down the chute to the Ghost main force in the bulrushes. 'Advance! Narrow file! For the Emperor and the glory of Tanith!'

With a deafening bellow, Gaunt's Ghosts charged forward en masse, breaking down into files of three, surging into the throttling entrance to hell.

Up ahead, in the dark, close, smoky killing zone, Rawne slumped against a buttress, splashed in gore, and panted. By his side, Larkin squatted and fired shot after shot into the darkness.

Corbec suddenly loomed out of the smoke, a terrible apparition drenched in blood.

'Back!' he hissed. 'Back down the chute! Sound the retreat!'

'What is it?' Rawne said.

'What's that rumbling?' Larkin asked, distracted, pressing his ear to the stone work. 'Whole tunnel is vibrating!'

'Water,' Corbec said grimly. 'They've opened the sluices. They're going to wash us out!'

THE CULTISTS WERE everywhere.

Sergeant Cluggan's secondary expedition force poured in through the stinking crypts of the western sanitation outfalls, and the enemy rose to meet them all around. It was hand to hand, each step of the way won by strength and keen blades. The dark, tight confines of the drainage tunnels were lit by the flashes of las-fire, and shots ricocheted from the roof and walls.

'What the hell is that smell?' Forbin wailed, blasting away down an airless cavity with his lasgun.

'What do you think? This is the main sewage drain,' Brodd snapped, a one-eyed man in his fifties. 'Notice how the others get the nice clean watergate.'

'Keep it together!' Cluggan snarled, firing in a wide sweep and cutting down a trio of attacking cultists. 'Forget the smell. It's always been a dirty job.'

More, heavy fire came their way. Forbin lost his left arm and then the side of his head.

Cluggan, Brodd and the others returned fire in the close channel. Cluggan eyed the cultist troops they cut through: bloated, twisted men in robes that had been white silk before they had been dyed in vats of blood. They had come from off-world, part of the vast host of Chaos cultists that had descended like locusts onto Voltemand and destroyed its people. The sigils and runes of the blasphemy Khorne were cut into the flesh of their brows and cheeks. They were well equipped, with bolters and lasguns, and armoured. Cluggan hoped to the sweet, dead gods of Tanith that his commissar was faring better.

THE GHOSTS STAGGERED and stumbled back from the spewing watergate, through the reed beds, towards the comparative cover of the riverbank. Enemy fire from the walls high above killed dozens, their bodies joining the hundreds swept out, swirling and turning, by the torrent of brown water roaring from the watergate.

Micro-bead traffic was frantic with cross-chatter and desperately confused calls. Despite their discipline, the madness of the flight from the water had broken Gaunt's main force into a ragged jumble, scrambling for their lives.

Soaked through, furious, Gaunt found himself sheltering by some willows in a scummy river bend eighty metres from the watergate. With him were Caffran, Varl, a corporal called Meryn and two others.

Gaunt cursed. Cultists he could fight… World Eaters, daemons…anything. He'd set square with any beast in the cosmos. But seventy million litres of water pressured down through a stone conduit…

'May have lost as many as forty to the flood,' Varl said. He'd dragged Caffran by the tunic from the water and the young man could only retch and cough.

'Get a confirmed figure from the squad leaders! I don't want rumours!' Gaunt snarled, then keyed his own radio link and spoke into his bead. 'Squad leaders! Discipline the radio traffic. I want regroup status! Corbec! Rawne!'

The channels crackled and a more ordered litany of units and casualties reeled in.

'Corbec?' Gaunt asked.

'I'm west of you, sir. On the banks. Got about ninety men with me.' Corbec's voice hissed back.

'Assessment?'

'Tactical? You can forget the watergate, sir. Once they realised they couldn't hold us out in a straight fight, they blew the sluices. It could run at flood for hours. By then they'll have the chute exits on the city side sewn up with emplacements, maybe even mines.'

Gaunt cursed again. He wiped a wet hand across his face. They'd been so close and now it was all lost. Voltis would not be his.

'Sir?' Meryn called to him. The corporal was listening to other frequencies on his bead. 'Channel eighty. The word has just been given.'

Gaunt crossed to him, adjusting his own setting. 'What?'

'The word. "Thunderhead",' Meryn said, confused.

'Source that signal!' Gaunt snapped, 'If someone thinks that's a joke, I'll–'

He got no further.

The blast was so loud, it almost went beyond sound. The shockwave mashed into them, chopping the water like a white squall.

A kilometre away, a hundred metre section of the curtain wall blew out, ripping a vast wound in the city's flank, burning, raw, exposed.

The channels went mad with frenzied calls and whoops.

Gaunt looked on in disbelief. Corbec's voice cut through, person to person on the link.

'It's Cluggan, sir! The old bastard got his boys into the sanitation outfalls and they managed to dump all of their high-ex into a treatment cistern under the walls. Blew the crap out of the cultists.'

'So I saw, colonel,' Gaunt said wryly.

'I mean it literally, sir,' Corbec crackled innocuously. 'It was Cluggan sent the signal. We may have lost the fight to take the watergate, but Cluggan has won us the battle!'

Gaunt slumped back against a tree bole, up to his waist in the stinking river. Around him the men were laughing and cheering.

Exhaustion swept over him. And then he too began to laugh.

GENERAL STURM TOOK breakfast at nine. The stewards served him toasted black bread, sausage and coffee. He read a stack of data-slates as he ate, and the message-caster on the sideboard behind him chattered and dealt out a stream of orbital deployment updates.

'Good news,' said Gilbear, entering with a coffee and a message slate in hand. 'The best, in fact. Seems your gamble paid off. These Ghost fellows have taken Voltis. Broken it wide out. Our attack units followed them in en masse. Colonel Maglin says the city will be cleansed by nightfall.'

Sturm dabbed his mouth with a serviette. 'Send transmissions of congratulation and encouragement to Maglin and to Gaunt's mob. Where are they now?'

Gilbear eyed his slate and helped himself to a sausage from the dish. 'Seems they've pulled out, moving back to Pavis Crossroads along the eastern side of the Bokore Valley.'

Sturm set down his silver cutlery and started to type into his memo-slate. 'The greater half of our work here is accomplished, thanks to Gaunt,' he told the intrigued Gilbear. 'Now we thank him. Send these orders under extreme encryption to the C.O. of the Ketzok Basilisks at Pavis. Without delay, Gilbear.'

Gilbear took the slate. 'I *say...*' he began.

Sturm fixed him with a stare. 'There are dangerous cultist units fleeing along the eastern side of the valley, aren't there, Gilbear? Why, you've just read me the intelligence reports that confirm it.'

Gilbear began to grin. 'So I did, sir.'

COLONEL ORTIZ SNATCHED the radio from his com-officer and yelled 'This is Ortiz! Yes! I know, but I expressly query the last orders we received. I realise that, but– I don't care! No, I– Listen to me! Oh, general! Yes, I... I see. I see, sir. No, sir.

Not for a moment. Of course for the glory of the Emperor. Sir. Ortiz out.'

He sank back against the metal flank of his Basilisk.

'Make the guns ready,' he told his officers. 'In the name of the Emperor, make them ready.'

THE GUNS HAD been silent for ten hours. Ortiz hoped he would never hear them blaze again. Dawn frosted the horizon with light. Down in the valley, and in the Blueblood emplacements, victory celebrations continued with abandon.

Dorentz ran over to Ortiz and shook him. 'Look, sir!' he babbled. 'Look!'

Men were coming up the Metis Road out of the valley towards them, tired men, weary men, filthy men, walking slowly, carrying their dead and wounded. They were a straggled column that disappeared back into the morning mist.

'In the name of mercy...' Ortiz stammered. All around, shocked, silent Basilisk crew were leaping down from their machines and going to meet the battered men, supporting them, helping them, or simply staring in appalled disbelief.

Ortiz walked over to meet the arrival. He saw the tall figure in the long coat, now ragged, striding wearily out of the mist. Ibram Gaunt was half-carrying a young Ghost whose head was a bloody mess of bandages.

He stopped in front of Ortiz and let medics take the wounded Ghost from him.

'I want–' Ortiz began.

Gaunt's fist silenced him.

'HE'S HERE,' GILBEAR said with an insouciant smirk. Sturm got to his feet and straightened his jacket. 'Bring him in,' he said.

Colonel-Commissar Ibram Gaunt marched into the study. He stood, glowering at Sturm and his adjutant.

'Gaunt!' Sturm said. 'You opened the way for the Royal Volpone. Good show! I hear Chanthar turned a melta on himself.' He paused and absently tapped at a data-slate on his desk. 'But then this business with what's-his-name...?'

'Ortega, sir,' Gilbear said helpfully.

'Ortiz,' Gaunt corrected.

'The Ketzok fellow. Striking a fellow officer. That's a shooting offence, and you know it, Gaunt. Won't have it, not in this army. No, sir.'

Gaunt breathed deeply. 'Despite knowing our position, and line of retreat, the artillery unit pounded the eastern flanks of the Bokore Valley for six hours straight. They call the phenomenon "friendly fire", but I can tell you when you're in the target zone with nothing but twigs and dust for cover, it's nothing like friendly. I lost nearly three hundred men, another two hundred injured. Amongst the dead was Sergeant Cluggan, who had led the second prong of my assault and whose actions had actually won us the city.'

'Bad show indeed,' Sturm admitted. 'but you must learn to expect this kind of loss, Gaunt. This is war.' He tossed the data-slate aside. 'Now this hitting business. Chain of command and all that. My hands are tied. It's to be a court martial.'

Gaunt was level and unblinking. 'If you're going to shoot me for it, get on with it. I struck Ortiz in the heat of the moment. In hindsight, I realise he was probably following orders. Some damn fool orders from HQ.'

'Now look, you jumped up–' Gilbear began, stepping forward.

'Would you like me to demonstrate what I did to Ortiz?' Gaunt asked the bigger man acidly.

'Silence, both of you!' snarled Sturm. 'Commissar Gaunt… *Colonel*-commissar… I take my duty seriously, and that duty is to enforce the discipline and rule of Warmaster Macaroth, and through him the beloved Emperor himself, strictly and absolutely. The Imperial Guard is based upon the towering principles of respect, authority, unswerving loyalty and total obedience. Any aberration, even from a officer of your stature, is to be– *What the hell is that noise?*'

He crossed to the window. What he saw made him gawp speechlessly. The Basilisk tank thundering up the drive was dragging part of the main gate after it and scattering gaudcocks and drilling Bluebloods indiscriminately in its path. It slewed to a halt on the front lawn, demolishing an ornamental fountain in a spray of water and stone.

A powerful man in the uniform of a Serpent colonel leapt down and strode for the main entrance to the house. His face was set and mean, swollen with bruises down the left side. A door slammed. There was some shouting, some running footsteps. Another slamming door.

Some moments later, an aide edged into the study, holding out a data-slate for Sturm. 'Colonel Ortiz has just filed an incident report. He suggested you saw it at once, sir.'

Gilbear snatched it and read it hastily. 'It seems that Major Ortiz wishes to make it clear he was injured by his own weapon's recoil during the recent bombardment.' Gilbear looked up at Sturm with a nervous laugh. 'That means–'

'I know what it means!' Sturm snapped. The general glared at Gaunt, and Gaunt glared right back, unblinking.

'I think you should know,' Gaunt said, low and deadly, 'it seems that callous murder can be committed out here in the lawless warzones, and the fact of it can be hidden by the confusion of war. You should bear that in mind, general, sir.'

Sturm was lost for words for a moment. By the time he had remembered to dismiss Gaunt, the commissar had already gone.

'OH, FOR FETH'S sake, play something more cheerful,' Corbec said from his troop-ship bunk, flexing his bandaged hand. He was haunted by the ghost of his missing finger. Appropriate, he thought.

In the bunk below him, Milo squeezed the bladder of his pipes and made them let out a moan, a shrill, sad sigh. It echoed around the vast troop bay of the huge, ancient starship, where a thousand Tanith Ghosts were billeted in bunks. The dull rhythm of the warp engines seemed to beat in time to the wailing pipes.

'How about… "Euan Fairlow's March"?' Milo asked.

Above him, Corbec smiled, remembering the old jig, and the nights he heard it played in the taverns of Tanith Magna.

'That would be very fine,' he said.

The energetic skip of the jig began and quickly snaked out across the iron mesh of the deck, between the aisles of bunks, around stacks of kits and camo-cloaks, through the smoky groups where men played cards or drank, over bunks where others slept or secretly gazed at portraits of women and children who were forever lost, and tried to hide their tears.

Enjoying the tune, Corbec looked up from his bunk when he heard footsteps approach down the deck-plates. He jumped up when he saw it was Gaunt. The commissar was dressed as he had first met him, fifty days before, in high-waisted dress breeches with leather braces, a sleeveless undershirt and jack boots.

'Sir!' Corbec said, surprised. The tune faltered, but Gaunt smiled and waved Milo on. 'Keep playing, lad. It does us good to hear your merrier tunes.'

Gaunt sat on the edge of Milo's bunk and looked up at Corbec.

'Voltemand is credited as a victory for the Volpone Blue-bloods,' he told his number two frankly. 'Because they seized the city. Sturm mentions our participation with commendations in his report. But this one won't win us our world.'

'Feth take 'em!' spat Corbec.

'There will be other battles. Count on it.'

'I'm afraid I do, sir,' Corbec smiled.

Gaunt bent down and opened the kit-bag he was carrying. He produced a half-dozen bottles of sacra.

'In the name of all that's good and holy!' Corbec said, jumping down from his bunk. 'Where–'

'I'm an Imperial commissar,' Gaunt said. 'I have pull. Do you have glasses?'

Chuckling, Corbec pulled a stack of old shot glasses from his kit.

'Call Bragg over, I know he likes this stuff,' Gaunt said. 'And Varl and Meryn. Mad Larkin. Suth. Young Caffran... hell's teeth, why not Major Rawne too? And one for the boy. There's enough to share. Enough for everyone.' He nodded down the companion way to the three bewildered naval officers who were approaching with a trolley laden with wooden crates.

'What do we drink to?' Corbec asked.

'To Sergeant Cluggan and his boys. To victory. And to the victories we are yet to have.'

'Drink to revenge, too,' Milo said quietly from his bunk, setting down his pipes.

Gaunt grinned. 'Yes, that too.'

'You know, I've got just the treat to go with this fine brew,' Corbec announced, searching his pockets. 'Cigars, liquorice flavour…'

He broke off. What he had pulled from his coat pocket had ceased to be cigars a good while before. There were a matted, frayed, waterlogged mess.

Corbec shrugged and grinned, his eyes twinkling as Gaunt and the others laughed.

'Ah, well,' he sighed philosophically, 'Some you win…'

HEAVY, SPOON-BILLED wading birds flew west across the lines, white against the encroaching dark. In the thickets, the day-time chirruping insects gave up their pitches to the night beetles, the nocturnal crickets, the tick-flies, creatures that spiralled and swam in the light of the stove fires and filled the long hot darkness with their percussion. Other cries rolled in the sweaty air: the whoops and gurgles of unseen climbers and grazers in the swamp. The distant artillery had fallen silent.

Gaunt returned to the command shed just as the grille-shaded watch lights came on, casting their greenish glow downwards into the slush, bull's-eye covers damping their out-flung light in any direction other than down. No sense in making a long range target of the base. Furry, winged insects the size of chubby hands flew in at once to bounce persistently off the lit grilles with a dull, intermittent thok thok thok.

Gaunt took one last look around the base site, now distinguished only by the points of light: the cook-fires, stoves, watch lights and moving torches. He sighed and went inside.

The command centre was long and low, with a roof of galvanised corrugate and walls of double-ply flak-board. The floor was fresh-cut local wood sawn into planks and treated with vile-smelling lacquer. Blast shutters on the windows stood half-open and the wire screens inside them were already thick with a fuzzy, quivering residue – the mangled bodies of moths and night-bugs which had thrown themselves at the mesh.

Gaunt's command equipment and his duffel bags of personal effects were set off the floor on blocks of wood. They'd been sat directly on the floor for the first two days until it was discovered that where damp didn't seep up, burrowing worms did.

He draped his coat on a wire hanger and hung it from a nail on the overhead rafter, then pulled up a camp chair and sat down heavily. Before him, block-mounted, sat a cogitator, a vox-uplink and a flat-screen mimeograph. A tech-priest had spent over an hour diligently intoning prayers of function as he made the sacred machines ready. They were still propped in their half-open wrought-iron casings to protect against the damp, and thick power feeds snaked off from them and ran from clip supports on the rafters, out of a socket-shutter and off to the distant generator. Lights and light images shimmered and flickered on glass plates glossed by condensation. Setting dials throbbed a dull orange. The vox-link made a low-level serpent hiss as it rose and fell through frequencies.

Gaunt leaned forward and idly surveyed the latest information and tactical data coming through from the orbital fleet and other units. A skein of coded runes crossed and blinked on the dark glass.

Quiet as nightfall, Milo entered from the ante-room. He offered a pewter beaker to his commissar. Gaunt took it with a nod, delighting at the beaded coolness of the metal.

'The tech-priests got the cooling units working again just now,' Milo muttered by way of explanation. 'For a few minutes. It's only water, but it's cold.'

Gaunt nodded his appreciation and sipped. The water was metallic and sharp, but it was deliciously cool.

There was a thump on the outside step, then a quiet knock at the door. Gaunt smiled. The thump had been deliberate, a reassuring advance warning from a man who made no sound if he did not wish to.

'Come in, Mkoll,' Gaunt said.

Mkoll entered, his lined face a little quizzical as if surprised at being recognised in advance.

'Patrol report, sir,' he said, standing stiffly in the doorway.

Gaunt gestured him to a seat. Mkoll's battledress and cloak were drenched in wet mud. Everything including his face was splattered – everything except his lasgun, miraculously clean.

'Let's have it.'

'Their positions are still far back,' Mkoll began, 'beyond the offensive line coded alpha pink. A few forward patrols.'

'Trouble?'

The powerful, wiry man grimaced noncommittally. 'Nothing we couldn't handle.'

'I've always admired your modesty,' Gaunt said, 'but I need to know.'

Mkoll screwed up his mouth and nose. 'We took six of them in the western swamps. No losses on our side.'

Gaunt nodded approval. He liked Mkoll, the Tanith's finest scout. Even in a regiment of stealthers and covert warriors, Mkoll was exceptional. A woodsman back home on lost Tanith, he had reconnaissance skills that had proved themselves time and again to the Ghosts. A ghost amongst ghosts, and modest with it. He never bragged, and it was certain he had more to brag about than most.

Gaunt offered his beaker to the man.

'Thank you, sir, no.' Mkoll looked down at his hands.

'It's cold,' Gaunt assured him.

'I can tell. But no. I'd rather go without something I could get used to.'

Gaunt shrugged and sipped again. 'So they're not moving?'

'Not yet. We sighted a… I'm not sure what it was, an old ruin of some kind.' Mkoll rose and pointed to a position on the wall chart. 'Around here, far as I can tell. Could be nothing, but I'd like to follow it through with a survey in the morning.'

'An enemy position?'

'No, sir. Something… that was already here.'

'You're right: deserves a look. In the morning then,' Gaunt agreed.

'If that'll be all, sir?'

'Dismissed, Mkoll.'

'I'll never get the measure of him,' Gaunt said to Milo after Mkoll had left. 'Quietest man I've ever known.'

'That's what he does, isn't it, sir?' Milo said.

'What?'

'*Quiet.*'

# THREE
# SOUND AND FURY

ALL AROUND THERE was a hushing sound, as if the whole world wanted to silence him.

Mkoll bellied in low amid the forest of ferns, trying to pick through the oceanic rushing sound they made as the wind stirred them.

The fern growth in that part of Ramillies 268-43, flourishing on the thin, ashy soils of the long-cold volcanic slopes, was feathery and fibrous, mottled stalks rough as cane rising three man-heights into swaying multi-part fronds as white as water-ice.

They reminded him of the nalwood forests back home, when there was still a back home, the nalwoods in winter, when he'd gone out logging and hunting. Frost had crusted the evergreen needles on the sighing trees then until they had tinkled like wind chimes.

Here, now, there was only the sigh, the motion of the dry ferns and the clogging dust that got into every pore and rasped the soft tissue at the back of the throat. The sunlight was bright and harsh, stabbing down through the pale, spare air out of a sky translucent blue. It made a striated web out of the ground cover under the ferns – stark sun-splashes and jagged shadows of blackness.

He crept forward twenty metres into a break of skeleton brush. His lower legs were already double-wrapped with chain-cloth to protect against the shredding thorns. He had his lasgun held to his chest on a tightly cinched strap to keep it clear of the dust but, every ten minutes or so, he checked its moving parts and cleared the dust, fern-fibres, twig-shreds and burrs that accumulated constantly.

Several cracks made him turn and freeze, sliding his gun into a firing grip between smooth, dry palms. Something was moving through the thicket to his left, cracking the occasional spent thorn underfoot.

To be fair, they were moving with extreme and trained stealth, but still their progress sounded like a careless march to Mkoll's acute hearing.

Mkoll drew his knife, its long silver blade deliberately dulled with ash. He backed into a thorn stalk and moulded his body to the kinking plant. Two steps, one.

He swung out, only pulling back his blade at the last moment.

Trooper Dewr cried out and fell backwards, splintering dry stalks as he dropped. Mkoll was on top of him in a second, pinning his arms and pushing the blade against his neck.

'Sacred Feth! You could've killed me!' Dewr barked agitatedly.

'Yes, I could,' said Mkoll, a whisper.

He relaxed his grip, rolled off and let the man rise.

'So could anything else out here, noise you were making.'

'I…' Dewr dropped his voice suddenly. 'Are we alone?'

Mkoll didn't answer. Chances were, if anything else was out here, it would have heard Dewr's fall too.

'I didn't mean anything,' Dewr began hoarsely, wincing as he plucked out the thorns he had fallen on.

Mkoll was scanning around, his gun ready. 'What the feth did they teach you during basic?' he whispered. 'You're meant to be a scout!'

Dewr didn't reply. All the scouts knew Mkoll's exacting standards, and knew just as well how they all failed to meet them. Dewr felt angry, in fact. During basic training, before that as a hunter in the southern gameland of Tanith Attica, he'd been reckoned as a good tracker. That was why they had selected him for the scout unit when the regiment mustered, for feth's sake! And this old bastard made him feel like a fool, a clumsy fool!

Wordlessly, ignoring the stare he knew Dewr was boring into the back of his head, Mkoll signalled an advance, heading down the slope into the fern-choked vale.

The Tanith had arrived on Ramillies two weeks before, just in time to miss the main action. The Adeptus Astartes had cleaned out and secured the four enemy strongholds, banishing Chaos from the world. The Ghosts had assembled on the low plains near one burning fortress, seeing Space Marines, threatening bulks in the smoky distance like the giants of myth, piling the ragged corpses of slain cultists onto pyres. The air had been thick with filthy char.

It seemed some small components of the enemy had fled the defeat, making into the fern forests in the north, too small and insignificant for the glorious Space Marines to waste time upon. The commissar was charged with a search and destroy detail. The Ghosts had advanced into the low hills and the dense forestation, to smoke out the last of the foe.

There were a few early successes: enclaves of cultists, some well-armed, dug into bolt-holes and lodges, making a last stand. Then, after a week, as they reached the colder, higher plateaux and the real thickness of the fern-cover, a working pattern developed. Mkoll would plan recon sweeps each day, deploying a couple of dozen scouts in a wide fan into the thickets. They would quarter each area and report back, signalling in the main Ghost forces if contact was made.

Perhaps they had become lazy, complacent. Major Rawne averred that they had silenced the last of the enemy and were now wasting their time and patience cutting deeper and deeper into the lonely territories of the hinterland. The commissar himself seemed devoted to discharging the task properly, but even he had doubled the reach and range of the scout sweeps. Another few days and they would quit, he had told Mkoll.

This day, this high cold windy day, with the ever present whisper of the ferns, the scouts had gone deeper and wider into the hills. There had been no contact with anything for two whole sweeps. Mkoll sensed that less dedicated troopers like Dewr were getting slack with the routine.

But he himself had seen things that kept him sharp and made him determined to press on. Things he had reported to Gaunt to convince him to work the forests a little longer: broken paths in the vegetation; trampled areas; torn, apparently random trails in the underbrush. There was something still out here.

They crossed the valley floor and came up the shaded side, where the ferns listed restlessly, like shadow-fans. Every dozen or so steps, Dewr's feet cracked a thorn or a seed case, or chinked a rock, no matter how delicately he walked. He cursed every sound. He was determined to prove his ability to Mkoll. And he had no clue how Mkoll moved so silently, like he was floating.

The ferns hissed in the wind.

Mkoll stopped to check his compact chart and referred his eyes to sun and compass. Within a quarter of an hour their circuit should bring them into contact with Rafel and Waed, on a mirror sweep towards them.

Mkoll suddenly held up a hand and Dewr stopped sharp. The scout sergeant fanned his fingers twice to indicate Dewr should cover, and the other slid in low beside a thick fern stem, knelt and raised his lasgun. There was dust on the exchanger and he wiped it off. Dust in his eyes too, and he wiped them. He braced and then took aim, rolling it left and right as Mkoll advanced.

Mkoll dropped down another few metres and found another torn trail in the fern. As wide as three men walking abreast, ferns uprooted or snapped and trampled. Mkoll gingerly touched one sappy, broken twist of stalk. It was as thick as his thigh, and the bark was tough as iron. He could not have severed it this clean even with a wood axe. He checked the ground. Trample marks, deep and wide, like giant footsteps. The trail snaked away both ahead and behind as far as he could see, uneven, weaving. Mkoll raised three fingers and circled them. Dewr advanced to join him.

The younger man looked at the trail, questions in his mouth, but the look in Mkoll's eyes told him not to ask them. Not to say anything. There was no sound at all except the hissing of the fronds. Dewr knelt and looked at the trail for himself. Something… someone… big, moving blindly. His fingers touched something buried in the ashy soil and he plucked it out. A chunk of blackened metal, part of the rim of something, large as a cupped hand. He held it out to Mkoll. The sergeant took it with genuine interest, studied it, and tucked it into his thigh pouch. He nodded a firm acknowledgement to Dewr for his sharp eyes. Dewr felt greater pride in that fleeting moment than he had ever done in his life before. Or would again.

They moved on, down the trail line, following the bent-forward fronds which indicated the direction of motion. After sixty metres, the trail veered uphill. Mkoll stopped and wiped his weapon again.

A scream cut the air, as bright and sharp as a Tanith blade. They both started. It shut off abruptly, but while it lasted it had been unmistakably human. Mkoll was moving in an instant, following the source of the sound. Dewr went after him, trying to keep his hurried steps silent. They moved off the trail into the thickets. Ahead, the foliage changed. Under the crest of the slope, thicker, spined cacti grew in clusters; fibrous, gourd-like growths lined with long needles were arrayed down each seam of the plant sac. There were hundreds of the plants, some knee high, some higher and fatter than a man, a forest of needle-studded bulbs.

Another, weaker scream came, as from a man waking from a nightmare and abruptly dying away as he realised it was but a dream. And another sound, close on the heels of the scream. A hollow, plosive, spitting sound, like someone retching fruit pits from his throat.

They found Rafel crumpled amid the gourd-bulbs. A trail of blood, bright spatters on the ashy ground, showed where he had dropped and how he had crawled. Over a dozen needles, some more than a foot long, impaled him. One went through his eye into his brain. Dewr, in horror, was about to speak, but Mkoll whirled and clamped his hand over the younger man's mouth. Mkoll pointed to the nearest of the large cactus growths, indicating where a line of spines were absent, leaving only a line of sap-drooling orifices.

'I say again, Trooper Rafel! What is your position?' The voice crackled out of the corpse's intercom. Mkoll drove himself into Dewr, knocking him aside, away from Rafel as the three bulbs nearest the body shuddered and spat spines. A salvo of those hollow spitting coughs again. Needles stabbed into Rafel's corpse like arrows and bounced off the ground around them.

One went through Dewr's shin. He wanted to scream but managed to master it. The pain was sharp, then dull. His leg went cold. Mkoll rolled off him. Dewr pointed feebly at his leg, but the sergeant seemed to ignore it. He made a quick adjustment to the intercom at his collar and then reached down to Dewr's, switching it off.

Only then did he turn to the wound. He took out his knife and cut the cloth away from Dewr's shin, slicing the straps holding the chain-cloth bandages in place. The needle had passed right through the chain, directly through the eye of some links and severing others. Mkoll turned the knife round and forced the hilt into Dewr's mouth. Instinctively, Dewr bit down and Mkoll yanked the needle free.

There was very little blood. That was bad. The blood was clotting and turning yellow fast and the sticky residue on the spine suggested venom. But the needle had only punctured flesh, which was good. The force of it could have shattered the shin bone.

Dewr bit hard on the hilt a while longer. As the pain ebbed, he slackened his mouth and the knife slid out down his cheek onto the ground. Mkoll rose. He would get Rafel's field dressings and bind the wound. Rafel wouldn't need them now. He turned. His foot cracked a thorn on the ground. A moment of carelessness, triggered by his concern for Dewr. A bulb shuddered at the crack and spat a needle.

It passed through the stock of Mkoll's lasgun and the point stopped an inch from his belly.

He unfroze and breathed, then pulled it out. Mkoll crossed to Rafel and freed his field dressing pouch, pinned to his waist by another needle through the strap. He returned to Dewr and bound the wound.

Dewr's head began to spin. It was an easy, fluid feeling, like his cares were ebbing away. There was a gnawing feeling in his leg and hip, but it was somehow pleasant.

Mkoll saw the vacant glaze coming over Dewr's eyes. Unceremoniously, he took another length of gauze dressing and jammed it into Dewr's mouth, taping the gag tightly in place. A delirious man may not realise the sound he is making.

He was about to lift Dewr onto his shoulder when another sound came. A ripping and crashing, distant at first, accompanied by the relentless retching spit of the bulbs as the tearing sound set them off. Something was coming, something drawn by Rafel's last scream. Something gigantic.

As it burst into the clearing, all of the cacti around them spontaneously shed their needles in a blitz of venomous barbs. The fusillade rattled off the metal carapace and legs. Mkoll threw himself over Dewr and they lay there, silent and still under the storm of darts.

The Chaos dreadnought came to a halt on its great hydraulic feet, sighing and hissing. There was a stench of heat and a throb of electromagnetic power that prickled the hairs on Mkoll's neck. It was four metres tall, wider than three men, blackened and scorched as if it had walked through hell and back. All signs of paint or insignia had been burnt off, to bare metal in some places. A malign presence oozed from it, filling the atmosphere. Such a great machine was terrifying enough in itself, but the malevolent feeling of it… Mkoll felt his gorge rise and clamped his jaws. Dewr seemed unconscious.

The dreadnought took a step forward, almost tentative and dainty though the great steel hoof shook the earth as it fell and triggered another volley of spines. Its body rotated as if scanning, and it took another step. Another plank-plank of rebounding spines.

It was blind. Mkoll could see that at a glance. The wounds of the Adeptus Astartes were deep and fearful across its visor. Its optical units had been blown away in some great act. Mkoll knew the semi-circle of burnt metal Dewr had found was from the recess socket of one of its eyes. It had been blundering around the fern forests for days, hunting by sound alone.

Another step. Another hiss of pistons and a growl of moti-vator. Another thump of footfall, and other rain of darts. It was only three metres from them now, still cranking its body around, listening.

Dewr started and woke up. He saw the dreadnought – and his filmy, poisoned eyes made even greater nightmares out of the existing one. He convulsed and screamed. Despite the gauze gag, the scream was fierce and high pitched, strangu-lated and horrible through the choke.

Mkoll knew he had an instant to react, even as Dewr stirred. He dived aside.

The dreadnought swung and targeted the source of the scream as rapidly as the plants around them did. Poison needles spat into a body that had, mere microseconds before, been incinerated by a belching plasma gun.

Needles rattled off the dreadnought again.

Mkoll moved low, sliding round the bulk of the bulbs, try-ing to keep the listening death machine in sight. His heart was thumping. He cursed it for being so loud.

Behind the next break of growth, he slid in low and checked his weapon. There were fern fronds caught in the trigger. He thought at once to pull them free and then stopped. It would make a sound, and what was the use? What good would a lasgun be against that?

He moved again, his foot skittering a stone. Needles spat ineffectually. The dreadnought began to move, following the sound, walking through rains of needles that convulsed and flew at each footfall.

Mkoll thought to run. It was blind, the plants were blind. If he could only stay silent – and that was his gift – he could slip away and take the information to Gaunt. But would they find it again? Out here, in such a wilderness? It could take weeks to relocate the dreadnought, the lives of many to neutralise it. If he could only…

No. Madness. Suicide.

Then he heard the voice. Distant. It was Waed, calling for Rafel. He was beyond the needle bulbs, searching, querying why Rafel had stopped transmitting. In moments, surely, he would be triggering needles.

Or summoning the dreadnought. Already, the blind beast had turned and begun to stride through the thicket, crushing the spitting cacti into ochre mash.

Mkoll had seconds to think. He would not lose another of his scout cadre, not like this.

He took out a grenade, primed it and threw it left. The crump took out a cluster of bulbs in a spray of fire and matted fibres, and caused a flurry of spines to shoot. Mkoll then headed directly for the blast site. He slid in with his back to one of the bulbs that had triggered at the sound of the explosion. Its needle apertures were spent. He could use it as cover safely now it was unarmed.

The dreadnought was thumping his way, drawn by the sound of the grenade. Waed had fallen silent.

Mkoll adjusted his gun and set it on the ground. Then he spoke.

'Over here, you bastard!'

It sounded impossibly loud. A final taunt to follow the grenade. Bulbs popped around him. But none had spines left on the sides facing him.

The dreadnought crunched into the clearing. Its left foot clinked against something in the dust. It bent to retrieve it.

Mkoll's lasgun.

The dreadnought raised it in its bionic claws, holding the gun up to its already ruptured frontal armour as if to sniff or taste it.

Mkoll started to run.

By his estimation, there were five seconds before the lasgun magazine overloaded as he had set it.

He threw himself flat as it went off.

Hundreds of cacti loosed needles at the roar.

Then silence.

WITH WAED, silently, Mkoll re-entered the thicket. They found the dreadnought broken open in the blackened clearing. The overload had not killed it, but it had split its armour as the towering machine had strode forward. Poison darts had done the rest, puncturing and killing the now-vulnerable once-man inside. Mkoll could see where the maddened Chaos beast-machine had strode arrogantly on for a few heavy steps after the puny laser blast. Then it had toppled, poisoned, dead.

They headed back onto the trail.

'You're a fething hero!' Waed said finally.

'How is that?'

'A fething dreadnought, Mkoll! You killed a dreadnought!'

Mkoll turned and faced Waed with a look that brooked no denial.

'We'll tell the commissar that the area is cleared. Understood? I don't want any stupid glory. Is that clear?'

Waed nodded and followed his sergeant. 'But you killed it...' he ventured softly.

'No, I didn't. I listened and waited and was silent... and when I made the opening, Ramillies did the rest.'

COLM CORBEC WAS sat outside his habitat unit. As regimental second officer, he was given a bivouac like Gaunt's, but the commissar knew that he preferred to sleep in the open.

As Gaunt approached, he saw that Corbec was whittling a piece of bark with his Tanith knife. Gaunt slowed and watched the thick-set man. If he himself died, Gaunt mused, could Corbec hold them together? Could he lead the Ghosts with Gaunt gone?

Corbec would say 'no', Gaunt knew, but he was confident of Corbec's abilities. Even though he had chosen his second in command on a decision that was as simple as a flick of a coin.

'Quiet night,' Corbec said as Gaunt crouched next to him and his fire.

'So far,' Gaunt replied. He watched the big man's hands play the blade over the pale wood. He knew Corbec hated the role of command, would do almost anything to distract himself. Gaunt also knew that Corbec hated ordering men to their deaths or glories. But he did it well. And he took charge when it was needed. Never more so, than on Caligula…

# FOUR
# THE HOLLOWS OF HELL

HE WOULD BE sick. Very soon, very violently. Of this sole fact, Brin Milo was absolutely sure.

His stomach somersaulted as the troop-ship plunged out of the sky, and every bone in his body shook as the impossibly steep descent vibrated the sixty-tonne vessel like a child's rattle.

Count...

...think happy thoughts...

...distract yourself...

...counselled a part of his mind in desperation. It won't look good if the commissar's aide, the regimental piper, wonderboy and all round lucky bloody charm hurls his reconstituted freeze-dried ready-pulped food rations all over the deck.

And whatever you do, don't think about how pulpy and slimy those food rations were... advised another, urgent part of his brain.

Deck? What deck? wailed another. Chuck now and it'll wobble out in free fall and–

*Shut up!* Brin Milo ordered his seething imagination.

For a moment, he was calm. He breathed deeply to loosen and relax, to centre himself, as Trooper Larkin had taught him during marksman training.

Then a tiny little black-hearted voice in his head piped up: Don't worry about puking. You'll be incinerated in a hyper-velocity crash-landing any second now.

LIKE PEPPER FALLING from a mill, thought Executive Officer Kreff, gazing down out of the vast observation blister below the prow of the escort frigate, *Navarre*.

Behind him, on the raised bridge, there was a murmur as the systems operators and servitors softly relayed data back and forth. Control systems hummed. The air was cool. Occasionally, the low, reverential voices of the senior helm officers would announce another order from the ship's captain, who lurked alone, inscrutable, in his private strategium, an armoured dome at the heart of the bridge.

The frigate's bridge was Kreff's favourite place in the universe. It was hushed like a chapel and always serene, even though it controlled a starship capable of crossing parsecs in a blink, a starship with the firepower to roast cities.

He returned to his study of the vast bright bulk of Caligula below him, plump and puffy like an orange, speckled with white-green blotches of mould.

Imperial starships hung in the blackness between it and him: some vast, grey and vaulted like cathedrals twenty kilometres long, some bloated like oceanic titans; others long, lean and angular like his own frigate. They floated in the sea of space and tiny black dots, thousands upon thousands of dots, tumbled out of them, fluttering down towards the ripe planet.

Kreff knew the dots were troop-ships: each speck was a two-hundred tonne dropcraft loaded with combat-ready troops. But they looked just like pepper ground from a mill. As if the Imperial fleet had come by to politely season Caligula.

Kreff wondered which of the pepper grains contained Commissar Gaunt. Things had certainly livened up since Gaunt had arrived: Ibram Gaunt, the notorious, decorated war hero, and the rag-tag regiment known as the Ghosts that he had salvaged from the murdered planet Tanith.

Kreff smoothed the emerald trim of his Segmentum Pacificus Fleet uniform and sighed. When he had first heard the *Navarre* had been assigned to Gaunt's mob, he had been dismayed. But true to his track record, Gaunt had shaped the so-called Ghosts up and taken them through several courageous actions.

It had been an education having him aboard. As executive officer, the official representative of the captain in all shipboard organisational matters, he'd had to mix with the Ghosts more than other Navy personnel. He'd got to know them: as well as anyone could know a band of black-haired, raucous, tattooed soldiers, the last survivors from a planet that Chaos had destroyed. He'd been almost afraid of them at first, alarmed by their fierce physicality. Kreff knew war as a silent, detached, long-distance discipline, a chess-game measured in thousands of kilometres and degrees of orbit. They knew war as a bloody, wearying, frenzied, close-up blur.

He'd been invited to several dinners in the Guard mess, and spent one strange, only partially-remembered evening in the company of Corbec, the regiment's colonel, a hirsute giant of a man who had, on closer inspection, a noble soul. Or so it had seemed after several bottles and hours of loose, earnest talk. They had debated the tactics of war, comparing their own schools and methods. Kreff had been dismissive of Corbec's brutal, primitive ethos, boasting of the high art that was Navy fleet warfare.

Corbec had not been insulted. He'd grinned and promised Kreff would get to fight a real war one day.

The thought made Kreff smile. His eyes went back to the dots falling towards the planet and the smile faded.

Now he doubted he would see either Gaunt or Corbec again.

Far away, below, he could see the scorching flashes of anti-orbit guns, barking up at the fluttering pepper grains. That was a dog's life, going down there into the mouth of hell. All that noise and death and mayhem.

Kreff sighed again, and felt suddenly grateful for the tranquil bridge around him. This was the only way to fight wars, he decided.

MILO OPENED HIS eyes, but it hadn't gone away. The world was still convulsing. He glanced about, down the hold of the troop-ship where another twenty-five Guardsmen sat rigid, clamped in place by the yellow-striped restraint rigs, their equipment shuddering in mesh packs under every seat. The air was sweet with incense, and the ship was shaking so hard that he could not read the inspirational inscriptions etched on the cabin walls. Milo heard the roaring of the outer hull, white-hot from the steep dive. What he couldn't hear was the booming cough of the anti-orbit batteries down below, welcoming them.

He glanced around for a friendly face. Hulking Bragg was gripping his restraints tight, his eyes closed. Young Trooper Caffran, only three years older than Milo, was gazing at the roof, muttering a charm or prayer. Across from him, Milo found the hard eyes of Major Rawne.

Rawne smiled and nodded his head encouragingly.

Milo took a breath. Being encouraged by Major Rawne in these circumstances was like being patted on the back by the Devil at the gates of Hell.

Milo shut his eyes again.

IN THE REAR of the slender cockpit, strapped in his G-chair, Commissar Gaunt craned his neck round to see past the pilots and the astropath and look through the narrow front ports. Chart displays flickered across the thick glass and the ship was bucking wildly, but Gaunt could see the target coming up: the hive city called Nero, poking up out of the ochre soil through a caldera ninety kilometres wide, like an encrusted lump of coal set in a plump navel.

'Sixty seconds to landfall,' the pilot said calmly. His voice was electronically tonal as it rasped via the intercom.

Gaunt pulled out his bolt pistol and cocked it. He started counting down.

\* \* \*

HIGH ABOVE THE sunken city of Nero, the troop-ships came down like bullets, scorching in out of the cloud banks. Anti-air batteries thumped the sky.

Then the cotton-white clouds began to singe. The fluffy corners scorched and wilted. A dark purple stain leached into the sky, billowing through the cumulus like blood through water. Lightning fizzed and lashed.

LEAGUES ABOVE, Kreff paused and stared. Something was discolouring the atmosphere far below.

'What the–' he began.

'WEATHER FORMATION!' the co-pilot yelped, frantically making adjustments. 'We're hitting hail and lightning.'

Gaunt was about to query further but the shaking had increased. He glanced round at the astropath, suddenly aware that the man was uttering a low, monotone growl.

He was just in time to see the astropath's head explode. Blood and tissue painted the pilot, co-pilot, Gaunt and the entire cabin interior.

The pilot was screaming a question.

It was a psychic storm, Gaunt was horribly sure. Far below them, something of unimaginable daemonic power was trying to keep them out, trying to ward off the assault with a boiling tempest of Chaos.

The ship was shaking so hard now Gaunt could no longer focus. Multiple warning runes flashed up in series across the main control display, blurring into scarlet streaks before his rattling eyes.

SOMETHING, SOMEWHERE exploded.

The vibration and the shrieking didn't stop, but they changed. Milo suddenly knew that they were no longer crash-diving into attack.

They were simply crash-diving.

He wasn't feeling sick any more. But the wicked inciner-ated-in-a-hypervelocity-crashlanding-voice started to crow: *I told you so.*

* * *

THERE WAS IMPACT...

...so huge, it felt like every one of his joints had dislocated.

There was sliding...

...sudden, shuddering, terrifying.

And finally...

...there was roaring fire.

And, as if as an afterthought...

...complete excruciating blackness.

HUNDREDS OF IMPERIAL troop-ships were already well below the cloudbank when the psychic typhoon exploded into life, and so escaped the worst of its effects. Levelling out, they descended on the massive citadel of Nero Hive like a plague of locusts. The air was thick with them, ringing with the roar of their thrusters as they banked in and settled on the wasteland outskirts of the towering black city-hive. Traceries of laser and plasma fire divided the sky in a thousand places, making it look for all the world like some insanely complex set of blueprints. Some struck landing ships which flared, fluttered and died. Flak shells sent loud, black flowers up into the air. Marauder air-support shrieked in at intervals, moving in close, low formations like meteorites hunting as a pack, strafing the ground with stitching firestorms.

Above it all, the purple sky boiled and thrashed and spat electric ribbons.

At ground level, Colonel Colm Corbec of the Tanith First-and-Only led his squad down the ramp of the troop-ship and into the firezone. To either side, he could see lines of ships disgorging their troops into the field, a tide of men ten thousand strong.

They reached the first line of cover – a punctured length of pipeline running along rusted pylons – and dropped down.

Corbec took a look each way and keyed in his micro-bead comm link. 'Corbec to squad. Sound off.'

Voices chatted back along the link, responding.

By Corbec's side, Trooper Larkin was cradling his lasgun and looking up at the sky with trembling fear.

'Oh, this is bad,' he murmured. 'Psyker madness, very bad. We may think we had it hard at Voltis Watergate or Blackshard deadzone, but they'll seem like a stroll round the garden next to *this*...'

'Larks!' Corbec hissed. 'For Feth's sake, shut up! Haven't you ever heard of morale?'

Larkin turned his bony, weasel face to his senior officer and old friend in genuine surprise. 'It's okay, colonel!' he insisted. 'I didn't have me comm link turned on! Nobody heard!'

Corbec grimaced. 'I heard, and you're scaring the crap out of me.'

They all ducked down as a swathe of autocannon fire chewed across the lines. Someone a few hundred metres away started screaming. They could hear the piercing shrieks over the roar of the storm and the landing troopships and the bombardment.

Just.

'Where's the commissar?' Corbec growled. 'He insisted he was going to lead us in.'

'If he ain't landed, he ain't coming,' Larkin said, looking up at the sky. 'We were the last few to make it through before that happened.'

Next to Larkin, Trooper Raglon, the squad's communications officer, looked up from the powerful voxcaster set. 'No contact from the commissar's dropcraft, sir. I've been scanning the orbital traffic and the Navy band, colonel. This filthy psyker storm took out a whole heap of troop-ships. They're still counting the crash fires. We was lucky we got down before it really started.'

Corbec shivered. He didn't feel lucky.

Raglon went on: 'Our psykers upstairs are trying to break the storm, but...'

'But what?'

'It looks pretty certain the commissar's troop-ship was one of those vaporised in the storm.'

Corbec growled something indistinct. He felt cold, and could see the look on the faces of his men as the word spread down the line.

Corbec lifted his lasgun and keyed up his micro-bead. He had to rally them fast, get them moving. 'What are you waiting for?' he bawled. 'Diamond formation fire-team spread! Double time! Fire at will! Advance! For the memory of Tanith! Advance!'

BRIN MILO woke up.

He was upside down, blind, suspended painfully from his restraint rig, his ribs bruised blue and a taste of blood in his mouth. But – unless someone was about to play a really nasty trick on him – he was alive.

He could hear… very little. The trickle and patter of falling water. A creaking. Someone moaning softly.

There was a loud bang and light flared into his dark-accustomed eyes. He smelled thermite and realised someone had just ejected the emergency hull-plates using the explosive bolts. Daylight – thin, green, wet daylight – streamed in.

Bragg's huge face swam up in front of Milo's, upside down.

'Hang on, Brinny-boy,' Bragg said softly. 'Soon have you down.' He started rattling the restraints and slamming the lock handle back and forth.

The restraints abruptly stopped restraining and Milo uttered a little yelp as he dropped two and a half metres onto the sloping roof of the troop-ship.

'Sorry,' Bragg said, helping him up. 'You hurt, lad?'

Milo shook his head. 'Where are we?' he asked.

Bragg paused as if he was thinking about this carefully, Then, with deliberation, he said 'We're earlobe deep in doo-doo.'

THE TROOP-SHIP, now just a crumpled sleeve of metal, had impacted at a steep angle on its roof.

Milo climbed down and gazed back up at the mangled wreck. What amazed him only slightly less than the fact he was still alive, was that they had come down in what appeared to be a jungle. Enormous pinkish trees that looked like swollen, magnified root vegetables, formed a dense forest of flaccid trunks around them. The huge growths were strung with thick ropey vines, creepers and flowering tendrils, and thorny fern and horsetail covered the moist, steaming ground. Everything was green, as all light – except for a single clear shaft which slanted down through the trees where the troop-ship had burst through – was filtered by the dense canopy of foliage above their heads. It was humid, and sticky, and sappy water dripped from the trees. There was a sweet stink of fungoid flowers.

Bragg clambered down from the wreck, and joined the boy. A dozen other Ghosts had clambered out and were sat down or leaning against trees, waiting for spinning heads and ringing ears to clear. All had minor cuts and scrapes, except Trooper Obel who lay on a makeshift stretcher, his chest bloody and torn. Corporal Meryn had taken charge. He and Caffran were trying to open other emergency hatches to look for more survivors.

Milo saw Rawne had survived. The major stood to one side with a tall, pale Ghost called Feygor, who served as his aide.

'I didn't know there were any jungles on this world,' Milo said.

'Me neither,' Bragg answered. He was catching and piling equipment packs Meryn was tossing down from the side of the wreck. 'Actually, I didn't even know what this world was called.'

Milo found Rawne by his side.

'We're in a forest hollow,' Rawne said. 'The surface of Caligula is barren pumice, but it's punctured in many places by deep rift basins, many of them old craters or volcanic sinks. The cities are built down into the largest of them, but others sustain microclimates wet enough for these forests. I think some of them were actually farmed... before the fething enemy came in.'

'So... where are we?' Feygor asked.

Rawne rubbed his throat, thoughtful. 'We've come down a good way off target. I think there were some forest calderas north of Nero. On the wrong side of the lines.'

Feygor swore.

'I think the major is correct,' said a voice.

Gaunt appeared, sliding down from a side vent in the punctured hull. He was tattered and bruised, with blood soaking the shoulder and side of his tunic under his coat. Meryn hurried over to him to assist.

'Not me,' Gaunt said, waving him off. 'The co-pilot's alive and he needs to be cut free.'

'It's a miracle anyone got out of that front end,' Meryn said with a whistle.

Gaunt crossed to Milo, Rawne and the others.

'Report, major,' he said.

'Unless we find anyone else alive in there, we've got twelve able-bodied men, plus yourself, the boy Milo and the co-pilot. Minor injuries all round, though Trooper Grogan has a broken arm. But he can walk. Obel has chest injuries. Pretty bad. Brennan is inside. He's a real mess and pinned, but he's alive. The rest are pulp.'

Rawne looked up at the wreck. 'Lucky shot got us, I guess. Missile–'

'Psykers!' Gaunt growled. 'They threw some freakshow storm up. Smashed us out of the sky.'

Everyone fell silent at the thought. Fear prickled them. Some looked away, uneasy and shaken.

Gaunt crossed to the pile of equipment packs Bragg and Caffran were offloading and opened a compact carry-box. Out of this he slid a topolabe from its cushioned slot and held it up by the knurled handgrip. The small brass machine whirred and the concentric dials span and clicked as the gravimetric gyros turned in the glass bubble of inert gas.

After a moment, the machine chimed and published a read-out on a back-lit blue display.

'We're in a forest caldera called K7-75, about forty kilometres north north-east of the Nero city perimeter. Your assessment was good, major. We're on the wrong side of the lines and in pretty damn inhospitable country. There's dense forest for at least eight kilometres in any direction, and this sinkhole's about a kilometre deep. We'd better get ready to move.'

'Move?' Feygor asked. 'Commissar… we can get the crash beacon up and running…'

'No we can't,' Meryn said. He showed them the molten resdue of the beacon unit.

'And even if we could, Feygor?' Gaunt shook his head sadly. 'About fifty kilometres south of us, the Imperial Guard is engaged in a massive assault. Thousands are dying. Every ship, and craft and man is committed to the attack. There will be nothing to spare to come looking – across enemy lines, mark you – for a few lost souls like us. They'll have already written us off. Besides, there's a psyker-bred storm raging up there, remember? No one could get to us even if they wanted to.'

Rawne spat and cursed. 'So what do we do?'

Gaunt grinned, but without humour. 'We see how far we can get. Better that than just wait here to die.'

IN FIFTEEN MINUTES, the survivors were assembled and injuries tended. Salvageable equipment and weapons were divided up. Both Milo and the dazed co-pilot were given a laspistol and a few spare power cells. Obel and the now-freed Brennan lay unconscious on stretcher pallets.

Rawne looked grimly at Gaunt. He nodded his head at the two injured men. 'We should… be merciful.'

Gaunt frowned. 'We're taking them with us.'

Rawne shook his head. 'With respect, they'll probably both be dead in an hour. Taking them will tie up four able-bodied soldiers as stretcher bearers.'

'We're taking them,' Gaunt repeated.

'If you lashed 'em both to a frame,' Bragg put in thoughtfully, 'I could drag 'em along. Better me than four other boys.'

Meryn and Feygor raised the two stretcher cases onto an A-frame of wood and Bragg took the weight of the point on his shoulder. Caffran had used his silver Tanith knife to cut lengths of waxy creeper and bound them on for a grip.

'I won't be fast, mind,' Bragg noted. But with the party clearing the way, he could pull them along on the sling-bed efficiently enough.

The commissar checked the topolabe again, scanning for closer detail.

'Interesting,' he murmured. 'About four kilometres east there's some kind of structure. Maybe an old farming complex or something. Might provide us with some shelter. Let's see.' Gaunt had armed himself with a lasgun from one of the dead. He handed his chainsword to Rawne. 'Take point please, major,' he said.

Rawne moved to the head of the column and started to slice his way through the dense, wet forest.

THE TANITH GHOSTS advanced through the outer complexes of the hive city, surging down an embankment and across the blasted ferrocrete of a six-lane arterial highway.

Broken vehicles littered the lanes, and great pools of motor oil blazed up curtains of fire. Corbec urged the Ghosts forward, under traffic control boards that still flashed and winked speed limits and direction pointers. Guns blazing, they began to assault a vast block of worker residences on the far side.

As the battle group swept into the shattered hallways of the old worker residences, where peeling placards exhorted the citizen workers to meet production targets and praise the Emperor at all times, fighting became a close-quarter business with the enemy forces, now seen face to face for the first time. Humans, corrupted by Chaos, cult worshippers whose physical forms had become twisted and warped. Most wore the black, vulcanised work suits of the hive workforce, daubed now with Chaos patterns, their heads protected with tight grey hoods and industrial glare visors. They were well armed, too.

Bodies littered the concourses and galleries of the residences, shattered glass and twisted plastic covered the ground. Intense fires blazed through some areas, and the air was full of drifting cinders, like incandescent snow.

And flies: dark, fat-bodied flies.

Blasting as he advanced, Corbec fired to left and right, through doorways and thin plastic-board walls, cutting down or exploding the foe all around.

Flanked in a fire-team, Larkin, Suth, Varl, Mallor, Durcan and Billad worked in immediate support. Larkin snatched off the occasional shot, his aim as fine as usual, though Corbec knew that thanks to the storm, he was closer to snapping than ever. Suth had the squad's melta, and seared them a path.

Bolt fire and las-shot cut their way. Billad jerked as he was hit repeatedly, sprawling back against a wall and sliding down.

Corbec sent a steady stream of shot into the smoke haze. The flies buzzed.

Radio chatter was almost as deafening as the firefight. Guard forces had begun to pincer the city. A combined force of Royal Volpone 50th and Raymian 13th and 16th had driven a steel fist into the ore-smelter heartland of the hive, meeting the enemy's main motorised units in an armoured battle in the vast, echoing barns of the starship yards and drydocks. Rumours were a battalion of Lakkarii Gundogs and some Raven Guard Space Marines had punched through into the upper levels, into the Administratum tower itself.

But an overall victory seemed so far away, especially given the psychic storm, which effectively shut off any further reinforcements. Or anything else.

'Any joy with the air-cover?' Corbec asked over the crackle of laser fire.

Trooper Raglon answered on the bead-link. 'Marauder flights are all out of action, sir. Fleet Command recalled them because of the storm. The Chaos effects are screwing their guidance.'

Corbec glanced up at the corrosive purple turbulence that passed for sky. Forget the aircraft, that nightmare was screwing with his guidance. This close to a manifestation of Chaos, his senses were whirling. His balance was shot and he felt nauseous, with a throbbing pain in his temple. Terror dimpled his skin and ached in his marrow. He dared not think about what was out there, waiting for him.

And he knew his men were the same. There had been a dozen spontaneous nosebleeds already, and several men had convulsed, vomiting.

Still, they were making headway, clawing through the grim habitat towers and the workforce residence blocks where things came down to knife and pistol, room to room, in the old, dirty tenements where the lowest level of worker had dwelt.

The commissar would have been proud, Corbec thought. The Ghosts had done the job. He spat out a fly and listened carefully to the flow of radio traffic again for a moment. The Fleet Command channel repeated its overriding directive: unless the enemy psykers could be neutralised, the Fleet couldn't land any more reinforcements, any more of the five million Imperial Guard troops still waiting in troop-ships in orbit. Or deploy air-cover. The fate of the entire battle teetered in the balance.

Corbec brushed off another fly. The air was thick with them now, choked with flies and cinders and ash. The smell was unbearable. Colm Corbec took a deep, shuddering breath. He knew the signs: they were close to something, something bad. Something of Chaos.

'Watch yourselves!' he warned his group over the link. 'We're getting into a real nest of Hell here!'

Through the swarming clouds of buzzing flies, the fire-team edged along a corridor littered with clear plastic shards and torn paper. Out in the concourse below, a fierce hand-to-hand battle was ending in screams and sporadic pistol fire. Something blew up a kilometre or so away, shaking the ground.

Corbec reached the turn in the hall and waved his men back.

Just in time, his fire-team sheltered in doorways as heavy stub gun fire raked up and down the old back-stairway, disintegrating the steps and tearing down the stained wall tiles.

Corbec looked round at Larkin, who was murmuring some Imperial Prayer under his breath, waving off the flies. It was probably the oath of allegiance to the Emperor they'd all been taught at school back home on Tanith.

Home...

This had once been someone's home, thought Corbec, snapping back to the hard facts of real time. A dingy old hallway in a dingy old high rise, where humble, hardworking people came back from the shift-work at the fabrication plants in the hive and cooked meagre meals for their tired children.

'Larks!' He gestured up the stairwell. 'A little Mad Magic on that stubber!'

Larkin wiped his mouth and shook out his neck like a pianist about to play. He took out his nightscope, a little heat-sensitive spotter he'd used back home poaching larisel out in the woods at night. He trained it up the hall, found a hub of heat emanating from the wall.

Most would have aimed for that, thinking it the body heat of the gunner. Larkin knew better. The source was the muzzle heat of the big cannon. That put the gunner about sixty centimetres behind it, to the left.

'A bottle of sacra says it's a head shot,' whispered Corbec as he saw Larkin snuggle down and aim his lasgun.

'Done,' Varl said.

Larkin punched a single shot up the stairwell and through the wall.

They moved forward, cautious at first, but there was no further firing.

Covering each other, they moved up the smashed staircase, past the landing where the cult soldier lay dead across his stub gun, head half gone. Corbec smiled and Varl sighed.

Then they entered a further landing and fanned out. There was a smell of burning flesh here, and the flies were thicker than ever.

Larkin edged along one wall, looking at the trash and broken possessions that had been dropped in the rubble. Along the wall, under a series of Chaos markings rendered in dark paint, someone had nailed up a series of dolls and other childrens' toys. Something in Larkin's heart broke as he gazed on the crucified dolls, remembering a world of family and friends and children forever lost to him.

Then he realised that not all of the dolls were dolls.

Larkin fell to his knees, retching.

On the far side of the gallery, Corbec, Durcan and Suth burst into a long concrete chamber that had once been a

central meeting hall for the tenement block. It was dark
inside. Several thousand eyes blinked in their direction.

They all belonged to the same... thing.

Something immeasurably vast began to coil up out of the
darkness, extending the flaccid, blue-white mass of its
bloated body, toxic spittle drooling from its befanged
mouths. Jellied things quivered in the dark spaces of its
translucent skin and flies billowed around it like a cloak.

Corbec's nose spurted blood and soaked his beard as he
backed away, his mind seized in horror. Suth dropped the
melta with a clatter and started to retch, sliding down the
wall, unable to stand. Durcan seemed unable to move. He
began to cry, wailing as he fumbled to raise his lasgun.
Limpid, greasy coils lashed out of the dark chamber and
encircled him, embraced him, and then crushed him so
hard and so suddenly he burst like a tomato.

Mallor and Varl turned and saw the horror slithering up
from the chamber, saw Suth helpless and Corbec frozen, saw
the pulpy red slick that had been Durcan.

'Daemon! Daemon!' Varl screamed down the comm link.
'DAEMON!'

GAUNT HELD UP a hand and announced a ten minute rest. The
group eased back and took the weight off their feet, leaning
on tree trunks, hunkering down.

Meryn took the medi-pack back to Bragg and helped him
lower the stretcher-bed.

'Oh, feth!' Milo heard him say.

Milo crossed over as Gaunt himself approached.

Meryn looked up, treating the ugly wounds of the two
unconscious men. 'It's this place,' he explained, 'hot, wet...
spores in the air... insects. Their wounds get re-infected as
fast as I clean them. Obel's fading fast. Some kind of fungus
necrotizing the raw flesh. Maggots too.' He shook his head
and continued with his work.

Milo moved away. The smell rising from the wounded
men was not pleasant.

Nearby stood the co-pilot. He'd pulled his flight helmet
off, and was staring nervously into the green darkness

around them, clutching his laspistol. Milo thought he looked young, no older than him. The flesh around his cranial implants looked raw and fresh. He probably feels just like me, Milo decided. In over his head.

He had just considered approaching the navy cadet and speaking to him when the low whine of gunfire sang through the trees. Everyone ducked for cover, and there was a staccato series of safety locks disengaging and power-cells humming to life.

Near to Milo, Gaunt crawled forward, tapping his microbead.

'Rawne? Answer!' he hissed. The major, with Feygor, Caffran and a trooper called Kalen, had scouted ahead towards the mysterious structure.

'Firefight!' came Rawne's response, Milo picking it up via his own comm-bead. 'We're pinned! Daagh! Throne of God! There's–'

The link went dead.

'Damn!' Gaunt hissed. He clambered to his feet. 'Meryn! Bragg! Guard the wounded! You, Navy boy! Stay with them! The rest with me, fire-team spread!'

The Ghosts moved forward and Milo moved with them, checking his pistol was cleared to fire. Despite the fear, he felt pride. The commissar had needed all the men he could muster. He had not thought twice about including Milo.

CORBEC WAS SURE his life was over when Larkin started shooting. Driven over the edge by what he had seen nailed along the wall, Larkin just went crazy; mindless, oblivious to the otherwise transfixing image of Chaos in that old tenement. Larkin simply opened fire and kept firing.

'Larkin! Larkin!' Corbec hissed.

The little man's howl was drying away into a hoarse whisper. A repetitive clicking came from the lasgun in his hands, the power cell exhausted.

The lashing tentacles of the vast thing in the hallway had been driven back by the hammerblow of relentless laser fire.

They had a moment of grace, time to retreat.

Corbec led his scrambling fire-team back down the tenement hall, half-carrying Larkin.

'Oh feth! Oh feth! Oh feth!' Larkin repeated, over and over.

'Shut up, Larks!' warned Corbec. 'Contact Fleet Command!' he yelled to Raglon over his bead. 'Tell them what we've found!'

IN THE COVER of a slumped tree-stump, Trooper Caffran sighted his lasgun to his shoulder and loosed a burst of laser shot that sliced explosively through the foliage ahead. Bolter fire returned, smacking into the wood around him, blasting sprays of splinters and gouts of sap.

'Major Rawne?' Caffran yelled. 'Comm link's dead!'

'I know!' spat Rawne, dropped down against a tree nearby as metal shot exploded the bark behind him. He threw down Gaunt's chainsword and swung his own lasgun up to fire.

Feygor took up a prone position, blasting with his own weapon, Kalen to his side. The four Ghost lasguns blasted an arc of fire into the dense trees, the dim grove flickering with the muzzle flashes.

Rawne span, his gun lowered, but dropped his aim with a curse as he saw Gaunt moving in behind them, the men in fire-team line.

'Report!' hissed Gaunt.

'We just walked into heavy bolter fire. Enemy positions ahead, unseen. Feels like an ambush, but who knew we were coming?'

'Comm link?'

'Dead… jammed.'

'Would help if we could see what we were shooting at,' Gaunt remarked. He waved a 'come here' to Trooper Brostin, who hurried over, cradling the single flamer they'd pulled intact from the troop-ship.

'Positions!' Gaunt yelled, and fanned his men out so that all could take a clear shot once the target was revealed. 'Brostin?'

The trooper triggered the flame cannon and a volcanic spear of liquid fire spat into the dense undergrowth.

Maintaining the spurt, like a horizontal fountain of fire, Brostin swept it left and right.

The trees, horsetails and giant ferns ahead flared and blazed, some of them igniting as if their sap was petrol, some wilting and withering like dust. In twenty seconds, a wall of jungle had been scorched aside and they had a clear view sixty metres into an artificially cleared area.

Silence. Not even the bolter fire which had got them ducking.

'Scope!' called Gaunt, and took the instrument as Milo offered it up.

'Looks like we have…' Gaunt paused as the self-focus dials on his scope whirred and spun. 'An Imperial installation. Three armoured, modular cabins, two larger hardened shelters… they've all had the insignia spray-painted out. Communicator-array and up-link mast for a voxcaster, that's probably what's jamming us… perimeter defence net… slaved servitors mounted into autoloader bolt cannons. You must have tripped a sensor as you came in, major. Triggered them off. I think we've fried a couple of them.'

'What is this place?' Caffran murmured.

'A way out… a chance we never thought we had. If we can get in there alive, that is.' Gaunt fell silent.

'But what's it doing out here in the middle of this jungle?' Milo found himself asking.

Gaunt looked round at him. 'Good question.'

THE WORD WASN'T good. All ground forces were stretched to breaking point maintaining the gains they had made. There was no one to move in to support the Ghosts.

'How can we fight that kind of stuff?' stammered Suth.

Corbec shook his head. He'd pulled the entire battle group back to the embankment overlooking the highway and the tenements beyond.

Tenements that held the most abominable thing he'd ever seen.

'But it has to die!' Larkin whispered. 'Don't you see? It's causing the storm. Unless it dies, we're all stuck here!'

'You can't know that, Larks!' Varl sneered.

Corbec wasn't so sure. Larkin's gut instincts had always been good bets. 'Emperor save us all!' Corbec said, exasperated. He thought hard. There had to be something… something… what would Gaunt have done? Something arrogant, no doubt. Pulled rank, broken the rules, thrown the strategy books out of the window and used the resources he knew he could count on…

'Hey, Raglon! Over here, lad!' he yelled to his comm-officer. 'Patch me a link to the *Navarre*!'

EXECUTIVE OFFICER Kreff cleared his throat, took a deep breath and stepped into the Strategium, the captain's armoured inner sanctum at the centre of the *Navarre*'s bridge.

Captain Wysmark sat in dark, contemplative silence on a reclined throne, quietly assessing the flickering overlays of runic and schematic data that flowed across the smoothly curved walls and roof of the room.

He turned in his chair slightly. 'Kreff?'

'I have, um, this is unorthodox, sir, but–'

'Out with it, man.'

'I've just spoken with Colonel Corbec, the acting chief of the Tanith First. His battle group is assaulting the western edge of the Nero Hive. He requests we… activate the main batteries and present on a target he has acquired.'

Wysmark sneered, the glow of the readouts flickering across his face in the gloom.

'Doesn't this idiot know anything about Naval tactics?' he chuckled. 'Fleet weapons will only engage a surface target from orbit before troop deployment. Once the ground forces are in, air-strikes are the responsibility of the attack squadrons.'

Kreff nodded. 'Which are grounded due to the psychic storm, sir. The colonel is aware it is counter to usual tactics, as orbital bombardment is not known for its… um… finesse. However, he claims this is a critical situation… and he can supply us with pinpoint co-ordinates.'

Wysmark frowned, thoughtful. 'Your assessment, Kreff? You've spent more time with these footsloggers since they've been aboard than anyone. Is this man mad, or should I grant his request?'

Kreff dared a little smile. 'Yes… and yes, sir.'

Wysmark grinned back, very slightly. He rotated his chair to face Kreff. 'Let's see those co-ordinates.'

Kreff jumped forward and handed him the data-slate.

Wysmark keyed his micro-bead intercom. 'Communications: patch me to Fleet Command. I wish to advise them of our next action. Fire control, energise the main batteries… I have a firing solution here. All stations, this is the captain… rig for main weapon firing.'

All so very neat and civil, Kreff smiled. This really was the only way to fight a war.

THERE WAS A blink of light, an astonishing shockwave that knocked them all down, and then a deafening roar that hammered across them.

Corbec rose, coughing dust and picked Raglon up.

'Right on the button,' he remarked jovially to his astonished men.

They scrambled up to the top of the slope and looked over the balustrade. Below them, the ruinous expanse of a ten-lane highway stretched into the dark industrial high rises of the hive. Across the highway, a vast blazing crater stood where the tenements had been.

'Holy Throne of Earth!' Varl stammered.

'Friends in high places,' sniggered Corbec. He glanced down the slope at the hundreds of waiting troops below, troops who could already sense the change in the air. There was smoke, and fumes and cordite – but the stink of Chaos was retreating. The storm was blowing itself out.

'Let's go!' he yelled into his bead.

THE COMMS OFFICER saluted Kreff as he crossed the polished deck of the serene bridge.

'Signal from the surface, sir.'

Kreff nodded.

'Standard Guard voxcaster encryption, data and time as now, orbit lag adjusted. Message reads: "Ghostly gratitude to

the *Navarre*. Kreff, you bastard, we knew you had it in you."
Message ends. Sorry about the vulgarity, sir.'

The comms officer looked up from the slate.

'I'll take that,' Kreff said, trying to hide his grin as he saun-
tered away.

GAUNT MOVED IN close to the cabins, bolt pistol in hand.
Behind him came Feygor and Caffran, edging slowly.

There was a low whirr and one of the servitors nearby
detected the movement and swung around, bringing its
automated weapon to bear.

Gaunt blasted it apart with three quick shots. Diving forward, he slammed in through the doorway, rolling up in
the blue, cold, artificial light of the interior, hunting for a
target.

There was nothing but darkness. And dead stillness. Gaunt
moved into the low habitat, mindful of the gloom. Ahead, a
dull phosphorescence shone. There was a dark bunkroom
full of over-thrown furniture and scattered papers. Gaunt
took a look at one leaf and knew he would have to have them
all burnt.

Rawne and Feygor slid in behind him.

'What is this?' Rawne asked.

'We'll see…' murmured Gaunt.

They moved through the habitat into a greenhouse where
the air was humid.

There were things growing in the hydroponics vats that
Gaunt didn't want to look at. Fibrous, swollen, bulging
things, pulsing with hideous life.

'What is this place?' asked Feygor, horrified.

'The start of it… the beginning of Caligula's fall,' Gaunt
said. 'One of the industrialists of this world, hot-housing
something he could not understand. The competition for
better crops is fierce here. This poor fool didn't realise what
he was growing.'

Or at least, Gaunt thought, I hope he didn't. If this had
been done with foreknowledge, deliberately… He shook the
idea away.

'Burn it. Burn it all,' he told his men.

'Not all,' Kalen said, entering behind them. 'I scouted around the perimeter. Whoever owned this place has a shuttle bedded in a silo out back.'

Gaunt smiled. The Emperor will always provide.

'SO HE DIDN'T DIE?' mused Corbec, sat on his bunk in the troop bay. Bragg shook his head and swigged from the bottle of sacra. 'Don't think nothing's gonna kill old Gaunt. He said he was gonna get us all out, and he did. Even Obel and Brennan.'

Corbec thought about this. 'Actually,' he said finally, 'I meant Rawne.'

They both looked across the quiet bay to where Rawne and Feygor sat in quiet conversation.

'Oh, him. No, worse luck.' Bragg passed the bottle back to Corbec. 'So, I hear you had some fun of your own?'

A FORWARD POST, looking out into the water-choked thickness of the Monthax jungles. The flies were thick out here, like sparkling dust in the air. Amphibians gurgled and chugged in the mudbanks.

The sappers had raised the spit-post out beyond the broad levees of the main embankment, one of six that allowed the Tanith snipers greater reach into the front line. They were long, zagged and lined with frag-sacking and a double layer of overlapped flak-boards.

Gaunt edged along the spit, keeping low, passing the sentries at the heavy-bolter post at the halfway point. The mud, unmoving and stagnant in the dug-away bed, stank like liquescent death.

The sagging cable of a land-line voxcaster ran down the length of the sacking, held above the water by iron loop-pins.

Gaunt knew it ended at a vox-set at the sniper post. In the event of attack, he would want the earliest warning from his keen-eyed forwards, and one that could be conveyed by good old, reliable, un-scrambleable cable.

Larkin was his usual edgy self. At the loop hole at the end of the spit-post, he was sat on a nest of sacking, meticulously polishing his weapon.

A compulsive, Gaunt thought. The commissar stepped up to him. Larkin looked around, tense.

'You always look like you're afraid of me,' Gaunt said.

'Oh no, sir. Not you, sir.'

'I'd hate to think so. I count on men like you, Larkin. Men with particular skills.'

'I'm gratified, commissar.'

Larkin's weapon was sparkling, yet still the man worked the cloth to it.

'Carry on,' said Gaunt.

*But for how much longer*, he wondered?

# FIVE
# THE ANGEL OF BUCEPHALON

LARKIN THOUGHT ABOUT death. He thought he might well have begged for it long ago, had he not been so scared of it. He had never figured out, though he had spent whole nights wondering it, whether he was more afraid of death itself or the fear of death. Worse, there had been so many times when he had expected to find out. So many moments caught in Death's frosty gaze, snapped at by Death's steel incisors. The question had been nearly answered so many times.

Now perhaps, he would find out. Here. Death, or the fear of death.

If the Angel knew, she was saying nothing. Her stern face was turned down, demure, eyes closed as if sleeping, praying hands clasped at her breast.

Outside, below them, the war to take Bucephalon raged. The stained glass in the huge lancet window, what remained of it, shook and twinkled with reflections of tracer sprays, salvos of blazing rockets, bright air-bursts.

Larkin sat back against the cold stone pillar and rubbed a dirty hand around his lean jaw. His breathing was slowing now at last, his pulse dropping, the anxiety attack that had seen him wailing and gasping five minutes ago was passing like a cyclone. Or maybe he was just in the eye of that storm.

The ground shook. He felt it through the pillar. His pulse leapt for a moment. He forced himself to breathe deeply through his mouth, slow, deep inhalations of the sort he used to steady himself before taking a shot.

'You were telling me how you came to be here.'

Larkin looked round at the Angel. Though her head was still angled down, now she was gazing at him, smiling grimly. Larkin licked his lips and gestured idly around with one dirt-caked hand.

'War. Fighting. Fate.'

'I meant specifically,' said the Angel.

'Orders. The will of the Emperor.'

The Angel seemed to shrug her robed shoulders slightly. 'You are very defensive. You hide yourself and the truth behind words.'

Larkin blinked. For a moment, sickle-shaped moons of bright white light and fuzzy oblongs of red blackness lurched across his vision. A tiny moment of nausea. He knew the signs. He'd known them since childhood. The visual disturbances, the nausea, the taste of tin in his mouth. Then, the anxiety, the tunnel vision. After that, if he was lucky, a white hot migraine pain that would burst inside his skull and leave him dazed and helpless for hours. If he was unlucky: fits, spasms, blackouts and an awakening hours later, bruised and bloodied from the thrashing seizures; empty, miserable, destroyed inside.

'What's the matter?' asked the Angel.

Larkin tapped his forehead gently with his index finger. 'I'm… not right. Never have been, not in all my life. The fits used to scare my mother, but not half as much as they did me. They come on me from time to time.'

'Times like now? Under pressure? In the presence of danger?'

'That doesn't help. But it's just another trigger. You know what a ploin is?'

'No.'

'Round fruit. Soft, green-skinned, juicy. Lots of black pips in pink flesh. They used to grow in my uncle's orchard on Tanith. Divine things, but even the smell of them would trigger an attack.'

'Is there no medicine you can take?'

'I had tablets. But I forget to take them.' He took a little wooden pill-box from his jacket, opened the lid and showed her it was empty. 'Or I forget when I run out.'

'What do they call you?' asked the Angel.

'They call me Mad Larkin.'

'That is cruel.'

'But true. I'm not right in my mind. Mad.'

'Why do you think you are mad?'

'I'm talking to a statue of the Imperium, aren't I?'

She laughed and smoothed the folds of the white robes over her kneeling legs. There was a low and perfect radiance to her. Larkin blinked and saw glowing moons and oblongs in after-image again.

Outside, a hail of gunfire lit the evening and a ripple of explosions crackled the air. Larkin got to his feet and crossed to the nearest window. He looked out through interlocking pieces of coloured glass at the city below. Steepled, tall, rising within a curtain of walls eighty metres high, the capital city-state of Bucephalon clung to the ridge of the mountains. Smoke obscured the sky. Las-fire filled the air like bright sleet. Two or more kilometres away, he saw the pair of enormous storming ramps that the sappers of the Imperial Guard had raised against the walls. Huge embankments of piled earth and concrete rubble almost a kilometre long, rising high and broad enough to deliver armoured vehicles to the top of the wall. Heavy fighting within blooms of flame lit the ramps.

Below, nearer, the men on the ground looked like insect dots. Thousands, churning in trenches, spilling out across the chewed and cratered mess of the battlefront to assault the forbidding walls.

Larkin's vantage point was high and good. This shelled, ruined fortress was part of a stone complex which straddled and guarded the main aqueduct into the city, a huge structure that had defied the most earnest attempts of the enemy to fell with mines. Though heavily defended, it had seemed to Commissar Gaunt a good way in for a stealth team. Not the first time the commissar had been wrong.

Gaunt had told them that, before the clutch of Chaos fell upon it, the city-state had been ruled by thirty-two noble families, the descendants of merchant dynasties that had established the settlement. Their brilliant banners, the heraldic displays of thirty-two royal houses, were displayed on the walls, tatters of rich cloth draped from massive timber awnings. Those mighty awnings were now additionally decorated with the crucified bodies of the leaders of those noble families.

It had been Nokad's first act. Nokad the Blighted, Nokad the Smiling, the charismatic cult leader whose malign forces had risen to conquer Bucephalon from within, and win one of the most honourable of the Sabbat Worlds. In his great liberation address at the start of the crusade, Warmaster Slaydo himself had listed proud Bucephalon as one of the worlds he was most eager to save.

Shells burst outside the windows and Larkin ducked back into cover. Glass pattered and tinkled onto the stone floor. The flashes behind his eyes were getting worse and he could taste the tang of metal in his saliva. There was a moaning, too, a dull aching groan in his inner ear. That was a particularly bad sign. He had only got that a time or two before, just prior to the very worst madnesses. His vision was not entirely stable. Everything in the chapel around him seemed elongated and stretched, like in the mirror tent at the Attica carnival. In places his vision belled and warped, objects shimmering in and out of focus, drifting near and then away again.

He shuddered, deep in his bones.

The Angel was lighting tapers at the wrought iron offertory. Her movements were slow and lovely, pure grace.

She asked, 'Why don't you believe in angels?'

'Oh, I do.' Larkin sighed. 'Not just now, before. A friend of mine, Cluggan, a sergeant, he was a bit of a military historian. He said that at the Battle of Sarolo, angels appeared over the lines just before dawn and inspired the Imperial forces to victory.'

'Were they visions, do you think? Mass hallucinations brought on by fatigue and fear?'

'Who am I to say?' Larkin replied, as the Angel finished her taper-lighting and blew the long flame-reed out. 'I'm mad. Visions and phantoms appear to me on a daily basis, most of them conjured by the malfunctions of my mind. I'm not in a position to say what is real and what is not.'

'Your opinion is no less valid than any other. Did they see angels at Sarolo?'

'I…'

'Say what you think.'

'I think so.'

'And what were those angels?'

'Manifestations of the Emperor's will, come to vitalise his loyal forces.'

'Is that what you think?'

'It's what I'd like to think.'

'And the alternative?'

'Hnh! Group madness! The meddling of psykers! Lies constructed by relieved men after the fact! What you said… mass hallucinations.'

'And if it was any or all of those things, does that make it any less important? Whatever they saw or thought they saw, it inspired them to victory at Sarolo. If an angel isn't really an angel but has the inspirational effect of one, does that make it worthless?'

Larkin shook his head and smiled.

'Why should I even listen to you? A hallucination asking me about hallucinations!'

She took his hands in hers. The feeling shocked him and he started, but there was something infinitely calm and soothing in her touch. Warmth wriggled into his fingers, palms, forearms, heart.

He sighed again, more deeply and looked up into her shadowy face.

'Am I real, Hlaine Larkin?'

'I'd say so. But then… I'm mad.'

They laughed together, hands clasped, his dirty, ragged fingers wrapped in her smooth white palms. Face to face they laughed, his wheezing rattle tying itself into her soft, musical humours.

'Why did you abandon your men?' she asked.

He shivered and pulled his hands out of her grip, struggling away from her. 'Don't say that!'

'Larkin... why did you do it?'

'Don't ask me! Don't!'

'Do you deny it?'

He bumped against a pillar across the debris-littered aisle and turned back to her with ferocious eyes. His vision was pulsing now, lights and alterations dancing and flexing across his line of sight. She seemed far away, then huge and upon him. His guts churned biliously.

'Deny? I... I never left them... I...'

The Angel stood and turned away from him. He could see the way her silver-gold tresses fell to waist length between the powerful furled wings which emerged from slits in her samite gown. Her head was bowed. She spoke again after a long pause.

'Commissar Gaunt sent his fire-team into the aqueduct, on an insurgency mission to enter Bucephalon. The primary target was Nokad himself. Why was that?'

'K-kill the head and the body dies! Gaunt said we'd never take this place in a year unless Nokad's charismatic leadership was broken! The whole city-state has become his Doctrinopolis, the wellspring of his cult, to seed and spread the deceitful charm of his sensibilities to the other city-states on this world and beyond!'

'And what did you do?'

'W-we entered the aqueduct channels. Rawne's company led the way to draw fire and break the defence. Corbec's slid in behind to leapfrog the fighting as Rawne met it and enter the city through the canal trenches.'

'Wouldn't you drown?'

'The canals have been dry for six months. They were mined and wired but we had sweepers.'

'You were with Corbec's company?'

'Yes. I didn't want to go… Feth! I hated the idea of taking a suicide run like that, but I'm Corbec's sniper… and his friend. He insisted.'

'Why?'

'Because I'm Corbec's sniper and his friend!'

'Why?'

'I don't know!'

'Might it have been because you are the best shot in the entire regiment? That if anyone could get a shot at Nokad, it was you? Might Corbec, your friend, have been reluctant to take you? Might he have been afraid you could snap if the going got too hard?'

'I don't know!'

'Think about it! Might he have decided to take you in the end because, no matter what the risk and no matter how fragile your mind, you are still the best shot in the regiment? Might he have valued that in you? Might he have needed that asset despite the risk?'

'Shut up!'

'Might you have let him down?'

Larkin screamed and pressed his face into the stone floor. His wiry body began to twitch as the storm of madness, the tidal wave of anxiety, rose and crested in his thundering mind. He saw nothing but colours now: his vision was a neon kaleidoscope blur.

'And what did you do? That firefight in the canal. Close quarters. Lopra dead, head blown off; Castin disembowelled; Hech, Grosd, the others, the screaming, the misty smoke of burning blood. Corbec bellowing for reinforcements, daggers of light cutting the air. And what did you do?'

'Nothing!'

'Not nothing. You ran. You ran away. You scrambled and ran and ran and ran and ended up here. Sobbing, vomiting, soiling yourself.'

'No…' Larkin breathed, spread face down on the cold floor. He felt he was in a vacuum now. There was no sound, no vision, no pain. Just her voice.

'You deserted them. That makes you a deserter.'

Larkin looked up sharply. The Angel stood by the reliquary, lifting the studded wooden lid. She took something out and placed it upon her head, smoothing her silver-gold hair under the brim. It was a cap. A commissar's regimental cap. Gaunt's cap.

She reached into the holy box and lifted out something else, wrapped in dusty, mouldering cloth. Her perfect hands unwound it. A bolt pistol. With incongruous sureness, her slender hands slammed a sickle-pattern magazine into the slot, racked the slide and thumbed off the safety. She turned.

Her face, below the commissar's cap, was lean and angular. Larkin hadn't realised how chiselled and thin her cheeks and chin were before. Cut out of stone, firm and fierce, like Ibram Gaunt. She raised the bolt pistol in her right hand and pointed it at Larkin. Her wings opened and spread, twenty metres wide, a vast arch of perfect white eagle feathers.

'Do you know what we do to deserters, Larkin?' she said grimly.

'Yes.'

'We are created to inspire and uplift, to carry the spirit of battle forward, to maintain the sense of glory in the hearts of the Imperial warrior. But if that spirit falters, we are also here to punish.'

'Y-you sound like Gaunt…'

'Ibram Gaunt and I have much in common. A common purpose, a common function. Inspiration and punishment.'

It seemed as if the world outside the chapel had fallen silent. As if the war had stopped.

'Did you desert, Larkin?'

He stared at her, at the gun, at the terrible wingspan. Slowly, he got to his knees and then his feet.

'No.'

'Prove it.'

Every joint in his body ached, every nerve sang. His head was clear and yet racing and strange. He walked with measured care over to his fallen pack.

'Prove it, Larkin! The Emperor needs you with him at this hour! Muster your strength!'

He looked back at her. The gun and the gaze had not faltered.

'How did you know my name?'

'You told me.'

'My forename. Hlaine. I don't use that any more. How did you know?'

'I know everything.'

He laughed. Loud and hard, his thin chest shaking as he stripped open his pack. 'Feth take you! I'm no deserter!'

'Tell me why.'

'See this?' Larkin slid his sniper rifle from the sling across the back of his pack. He held it up and freed the firing mechanism with a deft twist of his hand.

'A gun.'

'A lasgun. Workhorse of the Guard. Solid, dependable, tough. You can knock it, drop it, club with it, submerge it and it just keeps on going.'

The Angel took a step forward, looking at the gun he held out to her. 'It's not standard. Not a standard M-G pattern. Where's the integral optics, the charge-setting slide? That barrel: it's too long, too thin. And that flash suppressor?'

Larkin grinned and reached into his pack. 'It's the sniper variant. Same body, but stripped down. I did some of the work myself. I took out the integral optics because I use this.' He held up a bulky tube to show her for a moment, then slotted it into a bracket on the side of the gun case. He flipped covers off both ends of the tube and the device spread a faint red glow ahead of the gun.

'Night spotter. My own. I tooled the bracket to fit. I used to use it to spot for larisel in the woods back home.'

'Larisel?'

'Small rodents with a fine pelt. Made a good income hunting them before the Founding.'

He slid his hands down the gun and tapped the barrel. 'XC 52/3 strengthened barrel. Longer, and thinner than the standard. Good for about twenty shots.' He kicked the pack at his feet, which clinked. 'I always carry two or three spares. They twist and pull out. You can switch them in about a minute if you know what you're doing.'

'Why the strengthened barrel?'

'Increased range for a start, tighter accuracy, and because I use these...' Larkin pulled a power pack from his kit and slammed it into place. 'We call them "hotshots". Overpowered energy clips, liquid metal batteries juiced to the limit. Bigger hits but fewer. Perfect for marksman work. And that's why there's no charge setting slider on my piece. One size fits all.'

'The stock is made of wood.'

'Nalwood, Tanith grown. I like what I know.'

'And that long flash suppressor?'

'I'm a sniper, Angel. I don't want to be seen.'

'Are you a sniper, Hlaine Larkin? I was sure you were a deserter.' The gloomy voice echoed around the chapel.

Larkin turned away from her, expecting a bolt round in the back of the head. His own head was clear, clearer than it had been in months.

'Think what you like. I'll tell you what I know.'

He crossed to the arched doorway of the chapel and settled down in a crouch, the lasgun resting on a finial of stonework. It afforded him a wide view down onto the half-ruined canal on the upper level of the great aqueduct.

Larkin settled himself, shook out his neck, flexed his arms. He took a sight through the eyepiece of his scope.

'My company's primary mission was to take Nokad. He's a charismatic. He leads by personality and that means he stays at the fore. This aqueduct has been recognised by both sides as the primary weakness of Bucephalon. We've attacked it. Hard. Nokad will want to defend it just as hard. And that means inspiring his troops along the length of it. And that, in turn, means he'll be here in person.'

'And if he's not?' asked the Angel.

'Then I'm just another nameless wooden marker in the cemetery.' He was no longer looking at her, no longer caring about her terrible presence. She could be holding that bolt-gun to his temple for all he cared.

'You trust that scope to make the shot?' she whispered.

'I calibrated it myself. And yes, I trust the scope. Funny thing, but whatever goes on around me, whatever madness…' – and at that Larkin dared a glance round at the hovering presence at his shoulder – 'I always see the truth through my scope. It shows me the world as it really is. Truth, not what my fethed-up mind tells me is there.'

A long pause.

'Maybe I should look through the scope at you some time?' he ventured.

'Haven't you got a job to do, Hlaine?'

'Yes. My job.' He turned back to the scope and shut his eyes.

'Your eyes are closed. What are you doing?'

'Shhh! To take a shot, your breathing must be controlled. More than that, your weapon must be pointing naturally at the target.' He opened his eyes again and fiddled with the lasgun as it lay in the lip of stone.

'What's the matter?'

'I need to baffle the barrel against the stone. I need cloth to wrap around it.' He began to pull at his cloak, trying to tear a strip off it. There was a shredding noise behind him. A perfect hand passed him a long strip of glowing white cloth, light and warm to the touch.

'Use this, Hlaine.'

Larkin smiled. He wrapped the silky material around the muzzle of his rifle and then nested it back into the stony over hang. It rested better now, bandaged with angelic satin, neatly snuggled into the turn of the hard buttress.

'Thanks,' he said, resuming his position.

'What are you doing now?'

Larkin flexed, as if fidgeting. 'I must have a stable firing position. If the gun wobbles even slightly, the shots can go wild. I need a firm grip, but not too tight. I want it to point naturally at the target. If I have to apply pressure to keep it aimed, then it's going to miss. See, here's the trick…'

He closed his eyes.

'Take aim and then close your eyes. Open them again. Chances are your aim will have wandered. Realign your body and repeat.'

'How many times?'

'As many as is necessary.' Larkin closed his eyes again, opened them, shuffled, closed his eyes.

'Eventually, when you open your eyes, the gun will be pointing precisely, naturally, exactly where your body falls and directs it.'

'You're breathing slowly,' said the Angel, a whisper in his ear. 'Why?'

Larkin smiled, but ever so slightly as to not disrupt the perfect pattern of his firing position. 'Once you're in position, breathe slow, a regular rhythm. Keep it going, nice and relaxed. When you get the shot, take a couple of deep breaths, pause, breathe out just a tad, and then hold. Then fire. Then breathe out fully.'

'How long will this take?' the Angel asked behind him.

'As long as it takes to get a target.'

NOKAD THE SMILING sang to his brethren as they advanced down the upper canal of the aqueduct. An echelon of things that had been men, now trailing long tattered robes sewn from the hides of those they had defeated. They brandished weapons, slapping them in dull time to the chant. They passed over the butchered and exploded remains of the foe who had assaulted their one weak link that afternoon.

Nokad the Smiling was well over two metres tall, his frame heavy set and powerful. Piercings studded his naked torso and arms: loops, rings, chains and spikes armouring his sheened skin and glittering as brightly as his perfect teeth.

'Make trophies of them!' Nokad grinned as he passed the corpses. Imperial Guard, weak, puny things, draped in dull fatigues and anonymous cloaks. There was fighting ahead, the barking returns of lasguns at close range.

CORBEC WAS IN the canal gully with three remaining men and Rawne yelling through the intercom.

'It's no good! They've got it sealed tight! We have to withdraw!'

'Feth you, Rawne! This is the only way! We move in! Bring your men forward!'

'It's suicide, Corbec, you fool! We'll all be dead in a moment!'

'Are you deserting me, major? Is that what you're doing? There's a price for that!'

'Feth you, you insane moron! You'd have to be utterly mad to go in there!'

NOKAD ADVANCED. His men loved him. They sang together, jubilant as they forced the invaders back.

On the canal lip, Nokad howled his inspirational verses to his men, arms uplifted, chainsword whirring.

There was a crack, a stab of light – and Nokad's head vanished in a film of blood.

LARKIN FELL BACK in the doorway, frothing and convulsing, spasms snapping his body as the brain fever took hold once more.

'LARKS? LARKS?' Corbec's voice was soft.

Larkin lay in a foetal ball, messed by his own fluids, in the doorway of the shattered chapel. As he came around he felt his mind was clear, violently clear, like it had been purged with light.

'Colm...'

'You son of a bitch, Larks!' Corbec pulled him upright, unsteady on his legs.

Larkin's lasgun lay on the floor, its barrel broken, burnt and spent.

'You got him! You got him, you old bastard! You smoked him good!'

'I did?'

'Listen to that!' Corbec crowed, pulling Larkin around towards the doorway. There was a cheering and chanting noise rising from below the aqueduct. 'They've surrendered! We've taken Bucephalon! Nokad is fried!'

'Shit...' Larkin sank to his knees.

'And I thought you'd run on us! Honestly! I thought you'd fething deserted!'

'Me?' Larkin said, looking up.

'I shouldn't have doubted you, should I?' Corbec asked, bear-hugging the wiry little sniper.

'Where's the angel gone?' Larkin said quietly.

'Angel? There's no angel here except her!' Corbec pointed to the damaged statue of the angel above the chapel font, a beautiful winged woman knelt in the attitude of prayer. Her perfect hands were clasped. Her head was bowed demurely. The inscription on the plinth rejoiced that she was a symbol of the God-Emperor, a personification of the Golden Throne who had come to the elders of Bucephalon in the first days of the colony and watched over them as they conquered the land.

An old myth. A hunk of stone.

'But–' Larkin started as Corbec dragged him to his feet.

'But nothing!' Corbec laughed.

Larkin began to laugh too. He convulsed and gagged with the force of laughter inside him.

Corbec dragged him from the chapel, both laughing still.

The very last thing Larkin saw before Corbec wrenched him away was his fallen lasgun, with the peerless, scorched white cloth still wrapped around the barrel.

A SUDDEN BARRAGE of enemy guns, distant, impatient, came on just before the middle of the night over Monthax, and stippled the belly of the low brown sky with reflected flashes of fire and light. Wet, hollow rumbles barked and growled through the swamps and ground mist like starving hounds. Leagues away, some brutal night-combat was underway.

Gaunt woke instinctively at the sound of the guns and took a walk out of the command shed. The sound was coming from the east and he had a sergeant circle around to check on the sentry lines. The artillery sounded like some-one flapping and cracking a large, sweat-damp sheet in the hot, heavy air.

He crossed a gurgling creek via a duck-board bridge and made it into the tree line just as the humidity broke and cold drooling rain began to fall through air suddenly stirred by chill breezes. It was almost a relief, but the rain was sticky and sappy and stung his eyes.

Gaunt found himself on the embanked approach to one of the main sentry towers and pulled himself up the ladder. The towers, set at hundred metre intervals along the main defile, rose some ten metres out of the surface filth. They were fashioned from groups of tree-trunks, shored together and stoutly buttressed with riveted beams, and supported large flak-board gun-nests mounted on the top.

Up in the dark nest, Trooper Bragg tended a cradle-mounted pair of twinned heavy bolters, drums of shells piled around his huge feet. A flak-board cover kept the rain off and the nest was shrouded by netting.

'Sir!' Bragg saluted, his big face cracking into a broad, embarrassed grin. He was making fortified caffeine over a little burner, his huge paws dwarfing the pot and cup. He tried to hide the flask of sacra behind the stove, but the scent of the liquor was pungent in the close air of the nest.

Gaunt nodded the salute. 'I'll have one myself,' he said. 'A stiff one.'

Bragg seemed to relax. He sloshed a generous measure of sacra into a second battered cup and fussed over the boiling pot. Gaunt was amused, as always, by the combination of brutal strength and timidity in this giant of a man. Bragg's hands were big and strong enough to crush skulls, but he moved almost meekly, as if afraid of his own strength – or afraid of what others might think him capable of.

He handed the commissar a hot cup and Gaunt sat on a pile of shell-drums, gesturing out across the jungle to the east. The nest's raised vantage point afforded a better view of the distant fighting. Flares and tracers showed above the trees, and as the rain dissipated the mist, there were ruddy ground fires to be seen amid the trunks.

'Someone's having fun,' he remarked.

Bragg nodded, sipping his own cup. 'I make four or maybe five enemy positions, infantry support teams. They've advanced and dug in, because the fire-patterns are static, but they've found something to shoot at.'

'If they move this way, we'll need to take action.'

Bragg patted his heavy weapons. 'Let 'em come.'

Gaunt grinned. Bragg was a good heavy weapons technician, but his aim had scarcely improved since the Founding. Still, with guns with that sort of cycle rate and that much ammo, he should hit something.

'Oh, while I remember,' Gaunt said, 'the western embankments are collapsing again. I told Major Rawne that you'd help the detail re-dig tomorrow. They need some heavy lifting.'

Bragg nodded without question. His great physical strength was an asset to the Ghosts, and was matched by his geniality and willingness to help. He reminded Gaunt of some great blunt weapon, like a club: deadly when delivered properly, but difficult to wield or aim.

Bragg batted a moth away from his face. 'Precious little place we've found here,' he remarked.

'Monthax is… short on charm,' Gaunt admitted, studying the hulking trooper quizzically. Bragg was a strange man. Gaunt had decided that long ago. He'd never met a human so physically powerful, yet mentally restrained, as if he was somehow afraid of the terrible power he could unleash. Others took it for stupidity and regarded big old Bragg as dumb. But the man patently wasn't stupid. In his own, quiet, mountainous way, he was the most formidable and dangerous Ghost of all. So preoccupied by his physical power, others always underestimated the mind behind it.

And the mind, Gaunt knew, was the strongest thing of all.

# SIX
# THAT HIDEOUS STRENGTH

CALIGULA, AFTER THE Imperial liberation. Nights as bright as day, lit by the burning hive cities; days as dark as night, choked by the petrochemical smoke. Soot, like fat, black snowflakes, fluttered down everywhere. Even out here, in the deadlands.

Steepled canyons of coral-bright rock. Wisps of fluorescent dust licking the high places and the rims of the calderas. Cracked, dry basins of hard, russet cake-earth. Wide, slumping ridges of glass-sand. And death, bleached and baked white, like bones that had been out in the sun for years.

Eighteen cargo transports, thirty-wheel monsters, coughing blue exhaust from their vertical pipe-stacks, ground down the red-rock pass in low gear. The tractor units at the front of each payload wagon were monsters, armoured cabs of scorched metal rattling on top of a huge engine unit, glaring forward through multiple fog-lamp eyes and grinning fly-flecked smiles of fender bars, radiator grilles and spiked running boards. Flanking the massive transports were the outriders, rushing through the dust on track-bikes and in armoured cars.

Palapr Tuvant, transport driver, Caligula born and bred, wrestled with the half-moon wheel of the convoy's lead freighter and glanced around at his co-driver. Tlewn Milloom was looking out of the cab window, occasionally regarding his chronometer.

They were both wringing with sweat, entombed by the heat from the roaring engine under their feet. Milloom had dropped the window armour panels and opened the metal vents in the hope of washing them with cool breeze from outside. But the surface temperature out in the deadlands was pushing forty degrees, and they baked. Occasionally, sprays of hot engine oil spurted back from the leaky head gasket and spattered in at them through the forward grille-screen.

Milloom sat back in his ripped leather seat and looked up at the cab's ceiling hatch. 'He's still up there?'

Tuvant nodded, wrenching the wheel. Both of them were all too used to the juddering, shaking motion of the vehicle. 'Probably sticking his head out of the turret like a dog, enjoying the rush of air.'

Milloom chuckled. 'Kec, but he's a dumb-ass, right? Never stood in line for brains.'

Tuvant nodded. 'Typical Guard, all muscle and no head. Where the kec were they when the hives fell? Huh? Answer me that?'

'In a troop-ship in transit,' Trooper Bragg answered plainly, his huge bulk clambering down the rungs from the top hatch to join them. He stood at the back of the cab, holding onto a roll-bar for support as the tractor lurched over uneven ground. 'Colonel-Commissar Gaunt said we got here as fast as we could.' He smiled sheepishly at the two-man driving team.

'I'm sure he did,' Tuvant murmured.

Bragg edged forward, using handholds to stop himself from falling. 'We're making good time, aren't we?'

'Brilliant time,' Milloom replied, turning away from the big Ghost. 'Calphernia Station will rejoice when we arrive.'

'I'm sure it will,' Bragg smiled, sinking into the bench seat behind the driver's position. 'That'll be good. When the colonel-commissar ordered me to command this convoy detail, I said to him I will get it through on time, trust me, colonel-commissar. I will. And we are, aren't we?'

'Yes, we are. Right on time,' Tuvant said.

'Good. That's good. The colonel-commissar will be pleased.'

Milloom muttered something unflattering about the high and mighty colonel-commissar.

'What did you say?' Bragg asked sharply.

Milloom stiffened. He looked across at Tuvant. They'd been in the company of this huge guardsman for maybe three hours all told, and had so far reckoned him to be dim-witted and slow. Of course, his sheer bulk was impressive, but they had felt confident about laughing at him behind his back. Now Milloom tensed, feeling perhaps he'd gone too far, feeling the giant behind them might suddenly unleash his undoubted physical power in a mindless tantrum.

'I... I didn't say anything.'

'You did. You said something about my colonel-commissar. Something bad.'

Milloom turned slowly to face the huge Tanith. 'I didn't mean anything. I was just joking.'

'So it was a bad thing. An insult.'

'Yes, but just a joke.' Milloom tensed, expecting the worst, reaching his left hand down beside his seat for the axle-bar he kept stowed there.

'That's okay,' Bragg said lightly, turning to look out of a window. 'Everyone is entitled to their opinion. The colonel-commissar told us that.'

Milloom sat back and exchanged knowing grins with the driver. A total dummy, they agreed wordlessly.

'So,' Tuvant asked, teasing, looking at Bragg in the rear-view mirror, 'you do everything this colonel-commissar tells you?'

'Of course!' the giant replied brightly. 'He's the colonel. And the commissar. We're his men. We're Imperial Guard. Tanith First-and-Only. We're loyal to the Emperor and we do everything the colonel-commissar tells us.'

'What if he told you to jump off a cliff?' Milloom laughed, conspiratorially sharing the baiting with Tuvant.

'Then we'd jump off the cliff. Was that a trick question?'

THE CONVOY ROLLED on into the deadlands. It had assembled that morning on a stained curtain road outside the half-burned ruin of the Aurelian Hive City, where a second front of Imperial Guard had seized control after the main assault on Nero Hive. The mammoth Imperium victory was in no doubt, but still pockets of enemy soldiers held out, fighting a lingering war of wastage and attrition to wear out the lines of supply.

The Imperial Guard closed in en masse to root out and eradicate all remnants of resistance, and the work to rebuild Caligula began. What resources were available – and despite everything Aurelian Hive was rich in storehouses – had to be redistributed. The convoy marked the first attempt to convey relief supplies to the stricken Hive Calphernia. That meant a two hundred kilometre crossing of the battlewaste recently dubbed 'the deadlands'.

Six convoys had departed Aurelian Hive that dawn. Four were headed to Nero Hive, one to Tiberius and one to Calphernia. Gaunt's Ghosts, the Tanith First, were given the protection duty. It was agreed that the run to Calphernia was the most dangerous, as it crossed the territories of bandits – ex-hive workers who had fled the war and set themselves up as feudal warlords in the waste. Not a single relief vehicle had made it through in the last six weeks and the rumours told of thousands of rebels, stockpiling weapons. Some even whispered that Chaos powers were involved.

Everyone, including Bragg himself, was amazed when Gaunt chose Bragg to command the defence of the Calphernia convoy. Gaunt had ignored all the protests and taken the bemused Bragg into his command bunker to brief him.

Caober, Rawne, Larkin and the other Ghosts decided that Gaunt's choice simply represented an acceptance that the Calphernia convoy wouldn't get through. It was a write-off and Gaunt wasn't going to waste any decent commander to such long odds.

'And so our caring commissar shows his true colours!' Rawne had hissed, playing with the hilt of his silver Tanith dagger. Others fidgetted nervously, unhappy with what seemed to be going on but unwilling to question Gaunt's authority directly.

Bragg simply grinned at the honour bestowed upon him. It seemed he missed the irony. He was oblivious to the fact that he was already given up as dead. Rawne spat in the dust.

At the behest of the men, Corbec had approached Gaunt fiercely, demanding to know why Gaunt had been so callous as to deem Bragg expendable. 'Sir, with me or Hasker or Lerod at the helm, we might get a chance to drive that convoy through. Don't throw it away, don't waste Bragg–'

'I know what I'm doing,' Gaunt had replied curtly, sending the proud Bragg and seventy other Ghosts off on the detail from which everyone was sure no one would come back.

THE CONVOY RUMBLED down a wide-bottomed crevasse and began to cross a cracked, red dust-plain of baked earth. Heat shimmered up, distorting the horizons. Outrider one roared ahead of the convoy, a track-bike driven by Corporal Meryn with Trooper Caffran manning the pintle-mounted twin autocannons in the rear. Both had their stealth cloaks wrapped up around their mouths against the heat and dust, and wore filmed, heat-crazed goggles.

Meryn heaved the cycle to a halt on a rise, the convoy a kilometre behind them, and pulled down his swaddling dust-veils to spit and cough.

'You feel that?' he called back to Caffran. 'Eyes watching us from all around?'

'Just your imagination,' Caffran returned, cranking the guns round all the same.

Caffran felt a pulse in his temple that wasn't simply the heat. He'd seen the expression on Colonel Corbec's face when Gaunt had given the convoy command to Bragg. They were dead out here, as good as written off. The hundred burnt and crucified bodies they had passed on the roadside an hour before had nothing to do with imagination. Caffran shuddered.

OTHER OUTRIDERS WHIRRED forward in hazes of dust. Trooper Kelve drove one cycle with Merrt, one of Corbec's favoured sharpshooters, in the rear cradle. Merrt had his sniper gun wrapped in oil-cloth in the footwell below him, ready to switch to it when the autocannon rig ran dry. Kelve pulled them up to a revving halt on a sand-rise.

To their left, engine idling, was Ochrin and his gunner Hellat. To their right, five hundred metres distant, Mkendrick and his gunner Beris. A signal, waved from bike to bike, then they all flew forward into the dusty basin beyond, racing parallel to the track left by Meryn and Caffran. The huge convoy thundered in after them.

Tailing it, and flanking the rear, came three more outriders: Fulke with Logris gunning, Mktea with Laymon at the weapons, and Tanhak with Grummed manning the cannons. Behind them, an Imperial Guard half-track driven by Wheln, with Abat and Brostin at the weapons stations, and another with long, double-tracks driven by Mkteeg with Rahan and Nehn crewing a missile launcher platform.

Bragg clambered up into the gun-turret over the cab of his tractor, half-hearing the whispered slanging of the Caligulan drivers, Milloom and Tuvant. Heat and dust assaulted his big face. The sun was a torrential heat. His nostrils immediately clogged with ash-dust and he had to hawk and spit to clear his head. As an afterthought, he wrapped his stealth cloak around his mouth and nose, pulling out the goggles he had been issued and also remembering to wipe zinc paste over his exposed skin.

The paste, clagging and damp in a small circular tin, smelled bad, but the colonel-commissar had told them all to use it. Bragg lifted his micro-bead comms-set and slid the plug into his ear.

'Bragg to all Ghosts, remember to use your sun-paint. The zinc stuff. Like the colonel-commissar told us. Over.'

Over the vox-link came a round of curses and protests.

'I mean it,' Bragg said. 'Wipe it on, Tanith. There's burning and there's burning, the colonel-commissar said, and our fair skins won't last a minute out in this.'

Sliding his bike to a halt, Ochrin pulled out his tin and grudgingly applied paste to his brow and nose. He held the tin out, straight armed, to Hellat in the back.

There was soft, distant ping, a hollow, empty sound.

Hellat took the tin from Ochrin's outstretched hand just as he realised Ochrin no longer had a face. Ochrin's corpse flopped stiffly back off the saddle.

Hellat cried out in alarm, gripping the yokes of his pintle weapon and raining metal fury on the distant dunes.

'Ochrin's down! We are attacked!' he screamed as he fired.

A second later a missile lifted his cycle into the air and blew Hellat and Ochrin's corpses into pieces of cooked meat each no larger than a clenched fist.

Vox-traffic suddenly tumbled in confusion over the static. Murmuring the litany of protection the Ecclesiarch had taught him back on Tanith, at the Primer Educatory, Mkteeg drew his half-track hull-down behind a salty dune and his weapon crew spat a rack of missiles into the cliff edges.

Meryn drove his cycle around in a wide arc, pulling to rejoin, puffing up a wide skim of dust. Caffran rattled round the gun mount and flickered off a curving row of tracer shells into the position marked by Hellat's last assault. Ochrin and Hellat's vehicle lay in a burning heap on a crisped sand-rise.

The main convoy slowed as the attack made itself known. The enemy fire whickered into them from the right hand side like rain – a few shots at first, then faster and more furious.

Mkendrick raced his bouncing bike in, screaming a Tanith warcry, and only when his gunner didn't begin firing did he turn to find Beris hanging dead over the pintle mount, sunlight shining through a vast hole in his torso. Mkendrick braked, leapt out of the driver's position and tossed Beris's corpse aside, maniacally training and firing the guns from a stationary position.

As his cycle raced into the firefight, Merrt knew he had a good angle, pumping round after round from the big calibre guns into the distant dust dunes. He screamed to his driver to go faster and to overrun the enemy. Kelve was about to reply, or was half-way through saying something, when a salvo of stub rounds tore the vehicle to pieces and over-turned them.

Merrt pulled himself out of the dust and looked round to see Kelve trapped under the wreckage, shrieking in pain. The control column had impaled him, ripping him open and pin-ning him into the sand under three tonnes of twisted, smouldering metal.

Merrt ran to him, trying to raise the wreck, trying to tip it over. Kelve bayed at him, begging, pleading.

When Merrt realised how heavy the wreck was and how grievous Kelve's wound, he did as his driver instructed him. He took out his laspistol and shot Kelve through the head, point blank. Kelve's body spasmed and died, gratefully.

Merrt dived flat as further fire found his position. He located his swaddled sniper gun, thrown clear out from the wreck. There was no time to check for damage. He pulled off the cloth, lay low, and sighted, snuggling a fresh power cell into the receiver. His long sight brought the enemy into view, magnified, hazy, distant figures milling around trying to reload a khaki-painted missile launcher.

He made his first shot. It went long. He adjusted his scope, as Larkin had taught him, breathed out, and made the sec-ond shot a clean kill. The enemy were turning in confusion when he made the next three shots in calm, cold series.

Three clean hits. Sniper Master Larkin would be proud.

ATOP THE main tractor, Bragg yelled into his micro-bead, ordering the convoy to form a defensive circle. Various counter-demands whipped into his ears over the link and he shouted them down, gripping the gun-yokes with both of his huge hands and sending tight bursts of hammer-fire into the starboard hills.

The convoy vehicles reluctantly obliged, following Bragg's orders, circling round and forming a defensive position that the remaining outriders circled. Vehicles two and four in the convoy took heavy hits, and vehicle six exploded outright as

a rocket torched into its tractor unit. The side-panelling of
the cargo-unit rippled off as internal explosions blistered out
through the metal skin, shredding it. Scraps of metal hull
span away from the boiling black-smoked fireball, puffing
hundreds of individual ripples in the ashy sand all around.

Relieved at the turret guns by Trooper Cavo, Bragg
dropped down into the cab to find Milloom and Tuvant
sheltering under window level, the grid-shields and hatches
pulled up.

'This is madness, you stupid kec!' Tuvant bellowed.
'They'll pin us down and murder us all!'

'I don't think these bandits are really so tough,' Bragg
began.

Tuvant turned on him. 'You kec-head! They're all over us!
God-Emperor, but there are thousands of bandits out here,
more than enough to kill us all! We should have kept moving!
Stopping like this, we'll give them all a chance to congregate
for the kill!'

Bragg shambled across to the Caligulan drivers. There was
a dull look in his eye Tuvant didn't like. With one meaty,
hairy-knuckled paw, Bragg lifted Tuvant off the cabin deck
by his throat.

'I'm in charge here,' he growled, his voice as deep and
solid as his build, reverberative. 'The colonel-commissar
said so. If we have to fight our way through to Calphernia a
micron at a time, we will. And we will all fight. Clear?'

'C-clear!' gasped Tuvant, going blue.

'Now, can you make yourself useful?'

'How?' snarled Milloom acidly from behind. Bragg
dropped Tuvant, who sprawled, retching, and turned to face
the other driver. Milloom had his greasy axle-bar in his
hands. 'You don't scare me, Ghost.'

'Then you must be very stupid,' Bragg muttered, turning
aside without interest. Milloom launched forward to crush
the big man's skull with five kilos of cold-stamped metal.
Bragg broke stride lightly, impossibly lightly it seemed for
such a great bulk. He caught the descending bar in one
palm. There was an audible slap. Milloom gasped as the bar
was pulled out of his hands. Bragg tossed it aside.

'You can start by not attacking me. You fething non-
combatants really wind me up. Where the feth would you
be if we hadn't come to pull your arses out of the Chaos
pit?'

'Safe and sound in Aurelian Hive, probably!' Milloom
jeered. 'Not out in the deadlands, surrounded by terrorist
infantry!'

Bragg shrugged. 'Probably. With the other cowards. Are
you a coward, Driver Milloom?'

'Kec you!'

'Just asking. The colonel-commissar told me to watch out
for cowards. Told me to shoot them on sight, as they were
treasonous dogs who didn't deserve the salvation of the
Golden Throne. I wouldn't shoot them, not me.'

There was a pause.

Bragg smiled. 'I'd just hit them. Has a similar result. Do
you want me to hit you, Milloom?'

'N... no.'

'Then don't assault me again. You can help even if you
don't know the business end of a weapon from your own
arse. Get on the voxcaster. Recite the Ecclesiarchy's Oath of
Obedience. You know that?'

'Of course I know that! Then what?'

'Then recite it again. Make it clear and proud. Recite it
again, then again and then again. If you get bored, insert the
Emperor's Daily Prayer for variation. Maybe the Imperial
Litany of Deliverance for good measure. Fill the vox-channels
with soothing, inspiring words. Can you do that?'

Milloom nodded and crossed to the vox-caster built into
the tractor's dash.

'Good man,' Bragg said. Milloom started to speak into the
caster horn, remembering the verses he had learned as a
child.

Outside, laser and stub fire whined into the circled convoy. The outriders were laying in hard. Meryn drew his bike
in so that Caffran could do real damage to the slowly encir-
cling bandits.

Fulke, Mktea and Tanhak ran the line. From the back of
Fulke's machine, Logris excelled and scored four kills.

Mktea's gunner Laymon made one of his own before the upper part of his head was scythed off by a las-shot at the mouth. Tanhak and Grummed made six, maybe seven, good kills before a short-range missile ended their lives and their glory. Debris and body parts flew out from a searing typhoon of ignited bike fuel.

'Bragg! Bragg! We have to retreat!' Wheln yelled from the half-track, Abat dead behind him and Brostin blazing with his flamer.

In the cab of his freighter, Bragg was calmly unwrapping his autocannons from a felt shroud. Behind him, Milloom was steadily reciting into the vox-horn. Bragg paused, fingering his micro-bead to open the vox-line.

'No, Wheln. No retreat. No retreat.' he said simply.

Rubbing his sore throat, Tuvant scrambled up from the floor, about to argue with the huge Ghost, but he stopped dead as he saw the weapon that the Tanith hulk was preparing. Not one but two autocannons, the like of which were usually fixed to tripod or pintle mounts. Bragg had them lashed together, with a makeshift trigger array made out of a bent ration-pack fork so he could fire them as a pair. Long belt loops of ammunition played out from the gun-slots, leading back to a parcel of round-boxes.

Bragg punched out the perspex window section from the rear of the cab and laid his twin muzzles across the sill. He looked back at Tuvant.

'You wanted something?'

'No,' Tuvant replied, ducking suddenly as stub-fire perforated the cab and showered them with metal shards and soot.

'I can fire this on my own if I have to, but it would be easier if I had someone to feed.'

Tuvant blinked. Then he scrambled forward and grabbed the ammo-belts, easing them around so they would pull unobstructed from the boxes.

'Thanks,' smiled Bragg quickly, then turned to hunch and squint out of the window port. He squeezed the trigger assembly. The twin guns barked deafeningly in the confines of the cab. Milloom paused in his recitation, and covered his ears with a grimace. Tuvant shuddered, but kept working dutifully to play the ammo-belts out clear and clean. Shell cases billowed through the air like chaff.

Bragg's first devastating salvo had gone wide, passing over the top of the nearby cliffs. He grinned at himself and adjusted his aim.

'Try again...' he murmured.

'What?' asked Tuvant.

'Nothing.'

Bragg opened fire again, the barking chatter of the paired guns filling the cab again. Now his shots were stitching along the valley wall and crossing the far dunes. Something he touched exploded in a violent plume of red fire. Bragg played his guns around that area again for a minute or so.

Out on the dunes, with the convoy circled behind him, Merrt crawled forward, re-adjusting his aim. He could hear the anxious but determined voice reciting the Emperor's Prayer over his ear-plug and it filled him with a sense of right and dignity. He blinked dust out of his eyes. He'd ditched his sand-goggles the moment he'd hit the ground. Larkin had told him that nothing should get between a sniper's scope and his naked eye. You only saw the truth of the world when your eye was clear and you were looking down your scope, Larkin had said in training. Merrt smiled at the memory. He remembered how Larkin would often carry his scope around in his thigh-pouch and take it out to look at people through it. 'To tell if they're lying,' he always said.

Merrt's scope wasn't lying now. He could see over three dozen bandits advancing over the dunes under cover of the foggy dust kicked up by the firefight. They were running low, heads down, hugging the contours of the ground. Merrt took aim at the nearest one. He sighed and fired, timing his finger to the moment of respiratory emptiness so nothing in his torso would jerk the aim. The laser burst punched through the top of the bandit's bowl-helmet, presented as it was by his head-down approach. The shot probably passed down through his skull, his neck and his torso, following the line of his spinal column, Merrt thought, as the figure dropped stone dead in a crumpled pile.

He adjusted his aim and took another bandit in the face when he looked up to take a bearing. A slight swing to the left, and another came into his sight, scurrying forward to gain new cover. A sigh. A squeeze. A slight recoil. The figure flipped back and fell still.

Merrt readjusted and was about to target a small group of infantry when their position dissolved in a haze of heat and outflung debris. Missile hit, he thought.

Rahan and Nehn were keeping the aim of the missile turret low, sliding off single shots that hugged the ground cover and buried themselves in the foe. Mkteeg edged the half-track along the lip of the folded dunes, skirting the enemy as best he could. His weapon crew had almost expended their missiles, so he set the drive in idle and clambered back into the turret bed to set up the stub-gun folded away in a deck-locker.

He had it up and lashed in to the armoured side panel of the track as Rahan volleyed off five missiles high into the air. They looked like burning javelins as they arched over the desert and flew down onto unseen targets below the dune.

Mktea fired the autocannon mount Laymon had been manning until the feeder belt jammed and the gun glowed red. With a curse, he snatched up his lasrifle and dived over the side. Enemy las-fire reached his vehicle a moment later and blew it up in a shower of metal debris that pattered around him as he crawled through the sand. Mktea felt a sharp and painful impact in his ankle. Looking back, prone on his belly, he realised his combat trousers were smouldering from the wash of cinders and a thick piece of metal debris had pierced his foot.

He beat down the fire then rolled over to yank the debris from his ankle. It was the shattered handle of his vehicle's autogun return, he realised. The pain was immense. He pulled at it and passed out momentarily. Coming to, he realised that the shrapnel wasn't going to come free from the bones of his foot without a surgeon. He chewed down a handful of painkillers, and as the heady high smacked into his brain, he rolled over and began firing his lasgun into the dune crest behind him.

Wheln blasted away from his vehicle's turret next to
Brostin, who had ditched his flamer for a lasrifle. Bandits
were running at them from a scoop of low-lying desert, and
they shot everything that moved.

Mkendrik realised his guns were out as the last of the belt-
feed whickered through the slot and the weapons coughed
dry. Bandit troops were all over him, charging up to take his
machine. He pulled out his laspistol and shot the first one
through the head, gutting the second and blowing a knee off
the third. Then he took a glancing wound in the left shoulder that turned him sideways and knocked him to the deck.

There was a roaring sound.

Meryn's bike came over the rise in a puff of dust, landing
hard, Caffran hammering the enemy with his guns. Meryn
slewed to the left as Caffran played the cannons around,
exploding most of the enemy who were in eye-shot. The
others scrambled for cover.

'Come aboard!' Meryn shouted over the roar of his engine
and Mkendrik leapt onto the flat-bed next to Caffran. Meryn
gunned the engine and they hammered straight at the
enemy lines.

Firing from the back of his vehicle, Logris, one of Mkoll's
elite scout brigade, realised his driver was losing it. Fulke was
crying out, screaming, resisting the hammer of weaponsfire.
He slewed the bike around, away from the action.

'Pull us back around! The war's over there!' Logris bellowed. Fulke said something absurd and gunned the motor
of the outrider towards the comparative safety of the convoy
circle. Logris climbed forward over the ammo boxes and
feeder-cables strewn across the back-platform of the bike.
He came upon the whimpering Fulke from behind and
slammed his head sideways into the armour panel of the
pilot's door. The bike shuddered to a sidelong halt as Fulke
went limp.

Logris spat on the driver. 'Coward,' he said, then turned
back. Enemy troops were scurrying across the cracked dust-
land towards him. He took out his lasgun and armed it.

'Let's go,' he said to them, though they couldn't hear.

* * *

BRAGG PULLED back from the window and released his finger on the trigger assembly.

'What?' Tuvant asked.

'Get out,' Bragg said suddenly. 'You and Milloom, get out of the cab and back onto the trailer.'

'Why?'

'Fire-patterns...'

'What?'

Bragg turned and cursed at the Caligulan driver. 'Fire-patterns! Fire-patterns! They're concentrating their fire on the tractor units. It's the freight they want! If you want to be safe, get into the sections they don't dare shoot at!'

Tuvant and Milloom hurried back through the communicating door into the freight section. Bragg wiped his brow. His hand was rich with sweat and soot. Over the vox-link, he ordered all his crews to do the same. *The bandits want this cargo... and so, Throne help me, they'll be less sure of shooting at us when we're part of it.*

He yanked his autocannons off the sill and dragged them and the ammo boxes out onto the top of the freight unit.

'We're gonna die here!' Tuvant said, looking out from the top of the freight unit at the hundreds of bandit troopers who were advancing on their circle of machines.

'No, we're not,' Bragg told him.

'You're mad!' spat Tuvant. 'We're surrounded by them! Thousands of them! They'll pick us off, every last man!'

Bragg sighed and closed his eyes.

The Maurader bombers came low over the ridge, annihilating the enemy with their belly-slung payloads.

'There are bandits... hiding out there in the deadlands, impossible to target.' Bragg smiled, repeating what Gaunt had told him. 'Unless there is something to draw them out and unify them. Something like... this convoy.'

Tuvant looked at the huge ghost in disbelief. 'We were bait?'

'Yes.'

'Kec you for using us!'

'I'm sorry. It was the colonel-commmissar's idea.'

Tuvant sagged down onto the freighter-top walkway.

Bragg hunkered next to him. Around them, sheets of incendiary bombs and phosphor fire scorched the hills. The Imperial fighter-bombers shattered the air as they went supersonic and crossed the low hills to pull around for another massacre run.

'Tuvant?'

Tuvant looked round at the giant.

'We were bait, but we still have a purpose. We'll get this convoy through. Calphernia will rejoice, just like I said. It's just the colonel-commissar–'

Tuvant turned, eyes red. 'I'm getting kec tired of hearing that title!'

'His name's Gaunt. A good man. General Thoth ordered him to supervise the relief work here on your world. He knew that couldn't happen all the while the terrorists and bandit-clans were out here. So he set a lure. A lure of fat, tasty freight trucks bound for Calphernia.'

'Great.'

'We got them all in one place so that the Navy air-wing could dispose of them. Be happy, man! We've won a great victory here!'

Tuvant looked up at him. His face was pale. 'All I know is I've been used as bait by your colonel-commissar. You knew that all along.'

Bragg sat back against the guard rail, smelling the acid-rich reek of the burning napalm. 'Yes. The bandits aren't working blind, you know. Hive workers in Aurelian are tipping them off as to the movement of supply convoys. Why else do you think the colonel-commissar put me in charge of this run?'

Tuvant blinked at him, uncertain.

Bragg patted his vast chest with huge hands. 'I'm big... I must be stupid. No brain. The sort of – what was it again? – "kec" who would drive the convoy into trouble and then circle it in a defense position for easy pickings. The sort of idiot who was likely to deliver the convoy right into the hands of the bandits.'

'Are you telling me you were part of the lure too?'

'The sweet part, the part they couldn't resist. The part the workers on the inside would vox to their bandit friends about. Convoy's coming, boys and there's an idiot in charge. Right, Milloom?'

Milloom glared back at them from his place against the rail.

'Kec you!'

Bragg shook his great head. He held up a data-slate. 'Friend of mine, Trooper Raglon... Comms-Officer Raglon, was monitoring your cipher traffic. I've got you here, tipping off your bandit friends as to the time, schedule, make-up and strength of this convoy. Colonel-Commissar Gaunt told me to do it.'

'Milloom?' Tuvant stammered.

A compact auto-pistol was suddenly in Milloom's hand as he leapt up. 'Kec you, Guard filth!'

Bragg was up in an instant, shielding Tuvant and swinging a massive fist at Milloom.

The gun went off. There was a sickening gristle-crack of impact. The shot went wild.

His face mashed beyond recognition, Tlewn Milloom tumbled off the walkway of the freight unit and was dead before his body snapped on the hard-packed desert twenty metres below.

Bragg turned back to Tuvant and helped him up. There was blood on his bulky knuckles. Behind them, the sky was washed with heat-wash and cinder-smog from the bombing runs.

'He was a traitor. And a coward,' Bragg explained to Tuvant.

'Colonel-Commmissar Gaunt told you that, right?'

'No, I worked that out all by myself. Now, I believe we have a date with Calphernia Hive.'

A RUSTY DAWN split the sky over Monthax. The air reminded Gaunt of the tall windows at the Schola Progenium back on Ignatius Cardinal where he had been reared and trained years ago, after his father's death. Smoky, like glass, fading through scattered panels of reds and ochres to the frostier tones of mauve and purple high above where the stars still twinkled. All it lacked was the lead-edged figure of some champion of the Imperium, some holy saint frozen in an attitude of victory over the piled heads of the slain.

For a moment, he thought he heard the plainsong of the Schola choir, singing the dawn celebrant as the star Ignatius rose. But he shook himself. He was mistaken. Across the long daybreak shadows that laced the stinking, muddy trench lines, he heard men singing a rougher, more brutal Guard anthem as they set their cooking fires and made breakfast. Milo was amongst them, edging the throaty music of the men's husky, dreamy voices with silvery notes from a slender reed-pipe.

Just as much an offering, just as celebrational for the providence of a new day, safe-delivered from night, Emperor be thanked. Beyond the lines, the unyielding jungles steamed as the heat of the rising sun boiled the damp out of them. Mist coated the dark trees. In that darkness of foliage and water and mud and flies, what miseries awaited the Imperial Guard?

Near to him, one man wasn't singing. Major Rawne sat back on a folded bedroll set by the fire before his tent. He was shaving, using a bowl of hot water, a broken mirrored tile and the razor edge of his silver Tanith knife. He had lathered with a tiny hunk of soap and Gaunt could hear the scratch of the blade against the bristles of his cheek and throat.

The commissar found himself almost hypnotised by the practised, meticulous motions; the way Rawne held the skin of his cheek taut with his free hand as he looked sidelong into the propped mirror, drew the knife in a short scrape and then rattled it clean in the shallow bowl.

A knife against a knife, Gaunt thought. He always saw Rawne's face as a thin dagger, sleek and handsome. A dagger... or a snake, perhaps.

Both would be appropriate. Gaunt admired Rawne's abilities, and indeed even his ruthlessness. But there was no love lost. He wondered how many throats had been opened by the knife Rawne now stroked delicately across his own vulnerable flesh.

Watching him shave, without so much as a nick, it emphasised the dangerous control of the tall, slender man. Precise, perfect, the tiny difference between a clean shave and killing stroke.

And with *that* knife in particular...

Rawne looked up and caught Gaunt's eye. He made no other sign of recognition and continued with his work. But Gaunt knew how dearly Rawne would love to rattle that blade clean of soap-foam and bristles, and plunge it into his heart.

Or turn into a serpent and bite him.

Gaunt turned away. He would always have to watch his back against Rawne. Always, *forever*. It was the way of things. Ibram Gaunt had a billion enemies out there, but the bitterest was at his side, amongst his own, waiting for the moment to come where he could make a ghost of Gaunt.

# SEVEN
# PERMAFROST

THERE IS A VALLEY on Typhon Eight where frozen screams saw at the air, day and night, through eternity. The valley is a glacial cleft, its sheer sides nine kilometres deep. Where the starlight catches the top flanks, the ancient ice is so white, the eye can only take it briefly. Deeper, as it plunges, the ice becomes translucent blue, mauve, then crimson. Algae forms, frozen billions of years before into the rock-ice, stain it with their dyes and fluids.

It is the wind that screams, shredded and sliced by the razor-edged outcrops of ice along the valley crest, twisted and amplified by the gorge. Typhon Eight is an ice moon, its surface a crust of frozen water sometimes a hundred kilometres deep. Below that, boiling oceans of hydrocarbons pulse with the tidal rhythms of the planetoid's living core.

The screaming loud in his ears, Rawne rolled and slipped down a slope of scarlet ice at the bottom of the valley. The piercing wind raked at him, trying to steal his camo-cloak. Despite the cloak and his gloves and the insulation of his cold-weather fatigues, he was numb and leaden. The feeling – or the lack of feeling – replaced the rawness of an hour

before and was no more welcome. He lay still, fumbling
with his lasgun. Ice crystals formed on the metal of the
weapon. He could barely hold it.

More shots came his way. Rawne had become used to the
peculiar sound the impacts made in this place: a wet pop-
ping and a sizzle as superheated rounds punched into ice
which melted around them and refroze. Blackened wounds,
perfect circles, dotted the red ice sheet around him. He slithered into a deeper depression in the icescape and held
himself low. More shots, low and desperate, one buzzing a
hand's breadth over his head.

Then silence, or as close to silence as the perpetual
screaming would allow. He rolled onto his back and, with
his chin on his chest, looked back along the valley the way
he had come. There was no sign of anyone or anything,
except a crumpled black shape one hundred metres behind
him that he knew was Trooper Nylat.

Dead. They were all dead, and he was the last.

He wriggled up and took a sight. The lens of the lasgun
spotter was cracked and filmed with ice, ice which had
formed from the moisture of his own eye. He pulled back,
cursing. A day before, Trooper Malhoon had frozen his eye-
ball to his sight while spotting for targets on the ice floes. He
could still hear the man's screams as they had separated him
from his weapon.

He fired a triple salvo blind, wayward, into the dark of the
gorge. In answer, a dozen guns opened up on him, and blew
up an artificial blizzard in the ice-dust.

CAVES: LOW, arched, steepled defiles in the ice-cliff wall carved
by the slow shift of the crust. Short of breath and with a
shrapnel wound stinging his thigh, Rawne half-fell into the
nearest and lay on his face until the cold ache of the ice made
him roll over. It abruptly seemed breathlessly hot in the cave.
Rawne realised that it was because he was suddenly shielded
from the slicing wind. Though only a few degrees above zero
in the ice cave, out of the wind it felt almost tropical in there.
He pulled off his cloak and his gloves and, after a moment,
his insulated vest too. He shuddered, damp and too hot,

sweat built up under his insulating garments trickling like sauna moisture off his back.

He checked his leg. There was a hole in his fatigues at mid-thigh and it looked like he had been burnt by a melta. Then he realised the blood had not clotted on the flesh wound. It had frozen. He snapped the black ice off his flesh and, wincing as the action pinched, looked at the oozing wet gash in his leg.

Not for the first time in his military career and certainly not for the last, he cursed the name of Ibram Gaunt.

Rawne reached for his medi-pouch and pulled it open. He took the flesh clamps out and worked with them as the medic, Dorden, had instructed them all during Foundation Training. But the wire clamps were frozen and his numb fingers managed little more than to ping them off across the floor instead of opening them.

It took him an age to extract a needle from the sterile paper packets. He dropped four or five before he grasped one, and then set it between his teeth as he tried to find the loose end of the surgical thread.

Finally, it was pinched between unfeeling fingers. He took the needle and tried to thread it. He'd have had more chance making a bull's-eye on a target ten kilometres away with a wrong-sighted lasgun. After twenty attempts, he put the needle back between his teeth and tried to twist together the now frayed ends of the thread.

Something hit him hard from behind, smashing him head first into the snow floor.

He lay on his face, fazed, slowly becoming aware of the snorting and sniffling behind him. His tongue hurt and his mouth was full of blood which drooled out and frosted down into the ice. A big shape was moving behind him.

He turned his head slowly and dared to take a look. Circumspect, sidelong, as one might do into a mirror whilst shaving.

The ork was nearly three metres tall and almost as wide. Impossibly large muscles corded its shoulders and arms and stinking furs swaddled its bulk. Its head was huge, twice the size of a human's, thrust forward and seated on the vast lower jaw. Blackened teeth stuck like chisel blades out of the rotten gums. He couldn't see the eyes. He could smell the reeking breath, the corrosive saliva that spattered and dripped from the half-open mouth.

Playing dead, he watched as it toyed with his medi-pouch, rooting through the contents with hands big enough to break a human throat like a twig. It took out a roll of gauze and bit it, munching and then spitting out.

It's hungry, thought Rawne, and his guts iced and tightened at the idea.

Suddenly, it moved to him, pulling him up by the hair and jerking him back like a puppet, rummaging in his clothing with the other hand for food pouches, rations, munitions.

Blood spilled out of Rawne's jerked-open mouth, spattering down his chest. He tried to remain limp, but his left hand crept down towards the knife sheathed at his waist. The huge ork jerked and twisted him like a sack of bones, sniffing and gurgling behind his ear, hot breath on Rawne's neck, rancid smell in his nose.

Rawne found his knife and slid it out. He must have tensed doing so because the ork froze and then muttered something in its arcane tongue. Rawne moved to swing his knife, but the ork's huge paw was suddenly around his blade-hand, crushing it and slamming it into the icy wall beside them. Two slams and Rawne's hand gave up. The Tanith dagger whipped away.

The ork roared, a guttural bellow that deafened Rawne and shook his diaphragm. Holding him from behind, it bear-hugged, pulling its arms apart, determined to rip his torso in two. Rawne screamed, fighting futilely at the greater strength, tearing his arms free. He was dead, he knew that. Death was a moment away.

Pain made him reach into his mouth, to pull at whatever throbbed in his tongue. He found the end of the surgical needle, protruding from the flesh of his tongue. He yanked it out. A shockingly long spurt of blood followed it. Then he stabbed back behind his head with the little sliver of metal.

The ork screamed and dropped him. Rawne landed, spitting and coughing blood from his pulsing tongue. The ork was flailing around the cave wildly, holding one eye that dribbled with clear fluid and stained ichor. The noise of its rage was deafening in the ice-hole.

Rawne scrambled for a weapon, but the ork turned and sent him flying across the cave with a flat backhand. Rawne hit the ice wall hard with his shoulders, upside down and horizontal. His shoulder blade cracked and he dropped to the floor.

The ork charged him, one eye half-closed and oozing around the stub-eye of the surgical needle impaling it. Rawne rolled. His lasgun was on the far side of the cave, but his knife was in reach.

His knife. How many fights had he won with that? How many throats had he cut, how many hearts had he burst, how many stomachs had he opened?

He reached it, grasped it, turned in a low crouch to meet the attacker, a gleeful look on his face.

The ork faced him, its back to the cave mouth, a huge, crude bolt-pistol in its ichor-spattered fist.

The ork spoke, slow, rumbling, alien. Rawne didn't know what it said, but he knew what it meant.

There was a blinding flash and the roar of a weapon loosed in the confines of the cave.

Rawne had always wondered what it would feel like to take the killing hit. To be shot mortally. To die. But there was no feeling. No sense. In the blink of an eye, he saw the ork explode, its mid-section disintegrating in a burst of light.

It fell, almost in two parts. Its body fluids froze as it flopped to the ground.

There was a tall figure in the care entrance, blocking the light.

'Major Rawne?'

Ibram Gaunt entered the cave and holstered his bolt pistol.

IT SEEMED THAT the commissar had fared no better than him. The ork warband had decided to take advantage of the chaos of the crusade's push to seize Typhon as part of its attempt to build a raiding foothold into the Sabbat Worlds. Charged with destroying the menace, the Ghosts had deployed into the long gorges and ice-floes of the moon and come undone. As Rawne's platoon had been cut down along the eastern edge of the screaming valley, so Gaunt's had to the west. In retreat, the greenskins had proved the more determined adversaries.

The commissar and the major crouched down in the ice cave together. Rawne had made no sign of gratitude. In many ways he knew he would rather be dead than remain beholden to the off-worlder.

'How's your tongue?' Gaunt asked, getting a fire lit with chemical blocks.

'Why?'

'You're not saying much.'

Rawne spat. 'It's fine. A clean wound with a sharp instrument.' Truth was, his swollen tongue felt like a bedroll in his mouth, but he would not let the commissar have the satisfaction of knowing his discomfort. But he could not disguise the pain his leg gave him.

'Let me see to that,' Gaunt said.

Rawne shook his head.

'That was an order,' Gaunt sighed.

He moved over, pulling his own medi-pouch open. His clips were frozen too, but he warmed them over the chemical flame and then pinched the lips of Rawne's thigh wound shut. He sprayed the area with antiseptic from the one-use flask. Rawne felt his limb go dead.

Then Gaunt warmed his numb fingers and threaded surgical cord into a fresh needle. He handed Rawne his dagger. 'Bite the hilt.'

Rawne did so and stayed silent as Gaunt sewed the torn flesh together.

Gaunt bit off the cord and tied it, wrapping a dressing over the wound.

Rawne spat the dagger out.

Gaunt packed the kit away and then settled a kettle pan over the flames, dropping a scoop of ice into it.

'Seems to me Typhon has levelled us, major,' he said after a while.

'How so?'

'The high-born commissar, with all his airs and graces and rank, his schola training and his expertise; the low-life Tanith gangster with his wiles and tricks and diversions – it's put us on a level. Equals. Both fighting the same hostility with the same chances.'

Rawne didn't manage his retort. His tongue was too swollen and sore. He managed to spit again.

Gaunt smiled and watched the ice-water boil in the pan.

'Good. Maybe not. If you can still spit at me and hold me in contempt, we're not equal. I can lower myself down towards your level to help you… Feth, save you. But the day we're both on a level, your level, I'll kill myself.'

'Is that a promise?' Rawne asked.

Gaunt laughed. He dropped some dehydrated food cubes into the bubbling pan and stirred them. Dry-powdered bean soup puffed and formed. He was still laughing as he poured the soup into two tin cups.

THE WIND ROSE as night fell. It howled outside the mouth of the cave, raising the volume and intensity of the screaming. They sat together in the dark, watching the fire. There were only four fuel-blocks left to feed the blaze and Gaunt was being careful.

'You want to know some other differences between us, Rawne?'

Rawne wanted to say 'No', but his tongue was now too swollen and useless. He spat at Gaunt again instead.

Gaunt smiled and nodded down at the spittle freezing on the ice.

'There's one: this place might be a ball of frozen moisture, but you won't see me going around losing body moisture like that. The wind will freeze you dry in a few hours. Conserve your body water. Stop spitting at me and you might live.'

He held out a bowl of tepid water to Rawne and after a moment, the major took it and drank.

'Here's another. It's warm in here. Warmer than outside. But it's still close to zero. You're half-stripped and you're shivering.'

Gaunt was still dressed in his full uniform and his cloak was pulled around him. Rawne realised how numb he had become and began to pull his vest and cloak around him again.

'Why?' the major asked thickly.

'Why? Because I know... I've fought through cold zones before.'

'Not that... why? Why would you want to keep me alive?'

Gaunt was silent for a while.

'Good question...' he said at last. 'Given that you'd like nothing better than to see me dead. But I'm a commissar of the Imperial Guard, charged by the Emperor to keep his fighting legions able and intact in the face of battle. I won't let you die. That's my job. That's why I saved you here, that's why I saved the Tanith from the destruction of their world.'

There was a long silence, broken only by the crackling chemical bricks of the fire.

'You know I'll never see it that way,' Rawne said, his voice cold and small. 'You left Tanith to die. You didn't let us stand and fight. I will never forgive you that.'

Gaunt nodded. 'I know.' Then, after a moment, 'I wish it wasn't so.'

Rawne rolled himself up into a cleft of the ice cave and pulled the cloak around him. He felt only one thing. Hate.

SOMEHOW, SOMEWHEN, dawn had come up. Thin, frail light poked into the cave.

Gaunt was asleep, huddled down under his cloak, covered in frost. Rawne slowly got to his feet, fighting the ache in his bones and the almighty cold. The fire had long since gone out.

He edged around the cave, staring down at Gaunt. Pain ebbed through his sewn leg, his shoulders, his mouth. The pain cleared the fuzziness of his head and made him sharp. He picked up his Tanith knife, wiped the frost from it, and knelt to place its blade against Gaunt's throat.

No one would know. No one would ever find the body. And even if they did...

Gaunt shuddered in his sleep. He spoke the name of Tanith twice as his eyelids rolled and flicked. Then he spoke, curling up on himself: 'Won't let them die! No, not all of them! In the name of the Emperor, Sym!'

Then his voice died away into mumbling. Rawne's hand tensed on the knife. He hesitated.

Gaunt spoke again, his dreaming voice a low monotone. 'No, no, no, no... it's burning... burning... I would never... I would never....'

'Never what?' Rawne hissed, about to pull the dagger up in a quick killing slice.

'Tanith... In the name of the Emperor...'

Rawne twisted where he crouched. He pulled the dagger up, not in a killing slice but in an arc that threw it across at the mouth of the cave and impaled the throat of the ork creeping inside towards them.

As it fell back, gurgling, Rawne heard raucous baying from outside. He kicked Gaunt in the ribs to rouse him and swung up his lasgun, firing wildly at the cave mouth.

'They're on us, Gaunt, you bastard!' he screamed. 'They're on us!'

EIGHT FIERCE, WORDLESS minutes, weapons spitting and cracking in their hands. Gaunt roused from deep, troubled sleep to combat readiness with the speed of long experience. Six orks had come right up to the mouth of the cave, and without cover could do little but shoot and die. Caught in the mouth of the cave, the two Imperial soldiers had better cover and the advantage of the slope. Huge carcasses fell and slid, smoking down the crimson ice.

Rawne dropped the last of them and turned to find Gaunt scanning the valley floor with his scope.

'We can't stay here,' the commissar said. 'That exchange will bring them from all around.

'We have cover here,' Rawne argued.

Gaunt kicked the ice at the cave mouth. 'All we have is a tomb. Get enough of them around to pen us in and they'll bring the ice-cliff down and bury us. We have to move. And fast.'

They ditched bed rolls and anything else it would take too long to repack. Gaunt prioritised ammo, food, Rawne's small satchel of tube-charges, their cold weather gear. In less than a minute they were fleeing down the slope outside, cloaks flying, into the dawn chill.

Twelve kilometres away, the steep angles of the rising sun lit the far wall of the valley, but they were in twilight here, a frosty darkness in which the scarlet ice around them glowed and shone like marble. Or meat in a butcher's shop. Distantly, the crump of weapons fire. They hugged the valley wall, using ice rocks as cover as the wind wailed and agonised around them.

A kilometre or so from the cave, they rested, sweating in their insulated fabrics, crouched down in the cover of a block splinter fallen from high above.

Rawne wiped the ork blood off his knife and cut a hank of cloth from the edge of his stealth cape. He'd lost a glove somewhere, and his hand was aching and raw with the cold. He bound the cloth around his hand, tying it tight like a mitten.

Gaunt touched his shoulder and pointed back the way they had come. Lights, big gleaming lamps, bobbed and bounced along the valley floor: vehicles. The wind was too loud to make out engine notes.

'Come on,' said Gaunt.

FROM SHELTER, a scoop cut in the ice floor, they watched the vehicles pass five hundred metres away. Four big ork machines, black and pumping blacker smoke from crude combustion engines. Thick-treaded tyres with chains gave the front end of the machines traction, and the rear sections were carried on sled runners or tracks. Each vehicle carried at least two other warriors beside the driver, and hefty weapons on pintle or turret mounts. They howled past, spraying up sheets of ice particles, close enough for the men to see the tribal markings on the battered flanks of the machines and smell the stink of their burning oil.

Once they had passed, Gaunt made to continue, but Rawne pulled him back.

'They know how fast we can run,' he said. Sure enough, a roar reached them over the howling wind a minute or so later and the vehicles sped back past they way they had come, searching back over the ground to see what they had missed. One pulled away west and two more raced onwards. The fourth curved around in a spray of ice and moved towards them to search along the wall of the valley.

They were trapped. They could not run because there was nowhere to run to without exposing themselves to the orks if they rose from the scoop. Huddled low, they watched.

The ork half-sled slowed and one of the burly warriors jumped down, running alongside the vehicle, firing into caves along the valley wall. The other warrior traversed the heavy weapon of the trundling vehicle from side to side. Closer...

Gaunt turned to Rawne and nodded to his lasgun. 'More range, better sight. Take the weapon's operator.'

'Not the driver?'

'If his gunner's dead, all he can do is drive. If he dies, the gunner can still fire. Target the gunner... and when you've got him, re-aim on the foot soldier.'

Rawne nodded and breathed hard on his sight to warm the lens. He clicked in a fresh energy clip as quietly as he could. Though the wind was screaming, the hard metal clack would carry like a shot.

He saw Gaunt carefully doing the same with the sickle-pattern magazine of his bolt-pistol.

The motor sled turned their way, its harsh lights catching the lip of their ice scoop, making the scarlet ice translucent and all the more like fresh meat. Rawne took his aim. He knew he was no marksman like Larkin or Elgith, but he was passable. Even so, he let the sled slip closer in before he felt confident of a shot. His only target, the silhouette of the vehicle behind the lights. Closer... almost on them.

Rawne fired.

His blazing shot hit the black shape behind the lights. There was a double flash and then a series of loud, fierce explosions, like gunshots. The sled veered sideways, bumping to a halt. Rawne realised they had been gunshots. He had hit- the gunner squarely, but his shot had passed through the weapon mount on the way, exploding the heavy bolter and igniting the ammo drum. The gunner's smoking corpse hung from the burning weapon and, even as they watched, stray rounds super-heated and went off like fireworks. The driver was also dead, the back of his skull and neck riddled with shrapnel from the exploding ammo.

Gaunt and Rawne leaped up out of the scoop and ran towards the motorised sled. The ork left on foot was running their way, firing from the hip. Bolt rounds whizzed and sang around them, fizzling into the ice. Yelling as he charged the advancing ork, Rawne fired on full auto, his lasgun bucking as he carried it low against his side. Two laser shots spun the monstrous ork off his feet and dropped him on the ice, where he lay twitching.

Gaunt reached the sled, screwing up his nose at the smell of burning flesh. The gun and the gunner were still burning, but fire had not spread to the rest of the machine. He stepped forward, but darted back as another round went up. Then it was quiet.

He leaped up onto the tail-boards and put a point-blank round through the gunner's back, though he was sure the ork was dead. He had heard too many tales of the greenskin resilience to injury. Gaunt pitched the cadaver off the platform onto the ice, then grabbed hold of the smouldering, ruined weapon. There was a handle release to free the gun and its drums from the mount. He heaved on it, his hands slipping in thick grease. No human strength had tightened this latch. He put his weight behind it, cursing and grunting, expecting another round to explode in his face at any moment.

The latch gave. With a gasp, and an effort that tore ligaments in his back and arms, he hefted the entire gun and ammo carriage off the metal bars of the mount frame and tipped it over off the vehicle. As it landed, three more rounds went off, one scudding across the surface of the ice in slithering jags like a phosphorescent sprite.

Gaunt's gloves had caught fire from the red-hot metal and he jerked them off, throwing them aside. He clambered forward onto the driver's position and tried to pull the driver's body out of the cockpit. Nearly four hundred kilos of dead weight refused to budge.

He looked back at Rawne, in time to see him finishing the fallen footsoldier with his blade. Gaunt yelled him over, his voice lost in the keening wind.

Together they pried the driver's corpse free and flopped it into the ice. It had already begun to freeze and fell like a sack of rocks. Gaunt got into the cockpit, felt the space roomy and too big for a human operator. It stank of sweat and blood in the enclosed cabin. He tested the handlebar grips and found the foot pedals. His first tries at control revved the engine to a scream and then braked the sled in a jolt that threw the cursing Rawne onto his back in the troop bay behind him. Then he had the measure of it. It was a crude version of the landcars he had driven with his father back home, years ago. There was a foot throttle and also a foot brake, though that did little but dig a massive spike down from the underside into the ice to retard motion. The anchor would only work in conjunction with de-throttling. With the engine racing, the spike would shatter and pull the guts out from under the motor sled. The gears, three of them, were set by a twist on the left handlebar grip. There were gauges on the crude dash calibrated in greenskin script which he couldn't read or understand, but he began to measure the way the juddering needles spiked and dipped.

'Hold on, major!' he warned and raced them off towards the distant end of the valley. Rawne, in the back, clung on tight, the wind whipping his face and neck.

Gaunt focussed all his will into control. The massive machine bucked and jinked on every irregularity in the ice, but Gaunt quickly came to judge the way ahead, and knew what conditions would skid them round, or slide them, or make them spin treads. There was no power assist to the steering, and he fought it. It was beyond his strength to keep the steering true and he realised that he would never be able to drive the machine as fast as the stronger orks could. It fought too much and his strength was human, not inhuman.

They rocked and bumped and jolted. More than once, they spun out as he failed to keep the drive wheels true and the back end came around in a flurry of ice shards. After the last such lapse, the raging engine stalled and refused to restart. There was a starter switch under the steering column, but it flopped slackly.

Gaunt peered down and found the kick start stirrup to the left of the brake. He bent and flopped it down, trying it with his boot.

'Gaunt!'

He looked up. Rawne was standing on the flatbed, pointing back. A kilometre away, three dark shapes were kicking up ice-smoke as they raced after them. The orks, with their superior strength and experience of the snow machines, were making better speed in their pursuit.

Gaunt kicked viciously at the starter bar time and again until the engine yowled alive, and then hastily adjusted the protesting throttle.

They spun again, fishtailed, then chugged away. Gaunt pushed the machine as fast as he thought he could control it. Another misread flaw in the ice, another spin out, another stall, and they would be overrun. Or overturned, necks snapped under the rolling tonnage of the motor sled.

THEY CAME OUT of the night shadows of the valley onto the wide expanse of the ice floe. Sunlight seared them and Gaunt and Rawne were blind for a moment, even after they pulled their glare goggles down.

Ahead was the ice sea. White, scarlet, purple, green in patches, the ice was scalloped and curled like foam. Thousands of kilometres of open, frozen sea, spread out to a horizon where it met the blackness of space. The sunlight was a hostile white menace.

The sea and all its waves had frozen as if in mid-ebb, and now the sled bounced and flew, rose and fell, across the dimpled peaks of breakers that had frozen a millennium before.

The motor sled over-revved each time it left the ground and kicked ice chunks each time it landed. Gaunt could barely control the machine as the drive wheels and slithering skids kissed ice again. Rawne had thought about firing back at the ork machines closing on them, but the bumpy ride had thrown him to the greasy deck and it was all he could do to cling on and lie flat. Face to the metal deck-boarding, he saw the punctures for the first time. Shrapnel holes, from the exploding bolter drums. There was a stink of oil rising from them. He crawled, hand over hand, to the tail gate as the sled jumped and crashed, and saw a staining line of brown marking their wake.

He turned and yelled. 'We're bleeding fuel! The tank is punctured!'

Gaunt cursed. Now he understood what one of the gauges – the one with the rapidly dipping needle – really meant.

The ork pursuit was closing. Heavy bolter rounds and other explosive munitions rained down around them, blowing geysers of ice and steam up from the frozen sea.

Gaunt realised his naked, glove-less hands were beginning to freeze solid around the steering grips. The pain brought tears to his eyes, tears which froze behind his goggles and blurred his vision, biting his cheeks.

Two over-shot projectiles from the orks brought bigger explosions to the left of them. Sprays of glutinous, boiling liquid erupted far into the air from their impacts. Gaunt saw that the rushing landscape ahead of them was duller blue, more like frosted glass, cracked and crazed.

They made the next rise. Then the engine coughed, spluttered, died. They slid sideways in a long, wide deceleration, ice gouged up by Gaunt's desperate use of the anchor. He kicked the starter. The engine flared once, then died forever in a cough of stinking oil smoke. Dry rotors and cylinders burst and ground.

The ork machines were a hundred metres behind them. They could hear them whooping in victory. For the first time, Rawne realised that the wind was no longer screaming now they were out of the valley.

Gaunt clambered out of the cockpit. 'Tube-charges, Rawne!' he bawled.

'What?'

Gaunt pointed to where other wide shots from their pursuers dug steaming vents from the glassy ice.

'The ice is thin here. We're riding over a thin skin. The living ocean is right below us.'

Another shot whinnied down and exploded the steering section of the sled where Gaunt had just been sitting.

'Now!'

Rawne understood the commissar's idea just as suddenly as he recognised the insanity of it. But the orks were only fifty paces away. Rawne realised the desperation too.

He had twelve stick mines in his satchel and he pulled them all out, handing half to Gaunt. He kicked the glass off one of the vehicle's lamps and used the white-hot filament to light the fuses. The two humans took three in each hand and hurled them as far and as hard as they could, scattering them wide.

Twelve huge explosions, each big enough to kill a tank. They split the world apart. But more particularly, they burst and shattered the ice. The steaming hydrocarbon sea, so close beneath, rushed up to plume and boil and froth in the air.

One ork machine cartwheeled, an explosion taking it over. It tore itself and its occupants into fragments as it landed on ice that was beginning to separate and fracture in huge bobbing sections. Another dodged the rain of blasts and flew straight off the edge of an ice chunk into the sea, where it vaporised and burned. The last stopped short, the riders bellowing, just missing a gap in the ice. Then the ice chunk it sat on collapsed and they all dropped shrieking into the frothing, flaming liquid.

The ice was coming apart, fracturing into chunks that burned and steamed as the rising ocean, locked in for so many thousands of years, welled up and conquered the surface. On the back of their dead machine, Gaunt and Rawne leapt and yelled in triumph until they realised the ice collapse was spreading their way fast.

The ocean fizzed and thrashed up around their sled runners and the motor-sled dipped suddenly. Gaunt jumped clear onto a nearby iceberg, newly formed and sizzling in the hideous liquid.

He held out his hand. Rawne jumped after him, grabbing Gaunt's hand, allowing himself to be pulled clear as their ruined machine slid backwards into the liquid and exploded.

'We can't stay here,' Gaunt began. It was true. Their iceberg was rocking and dissolving like an ice cube in hot water. They leapt off it to the next, and then the next, hoping that the fractured sections of ice would remain intact long enough for them to reach some kind of shore. Vapours gasped and billowed around them.

On the fourth, Rawne slipped and Gaunt caught him just centimetres from the frothing water.

They made the next floe and Rawne moved ahead. He heard a cry behind him and turned to see the ice plate upending and Gaunt sliding backwards on his belly, clawing the surface as he slipped down towards the seething ocean of hydrocarbons.

He could let him die. Rawne knew that. No one would know. No one would ever find the body. And even if they did… Besides, he couldn't reach him.

Rawne pulled out his knife and hurled it. It stuck fast, blade down, in the tilting ice just above Gaunt's hand and gave the commissar a grip. Gaunt pulled himself up on the dagger and then got his foot braced on it until he could reach up and take Rawne's hand. The major hauled him up high enough for the pair to make a safe jump to the next berg. This was larger, more solid. They clung to it, side by side, panting and out of strength.

The ice chunk behind them fell back into the ocean, taking Rawne's silver dagger with it.

THEY SAT TOGETHER on top of the iceberg for six hours. Around them, the ocean refroze and its seething hiss died away. But they could go nowhere. The reforming ice skin was but a few centimetres thick – thick enough to enclose the lethal liquid but not so hard as to bear weight. The distress beacon from Gaunt's pack blinked and sighed behind them on the top of the ice chunk.

'I owe you,' Gaunt said at last.

Rawne shook his head. 'I don't want that.'

'You pulled me up there. Saved me. I owe you for that. And frankly, I'm surprised. I know you'd like to see me dead and this was an opportunity that spared your hands from blood.'

Rawne turned to look at Gaunt, his face half-lit by the dwindling starlight. His cheeks and chin seemed to catch the light more like a dagger now than ever before. And his eyes were hooded like a snake's.

'One day, I will kill you, Gaunt,' he said simply. 'I owe it to Tanith. To myself. But I'm no murderer and I respect honour. You saved me from that greenskin in the cave and so I owed you.'

'I would do as much for any man in my command.'

'Precisely. You may think I'm a malcontent, but I stay loyal to the Emperor and the Guard always. I owed you and, though I hate myself for it, I repaid. Now we're even.'

'Even,' Gaunt murmured, measuring the word softly in his mouth. 'Or level, perhaps.'

Rawne smiled. 'The day will come, Ibram Gaunt. But it will be on equal terms. *Level* terms, as you put it. I will kill you, and I will rejoice in it. But now is not the time.'

'Thank you for being so forthright, Rawne.' Gaunt pulled out his Tanith knife, the knife given to him by Corbec when they first mustered for war.

Rawne tensed, jerking back. But Gaunt held it out to him, hilt first.

'You lost yours. I know any Tanith would be incomplete without a long blade at his hip.'

Rawne took the knife. He held it in his hands for a second, spun it with deft fingers, and then slid it into his empty belt sheath.

'Do with it as you see fit,' Gaunt said, turning his back on Rawne.

'I will… one of these days,' replied Major Elim Rawne.

THE INFIRMARY LAY well back from the main embankment
defence here on Monthax. Like Gaunt's modular hut, it was
raised out of the soupy ground on stacks. Long, swoop-
roofed, the Infirmary's wall planking was washed an arsenic
green, while the roof was black with bitumen. Grey blast-
curtains protected the doors and window hatches, and
bunches of pipes and cables carried in air from the scrubbers
and power from the chattering turbine behind the place.
Symbols of the Imperium, and of the medical corps, were
stencilled on the walls, for all that Chaos would notice them
if they stormed over the bulwark. Gaunt climbed up a metal
ladder next to the rush-ramp for stretcher parties, and
pushed inside through the screens and heavy curtaining.

Inside he found a paradise and a surprise. It was by far the
coolest and most fragrant place in the camp, probably the
coolest, most fragrant place on Monthax itself. Sweet odours
of sap rose from the fresh timber of the floor and the clean
rush matting. There was a scent of antiseptic fluids, rubbing
alcohol and some purifying incense that burned in a bowl
next to the small shrine set near the western end. The forty

beds were made up and empty. Pale, artificial light shone from gauze-hooded lamps.

Gaunt wandered the length of the ward and let himself through a screen door at the end. There, access led off into storerooms, latrines, a small operating theatre, and the Chief Medical Officer's quarters. Dorden wasn't in his little, tidy office, but Gaunt saw his distinctive handiwork in the careful arrangement of medical texts, chart folders, and the labels-front regimentation of the flasks and bottles in the locked dispensary cabinet.

The medic was in the operating theatre, polishing the stainless-steel surface and blood drains of the theatre table. Gleaming surgical tools, an autoclave and a resussitrex unit sat in corners.

'Commissar Gaunt!' Dorden looked up in surprise. 'Can I help you?'

'As you were. Just a routine walkabout. Anything to report, any problems?'

Dorden stood up straight, balling the polishing cloth in his hands and dropping it into a ceramic bowl of disinfectant. 'Not one, sir. Come to inspect the place?'

'Certainly an improvement on the last few facilities you've had to work with.'

Dorden smiled. He was a small, elderly man with a trimmed grey beard and genial eyes that had seen more pain than they deserved. 'It's empty yet.'

'I admit that surprised me when I came in. So used to seeing your places overflowing with wounded, Emperor spare us.'

'Give it time,' Dorden said, ominously. 'It unnerves me, I have to say. Seeing all those empty beds. I praise the Golden Throne I'm idle, but idleness doesn't suit me. Must've polished and swept the place a dozen times already.'

'If that's the worst work you have here on Monthax, we may all give thanks.'

'May we all indeed. Can I offer a cup of caffeine? I was about to light the stove.'

'Perhaps later, when I come back this way. I have to inspect the magazines. There are stirrings beyond us.'

'So I heard last night. Later then, sir.'

Gaunt nodded and left. He doubted he'd have time to stop by later, and he doubted too that this little paradise would remain unsullied much longer.

Dorden watched the commissar leave, and stood for a while longer surveying the clean ward with its empty cots. Like Gaunt, he had no illusions as to the horror-hole this place would become. It was inevitable.

He closed his eyes, and for a moment he could see the floor matting drenched in black blood; the soiled sheets; the moaning, screaming faces. And the silent ones.

His nostrils seemed to detect blood and burned flesh for a second, but it was just the incense.

Just the incense.

# EIGHT
# BLOOD OATH

THE FALLEN MEN, scattered on the roadway and across the
low, muddy fields of Nacedon, looked like they were wear-
ing black mail armour. But they weren't. The meat-flies
were busy. They covered the flesh like seething black links
of armour. They glittered furiously, moving like a single
thing.

'Medic!'

Tolin Dorden looked away from the flies. The afternoon
sky lay wide and misty over the low, flat fens. Trackways and
field boundaries were marked with dykes and hedge ways,
all of them ruined and overrun with razor-posts, concertina
wire and churned tank paths. The mist smelled of thermite
powder.

'Medic!' The call again. Sharp and insistent, from down
the roadway. Slowly, Dorden turned and trudged from the
gutter of the road where, for a hundred metres, more corpses
lay twisted and crumpled and coated in flies.

He advanced towards the buildings. Feth, but he'd seen
enough of this war now, no matter what the world. He was
tired and he was spent. Sixty years old, older by twenty years

than any of the other Ghosts. He was weary: weary of the death, the fighting, weary of the young bodies he had to patch back together. Weary, too, of being regarded as a father by so many men who had lost their own at the fall of Tanith.

Smoke clogged the late afternoon sky across the low fields. He approached the old red-brick buildings with their blown-out windows and crumpled walls. It had been a farm complex once, before the invasion. A feudal estate with a main house, outbuildings and barns. Agricultural machinery lay rusting and broken in waterlogged swine pens. A wide trench gully and a double fence of seared flak-boards topped with more spools of wire enclosed the complex in a horseshoe, with the northern side, the one that faced away from the frontline, open. Ghosts stood point all around, weapons ready. Trooper Brostin nodded him inside.

Dorden passed a sandbagged gunnery post from which the weapon had been hastily removed and entered the first of the buildings, the main house, through a doorway that had been shot out of the brick by sustained las-fire. More flies, billowing in clouds in the afternoon sunlight. The smell of death he was so, so used to. And other smells: antiseptic, blood, waste.

Dorden stepped across a tiled floor. Half the tiles were broken, littered with glass and pools of oil that shimmered rainbow colours. Corbec loomed out of the shadows nearby, shaking his weary head. 'Doc,' he acknowledged.

'Colonel.'

'Field hospital…' Corbec said, gesturing around himself. Dorden already knew as much.

'Anyone alive?'

'That's why I called for you.'

Corbec led him through to a vaulted hallway. The various stenches were stronger in here. Perhaps five dozen men lay on pallet beds in the chamber, half-lit by pallid yellow sunlight that streaked down through shattered lights in the sloping roof. Dorden walked the length of the room and then back.

'Why have they been left here?' he asked.

Corbec shot him a questioning look. 'Why do you think? We're all retreating. Too much to carry. Can you... sort them?'

Dorden cursed quietly. 'These men are what?'

'Bluebloods. Volpone 50th. You remember those devils from Voltemand? Their command units pulled out this morning, as per orders.'

'And they left the wounded here?'

Corbec shrugged. 'Seems so, Doc.'

'What kind of animal leaves his sick and wounded behind to die?' Dorden spat, moving to change the dressings on the nearest man.

'The human kind?' Corbec asked.

Dorden looked round sharply. 'This isn't funny. Corbec. It's not even whimsical. Most of these men will live with the proper attention. We're not leaving them.'

Corbec groaned softly. He rubbed the top of his scalp, folding the thick black hair between his big, swarthy fingers. 'We can't stay here, Doc. Commissar's orders...'

Dorden turned and looked at the colonel with fierce, old eyes. 'I'm not leaving them,' he stated plainly. Corbec seemed to start to say something, then hesitated and decided better of it. 'See what you can do for them,' he said, and left Dorden to his work.

DORDEN WAS TREATING a leg wound when he heard the crunch of gravel on the roadway outside and the rumble of a troop carrier. He looked up to locate the source of the sound only after he had finished what he was doing.

'Thank you, sir,' said the young man whose leg he had treated. The boy was pale and sallow, too weak to rise from his pallet bed.

'What's your name?' Dorden asked.

'Culcis, sir. Trooper, Blueblood.' Dorden was sure that Culcis would have wanted to punctuate that statement with an exclamation mark, but he was too weak to manage it.

'I'm Dorden. Medic. Tanith. You need me, Trooper Culcis, you call my name.'

The boy nodded. Dorden went outside, approaching the Chimera parked below the leaning walls. Corbec was speaking to the tall figure perched on top.

The figure moved, dropped down to the soil, began to march towards him: Gaunt, his cap on, his face a shadow, his long coat flying.

'Sir!' Dorden said.

'Dorden – Corbec says you won't move.'

'Sixty-eight wounded here, sir. Can't leave them; won't leave them.'

Gaunt took Dorden's arm and led him across the muddy yard to the side wall that looked out across trampled farmland and vacant swine pens towards the setting suns beyond.

'You must, Dorden. Enemy forces are half a day behind us. General Muller has called us all to retreat. We can't carry them with us. I'm sorry.'

Dorden shook off the commissar's grip. 'So am I,' he said.

Gaunt turned away. For a moment, Dorden thought the commissar might round on him and discipline him with a fist. But he didn't. Instead, the man sighed. On reflection, Dorden knew violence wasn't Gaunt's first or chosen way of command. The endless war and his experience of other officer cadres in the field had soured Dorden's expectation, something he wasn't proud of.

Gaunt looked back at the medic. 'Corbec told me you'd say as much. Look, the counter-push for Nacedon is scheduled for tomorrow night. Then, and only then, Emperor willing, we'll retake this land and drive the enemy back.'

'Few of them will last the night and day unattended. And none if they are found and attended by the Chaos filth!'

Gaunt took off his cap and smoothed his cropped blond hair. The dying suns-light silhouetted his angular profile, but kept his internal thoughts in shadow. 'You have my respect, medic. You've always had it, since the Founding Fields even. The only Ghost who refuses to bear arms, the only man who can keep us alive. The Ghosts owe you, many of them owe you their lives. I owe you for that. I'd hate to have to give you an order.'

'Then don't, commissar. You know I'll refuse it. I'm a medic first and a Ghost second. Back on Tanith, as a community practitioner, I worked for thirty years ministering to the sick, the infirm, the new-born and the weak in the Beldane District and County Pryze. I did it because I took an oath at the Medical College in Tanith Magna. You understand allegiances and oaths, commissar. Understand mine.'

'I understand the weight of the medical oath well enough.'

'And you've honoured it! Never asked me to break my vow on confidentiality over men with private problems... drink, pox, mind-troubles... you've always let me do as my oath bids. Let me now.'

Gaunt replaced his cap. 'I can't leave you here to die.'

'But you'd leave these men to die?'

'They're not the Ghosts' chief medic!' Gaunt spat the answer and then fell silent.

'A doctor is vowed to serve any injured. Oh, I swore to the Emperor, on the Founding Fields, to serve him and you and the Imperial Guard. But I'd already sworn to the Emperor to uphold life. Don't make me break that vow.'

Gaunt tried logic. 'Our illustrious forces were routed on the delta at Lohenich. We are fleeing before a massed Chaos army that thunders at our heels, barely half a day away. You're a non-combatant. How could you hold this place?'

'With words, if I have to. With volunteers, if any will stay and you'll allow it. After all, it's only until tomorrow night. Until your counter-push retakes this place. Or was that a lie? Propaganda?'

Gaunt said nothing for a while, tilting his tall bulk into the evening suns, adjusting his muddy coat. Then he turned back to the old medic.

'No lie. We will retake this land, and beyond. We will drive them back as they come to us. But to leave you out here, even for a night...'

'Don't think of me. Think of the Volpone wounded in there.'

Gaunt did. It didn't change his mind much. 'They would have had us butchered–'

'Don't go to that place!' Dorden warned. 'Hate has no place between allies. These are men, Troopers, valuable soldiers. They could live to fight again, to turn another conflict for the better. Leave me to care for them, with whoever you can spare. Leave me, and come back for us all.'

Gaunt cursed. 'I'll give you a squad. I can spare no more. Ten men, volunteers. If it doesn't come to ten, tough. Muller will have my head for leaving any in the field as it is.'

'I'll take whatever I can get,' Dorden said. 'Thank you.'

Gaunt strode away abruptly, then turned, came back and took Dorden's hand tightly in his own.

'You're a brave man. Don't let them take you alive… and don't make me regret allowing you to be too brave.'

GAUNT AND THE retreating lines of Ghosts passed on and then they were alone. Dorden was working in the long hall, and only noticed the passing of time as the sunshine through the skylights faded to blue and dusk fell. He lit lamps on crates placed between the wounded and went outside into the yard. Overhead, alien stars were coming out in the mauve sky.

He saw three Ghosts at first: Lesp, Chayker and Foskin, who acted as his orderlies and were skilled field medics. They were sorting through the medical supplies Gaunt had left for them. Dorden had half-expected them to volunteer and stay, hoped for it, but to see his three staffers working as usual was refreshing and uplifting. He crossed to them, meaning to carry on as normal and ask about the supply level, but all he found in his throat was thanks. Each one smiled, took his hand as he offered it, grunted an acknowledgement of duty. Dorden was proud of them.

He started to give them dispersal instructions, and began to run through the needs of the sick in priority order, when other Ghosts stepped into view: Mkoll, the chief scout and Dorden's closest friend in the unit, accompanied by Troopers Brostin, Claig, Caffran and Gutes. They had just finished a patrol sweep of the horseshoe boundary and were preparing to dig in for the night.

Dorden greeted Mkoll. 'You needn't have stayed.'

'And leave you alone here?' Mkoll laughed. 'I'll not have the records say "Medic Dorden died and where was his friend, the warrior Mkoll?" The commissar asked for volunteers and so we volunteered.'

'I'll not forget this, however short my life,' Dorden replied.

'We have the flank guarded well,' Mkoll told Dorden, indicating the double fence. 'All ten of us.'

'Ten?'

'That's what the colonel-commissar allowed. Us five, your three, and the other two. All of the Ghosts were arguing over who could stay, did you know? Everyone volunteered for the duty.'

'Everyone? Not Major Rawne, I'd bet!'

Mkoll grinned ruefully, 'All right, not everyone. But there was a scramble for places. Gaunt finally decided on first come, first served. So you got your three, me, Brostin, Claig, Caffran and Gutes. Plus Tremard, on watch at the gates. And...'

'And?'

Dorden whipped round, sensing someone was suddenly behind him. He looked up into the smiling bearded face of Colm Corbec.

'And me. So, Doc, you're in charge. How do we play this?'

NIGHT FELL. The air cleared. Distantly, carrion-dogs howled. Three or more moons rose and set, duelling with each others' orbits. The darkness was clear and cold and smelled of death. Far away, on the southern horizon, amber clouds thumped and boiled, a storm approaching. A mighty land army was moving towards them. That, and a real storm. Lightning shuddered the sky in hazes of white-flash. The air became heavy and sweet.

Inside the farmhouse, one of the Bluebloods spasmed and died. Dorden was fighting for that life, his apron-smock slick with spurting blood. There was nothing he or Lesp could do.

Dorden stepped back from the cooling corpse and handed bloodied instruments to Lesp. 'Record time and manner of death, and the name and number from the tags,' he said darkly. 'Emperor willing, we can pass it to the Volpone adjutant's office and they can adjust their records.'

Lesp snorted. 'The Bluebloods have doubtless marked all these as dead already.'

Lesp was a tall, thin man from Tanith Longshore, with cold blue eyes and an Adam's apple that looked like a knee in his slender neck. He'd been a fisherman back on the Lost Place, part of a sea-fishing family which plied the ocean currents beyond the archipelago. He owned a fierce skill with a sail-cloth and net needle, and an almost surgical knack with a blade learned from gutting fish back in those days. Dorden had put those skills to use in the name of healing when he had co-opted Lesp as an orderly. Lesp had taken to it well, and enjoyed his work alongside the chief medic.

Dorden took all the willing, able help he could get. Most of the trained medics who had founded with the Ghosts on Tanith had never made it off-world. Originally, the only fully qualified medics had been Dorden, Gherran and Mtane, with twenty other troopers trained as field medics. Dorden had interviewed and studied all of the surviving men to recruit for the badly needed medical staff. Without devoted, constantly learning amateurs like Lesp, Foskin and Chayker, the health of the regiment would have failed long ago.

Mtane and Gherran had moved on with Gaunt's main force, though both had wanted to stay. Losing all three trained medics in one rash act was more than Gaunt would tolerate.

Dorden stepped out into the muddy yard and, as if on cue, the heavens opened and sheeting rain hammered down on him, washing another's blood out of his tunic. He stood there, dripping, as the downpour eased a little.

'You'll get wet out there,' came a voice from nearby.

Dorden swung round to face Corbec, who was smoking a cigar in the cover of the slumping side-roof. All Dorden could see was the shape and the red coal of the light.

Dorden crossed to him. Corbec offered up a waxy box of smokes. 'Liquorice. Got the taste of them on Voltemand and it's taken me an age to get some on the black market. Take one for now and one for later.'

Dorden took two, slid one behind his ear unlit and lit up the other from Corbec's half-smoked stick.

They looked out into the night.

'It's going to be rough,' remarked Corbec softly.

He was looking at the flash and howl of the storm, but Dorden knew what he meant.

'Yet you stayed.'

Corbec took a deep drag and white smoke plumed out of his hairy shadow. 'I'm a sucker for good deeds.'

'Or lost causes.'

'The Emperor will provide. And aren't we all just one big lost cause? The First and Last and Lost? You don't see me giving up on that.'

Dorden smiled. The cigar was strong and the flavour hellish, but he was enjoying it. It had been twenty years since he'd smoked. His wife had never approved, said it didn't set a good example to the patients Dorden tended to.

Then the kids came along, Mikal and Clara, and he'd kicked the habit, so–

Dorden shut off the thoughts. Tanith had taken his wife with it, and Clara and her husband and their baby too. All he had was Mikal, Trooper Mikal Dorden, vox-caster operator in Sergeant Hasker's platoon.

'You're thinking about home,' Corbec muttered.

Dorden broke his sad reverie. 'What?'

'I know that look.'

'It's dark, colonel!'

'I know that... feeling, then. The set of a man's shoulders. Comes on us all, time to time.'

'I'd guess the commissar has told you to stamp it out where ever you see it? Bad for morale.'

'Not in my book. Tanith still lives while we all carry it here...' Corbec tapped his forehead. 'And we don't know where we're going if we don't know where we came from.'

'Where are we going, do you suppose?'

Corbec flicked his butt onto the mud and let it sputter dead. 'On a bad day, to hell. On a good day, I'd say we were bound for that trophy world Gaunt's promised us. Slaydo's gift: the first world we truly win we can take and claim and settle as our own.'

Dorden gazed at the storm. 'New Tanith, huh? Like the men talk of when they're drunk or dying? Do you believe that? Might we ever take a world ourselves, get the credit clean and true? We're less than two thousand. Every theatre we enter, we do so alongside other regiments, and that muddies victory claims and credit. I'm not a pessimist, colonel, but I doubt any of us will ever find that New Tanith, except in drink or death.'

Corbec smiled, his white teeth shining in the gloom. 'Then lucky me. One way or another, I'll see more of it than most.'

A door banged to their left. Chayker, shrouded in his cape, emerged from the hospital and carried a tin drum over to the well. A few moments' cranking, and he struggled with it back to the buildings. Dorden and Corbec could already smell the broth Chayker and Foskin were brewing for all the company.

'Something smells good,' Corbec said.

'Foskin found tubers and grain in a field beyond the ditch walls, and we turned up dried pulses and salt meat in an old pantry. Should be the best supper any of us have had in a while. But first rations go to any of the patients who can take it.'

'Of course. They need it more than us. I've got a flask of sacra and a box of these smokes. Should keep me going awhile.'

'Come in when you're ready for proper nourishment,' Dorden instructed, as if issuing a prescription. 'Thanks for the cigars.' He headed back to the ward.

A CIRCUIT of the wounded took another hour and a half. Lesp and the other orderlies had done well, and many had eaten or at least taken fluid. There were twelve who were too far gone to remain conscious, and Dorden carefully rationed out his supply of drugs to prioritise them. The boy, Culcis, along with a few others, were now sitting up, chatting, grateful. All of them, Volpone aristo-blood, were disdainful of

the Tanith, but civil nevertheless. Being cut adrift by their
regiment, and spared from death only by a barbarian unit,
would seem to have altered many of their deeper prejudices
and snobberies. For that at least, Dorden felt pleased.

He saw Trooper Caffran, coming in soaked from a patrol
circuit, taking his bowl of broth to sit with Culcis. They were
about the same age, Dorden reckoned. The same age as
Mikal. He heard them share a joke.

Lesp took his arm. One of the critical cases was showing
signs of fading. With Chayker's help, they carried the man
out into what had once been the household kitchen, and
now served as a surgical theatre. A refectory table sat there,
long enough for a man, and they heaved him onto it.

The Blueblood, a Corporal Regara by his tags, had lost a leg
below the knee and taken shrapnel in the chest. His blood
was far from blue. The refectory table became slick and blood
drooled off onto the flagstones. Chayker almost slipped and
Dorden ordered him to fetch a mop and more wadding.

'There are no mops,' Chayker shrugged.

'Then find something *like* a mop.'

Dorden had to take off more of the ruined leg from the
shrieking Regara with his handsaw before he could staunch
and tie the haemorrhage. He directed Lesp's sure fingers in
to suture the breach with fine, sail-maker's stitches. By then,
Chayker had returned. Dorden found he was mopping the
floor with shredded strips from his cape tied to an old rake
handle. For a Ghost to tear up his treasured stealth cloak to
mop blood... Dorden's admiration for his volunteers' devotion to duty grew.

They carried the softly moaning Regara back to his bed.
With luck, and a fever-breaking shot of mascetamine, he
might yet live. But Dorden was called away almost at once
to a seizure that Foskin couldn't cope with, and then to a
man who had woken from near-coma, only to begin violently retching blood.

The ward fell quiet towards midnight, as other dramas
came and passed. Dorden was scrubbing his chrome rib-
spreaders in a bucket of scalding water when Mkoll came
in, shaking the water from his cape. The storm was still

booming outside and thunder rattled the casements and roofing. Every now and then, loose glass in a window some- where fell in, or tiles slipped off and shattered. The storm had continued all that evening, but until then, Dorden had blanked it out.

He watched Mkoll sit and clean his gun, the first thing he always did before seeing to other duties like food or warmth. Dorden took him a bowl of broth.

'Anything out there?'

Mkoll shook his head. 'If we're lucky, the storm is slowing their advance.'

'And if we're not?'

'They conjured the storm.'

Mkoll looked up at the rafters and the high roof. 'This must have been quite a place. A good homestead, worth the working. The soil is healthy and they had plenty of live-stock.'

'A family home,' Dorden pondered, who hadn't thought about it before. The thought of another home and family lost to the war now bit at him. He felt weary again. Old.

Mkoll spooned his broth quietly. 'There's an old chapel at the rear of the house. Blown in, of course, but you can still see the painted reredos commemorating the Emperor. The Volpone used it as a privy. Whoever lived here were devout servants of the Imperium, working the land, raising their kin.'

'Until this.'

Dorden fell silent. Chaos had taken this world, Nacedon, two months gone, as part of their counter-punch to thwart Macaroth's crusade. It hadn't been occupied, or even cor- rupted from within. Nacedon, an agricultural world with three million Imperial colonists, had been violated and invaded in the space of three nights.

What kind of universe was it, Dorden wondered, where humans could struggle and break their backs and love their families and worship the Emperor and build for years, only to lose it all in a few hours? His universe, he concluded, the same one that had taken Tanith away.

* * *

A LATE MOON was up, a lonely sentry in a sky suddenly clear of storm. The rain had stopped and silver clouds scudded across the purple openness of the heaven.

Counterpart to the moon, a lone sentry stood at the gate of the station. Trooper Tremard, sitting his second shift at the gate in the sandbag emplacement, watched the tree lines, black fuzzes of darkness edging the flats of the equally black fields and fens. He was tired, and he wished that the fething Volpone had left their heavy gun in the emplacement.

Mist rose across the fenland, drifting sideways like smoke. Something twinkled in the dark.

Tremard started up, grabbing his scope from the sandbags. He fumbled with the focus ring, pulling the green-on-green night vision view into true. Mist – and other things in it. The twinkle he had seen. Moonlight flashing back from the staring reflective retina of hunting eyes.

He triggered his micro-bead link. 'Gate to Ghosts! Can you hear me, colonel? To arms! To arms! Movement to the south!'

CORBEC ROSE abruptly from his cot, like a dead man lifting from a grave, making Dorden start. The colonel had been catching forty winks on a spare bed in the ward as the medic sorted pills into paper twists.

'What is it?'

Corbec was on his feet. 'Three guesses, Doc.'

Dorden was up too. He looked around at the fragile hall, the vulnerable, half-dead men, as Corbec readied his lasgun and voxed-in with the other troopers. Dorden felt suddenly stupid. He knew what a full-on assault of Chaos was like. They'd all be shattered like an egg-shell. He'd been stupid to insist on staying. Now he had them all dead – the Blue-bloods, the Ghosts... valuable, peerless Ghosts like Corbec and Mkoll. He'd wasted them all, over some foolish pride in an old oath. An old medical oath, taken in safer times, in a nice community practice where the worst injury was a laceration at the sawmill.

*Feth me for a fool! Feth me for my pride!*

'We'll front them as long as we can. The boys know some tricks,' Corbec told him. 'I'll need Chayker and Foskin... Lesp can stay with you. If we lose the first attack, you need to be ready to get as many of the wounded out into the back rooms. They're ruins I know, but it'll put more walls between you and the fighting.'

Dorden swallowed, thinking of the work it would take him and Lesp to carry sixty-seven men out into the rear of the dwelling on stretchers. He heard the distant wail of las-fire and realised it wouldn't be half the effort Corbec and his soldiers were about to make. So he simply nodded, beckoning Lesp to him.

'Emperor be with you and watch over you, Colm Corbec,' he said.

'And you, Doc.'

TREMARD HELD THE gate. Dark shapes moved across the fields and through the dim hedgerows towards him, crackling out green pulses of laser fire and white-hot bolt rounds. The treacherous moon showed movement and the occasional glint of armour, and he picked his targets well, barking orange slices of laser into the open fenland beyond the farm.

Ducking the incoming sprays of fire, a figure dropped into the position beside him. It was Colonel Corbec. Corbec grinned at Tremard, made some obscene remark as to the maternal origins of the enemy that had Tremard cackling at its vulgarity, and leaned up over the bags to loose a volley of shots from his lasgun down the lane into the fens.

Along the ditch walls, the other Ghosts opened up. Eight lasguns against the encroaching dark, eight lasguns picking their targets through scope and skill, matching the hundreds of fire-points blasting back at them from the fens.

'Where's Brostin?' Corbec barked into his micro-bead, over the howl of gunplay, sustaining a regular fire-pattern.

A second later, his query was lost in a withering assault which blasted down the lane and onto his position. A hundred or more warriors of Chaos were forcing their approach at the main gate, charging them, weapons blazing. Corbec and Tremard could see nothing but the light-blur of their guns.

Corbec ducked under the intense volley. He didn't even curse. It was over, he knew. The end of Colm Corbec. By his side, Tremard, a second too late in ducking, flew backwards, his left arm gone in a shredded waste of flesh below the shoulder. He fell on his back, screaming and writhing. His lasgun, with his left hand still holding the grip, sat miraculously on the parapet where he had rested it.

Corbec scrambled to him, under the hideous rain of bolt and las-fire, grabbing the struggling man and holding him close. He had to calm him and make him still before he could tie up that awful stump. *If he lived that long.*

Tremard screamed and screamed, fighting like a scalded cat, drenching Corbec and himself with the pumping arterial spray of his stump. Corbec glanced up to see black forms in quilted armour, faces covered by gas-hoods, scrambling over the lip of the sandbags towards him. He could smell their rank animal scent, and the badges of the Dark Gods blazoned on their armour burned in his mind even at a glimpse and turned his stomach.

There was a double click, dry and solid, and then a whoosh of heat as the night lit up. Corbec winced. Trooper Brostin stood over him, raking the tops of the sandbags and the lane beyond with his flamer. The hurricane force of the flame gout cut the enemy away like dry grass.

'I was wondering where you'd got to,' Corbec said to Brostin. Then he tapped his micro-bead. 'Medic! Medic!'

DORDEN AND LESP were halfway through transporting the injured into the rear of the house when the call came through. Stray shots were punching through the ward hall, exploding rafters and shattering wall-plaster and brick.

Dorden fumbled with his micro-bead, trying to steady the stretcher he was sharing with the backing Lesp.

'Dorden! What?'

'Tremard's down bad. Get out here!' Any more of Corbec's message was lost in crackling static, drowned by the gunfire.

'Set it down! I'll drag it!' Lesp cried to Dorden as a las-round punched a hole in the plaster near his head.

Dorden did so and Lesp hauled the stretcher through the archway, its wooden handles screeching on the floor. 'Just like a fish box back home!' Lesp yelled over the onslaught as he disappeared.

Dorden grabbed his kit. 'Corbec! I'm coming out, but you need to send someone in to help Lesp move the wounded!'

'Feth that! We're all engaged out here! Can't spare a man!'

'Don't give me that!' Dorden returned, scuttling under the puncture level of the las-range as the hall fell apart around him. 'Lesp needs help! These men need help!'

A hand took his shoulder. He looked round. It was the Blueblood Culcis. Several more of the less seriously injured Volpone were with him. 'I can't manage a stretcher with my leg, but I can man a fire-point, doctor. I'll take any lasgun free if it means able bodies can help you here!'

Dorden smiled at the young man's bravery. Pain was slashed into the Blueblood's thin face.

He nodded them forward to the door and they looked out into the rain of fire.

'Caffran!' Dorden called on the link. 'I'm sending a Blueblood over to you. Give him your weapon and then return!'

He didn't wait for an answer.

Using Chayker's mop as a crutch, Culcis scurried out into the yard and made the inner wall, where Caffran was blasting through a fire-slot. A nod, and Caffran gave up his gun and position to the Blueblood. Culcis settled in, leaning against the flak-boards, and resumed blasting. Caffran ran back to the farmhouse door where Dorden was waiting.

'Help Lesp! Go! Go!'

In three minutes, Dorden had substituted three more Volpones on the defence line, men with leg wounds or head wounds, but able-bodied. In return, he got Claig, Gutes and Foskin.

Dorden told Foskin the drill, and Foskin supervised the five able-bodied Ghosts into a slick pattern of removing the wounded into the rear sections of the house.

Shaken by the onslaught which lit up the feeble night, Dorden reached the gatepost, running in a stoop. Brostin and Corbec were blasting away. Brostin was now using Tremard's lasgun, switching to the big flamer every time the assault became too great.

Dorden knelt by Tremard, assessed his injury and set to work. 'I need a stretcher for him!' Dorden yelled at Corbec.

'Help him, Brostin,' Corbec snapped. As Dorden and Brostin carried Tremard back to the farmhouse, Corbec held the gate. Dorden's last view of him was clear: the huge Tanith warrior, his hair loose and flowing in the night wind as the storm came down again, crackling and flashing, flamer in one hand, lasgun in the other, dealing death to anything that moved.

The enemy assault had pivoted to the western side of the horseshoe, and heavy fire slammed against the flakboarding, throwing some sheets up out of the muck and shattering them. Mkoll felt more than saw the change in emphasis and rushed from his position at the east end to support Chayker and a Blueblood called Vengo who had substituted for Gutes. Chaos soldiers were pushing through the holes in the outer flak-board wall and the three Guardsmen, firing single, aimed shots to preserve power on Corbec's orders, dropped dozens into the slime pit of the ditch. Soon bodies blocked the fence holes as well as the missing boards had done.

Well enough when they come at us with boltguns and las-weapons, Mkoll thought to himself darkly. But what do we do when they bring up flamers, meltas, grenades... or worse?

The cacophony of the assault was ear-splitting and a double echo rolled back to them from the wide fens like thunder, almost as loud as the real thing. The storm or the storming shook the earth, and Mkoll wasn't sure which.

Vengo, bandaged up with a gut wound, found his strength failing and his vision swimming. The majesty and fury of the open assault, the desperation and the frantic effort, had quite numbed him to the dull pain of his injuries, but they were telling on him none the less. Drenched by the downpour, he tried to reposition himself, changing spent clip for fresh with cold, wet hands. The fresh power clip slipped away and dropped into the mud under his feet. He stooped.

A soldier of Chaos, cut down and presumed dead in the ditch, had crawled forward, and now loomed over the inner fence above the scrabbling Volpone. His chest had been blasted open, and blood and tissue dribbled from exposed ribs. His gas-hood was also gone, revealing the fanged snout and grey hide of his corrupted face. He swung up a rusty entrenching tool.

Chayker, dazzled by the volleys of las-light and the strobe effect of the lightning, saw his assailant in a flash of white, frozen mid-swing. He wrenched his lasgun out of the fire-slot and blasted down the gully, blowing the attacker out over the fence. Rising with the recovered clip, deafened by the sensory overload of the storm and fighting, Vengo had no idea how he had been spared or how close he had been to death.

Bolt rounds drummed into the flak-boards around Mkoll's slot, and nailed wooden splinters into his cheek and neck. He cried out and dropped back for a second. Rubbing at the bloody grazes in his face, he moved back to the slot, re-aiming. Other dark shapes were stirring in the filth at the bottom of the ditch. Vengo's close call had been a warning. Even killing shots didn't seem to finish all of these abominations. Many of those that they had cut down were far from dead, and now were crawling and clambering up to attack the inner fence.

'Brace!' he yelled over the comm-link to Chayker and Vengo. He had a few tube-charges left, and he hefted three over the inner fence into the ditch with its half-seen stirrings.

The triple blast rocked them and pelted the inner flak-boards with liquid mud and liquefied organics.

'Keep checking the ditch!' Mkoll voxed. 'They don't die easy.'

Vengo caught the hint at once, and lowered his aim to pick off two more of the supposed dead who were writhing through the mire towards him. Others clustered around the breaches in the outer fence, cut down by the trap as fast as they gathered and pressed in.

How many of them are there out there, Chayker wondered? The force of the assault seemed to be increasing with every moment.

On the eastern turn of the horseshoe, Culcis held the line with his other two Volpone substitutes, Drado and Speers. Brostin had returned from his stretcher run to the house and fell in beside Culcis, hefting a misfiring Volpone heavy stubber he'd found leaning against the wall in the long hall. It had a drum of sixty rounds left in it, and he'd resolved to use them all before switching to his laspistol. His flamer was in Corbec's meaty hands at the gate.

All they could hear or see from the gate area, at the southern point of the horseshoe, were belches of flame and las-chatter and Corbec's increasingly colourful exclamations over the vox-link.

Brostin settled in, getting to know the unfamiliar stubber. Its cyclic rate was poor and it jammed frequently, but when it fired, the thump and blast was satisfying. He shredded half a dozen shapes that loomed beyond the outer fence. At the eastern side, the tree-line and woods were closer than at the west, which looked out over fenland interrupted only by hedges and dykes. Here, the enemy was on them with little warning, rushing out of the trees to assault the double fence and the ditch.

Brostin found himself admiring the shooting skills of the Blueblood Culcis. Arrogantly, against Corbec's orders, he had adjusted the power setting to full and was firing off searing orange blasts. But each one counted.

His eye's as good as Mad Larkin's, thought the heavy-set Ghost, and that's a real compliment.

Drado and Speers were doing their part too, but Drado's aim was off. Though able-bodied, the man had a head wound and one eye bandaged. The lack of binocular range-finding was ruining his shot. Brostin hunkered down and moved along the fence to him.

'Aim left!' he yelled over the barrage and the thunder. 'You're shooting wide!'

Drado turned on him, his noble, half-bandaged face curled into a haughty sneer. 'No low-life gutter-dog tells a Volpone how to fight!'

Brostin smacked him hard with the side of his fist and slammed the Blueblood into the mud.

'Get up!' Brostin said fiercely, fist raised. 'This is a last stand of the Tanith First-and-Only. We're only here because of you and your kinsmen! Fight like a Ghost or stand aside and let someone else do it!'

Drado hauled himself up and spat at Brostin. 'You'll pay...' he began.

Firing his stubber out at the enemy, Brostin laughed. 'Pay? Of course I'll pay! But not to you! If we live through this, my Blueblood friend, you can hammer me to hell, and get your oh-so-noble brothers to help! See me care! If we don't die here, tonight, guarding the line to protect your precious wounded, then I'll go laughing into any retribution you care to dish out! What could be worse than this?'

Drado didn't answer. He set to firing again, and Brostin noted with approval that he was compensating now and favouring the left side. He made hits.

'Much better, you feth-wit,' he muttered.

INSIDE THE MANOR house, Dorden checked the state of the wounded they had moved. With the help of Lesp, Gutes, Caffran, Foskin and Claig, he had transferred the patients back, one at a time, through to the rear chambers and then down in the long undercroft. This low, vaulted cellar space was made of thick stone. The best protection they could afford. They might survive the attack here – or be buried like rats.

With Foskin's help, he treated Tremard's wound and got him stable. Then he ordered all the Ghosts back out to the defence, all except Lesp, whom he needed. Another comatose Volpone had woken during the rough relocation and was convulsing.

Caffran, Foskin, Gutes and Claig made their way up the cellar steps, taking their pick of the broken Volpone weapons stacked in the stable-block on their way to rejoin the defence.

The convulsing Volpone died. Though he showed no outward signs of injuring except severe bruising, Dorden knew his innards had been turned to jelly by artillery concussion. Lesp helped him haul the corpse back up the undercroft stairs and dump it in the hall.

They went back down. The undercroft was damp and pungent, lit by hissing chemical lamps the Ghosts had set up hurriedly. The injured moaned and sighed. Some slept like they were dead. The earth around them all shook and trickles of liquid mud spurted down from the roof every now and then as the onslaught rattled the foundations of the house.

'We're all going to die here, aren't we, sir?' Lesp asked, his voice clear and certain.

Dorden stammered for a moment, lost for words. He thought, desperately, what Gaunt might say in such circumstances. What would a trained political officer do here, trying to raise the spirits of men looking death in he face? He couldn't do it. It wasn't in him. He couldn't compose any deft line about 'the greater good of the Imperial Guard' or the 'lifeblood of the Emperor'. Instead, all he could manage was something entirely personal.

'I'm not,' he told Lesp. 'When I die, my wife and daughter and granddaughter die too, their memories lost with me. For them, I'll not die here, Lesp.'

Lesp nodded, his big Adam's apple gulping in his narrow throat. He thought of the memories he carried: mother, father, brothers, crew mates on the archipelago trawler.

'Neither will I, then,' he managed.

Dorden turned towards the stairs.

'Where are you going?' Lesp asked.

'You manage things here. I'm going to take a look up top. From the sound of things, they may need a medic.'

Lesp pulled out his laspistol and offered it, butt-first, to the chief medic.

Dorden shook his head. 'I can't start that now,' he said.

UPSTAIRS, THE OLD ruin was quiet. It seemed as if the storm and the assault had abated together for the moment. Dorden edged into the vacated long hall and tried his micro-bead but it was dead. The ceiling lamps swung and loose debris fluttered down. Free of bodies, the stinking cots looked pitiful and sadly spoiled. Dorden stepped over pools of blood and shreds of discarded clothing.

He strode into the outer kitchen, looking once at the stained table where he had excised a part of Regara's leg. He saw the old fireplace for the first time. Black iron, just like the one he had sat before at home on Tanith. He and his wife, at the end of a long night, with a book and a glass of something warming, before the grate-light.

Along the mantle, small blocks of what looked like chalk sat in a row. He moved over and took one in his hand. A tusk. The small, shed tusk of a pig. The inhabitants of this manor, whoever they were, had raised swine, cared for them enough to treasure the trophies of their growth and development. Pig teeth, each marked in a delicate hand with a name... *Emperor, Sire, His Lordship*... and dates.

This touch of frugal humanity, the day-to-day chronicle of a farmstead, affected him deeply. It wasn't mawkish, it mattered somehow. Why pigs? Who had lived here, raised the swine, toiled in the fens, brought up a family?

A sound from the long hall brought him up to the surface of his thoughts. He moved back to meet a gaggle of men as they limped and blundered in through the hall doors from the outside. The Volpone substitutes and the Ghosts, all except Corbec. They were shell-shocked and dazed, weary on their feet.

Dorden found Mkoll at the rear of the group.

'They've fallen back,' Mkoll said. 'It's dead quiet out there. That can mean only one thing...'

'I'm a medic, not a soldier, Mkoll! What does it mean?'

Mkoll sighed as Dorden attended to the splinter wounds in his face. 'They've failed with a physical assault. They're drawing back so they can bring up artillery.'

Dorden nodded. 'Get below, into the undercroft, all of you. Foskin – Lesp will help you cook up some food for all. Do it! Artillery or not, I want everyone sustained.'

The men filed away towards the steps into the cellar. Dorden was alone again in the hall.

Corbec entered, covered in blood and fire-soot. He dropped Brostin's empty flamer onto one cot and threw Tamard's spent lasgun the other way.

'Time's trickling away, Doc,' he said. 'We held them – feth but we held them! – but they're gonna hammer us now. I scoped movement over the fens, big guns being wheeled into place. An hour, if we're lucky, and then they'll level us from a distance.'

'Colm... I thank you for all you and the men have done tonight. I hope it was worth it.'

'It's always worth it, Doc.'

'So what do we do now? Bury ourselves in the cellar?'

Corbec shrugged. 'That won't save us from their shells. Don't know about you, but I'm going to do the only thing I can think of at a time like this?'

'Which is?'

'Pray to the Emperor. Mkoll said there was an old shrine out back of this place. Prayers are all we have left.'

TOGETHER, CORBEC AND Dorden pulled their way through a litter of rubble and debris and broken furniture into the little room at the back of the farmhouse. It had lost its roof and the stars twinkled above them.

Corbec had brought a lamp. He played its light over the rear walls, picking up the flaking painted image on the ornamental screen Mkoll had mentioned. It showed the Divine Emperor subduing the Heretics, and smaller figures of a man, a woman, and three small children, shown in obeisance to the central figure of the God-Emperor of Man.

'There's an inscription here,' Dorden said, scraping the dirt away from the wall with his cuff pulled up over the ball of his hand.

'A pig! What is this?'

Corbec raised the lamp and read off the inscription. 'Here's irony for you, Doc: this was a trophy world. A New Tanith. The master of this hall was a Farens Cloker, of the Imperial Guard, Hogskull Regiment. The Hogskulls won this world during the first advance into the Sabbat one hundred and ninety years ago. Winning it, they were awarded settlement rights. Cloker was a corporal in the Guard, and he took his rights gladly. Settled here, made a family, raised swine in honour of the mascot beast of his old regiment. His kin have honoured that ever since.'

Corbec faltered, something like sadness in his eyes. 'Feth! To get there, to win it, to take the trophy world... and still it comes down to this?'

'Not for all. How many trophy worlds are there out there where the soldiers of the Guard have retired and lived out their days?'

'I don't know. This is all too real. To fight for your lifetime, get the prize you wanted, and then this?'

Corbec and Dorden sank down together in the debris-strewn chapel.

'You asked me why I stayed with you, Doc. I'll tell you now as we're dead and we have nothing to live for.' With that last remark, Corbec flung his hand towards the reredos' inscription.

'Well?'

'You were the doctor for Pryze County for twenty years.'

'Twenty-seven. And Beldane.'

Corbec nodded. 'I was raised in Pryze. My family were wood workers there. I was born out of wedlock and so I took my father's name, when I knew him. My mother now... I was a difficult birth.'

Dorden stiffened, knowing somehow what must come next.

'She'd have died in labour, had it not been for the young medic who charged out in the night and saw to her. Landa Meroc. Remember her?'

'She would have died if I hadn't–'

'Thank you, Doctor Dorden.'

Dorden looked round at Corbec in wonder. 'I delivered you? Feth! Fething feth! Am I that old?!'

They laughed together until they were choking. And until the thump of artillery began, blasting the quiet of the night away.

* * *

THE IMPERIAL GUARD drove the enemy back with their shelling and Gaunt was on the foremost half-track as they ploughed back into the fenlands in the early light of dawn. They caught the enemy almost unawares, and were blasting the Chaos artillery and infantry even as the enemy wheeled their own blasphemous guns around into position in the dark.

The farmhouse, and its shattered defence of horseshoe fences, was almost unrecognisable. Mud, burnt flak-board and shattered corpses lay piled amidst the devastated ruins. He ordered the vehicle to stop, and it spun wheels on the fenland muck as it slid to a halt.

Trooper Lesp was on duty at the gateway. He saluted the colonel-commissar as he passed in. Dorden and Corbec were waiting for him in the littered yard.

'Medical evac is coming,' Gaunt told them. 'We'll get the Volpone wounded out of here.'

'And our own too?' Dorden asked, thinking of Tremard, and Mkoll's lacerated face.

'All of the wounded. So, you've had an adventure out here, it seems?'

'Nothing to speak of, sir,' Corbec said.

Gaunt nodded and moved off into the manor house ruin.

Corbec turned to Dorden and showed him the pig's tooth he had clutched in his hand. 'I won't forget this,' he said. 'It may not have worked here on Nacedon for this guardsman, but by this tooth, I'll trust it will work for us Ghosts. A trophy world, brighter and better than you can imagine.'

Dorden's hand held a pig-tooth too, marked 'The Emperor'.

'I trust you to do that, Colm. Do it. Doctor's orders.'

*Swing, address, stab, return… swing, address, stab, return…*

In the shade of the cycads at the edge of the Tanith encampment on Monthax, Trooper Caffran was practising bayonet discipline. Stripped to the waist, his powerful young shoulders glistening with sweat, he whirled his lasgun in time to his rhythmic chant, snapping it round, clutching it horizontally, lunging forward and killing the bole of one of the trees over and again. After each strike, he tugged it free with effort, and repeated the drill. The trunk was slashed and puckered, oozing orange sap from the wounds left by his nimble work.

'Good skill,' Gaunt said from behind him. Caffran snapped around, realising he was being watched. He shook sweat from his brow and began a salute.

'At ease,' Gaunt said. 'I'm just walking the lines. Everything alright with you? The men in your platoon?'

Caffran felt tongue-tied, as he always did when Gaunt addressed him directly. He still, after all this time, had mixed feelings about the commissar who had both saved them and made them Ghosts in the same action.

'We're all waiting for the word,' he said at last. 'Itching for action. This waiting…'

'It's the worst part, I know.' Gaunt sat down on a nearby log. 'Until the killing starts and you realise the waiting wasn't all that bad after all.'

Caffran caught the smile in Gaunt's eyes and grinned as well, unable to stop himself.

Gaunt was pleased. He was very aware of the stiffness Caffran always manifested around him. A good soldier, one of the youngest, but so very nearly one of Rawne's malcontents.

'Go again,' Gaunt suggested.

Self-consciously, Caffran turned and repeated his drill. Swing, address, stab, return… It took a moment to pull his blade free from the thick bark.

'Slide it,' Gaunt said. 'It'll come out easier if you slide it laterally before pulling.'

Caffran did so. It was true.

Gaunt got up, moving on with his circuit. 'Not long now, Caffran,' Gaunt said as he moved away.

Caffran sighed. No, not long. Not long before the frenzy and the madness would start.

*Swing, address, stab, slide, return… Swing, address, stab, slide, return…*

# NINE
# A SIMPLE PLAN

Engines screaming, the Imperial troop carriers fell upon the ocean world, Sapiencia.

Like swarms of fat, black beetles shrilling in over the edges of a pond, they assaulted the Bay of Belano. Their combined down-draughts boiled the choppy surface water into foam mist, an embankment of steam three kilometres long and two hundred metres high that stormed forward across the beach rocks and blinded the island's outer defences.

It entirely hid the merciless wall of solid water driven up under the spray by the concussive force, and this tidal wave exploded across the western sea-fall emplacements of Oskray Island twenty seconds after the steam cloud choked them. Rock and metal and flesh were pulverised, blasted into the air, then sucked back into the basin of the bay as pressures equalised and hydraulic action righted itself. A spume haze hung over the island, clogging the beaches and masking the final, slow approach of the gargantuan troop-ships.

The heavy emplacements higher on the cliffs of Oskray spat fierce salvos down into the mist, or up into the striated

clouds where further formations of troop-ships were beginning their final approaches to the island shore. The fire from
the batteries, blue and flickering, danced like luminous
damsel flies amongst the beetle-like ships. Some craft burst
as they were touched, and burned; some dropped, bleeding
smoke and trailing lines of debris.

The twenty kilometres of Oskray Island was only partly
rock. It was, in point of fact, a cluster of islets, linked as one
by the massive industrial fortification built up upon the
shoulders of submarine mountains. Behind ocean-blocking
walls of stone a hundred metres thick, pump structures, drill
towers, flame-belching waste stacks and pylons rose against
the sky. The primary target, the great refinery hive of Oskray
Island One.

Red hazard lights flashed and hooters started their deafening caterwaul as the jaw-hatch locks of troop-ship *Lambda*
disengaged with a massive leaden thump. Dim light began
to pour in from outside as the jaw-sections hinged open.
Caffran, tensed tight and ready, knew they were assaulting a
sea-bound target, and that the way in for the infantry was up
the beach. That was the plan. But as the troop-hatch opened,
he believed for a moment they had come in too low and it
was translucent torrents of water that were spurting into the
dispersal deck. He gulped in his breath, held it, but it was
only steam and pale light that rushed over him.

The yells of men, of boots racing on metal decking, and of
the hooters, were overwhelming. With fifty others, lasguns
raised, he charged out of the hatch mouth. For a second, on
the ramp, the dispersal deck noises were swamped by the
greater volume of the thundering drop-ships all around.
Caffran could see nothing beyond the men closest to him
and the solid atmosphere of mist and smoke. He could
smell salt and ozone, oil and thermite.

Then nothing. Rushing silence, roaring dullness, a cold-
ness all over him, enveloping him, dark grey blurs in his eyes.

He was underwater, floundering in the chilly, muffled
dark of the sea, writhing black bodies struggling and flailing
around him, each one bejewelled with trapped baubles of
silver air.

The troop-ship had come up short of the beach slope, and all the men dropping blind off the ramp were falling into thirty metres of ocean where the island shelved steeply away.

Caffran couldn't swim. He'd been born and raised in a forest a thousand kilometres from any open water. He'd never seen the ocean, any ocean, though he'd heard others, like the medic-fisherman Lesp, speak of it. He was going to do the last thing he had ever expected to do: drown.

Momentarily, he realised he had not yet released the deep breath he had instinctively sealed into his lungs when he thought the dispersal deck was going to flood, and he almost laughed, almost releasing the air.

Instead, he held on to it, felt it burning and exhausting inside him as he rose slowly to what seemed the surface. It saved his life, where others had gone screaming and exhaling off the ramp.

Sinking, blundering, black shapes thrashed around him: Tanith combat dress, dark as dry blood, faces pale like phantoms or ghouls. A body sank beside him, arms frozen in claws, mouth open to emit a dribble of bubbles, eyes glazed. Caffran kicked upwards again.

Something struck him stunningly hard on the back of the neck and he lost his precious saved breath in a blurt of silvery air pebbles. Men were still coming off the ramp-end above, falling on those Ghosts now coming up from below. A boot had hit him. The man it belonged to was inverted in the water behind him, panicking, dying. Caffran kicked away, trying to rise and not breathe in to ease his emptied, screaming lungs. He saw men explode into the grey, dreamy world from above, fighting the water as they hit and sank. But that at least told him the surface was only a few metres away.

The man who had kicked him on his way down had become entangled with another by the slings of their lasguns. One of them fired his lasgun in desperation, twice, three times. The water boiled around each slicing minnow of orange light. Caffran's ears throbbed as they heard the fizzing report of the underwater shots. One of the las-rounds punctured a drifting corpse nearby; another punched through the leg of a desperate swimmer next to Caffran. Blood fogged the water. Caffran heard the distant voices of his ancestors in his ears, muffled by pressure and fluid and distance and time.

He surfaced in a gasping explosion, retching, treading water, blood streaming from his nose. He looked around to see Ghosts surfacing all around, kicking towards the shore or just panicking. Some were floating in the surge, lifeless, already lost. Noise rushed back to him, the momentous noise of combat now unfiltered by the deadness of the sea. Screaming, the whicker of lasguns, the roar of troop-ship downwash. He could smell blood, water and smoke, but was thankful, because that meant he was breathing. Behind him, las-rounds punched up out of the water into the fog as other unfortunates lost their grip on everything but their triggers as they drowned.

Caffran paddled forward, hacking up each and every slop of sea-water he accidentally swallowed. The pall of smoke and fog cut visibility at the surface to ten metres. For a moment, he heard the voices of his ancestors again – then realised that wasn't what he'd heard at all. It was his micro-bead intercom, crackling with staccato traffic, screeching into his ear-plug. Underwater, it had been the tinny whisper of ghosts.

Caffran felt gravel or sand under his boots, a slope. He felt weight and momentum return to him as he churned up through shallower and still shallower water, falling twice and choking. Bolt rounds and las-fire whipped and stitched the breakers around him, cutting down the Ghost beaching next to him. The man fell face-down, his body lifted and pulled back, lifted and pulled back again by the choppy waves.

Caffran fell again as a las-round scorched across the top of his left shoulder, dropping him to his knees. His shins scraped on the stony gravel, shredding his fatigue pants from the knee down. He felt his lasgun grow heavier and flop away. The shot had cut his gun-strap across the shoulder.

Hands pulled him up as he grabbed hold of his weapon.

'Caffran!'

It was Domor, the squad's sweeper. He was laden down with the heavy backpack of the sweeper unit and its long handled sensor-broom. Domor had lost his eyes – and almost his life – in that final push on Menazoid Epsilon six months before. They had been there together for that fatal time, in the thick of it as they were here. Domor's metal-irised artificial implants shuttered and whined as they adjusted to look down at Caffran. The sweeper's cybernetic implants looked like truncated binocular scopes crudely sutured into the scar tissue of his eye-sockets.

'We can make the beach!' Domor yelled, pulling the young trooper to his feet. They ran, blundering through the breakers. Others charged or staggered in with them, a ragged line of Ghosts making landfall on the fog-washed shore, some falling over submerged barricade crosses or entangling themselves on rolls of rusting razor-wire. The fire-storm fell amongst them and some dropped silently, or screaming, or in minced pieces.

Now, the flinty shingle slope of the beach. They crashed up it, pebbles flying from each footfall. Twenty metres up, they ducked below the lichen-fronded line of an old wooden groyne, black as tar. Las-fire slammed into its weighty bulk.

'What's the plan? What have we got?' Caffran yelled.

'Nothing! Visibility is low! Heavy resistance from up there!' Domor pointed up into the spray-fog at something only his augmented vision could resolve, and then only barely.

Two more bodies flung themselves down next to them, then a third. Trooper Mkendrik with his flamer; Trooper Chilam, missing an ear and yowling like a cat as he dabbed his salty hand at the bloody hunk of cartilage on the side of his head. And then, Sergeant Varl.

Varl was a popular officer amongst the Ghosts; young, field-promoted from the rank of trooper, a wise-cracking, hard-nosed bastard refreshingly lacking all the airs and graces of the officer class. He'd lost his shoulder on Fortis Binary, and his black tunic bulged over the cybernetic joint

the medics had given him. It was clear to Caffran that the
sergeant was in some pain. Varl cursed and struggled with
his artificial shoulder.

Sea-water had soaked into the shoulder joint, shorting
out servos and fusing linkages. His arm was dead and useless, but still the raw neural connections transmitted flickers
of shorting electrical failure to his brain. Domor had been
lucky. His ocular units had been sealed into his skull
enough to prevent such damage... though Caffran wondered how long it would take the insidious touch of
sea-water corrosion to blind the man.

With Mkendrik's help, Caffran stripped off Varl's tunic
and unscrewed the bolts on the small inspection plate in
Varl's metal shoulder blade. With the point of his Tanith
dagger, Mkendrik prised out the flat battery cells revealed
there, cutting the electrical relay which governed the limb.
Varl sighed as his arm went dead and Caffran strapped it up,
tight against the sergeant's body. It was a desperate gesture.
Without the booster relay of the cells, not only all neural
control, but all life support would be cut from the organic
parts of Varl's repaired arm. He needed proper help, or
within an hour or two his now-lifeless arm would begin to
decay and perish.

For now, though, the sergeant was grateful. He scrambled
over, supporting himself on his one good hand, and took a
look over the cover-line. Along the beach, under the downpour of fire, men were coming ashore. Most were dying;
some were making it to cover.

'Where in Feth's name is the armour?' Varl wailed. 'They
should have led the assault and opened this beach up!'

Caffran scoped around, and saw heavy Basilisk tanks half-
submerged, struggling up the beach a hundred metres away.
They were in too deep, drowning like beached whales,
squirming and coughing exhaust smoke as their engines
flooded and died.

'The troop-ships dropped us short,' he said to Varl.

Varl looked where Caffran pointed. 'They've drowned the
front end of this fething assault!' he bellowed.

'They were blind... This spray–' Caffran began

'Feth them for not doing their job!' Varl spat.

A whinnying bolt round ricocheted off the top of the groyne's solid woodwork and took Chilam straight in the face, exploding his head. He flew back onto the shingle, full length.

'We have to advance! We have to!' Varl yelled. Micro-bead chatter, discordant and contradictory, rasped in their ears.

'There's no going forward,' Domor said quietly.

The spume of the spray-mist was receding, and now they could see what he saw. The vast white curtain wall of Oskray Island's sea-defences rose ahead of them, almost a kilometre high. Apart from some stray scorch marks, it was unblemished.

The Basilisks had been meant to flatten it and break through for the infantry. But the wall still stood, impassive, cold, like a denial of any possible future.

Varl cursed.

Caffran heard the protesting wail first. He looked back out to sea, then grabbed Domor and Varl and threw them flat into the painful jumble of the shingle. Mkendrik dived down too.

A troop-ship, one of the great fat beetles, on fire from end to end, was coming in low, half-sidelong, nose down, spilling burning fuel and shreds of fuselage. It was huge, blocking out the sky, six hundred tonnes of dying metal keening in towards the beach over their heads. Its jaw-hatches were still closed.

Men are cooking in there, Caffran thought, wondering which regiment, and then, as it came down on top of his head, his thoughts guttered out like a candle flame in a hurricane.

MKENDRIK SHOOK HIM awake. Caffran stirred, and woke up into the roar of the assault. 'How long have I been out?'

'Less than a minute,' Mkendrik said.

Caffran struggled up out of the shingle. It had felt like hours, like all his fatigue and pain had overwhelmed him and sent him to sleep. 'What happened?' he gasped. 'I thought for Feth we were dead then.'

Mkendrik pointed. At first there was little to see. The white steam and mist had become fouled with black smoke, and the ashy curls of it, thick with glowing cinders, enveloped the beach. Then, Caffran made out more. The stricken troop-ship had slammed over them, coming to rest at the head of the beach where the last few seconds of its crash-flight had been broken by the fortified seawall of Oskray Island. The impact had blown the wall in. For six hundred metres, its immeasurably old and solid stone was fused and fractured. A blackened chasm had opened into the heart of the refinery. The men aboard that troop-ship had bought a way into the target with their lives as surely as if they had fought their way up the beach.

Caffran gathered scattered items which had split from his burst pack, and recovered his fallen lasgun. Mkendrik was changing las-cells. A short way off, Varl and Domor were making ready, and small groups of Ghosts in foxholes along the beach were also preparing to make use of this new way in.

Enemy fire still strafed down from the wall, though it was thinner now such a chunk of the wall had gone. The incoming troop-ships, still roaring and settling over the tide-line behind them, were jockeying into this blind spot to avoid the tracking fire from the main batteries on the cliffs. Caffran heard thunder, and turned to see four Basilisks hoving up the beach, properly delivered, moving past them into the breach and tracking to fire. They sizzled up wet stone flecks as they rolled, cranking their huge, decorated bulks up and over the groynes. Caffran recognised the markings. Ketzoks, the 17th Armoured Regiment, the so-called Serpents who had been gulled into slaughtering them back on Voltemand.

With Varl, Domor, Mkendrik and several others, Caffran moved in towards the breach, running over stone litter and smouldering fragments of blackened mechanicals, the last remnants of the troop-ship. Stray las-shots winged down at them and stubber rounds rattled with a curious clack-clack sound off the stone facings to their left.

Entering the chasm in the wall, Caffran passed into deep shadow. Ahead, one hundred metres down the V-shaped channel blasted by the crash, a dimness loomed. He felt a sense of pride. They would be the first – the Ghosts would be the first to break through the stalwart defences of the target.

He was close to the far end now, stumbling with the others through the shadow, picking his way around mangled hull fragments. Ahead, the dimness was becoming a forest of steel and iron. The refinery itself.

Gaunt had been precise in his briefing. The fleet could have vaporised Oskray Island from orbit, but it was too valuable. That meant a land assault to retake it from the legions of Chaos. The vile host here called themselves the Kith, some hive-fermented sub-cult of Khorne… Caffran had blanked on some of the briefing's complexities, partly because it was alien gibberish to him, and partly because the gibberish made him feel ill. He didn't want to listen to the details concerning the filth they were going up against. The Kith: that was all he focussed on. The Kith were the sub-human vermin he was here to eradicate. Their leader was a monster called Sholen Skara. Fragments of the Chaos armada stopped at Balhaut had run to Sapiencia for shelter, and their leaders had conjoined with a Chaos cult already thriving in the underclass of the vast hive to overthrow Imperial rule and seize the fuel-oil and promethium wells.

Colonel-Commissar Gaunt had spoken long and passionately about the Kith in his briefing. Caffran knew Gaunt had been part of the great Balhaut victory, back when he was still a political officer with the Hyrkan Eighth. Gaunt loathed all Chaos, but loathed especially the tendrils of it which had escaped destruction at Balhaut only to twist and pollute other worlds, thanks, as he saw it, to the tactical miscalculations of Warmaster Macaroth. Gaunt had spoken of Sholen Skara, renegade of the Balhaut murder-camps, as if he had known him personally. That was why the colonel-commissar had volunteered his Ghosts for the Oskray assault. He had made it plain to them all.

And that, mused Caffran, was why they had been drowned and blasted and torn apart on the razor-wire.

Caffran often thought about Gaunt. Ibram Gaunt. He rolled the name in his mind, a name he would never dare voice aloud. The colonel, the commissar. A strange man, and Caffran's feelings for him were strange too. He was the best, most caring, most charismatic leader Caffran could imagine. Caffran had seen, time and again, the way Gaunt looked after the Ghosts. Caffran had also seen enough of other regiments and their commanders and politicos to know how rare a thing that was. Many, like beloved Colonel Corbec, regarded Gaunt as a saviour, a friend, a brother, and Caffran could not deny he admired Gaunt and would follow him to the ends of any earth.

But Caffran knew Feygor, Rawne and the other malcontents well, and in bitter moments he shared their contempt for the colonel-commissar. For all his fatherly love, like their own private Emperor, Gaunt had left Tanith to die. From time to time, Caffran had been tempted to throw aside his reservations about Gaunt and worship him as so many others did. But always, that creeping resentment in his heart had stopped him from total devotion. Gaunt was ruthless, calculating, direct. He would never stint from sending men to their deaths, for his duty was to the Emperor and the rule of Terra long before it was to the lost souls of Tanith.

Caffran saw the boy Milo, the so-called adjutant, as a constant reminder of the lost youth of his homeworld. Milo was only a year or two younger than Caffran, but a gulf divided them. He never spoke to the boy. Gaunt, in his oh-so generous wisdom, had saved Milo from the fires of Tanith Magna. Saved one – but no one else.

Caffran thought, at such times, of Laria. How he had loved her. How very much. All Caffran knew for sure was that Laria was dead now. How she had died he had no idea, and frankly, he was thankful for that. But Laria haunted him. Laria embodied everything he had lost. Tanith itself, his friends, his life, his family. For Laria's sake, Caffran knew he would always remain one of those Ghosts in the middle way, one who would follow Gaunt to hell devoutly, but would never forgive him when they arrived.

Here, in the wall gully of Oskray, it was easy to hate Gaunt. The stink of death and fire filled the place. Caffran slid in low against a fallen tower of stone blocks as he approached the opening into the island proper. Varl, Mkendrik and Trooper Vulliam dropped in beside him.

Behind them, down the crash-chasm at the mouth of the breach, Caffran could hear shouts and grinding tracks.

He looked at Varl questioningly.

'The fething Basilisks!' the sergeant said. 'They want to storm in ahead of the infantry, but they can't get their fat arses into the gap.'

'Then we still have point,' Caffran smiled. 'Feth the armour!'

Varl chortled. 'Feth them indeed. Did us no favours on Voltemand, doing us no favours now.'

Varl signalled the advance beyond the breach gap, and fifty-nine Ghosts rose from cover and moved forward. Vulliam, two metres ahead of Caffran, was one of the first to break into the open. Stub rounds broke him messily into four.

Six more Ghosts died as they broke cover. Though hammered, the Kith had their side of the chasm in the wall soundly covered. Caffran fell back with the others as lasrounds and bolts and stub charges peppered the exit of the breach.

In cover, they lay trembling as the deadly rain continued to drum the opening ahead.

'Blocked as surely as we were before,' Domor said, scratching at his eye-sutures.

'You all right?' Mkendrik asked.

'Vision's a little foggy. Got water in there. Hope...' Domor said no more, but Caffran knew what he was thinking. The seawater had ruined Varl's arm, and now it seemed to be starting its slow work on Domor's eyes.

'Might as well have left this fething wall standing for all the good it's going to do us!' Trooper Callun said.

Varl nodded, nursing his strapped arm.

His laspistol, the only weapon he could handle now, lay in his lap.

'What about missiles? Munitions?' Mkendrik wondered. 'We could blow them out and—'

'What do we aim at?' Varl asked sourly. 'Do you even see them?

Mkendrik settled back with no answer. Ahead of them was nothing but a sliced mouth cut in the wall. Beyond, the steeple girders and scaffolds of the refinery, thirty storeys high. The enemy gunners could be anywhere.

Silence fell. Sand flies billowed around the dead, and oceanic carrion swooped in to peck at the cindered flesh with hooked, pink beaks. The birds mobbed the chasm, squawking and shrilling. Trooper Tokar drove them off with a scatter burst of las-fire.

There was movement and voices behind them. Caffran and the others turned to see several Ketzok gunnery troopers creeping their way, pausing to exchange words with each group of Ghosts.

One hurried over to them, bent double, and saluted Varl's sergeant patch as he crouched next to them.

'Corporal Fuega, Ketzok 17th Serpents.'

'Varl, sergeant, Ghost. And your purpose is?'

Fuega scratched his ear for a moment, unmanned by Varl's attitude. 'Our Basilisks can't manage this breach, so we're going to split it wider with shelling. My commander asks you to fall back out of the fire-zone.'

'Wish he'd given us such a warning on Voltemand,' Domor said icily.

Fuega stepped back. 'That black day is forever in our shame, Tanith. If we could give anything, even our lives, to change it, we would.'

'I'm sure you would,' Varl sneered. He got up to face the Ketzok corporal. 'What's the plan?'

Fuega coughed. 'Orders from General Kline. You pull out, we shell, then we advance with heavy infantry.'

'Heavy infantry?'

'The Volpone have just beached in legion strength. They have heavy armour and weapons. We will clear the way for their advance.' Fuega turned away. 'You have fifteen minutes to withdraw.'

The Ghosts sat in a stupefied gaggle. 'All this, all we lost, for nothing?' Domor sighed.

Varl was angry. 'Feth those Volpone, and the Ketzok too! We die in the wire to open the beach and then they march in and follow the tanks to glory!'

'I don't know about you, sergeant, but I don't want to be sitting here still, complaining about life, when those Basilisks open up.'

Varl spat and sighed. 'Me neither. Okay! By platoon team, call the retreat.'

The Ghosts all around scrambled up and prepared to fall back. Domor, looking up, caught Caffran by the arm.

'What?'

'Up there – do you see it?'

Domor pointed and Caffran looked up. The broken wall rose like a cliff above them, scabbed with slumping masonry and broken reinforcement girders. Fifty metres up, just above a severed end of pipe work, Caffran saw the door. 'Feth, but your eyes are sharp!'

'There were tunnels in the wall, troop tunnels buried deep. This hole has cut through one of them and exposed it.'

Caffran called Varl over, and a group of Ghosts gathered to look up. 'We could get a fire-team inside the wall… follow the tunnel to where ever it led us.'

'Hell?' supposed Trooper Flaven.

'It's high up…' Varl began.

'But the cliff is ragged and full of good handholds. The first man up could secure a line. Sergeant, it's a plan…'

Varl looked round at Caffran. 'I'd never make it, with one arm dead. Who'd lead?'

'I could,' said Sergeant Gorley of Five platoon. He was a tall, barrel-chested man with a boxer's nose. 'You get the wounded back onto the beach. I'll take a squad and see what we can do.'

Varl nodded. He began to round up the walking wounded, and seconded several able bodies to help him with the more seriously injured. Gorley selected his commando squad: Caffran, Domor, Mkendrik, Flaven, Tokar, Bude, Adare, Mkallun, Caill.

Mkendrik, raised in the mountains of Tanith Steeple, led off, clambering up the splintered wall, hand over hand. He left his flamer and its tanks with Gorley, to raise them later on a line.

By the time the ascent was made, and ropes secured, their leeway was almost up, and the ten Ghosts were alone in the chasm. Within moments, the Basilisks at the throat of the breach would start their bombardment.

The men went up quickly, following the ropes. Gorley was last, securing a line around the flamer unit and other heavy supplies. The team at the top, crowded into the splintered doorway, hauled them up.

Gorley was halfway up the ascent when the bombardment began. The nine Ghosts above cowered into the shelter of the concrete passageway they had climbed into and covered their ears at the concussion.

A shell hit the wall and vapourised Gorley, as if he had never been there.

Realising he was gone, Caffran urged the party to collect their equipment and move inwards. Soon this entire wall section would be brought down.

THE GHOST SQUAD crept up the unlit passageway. Though generally intact, the tunnel had slumped a little following the massive shockwave from the troop-ship crash. The ground was split in places, exposing crumbling rock. Pipes and cables dangled from the cracked roof; dust trickled down from deep fissures. In places, the shock-impact had sectioned the wall, cutting the originally straight and horizontal tunnel into a series of cleanly stepped slabs. The Tanith clambered on, probing the dusty darkness with the cold green glare of assault lamps.

Behind them, the stonework of the great sea wall began to shake. The Ketzok had redoubled their furious work. Caffran found himself leading, as if there had been an unspoken vote electing him in Gorley's place. He presumed it was because he had suggested this incursion in the first place. The Ghosts picked up their speed and moved deeper into the tunnel system that threaded the marrow of the wall.

They reached a vertical communications shaft, down the centre of which ran a great wrought-iron spiral staircase. The air was damp and smelled of wet brick and the sea. Shock damage was evident here too, and the bolts securing the metal stairway and its adjoining walkways to the shaft-sides had sheared off or snapped. The entire metal structure, hundreds of tonnes of it filling the shaft, creaked uneasily with each shuddering impact from the guns of the distant Basilisks.

The Ghosts stepped across the metal landing of the stair-coil to where the tunnel resumed beyond. It squealed and yelped with every step, sometimes threatening to tilt or fall.

Caill and Flaven were last across. A metal bolt-end the size of a man's forearm rang off the gantry, just missing Caill. It had come loose far above.

'Move!' yelled Caffran.

With a protesting, non-vocal scream, the staircase collapsed, tearing itself apart and rattling away down into the black depths of the bottomless shaft. Where larger parts of the structure remained intact – a few turns of steps laced together, a long section of handrail, a series of stanchion poles – they fell with heavy fury, raking sparks and hideous shrieks from the shaft walls.

Empty, the stairs fallen away, the brick shaft seemed immense, uncrossable.

Domor looked back at the tunnel they had come along, out of reach now across the gulf. 'No going back now…' he muttered.

'Good thing that's not the way we're going,' Caffran replied, pointing into the darkness to come with the barrel of his lasgun.

WIDE CISTERNS OPENED up around them. The cement floors were painted with glossy green paint and the wall bricks matt white. The walls tapered upwards so that the ceiling was narrower than the floor, and the whole tunnel turned a few degrees to the left. The entire passageway was following both the line and the profile of the wall it ran through. Grilled lighting panels, glowing phosphorescent white, hung at intervals from the roof. They looked like a giant stream of tracer rounds, arcing off down the line of the tunnel, frozen in time.

Caffran's Ghosts – and indeed now they were 'his' Ghosts, bonding to him as leader now that they were cut off from outside without asking or deciding – haunted the long passageways, hugging the walls in the fierce white glow of the lights.

Every sixty metres, tunnels bisected the main route on the inland side: deep, wide throats of brick and concrete that sloped downwards. Mkendrik thought they might be drainage channels, but if that was true, the size alarmed Caffran. They were big enough to take a man walking upright and just as broad. If that kind of liquid quantity flooded these tunnels from time to time…

Domor believed the channels to be for personnel movement, or for running carts of ammo and supplies up to the emplacements buried in the sides and along the top of the great sea wall. But they'd seen no vertical cargo shafts for munitions lifting, and Caffran doubted sheer manpower could roll enough shells up the sloping channels without mechanical assistance.

And they had met no one, not a trace of the Kith soldiery, not even a corpse.

'They're all fully engaged, deploying on the defences,' Caill suggested.

Caffran thought it a fair bet. 'We wanted to get inside, I figure we might get further than we expected.' They had just reached the latest of the mysterious sloping shafts. Caffran nodded to it. 'It leads into the heart of the island itself. Let's try it.'

'And then what?' Bude asked.

'Then?'

'I mean, what's your plan, Caff?'

Caffran paused. Getting in, that had been everything. Now… 'We're inside,' he began, 'no one's got this far.'

Bude and others nodded. 'But what then?' Flaven asked.

Again, Caffran was lost for words. 'We… we… we see how far we can get. Inside.'

None demurred. Lighting in the sloped tunnel was built into the wall and hidden behind transparent baffles. The concrete floor had a mesh grill set into it, providing greater purchase for walking.

They moved in formation. Half a kilometre, by Domor's gyro-compass. A kilometre. The air became damp-cold. The tunnel began to level out. The distant thump and shudder of the sea-wall assault dimmed behind them.

They heard the humming before they saw the end of the tunnel. A low, ululating throb that bristled the air. It reminded Caffran of the heavy fruit-wasps in the nal-forests of Tanith, crossing glades on iridescent wings to bury their long ovipositors into soft bark in search of nal-grubs to use as living kindergartens.

Adare, at the head of the pack with Mkallun, called out. The tunnel was sealed fifty metres ahead by a vast metal hatchway. A thick ironwork seal surrounded a man-sized hatch closed with lever-latches and greased hydraulic hinges. The door and its frame were painted matt green with rust-proof paint, all except the clean steel inner rods of the extended hydraulics, which glittered with filmy brown oils.

The throbbing was coming from the far side of the hatch.

Adare checked the hatch seals, but they were wound tightly shut and locked, it seemed, from the other side. Caffran shouldered his way forward and reached out a hand to the metal barrier. It was wet-cold but it tingled, vibrating gently with the reverberations behind it.

'How do we get through?' Caffran murmured.

'Do we want to get through?' Bude returned.

Domor knelt down and started to open the clasps of his sweeper pack. Caffran noticed with some concern that Domor was regularly pausing to fidget and scratch at his eyes now, as if irritated by persistent flies. Domor pulled the head of the sweeper broom out of the pack, removed the soft cloth bag it was wrapped in, and carried it to the wall with his set unit and his headphones. He plugged the headphones and the sweeper head into the unit and switched it on, listening patiently to the clicking returns in his earpieces as he moved the flat pad of the sweeper head across the metal door surround. Three or four times he stopped, went back to check, and then marked the green-painted metal with a graphite cross, using a stick he kept in his bicep pocket.

Domor turned back to Caffran, pulling his headphones back down around his neck. 'The main internal lock for the hatch is buried inside the frame. Those crosses mark the threads of the gears.'

Caffran let Tokar do the honours. He put a point-blank las-round through each of the crosses, leaving round puncture holes with sharp metal edges.

The latches and locks spun free easily now their mechanisms were ruined. Adare and Flaven hauled the green hatch open and the Ghosts crept forward into a blue, gloomy realm of smoke.

Caffran knew they were emerging on the land side of the great sea wall, deep in the refinery complex of Oskray Island. They were exiting onto a lattice walkway of scrubbed iron that jutted out of the fastness wall and crossed a gulf whose depths he had no way of judging. Above, below and around, everything was smoke.

The walkway was five metres wide, with a low handrail, and reached across forty metres to a tower that rose skeletally out of the haze.

The air smelled of cordite and salt. It was cold and clammy suddenly.

Caffran scanned around. Behind them, the way they had come, he was just able to make out the back of the vast sea wall rising up, lost in the fog. The throbbing and pulsing was much louder now and Caffran knew it must be coming from the fuel-mills, the promethium pumps and the other working systems of the vast refinery.

Domor was next to him, prying into the smoke with his prosthetic eyes. The focus rings were buzzing now, and he strained with them. Thick, discoloured tears trickled down his stubbled cheeks. The salt water had really done its devious work.

'This smoke is backwash from the enemy guns along the wall top,' Domor said. 'The sea air and the downdraft of our ships is blowing it back over the wall and it's pooling here in the inner basin of the refinery.'

All the better for them to move unseen, thought Caffran, but... to where? Adrenaline had brought them so far. Where was the plan?

They were nearly at the tower, a vast red-painted skeletal needle of girders with dull flashing lamps at the corners. Other walkways stretched away from it into the soupy air. Caffran was beginning to make sense of the place, and picked out other catwalks and walkways above, below and parallel to the one the Ghosts used, through the billowing smoke.

Laser fire peppered down at them suddenly, rebounding from the iron walkway or punching through it. Bude stumbled as a round hit him in the top of the left shoulder and exited through his right hip. Caffran knew he was dead, but he tried desperately to get to him nevertheless. Bude leaned on the rail for a moment, upright, then pitched over and fell away into the smoke below silently.

There were dark shapes on a catwalk forty metres above and to the left of them. More zinging fire spat down through the clouds. The Ghosts opened up in return, pasting shots up into the roof of the smoke. A body fell past them. Mkendrik swivelled his flamer and vomited huge curls of fire up at the enemy position. The catwalk above them collapsed and spilled four fire-streaming comets down into the chasm: burning, screaming, flailing human forms.

Caffran led the way to the tower at a run and entered a grilled-off section that faced an open-sided elevator car. Caill and Mkallun joined him first, the others close on their heels. A steep stairwell of open-backed mesh steps led both down and up the tower alongside the open elevator shaft.

More las-fire, and stub rounds, started spanking off the ironwork and tinging around the metal cage of the tower.

'Which way?' bellowed Caill.

'Up!' Caffran decided.

'Where's the sense in that? We'll be trapped like rats at the top of the tower with nowhere to run!'

'No,' Caffran countered, trying desperately to think.

He was trying to bring back the briefing. The commissar had shown them aerial views of the Oskray facility, concentrating on the sea wall area they were meant to assault. He tried to picture the other, inner derrick areas he had glimpsed. Towers, dozens of them, just like the one on which they stood, bridging to each other at various levels, including some higher than the sea wall. If that was true – if the memory was true – they could cross to other towers higher up as well as lower down.

'Trust me,' Caffran said and started up the stairs, blasting las-rounds over the side at distant walkways where muzzles flashed in their direction.

They ascended.

Caffran fought the panic in his mind. The way in, the chance to sneak inside, had seemed a good plan, a brave plan, but now they were here, eight men alone in a city of the enemy, he had no idea what they had even expected to be able to achieve. There was no plan, not even the raw materials for a plan. He dreaded any of the others asking him to explain their purpose here.

Fire from below; three or four storeys down, squads of Kith soldiery were moving up the tower, blasting upwards. Las-rounds popped and thumped through the mesh steps around them. Mkallun lost the front of his foot and toppled, screaming in pain. Adare, just a few steps below him, arrested his fall and hauled the whimpering man up with him. The others blasted downwards and an odd vertical fire-fight began, laser salvos spitting up and down the tower structure. Mkendrik, last of the ascending Ghosts, hosed the stairs below them with his flamer and belching clouds of fire drizzled down through the open metal edifice and torched the closest of the pursuers.

Six more flights up, a bridging walkway opened to their left, crossing the smoky chasm to another tower. There seemed to be no one on the other structure, and Caffran gestured the men across, stopping to help Adare with Mkallun. Adare grabbed Caffran's shoulder and pointed to the swiftly ascending elevator in the tower they were leaving. It was packed with enemy troopers, climbing far faster than those on the stairs. Caffran sent Adare hobbling onwards with Mkallun, then pulled a pair of tube-charges from his pack. He set short fuses and rolled them along the bridge onto the tower deck, then ran to join the others.

The blast tore through the tower assembly, blowing out stanchions and main-supports all around. With a deafening howl, the tower crumpled and collapsed, hundreds of metres of steeple section from above sliding down with almost comical slowness, splintering the body of the tower below. The packed elevator car fell like a stone. Power servos tore out and exploded. Secondary explosions rippled out into the gloom.

The collapse tore away the bridge they had just crossed by, and ripped the bridge supports out of their side of the cross-ing, shearing metal and girders around them, shaking the other tower. Heavier impacts shook them as bridges higher up tore loose with the descending tumult and came slam-ming or dragging down the length of their tower.

From below, as the tower mass crashed to the ground, other explosions fluttered out as fuel stores and pumps det-onated under the impact. Plumes of fire gusted around them.

'What the feth have you done?' bellowed Flaven.

Caffran wasn't sure. In desperation, he hadn't really thought through the consequences of mining the tower. One simple thing occurred to him.

'I've bought us some time,' he whispered.

NOW THEY moved downwards, partly because down seemed to make sense, and partly because none of them trusted the stability of the tower now that its neighbour had been torn so brutally away. They descended into thicker, blacker smoke. Bright cinders floated on the wind and there was a deep, rank smell of burning fuel and spilt promethium. Even from here, they knew the collapsing tower had done vast damage to the plant.

Down, thought Caffran. Still he had no plan he could speak of, but down seemed to be instinctively right. What could they do here except perhaps some small, specific act? Like… take out the Kith's command cadre.

He laughed to himself as he thought the words. Bold, ridiculous words. As if they could even find Sholen Skara and his seniors in an island-hive this size. But it was a notion worth hanging on to.

A few hundred metres from the ground, he instructed his men to work stealthily, to do what the Ghosts did best. They blackened their skin with soot from the handrails, and pulled down their camo-cloaks, melting into the darkness of the smoke and the blackened tower-scaffold.

Below them, around the base of the tower, twisted, burning wreckage lay scattered five hundred metres in every direction. Flames leapt from small lakes of petroleum and mineral gels. The debris from the fallen tower, some of it great chunks of tower-section intact and twisted on the concrete, crushed beneath it smaller buildings and storage blocks, cranes and other rig service vehicles. Charred bodies lay crumpled or burst here and there. They passed at least one section of walkway dangling from their tower like a loose flap, clanking as it swung back and forth against the girders. Reedy klaxons barked through the smoke like the sound of yapping guard dogs.

They strode out from the base of the tower into the wreckage in fire-team formation, Caffran and Tokar at point. Domor supported the hopping Mkallun; Caffran wasn't going to leave him behind.

Spools of chain, frayed wire hawsers, splashes of oil and metal litter covered the concourse. Caffran skirted around a pair of Kith corpses, men who had clung together as they fell and been mangled into one hideous ruin by the ground.

Sending Mkendrik ahead in his place, Caffran dropped back to check on Domor and Mkallun. A hefty shot of analgesic had left Mkallun vacant, lolling and useless. Domor was blind. The iris shutters on his bionic implants had finally failed and shut tight. Filmy fluid leaked around the focussing rings and wept down his face. It hurt Caffran to see his friend like this. It was like Menazoid Epsilon all over again, when Domor had lost his eyes and still fought on without them, playing his part with a valour and tenacity even Gaunt had been awed by.

'Leave us,' Domor told him. Caffran shook his head. He wiped away the sweat that beaded his brow and trickled down the blue dragon tattoo on his temple. Caffran opened Mkallun's pack and took out a one-shot plastic injector of adrenaline, stamping it into Mkallun's bare forearm. The injured trooper roared as he came out of his stupor. Caffran slapped him.

'Domor will be your legs – you have to be his eyes.'

Mkallun growled and then spat and nodded as he understood. The adrenaline rush was killing all his pain and refortifying his limbs.

'I can do it, I can do it...' he said, clutching hold of Domor hard.

They moved on. Beyond the area of debris, the hive complex was a warren of drum silos and loading docks, red-washed girder towers marked with the Imperial eagle and then defaced with sickening runes of Chaos.

In one open concourse there was a row of fifty cargo trucks, flatbeds, smashed and burned out. Along one wide access ramp, millions of sections of broken pipe and hose, scattered in small random mounds. Inside one damaged silo, countless pathetic bodies were piled and jumbled: a mass grave of those Oskray workers who would not join Skara's cause.

So Flaven suggested. 'Perhaps not,' Caffran said, covering his mouth and nose with the edge of his cloak as he looked in. 'Enemy insignia there, and armour. These aren't long dead.'

'When have they found time to gather and pile their dead? There's an assault going on!'

Caffran agreed with Flaven's incredulity, but the signs were there. What purpose... what peculiar intent lay behind this charnel heap?

They heard shots, a ripple of las-fire from beyond the silo and swung in close, moving with the shadows. More shots, another almost simultaneous volley. Perhaps... a hundred guns, thought Caffran? He ordered them to stay down and crept forward with Adare.

What they saw beyond the next bunker shocked them.

There was a wide concourse, almost a kilometre square, at the heart of this part of the island complex. From the markings on the ground, this had been a landing pad for the cargo lighters. Across the centre, a thousand Kith soldiers stood in ranks of one hundred. Facing them was a messy litter of bodies which tractors with fork shovels and dozer blades were heaping into freight trucks.

Caffran and Adare watched. The front rank of the Kith took twenty steps forward and turned to face the other rows. At a signal from a nearby officer, what was now the front rank raised their weapons and cut the file of a hundred men down in an uneven burst of gunfire. As the tractors pushed the bodies aside, the rank that had fired stepped forward and marched to where their targets had been. They turned, waited. Another order. Another ripple of fire.

Caffran wasn't sure what sickened him most: the scale of the mass firing squads or the willing, uncomplaining way each rank slew the last and then stepped forward and waited to be cut down.

'What the Feth are they doing?' Adare gasped.

Caffran thought for a moment, reaching into his memory to recover the parts of the briefing he had blanked. The parts where Gaunt had spoken about Sholen Skara.

It came back to him, out of the darker reaches of his mind, recollections rising like marsh-gas bubbles out of the mire of forgetfulness. Suddenly, Gaunt's voice was in his ear, Gaunt's image before him. The briefing auditorium of the mighty troop-ship *Persistence*, Gaunt, in his long storm coat and cap, striding onto the dais under the stone lintel of the staging, glancing up at the gilt spread-eagle with its double heads on the velvet drop behind him. Gaunt, removing his coat and dropping it on the black leather chair, standing there in his dress jacket, taking off his cap once to smooth his cropped hair as the men came to order.

Gaunt, speaking of the abominations and filthy concepts Caffran had blanked from his mind.

'Sholen Skara is a monster. He worships death. He believes it to be the ultimate expression of the Chaotic will. On Balhaut, before we came in, he ran murder-camps.

There, he ritually slaughtered nearly a billion Balhauteans. His methods were inventive and–'

Even now, Caffran could not bring himself to think of Gaunt's descriptions. The names of the foul species of Chaos that Sholen Skara had commanded, the symbolic meaning of their crimes. Now though, he understood why Ibram Gaunt, champion of human life and soldier of the divine Emperor, would so personally loathe the likes of the monster called Skara.

'He kills to serve Chaos. Any death serves him. Here, we can be sure, he will have butchered any Imperially-loyal hive workers en masse. We can also be sure that if he believes defeat is close, he will begin a systematic purge of any living things, including his own troops. Mass suicide, to honour Chaos. To honour the blasphemy they call Khorne.'

Gaunt coughed at the word as if his gorge was rising, and a murmur of revulsion passed through the assembled Ghosts.

'That is a way we have of winning. We can defeat him – and we can convince him he will be defeated and thus save us the bother of killing them all. If he thinks he is losing, he will begin to slaughter his own as a final hymn of defiance and worship.'

Caffran's mind swam round to the present. Adare was speaking.

'–fething more of them, Caff! Look!'

Kith soldiers, in their hundreds, were marching out onto the concourse to fall in behind the rows already slaughtered.

Not slaughtered, thought Caffran: harvested. It reminded him of the rows of corn stooks back on the meadows of Tanith, as the mechanical threshers came in reaping row after row.

Despite the sickness in his stomach, a sickness that pinched and viced with each echo of gunfire, Caffran smiled.

'What?' Adare asked.

'Nothing…'

'So what do we do now? What's the plan?'

Caffran grinned again. He realised he did have a plan, after all. And he'd already executed it. When he'd brought that tower crashing down, he'd made Sholen Skara believe a significant enemy force was inside Oskray Hive. Made him believe that defeat loomed.

As a result, Skara was ordering the Kith to kill themselves, one hundred at a time. One hundred every thirty seconds.

Caffran sat back. His aching body throbbed. There was a las-burn across his thigh he hadn't even noticed before.

'You're laughing!' said Adare, perplexed.

Caffran realised he was.

'Here's the plan,' he said at last. 'We wait.'

AFTERNOON SQUALLS from the ocean were clearing the smoke from Oskray Hive, but even the wind and rain couldn't pry the stink of death from the great refinery. Formations of Imperial gunships shrieked overhead, pummelling the rain clouds with their fire-wash.

Gaunt found Caffran asleep amongst several hundred other Ghosts under a tower piling. The young trooper snapped to attention as soon as he realised who had woken him.

'I want you with me,' Gaunt said.

They crossed the great concourse of the refinery city, passing squads of Ghosts, Volpone and Abberloy Guardsmen detailed at building-to-building clearance. Shouts and whistles rang commands through the air as the Imperial forces took charge of the island hive and marshalled ranks of dead-eyed prisoners away.

'I never thought you to be a tactical man, Caffran,' Gaunt began as they walked together.

Caffran shrugged. 'I have to say I made it up as I went along, sir.'

Gaunt stopped and turned to smile at the young Ghost. 'Don't tell Corbec that, for Feth's sake, he'll get ideas.'

Caffran laughed. He followed Gaunt into a blockhouse of thick stone where oil-drum stacks had been packed aside to open a wide space. Sodium lamps burned from the roof.

A ring of Imperial Guardsmen edged the open area; Volpone mostly, but there were some Ghosts, including Rawne and other officers.

In the centre of the open area, a figure knelt, shackled. He was a tall, shaven-headed man in black, tight-fitting robes. Powerful, Caffran presumed, had he been allowed to stand. His eyes were sunken and dark, and glittered out at Gaunt and Caffran as they approached from the edge of the guarding circle.

'The little juicy maggot of the Imperial–' the figure began, in a soft, sugar-sweet tone. Gaunt smacked him to the ground with the back of his fist to silence him.

'Sholen Skara,' Gaunt said to Caffran, pointing down at the sprawled figure who was trying to rise, despite his fetters, blood spurting from his smashed mouth.

Caffran's eyes opened wide. He gazed down.

Gaunt pulled out his bolt pistol, checked it, cocked it and offered it to Caffran. 'I thought you might like the honour. There's no court here. None's needed. I think you deserve the duty.'

Caffran took the proffered gun and looked down at Skara. The monster had pulled himself up onto his knees and grinned up at Caffran, his teeth pink with blood.

'Sir–' Caffran began.

'He dies here, today. Now. By the Emperor's will,' Gaunt said curtly. 'A duty I would dearly liked to have saved for myself. But this is your glory, Caffran. You wrought this.'

'It's… an honour, commissar.'

'Do it… Do it, little Ghost-boy… What are you waiting for?' Skara's sick-sweet tones were clammy and insistent. Caffran tried not to look down into the sunken, glittering eyes.

He raised the gun.

'He wants death, sir.'

'Indeed he does! It is the least we can do!' Gaunt snapped.

Caffran lowered the gun and looked at Gaunt, aware that every eye in the chamber was on him.

'No, sir, he wants death. Like you told us. Death is the ultimate victory for him. He craves it. We've won here on

Sapiencia. I won't soil that victory by handing the enemy what he wants.' Caffran passed the gun back to Gaunt, grip first.

'Caffran?'

'You really want to punish him, commissar? Let him live.'

Gaunt thought for a moment. He smiled.

'Take him away,' he said to the honour guard as it closed ranks around Skara.

'I may have to promote you someday,' Gaunt told Caffran as he led him away.

Behind them, Skara screamed and begged and pleaded and shrieked. And lived to do so, again and again.

BRIN MILO, Gaunt's young adjutant, brought the commissar a tin cup of caffeine brew and the data-slates he hadn't requested – though he had been about to. Gaunt was sat on a camp chair on the deck outside his command shelter, gazing out at the Tanith lines and the emerald glades of Monthax beyond them. Milo gave the data-slates to the commissar and then paused as he turned away, guilty as he realised what he had done.

Gaunt eyed the slates, scrolling the charts on the lit fascia of the top one. 'Mkoll's surveys of the western swamps... and the orbital scans of Monthax. Thank you.'

The boy tried to cover his mistake. 'I thought you'd want to look them over,' he began. 'When you attack today, you'll–'

'Who said I'd attack today?'

Milo was silent. He shrugged. 'A guess. After last night's action, so close, I thought...'

Gaunt got up and looked the boy squarely in the eyes. 'Enough of your guesses. You know the trouble they might cause. For me. For you. For all the Ghosts.'

Milo sighed and leaned against the rail of the command shed's stoop where he attended the commissar. Mid-morning light lit the marshy groves beyond, lighting the tops of the tree cover an impossibly vivid green. Armoured vehicles rumbled through the mire somewhere, kilometres away. There was the distant thump of guns.

'Is there some crime…' he ventured at last, 'in anticipation? Sir. Isn't that what a good adjutant is supposed to do? Anticipate his officer's needs and requirements ahead of time? Have the right thing to hand?'

'No crime in that, Brin,' Gaunt replied, sitting back down. 'That's what makes a good adjutant, and you're making a fine job of being one. But… you anticipate too well sometimes. Some times it spooks me, and I know you. Others might view it another way. I don't need to tell you that.'

'No…'

'You know what happened in orbit last week. That was too close.'

'It was a conspiracy. I was set up.'

Gaunt wiped the sweat from his temple. 'You were. But it was easy to do. You'd be an easy victim for a determined manipulator. And if it came to that again, I'm not sure I could protect you.'

'About that… I have a request, sir. You do protect me… you have since Tanith.'

'I owe you. But for your intervention, I would have died with your world.'

'And from that you know I can handle myself in a combat situation. I want to be issued with a gun. I want to fight with the Tanith in the next push. I don't care what squad you put me in.'

'You've seen your share of fighting, Brin,' Gaunt said, shaking his head. 'But I won't make a soldier out of you. You're too young.'

'I was eighteen three days ago,' the boy said flatly.

Gaunt frowned. He hadn't realised. He flapped away a persistent fly and sipped his cup. 'Not a lot I can say to counter that,' he admitted.

He sat back down. 'What if we make a deal?'

Milo looked back at him with bright eyes and a cautious smile. 'Like what?'

'I give you a brevet field rank, a gun, and stick you next to Corbec. In return, you stop anticipating – completely.'

'Completely?'

'That's right. Well, I don't mean stop doing your job. Just stop doing things that people could take the wrong way. What do you say?'

'I'd like that. Thank you. A deal.'

Gaunt flashed him a rare smile. 'Now go and find me Corbec and Mkoll. I need to run through some details with them.'

Milo paused and Gaunt turned, looking down off the stoop to see the colonel and the scout sergeant standing side by side, looking up at him expectantly.

'Milo suggested that we should stop by. When we had a chance,' Corbec said. 'Is now a good time?'

Gaunt turned back to find Milo but the boy, probably on the basis of another wise anticipation, had made himself scarce.

# TEN
# WITCH HUNT

VARL LIFTED THE Tanith camo-cloak off the censer on the floor like a magician about to perform a conjuring trick. There was a hushed silence around the ship's hold as the veil came away.

The game was simple and enticing and completely fixed, and Sergeant Varl and the boy mascot made a good team. They had a jar of fat, jumping lice scooped from the troop-ship's grain silos and that beaten old censer borrowed from the Ecclesiarch chapel. The censer was a hollow ball of rusty metal whose hemispheres hinged open so that incense could be crumbled into the holder inside and lit. The ball's surface was dotted with star-shaped holes.

'The game is simple,' Varl began, holding up the jar and jiggling it so all could see the half dozen, thumb-sized bugs inside. He held it in his mechanical hand, and the servos hummed and whirred as he agitated the glass.

'It's a guessing game. A game of chance. No trickery, no guile.'

Varl was something of a showman, and Milo liked him very much. He was one of what Milo regarded as the inner circle of Ghosts, a close friend of Corbec and Larkin, one of a gaggle of tight-knit friends and comrades mustered together from the militia of Tanith Magna at the Founding. Varl's sharp tongue and speak-your-mind attitude had retarded his promotion chances early on, but then he had lost his arm on Fortis Binary during the heroic reconquest of the forge world and by the time of the now-legendary actions of Menazoid Epsilon he had been made a squad sergeant. Many thought it was well past time. Next to the ruthless command styles of Rawne and Feygor, and the intense military mindset of the likes of Mkoll and the commissar himself, Varl, like the beloved Colonel Corbec, injected a note of humanity and genial compassion into the Ghosts' command structure. The men liked him: he told jokes as often as Corbec, and they were for the most part funnier and cruder; his prosthetic arm proved he was not shy of close fighting; and he could, in his own, informal, garrulous way, spin a fine, inspiring speech to rouse his squad if the need called for it.

Just now, though, in one of the troop-ship's echoing holds with an audience of off-duty guardsmen roused from their cots and stoves all around, he was turning his charismatic tongue to something far more important. The pitch.

'Here's the deal, my friends, my brave fellow guardsmen, praise be the Golden Throne, here's the deal.'

He spoke clearly, slowly, so that his sing-song Tanith accent wouldn't confuse the other guard soldiers here. Three other regiments were sharing this transport with the Ghosts: big, blond, square-jawed brutes from the Royal Volpone 50th, the so-called Bluebloods; sallow-skinned, idle-looking compact men from the 5th Slamabadden; and tall, tanned, long-haired types from the 2nd Roane Deepers. Worlds and accents, separated by a common tongue. Varl worked his crowd with care and precision, making sure nothing he said was lost or misunderstood.

He handed the censer to Milo, who opened it. 'See now, a metal ball, with surface holes. The grain-lice go in the ball…' He tipped a couple from his jar out into the censer as Milo held it ready. 'And my young friend here closes it up. Notice how I've scratched a number next to all the holes. Thirty-three holes, a number next to each. No tricks, no guile… you can examine the ball if you like.'

Varl took the rusty ball from Milo and set it on the floor where all could see. A large washer welded to the censer's base stopped it from rolling. 'Now, see, I sets it down. The lice want the light, right? So sooner or later, they'll hop out… through one of the holes. There's the game. We wager on the number.'

'And we lose our money,' said a Deeper near the front, his voice twanged with that odd, rounded Roane accent.

'We'll all make a bet, friend,' Varl said. 'I will, you will, anyone else. If you guess the right number or get closest, you win the pot. No tricks, no guile.'

As if on cue, a bug emerged from one of the star-shaped holes and lit off onto the deck, where a Blueblood crunched it sourly underfoot.

'No matter!' Varl cried. 'Plenty more where he came from… and if you've seen the grain silos, you'll know what I mean!'

That brought general laughter and keen sense of suffering comradeship. Milo smiled. He loved the way Varl could play a crowd.

'What if we don't trust you, Ghost?' asked a Blueblood, the big ox who had mashed the bug. He wore his grey and gold twill breeches and black boots, but was stripped down to his undershirt. His body was a mass of well-nourished muscles and he stood two heads taller than Varl. Arrogance oozed from him.

Milo tensed. He knew that some rivalry existed between the Ghosts and the Bluebloods, ever since Voltemand. No one had ever said, but the rumour was that the Blueblood's own commanders, steering the invasion force, had ordered the barrage on the Voltis riverbed where so many Ghosts had died. The Bluebloods, so high and Emperor-damned mighty, seemed to despise the 'common born' Ghosts, but then they despised everyone. This aristocratic giant, with his hooded eyes and bullying manner, had at least six friends in the crowd, and all were as big as him. What the feth do they feed them on back home to raise such giants? Milo wondered.

Varl, unconcerned, got down off the crates he had been using as a stage and approached the giant. He held out his hand. It whirred. 'Ceglan Varl, Sergeant, Tanith First-and-Only. I admire a man who can express his doubts... sergeant?'

'Major Gizhaum Danver De Banzi Haight Gilbear, Royal Volpone 50th.' The giant didn't offer to take the outstretched hand.

'Well, major, seems you've no reason to trust a low-life like me, but it's all a game, see? No tricks, no guile. We all make a bet, we all have a laugh, we all pass the voyage a little quicker.'

Major Gilbear did not seem convinced.

'You've rigged it. I'm not interested if you place a bet.' He swung his look past Varl and took in Milo. 'Let your *boy* do it.'

'Oh. Now, that's just silly!' Varl cried. 'He's just a kid... he knows nothing about the fine and graceful art of gamesmanship. You want to play this with gamblers!'

'No,' Gilbear said simply. Others in the crowd agreed, and not just Bluebloods. Some seemed in danger of walking away, disinterested.

'Very well, very well!' Varl said, as if it was breaking his heart. 'The boy can play in my stead.'

'I don't want to, sir!' Milo squeaked. He prayed his outburst had the right mix of reluctance and concern, and that it didn't sound too much on cue.

'Now then, lad,' Varl said, turning to him and putting a heavy bionic arm around his shoulders paternally. 'Be good now and play along so that the nice gentlemen here can enjoy a simple game.' Unseen to all others present, he winked at Milo. Milo fought the fiercest battle of his life not to laugh.

'O-okay,' he said.

'The boy will play in my place!' Varl said, turning back to the crowd and raising his arms. There was cheers and applause in reply.

They set to it. A larger crowd gathered. Paper markers were handed out and coin produced. Gilbear decided to play, as did two Roane Deepers and three of the Slammabadden. In the crowd, secondary bets were laid on winners and losers. Varl opened the censer and took up his jar.

Gilbear plucked it from his hand, opened it and dropped the lice out onto the deck, crunching them all underfoot. He held it out to one of his men. 'Raballe! Go fetch fresh lice from the silos!'

'Sir!'

'What is this?' Varl gasped, dropping to his knees and wiping away what seemed to Milo a real tear as he surveyed his crushed insects. 'Do you not even trust my lice, Major Gilbear, Blueblood, sir?'

'I don't trust anything I can crush with my boot,' Gilbear replied, looking down and apparently dangerously close to stamping on Varl too. A tidal change swept through the secondary betting, some of it in sympathy with the damaged Ghost and his crushed pets, some sensing trickery was routed and heaping money on the Blueblood major.

'You could have drugged them, overfed them – they seemed docile. You could place your money on the lower holes so that the sluggish things simply fell from the bottom as gravity pulled.' Gilbear smiled at his deduction and his men growled approval. So did several of the wily Slammabadden, and Milo was afraid the mood might turn ugly.

'I'll tell you what,' Varl said to the major as he got up. The Blueblood's second was returning with a jar packed full of agitated lice and semi-digested meal where he had scooped it from the dank silos. 'We'll use your pick of the bugs...and you can set the censer whichever way up you like.' Varl pulled a cargo hook from the crates behind him to use as a makeshift base. 'Happy?'

Gilbear nodded.

They made ready. The gamblers, Milo included, prepared to make their guess on the paper slips provided. Varl flexed his good shoulder, as if easing out an old hurt. A signal, the next cue.

'I'll play this too,' Caffran said, pushing forward through the huddle. He seemed to sway and he stank of sacra. Many gave him a wide berth.

'Cafy, no… you're not up to it…' Varl murmured.

Caffran was pulling out a weight of coins, rolls of thick, high-issue disks.

'Give me the paper… I like a bet,' Caffran mumbled, slurring.

'Let your Ghost play,' Gilbear growled with a smirk as Varl began to protest.

It looked to all present like the Tanith showman had lost control of his simple game, and if there had been any trickery in it, any guile, then all of it was ruined now.

The first lice went in. Gilbear spun the censer and set it down. Markers were overturned. A Slammabadden came closest, closest to guessing the exit by three holes. Milo was nowhere near and seemed to whimper.

Caffran raged as his money was scooped away. He produced more.

A Deeper won the next, the winner of the last round given the honour of placing the censer. He was no closer than five holes, but the others were grouped and very wrong. Milo begged Varl to let him stop but Varl shook him off, glancing sidelong at the glowering Gilbear.

Gilbear won the next by guessing within two. He collected a massive pile of coins and one of the Deepers dropped out in disgust. The level of the bets – and off-game bets – had risen considerably and now real money was at stake. Cash was changing hands all around. The Bluebloods were jubilant and so were others. Others still bemoaned their losses. Two more Slammabadden and another Deeper stepped up to play, their bets bolstered by whip-rounds amongst their friends. No Blueblood dared to play against Gilbear.

Flushed with success, Gilbear placed his won pot again, and doubled it. Some of the guardsmen present, especially the Deepers and the watching Ghosts, had never seen so much ready cash in their lives. Caffran made a fuss and swigged from a bottle of sacra, imploring his friend Brostin for a sub which was eventually, reluctantly, given.

The next round. Gilbear and a Deeper, each three holes away from the winning aperture, split the now considerable pot.

The next round. Playing was Gilbear, three of the Slammabadden, two Deepers, Caffran (now subbing from a worried-looking Raglon, Brostin having exited in a convincing rage) and Milo. A huge pile of wagers.

Caffran came out two off the mark, a Slammabadden was one off. Gilbear was on the other side of the censer. Milo was spot on.

Howls, anger, jubilation, tumult.

'He was just lucky,' Varl said, collecting up the winnings. 'Are we done?'

'The boy got a fluke,' Gilbear said, ordering his subalterns to empty their pockets. Another big wager was assembled. The Deepers had dropped out, and so had Caffran, leaving the chamber with Raglon. The Slammabadden mustered their strengths into one wager.

Milo turned the censer and set it down.

Silence.

The bug ticked and bounced against the inside of the metal ball.

It emerged.

Milo had it again, spot on.

Pandemonium. It seemed like a riot would overturn the troop bay. Varl collected the winnings and the censer and pulled Milo out of the chamber by the scruff of his tunic. Men were shouting, milling around, and a fight had begun over the outcome of one of the side-bets.

In the companionway that led back to the Tanith troop deck, Varl and Milo rejoined Caffran, Raglon and Brostin. They were all laughing, and Caffran seemed suddenly sober. He would have to wash his tunic to get the stink of sacra out of it, of course.

Varl grinned at them and held up the bulky pouch containing their winnings. 'Spoils to be divided, my friends!' he announced to them, slapping Milo across the back with his bionic arm. He had never got used to its strength and Milo nearly fell.

Caffran uttered a warning. Dark shapes loomed down the companionway behind them. It was Gilbear and four of his men.

'You'll pay for that trickery, whore's-son,' Gilbear told Varl.

'It was a fair game,' began Varl, but realised at once that his silver tongue was useless now.

There were five on each side, but each of the Bluebloods towered over Brostin, the largest of the Tanith present. In a close-quarter brawl, the Ghosts might score, draw even perhaps, but it would be bloody.

'Is there a problem?' asked the sixth member of the Tanith scam team. Bragg pulled his vast bulk into the light behind his comrades, squinting in a relaxed way down at the five Bluebloods. He seemed to fill the corridor.

The Ghosts parted to let Bragg lumber through. He adopted the slow gait Varl had trained him in, to emphasise his power. 'Go away, little Bluebloods. Don't make me hurt you,' he said, repeating the cue Varl had also given him. It came out stilted and false, but the Bluebloods were too amazed at his size to notice.

They turned. With a final scowl, Gilbear followed them.

The Ghosts began to laugh so hard, they wept.

BELOW HIM, Monthax, green, impenetrable.

Gaunt gazed down through the arched viewports of the hexathedral *Sanctity*, studying the distant surface of the planet that, within a week, his forces would be assaulting. From time to time, he referred to a data-slate map in his hand, checking off geographical details. The dense jungle cover was the biggest problem they faced. They had no idea of the hidden enemy's strength.

Advance reports suggested a vast force of Chaos filth had retreated from a recent engagement at Piolitus and dug in here. Warmaster Macaroth was taking no chances. Around the huge bulk of the orbiting hexathedral, a colossal towered platform designed as a mustering point for the invasion forces, great legions massed. Over a dozen huge troop-ships were already docked around the crenellated rim of the hexathedral's skirt platform, like fat swine at the teats of their obese mother, and tugs were easing another in now to join them. More were due. Further away, Imperial battlecruisers and escort ships, including the frigate *Navarre* on which Gaunt and the Ghosts had been stationed for a while, sat at high orbit anchor, occasionally buzzing out clouds of attack squadrons heading off for surface runs or patrol sweeps.

Gaunt turned from the windows and stepped down a short flight into the cool, echoing vastness of one of the *Sanctity*'s main tactical chapels, the Orrery. A vast circular dial was set flush in the centre of the chamber's floor, thirty metres across and made of intricate, interlocking, moving parts of brass and gold, like a giant timepiece. As it whirred and cycled, the three-dimensional globe of coloured light it projected upwards altered and spun, advancing data, chart runes, bars of information across the luminous surface.

Trim uniformed Guard officers, robed members of the Ecclesiarch and the Munitorium, Navy commanders in their Segmentum Pacificus deck dress, and the hooded deaconal staff of the hexathedral itself, prowled the edges of the great Light Orrery, consulting the data and conferring in small groups. Skeletal servitors, emaciated, wired into the machine banks via cables from their eyes, spines, mouths and hands, hunkered in booth-cribs, murmuring and chattering. Around the sides of the great chamber, under cloistered roofing, great chart tables were arranged at intervals, each showing different sections of Monthax. Staff groups stood around every table, engaged in more specific and detailed planning sessions. The air chimed with announcements and updates, some of these overlapping and chattering with data noise. The Orrery turned, whirring, and new details and deployments appeared.

Gaunt walked a circuit of the chamber, nodding to those fellow officers he knew, saluting his seniors. The whole place had an exceptional, expectant hush, like a great hunting animal, breathless, coiled to pounce.

The commissar decided it was time he took a walk down to the Ghosts' troop-ship. The men would be restless, awaiting news of debarkation and deployment, and Gaunt knew well that trouble was always likely to brew when guardsmen were cramped together in transportation, idle and nervous.

And bored. That was the worst of it. In any Guard regiment, disciplinary matters rose in number during such times, and he and the other commissars, the political enforcers of the Imperial Guard, would be busy. There would be brawls, thefts, feuds, drunkenness, even murder in some of the more barbaric regiments, and such disorder quickly spread without the proper control.

Across the chamber, Gaunt saw General Sturm, the commander of the Volpone 50th, and some of his senior aides. Sturm did not seem to see him, or chose not to acknowledge Gaunt if he did, and Gaunt made no effort to salute. The crime of Voltemand was still raw in his mind, despite the interval of months. When he learned that the Volpone Bluebloods and the Ghosts would encounter each other again at Monthax, for the first time since Voltemand, he had been apprehensive. The action on Menazoid Epsilon had shown him personally what a long-standing feud between regiments could do. But there was no chance of redeployment, and Gaunt comforted himself that it was only Sturm and his senior staff he had a problem with. The rank and file of the Ghosts and the Bluebloods had no reason for animosity. He would keep a careful watch, but he was sure they could billet side by side safely enough until the assault sent them their separate ways.

And, unlike on Voltemand, Sturm wasn't in charge here. The Monthax offensive was under the supreme command of Lord Militant General Bulledin.

Gaunt saw Commissar Volovoi, serving with the Roane Deepers, and stopped to talk with him. It was mostly inconsequential chat, though Volovoi had heard some word that Bulledin had consulted the Astropathicus. Rumours of psyker witchery on the planet below had started to spread. There was talk that auguries and the Tarot had been consulted to determine the truth of the situation.

'Last thing we need,' muttered Volovoi to Gaunt. 'Last thing I need. The Roane are the very devil to keep in line. Good fighters, yes, when they're roused to it, but damned idle for the most part. A few weeks of transportation confinement like this, and I'll have to kick each and every one of their arses to get them down the drop-ship ramp. Languid, lazy – and this makes it worse: they're superstitious, more than any band of men I've ever known. The rumours of witchcraft will get them spooked and that will make my work twice as hard.'

'I sympathise,' Gaunt said. He did. His old regiment, the Hyrkans, were tough as deck plate, but there had been times when the thought of psyker madness had balked them in their tracks.

'What of you, Gaunt?' Volovoi asked. 'I hear you're taken up with a low-tech rabble now. Don't you miss the Hyrkan discipline?'

Gaunt shook his head. 'The Tanith are sound, quietly disciplined in their way.'

'And you have actual command of them too, is that right? Unusual. For a commissar.'

'A gift of the late Slaydo, may the Emperor watch his rest. I resented it at first, but I've grown to like it.'

'You've done well with them, so I hear. I read the reports on that campaign in the Menazoid Clasp last year, and they say your men turned the key that opened the door at Bucephalon too.'

'We've had our moments.'

Gaunt realised Volovoi was studying something over Gaunt's shoulder.

'Don't turn, Gaunt,' Volovoi went on, without changing the timbre of volume of his talk. 'Are your ears burning? Someone's talking about you.'

'How so?'

'The Blueblood general. Sturm, is it? Arrogant piece of yak flop. One of his officers just came on deck and is bending his ear. And they're looking this way.'

Gaunt didn't turn. 'Let me guess: the newcomer is a big ox with hooded eyes?'

'Aren't they all?'

'This one's a piece of work even by the Volpone standards of breeding. A major.'

'That's what his rank pins say. You know him?'

'Not particularly, though even that is more than I'd care for. Name's Gilbear. He and I and Sturm had a… difference of opinion on Voltemand eighteen months ago.'

'What sort of difference?'

'They cost me several hundred men.'

Volovoi whistled. 'You'd think it would be you whispering about them!'

Gaunt smiled, though it was dark. 'We are, aren't we, Volovoi?'

Gaunt made to leave. Crossing the Orrery deck, he was afforded a better view of the Volpone staff. Gilbear was stood alone now, staring at Gaunt with a burning look that did not flinch. Sturm, escorted by his aides, was heading up the long flight of steps to the Lord Militant General's private chambers in the spire above.

WALKING THE TROOP decks with Gaunt, Corbec brought his commander up to speed.

'Quiet really. There was a fight over some rations, but it was nothing and I broke it up. Costin and two of his pals got falling down tipsy inhaling paint thinners in the armour shops and Costin then fell down for real, breaking his shin.'

'I've warned the armouries to lock that sort of material up…'

'They did, but Costin has a way with locks, sir, if you get me.'

'Put him and the others on report and punishment detail.'

'I'd say Costin's paid for his ill-gotten–' Corbec began.

'I won't stand for it. They've got rations of grog and sacra. I can't use men with fume-ruined heads.'

Corbec scratched his chin. 'Point there, sir. But the men get bored. And some of them use their sacra rations up in the first few days.'

Gaunt turned to his second, anger flickering in his eyes. 'Let it be known, Colm: the Emperor grants them recreational liquor and smokes. If they abuse that privilege, I'll take it away. From all of them. Understand?'

Corbec nodded. They stopped at the rail and looked down into the vast troop bay. The air was laced with smoke and rank sweat. Below them, bench cots by the hundred in rows, men by the hundred, sleeping, dicing, chatting, praying, some just staring into nothing. Priests walked the rows, dispensing solace and benediction where it was requested or simply needed.

'Is there something on your mind, sir?' Corbec asked.

'I think trouble's brewing,' Gaunt said. 'I'm not sure what yet, but I don't like it.'

THERE WAS SOMEONE moving in the outer room.

Gaunt awoke. It was night cycle on the troop-ship and the wall lamps had been doused by the automatic control. He had fallen asleep on his cot with a weight of data sheets and slates on his chest.

Movement from the ante-room beyond his bed quarter had roused him.

Gaunt rose silently, placing the data sheets on a wall shelf. His boltgun and chainsword were slung over a wooden stand in the outer room, but he pulled a compact laspistol from his foot locker and slid it into the back of his waistband. He was dressed in his boots, trousers, braces and an undershirt. He thought for a moment about re-donning his jacket and cap, but cast the idea aside.

The cot-room door was ajar. The light of a tight-beam flashlight stabbed the darkness beyond. Someone was going through his things.

He moved in an instant, kicking open the door and grabbing the intruder from behind, turning him, twisting his arms, and slamming him face first into the round observation port of the outer room. The man – robed, struggling – protested until the moment of impact. His nose broke against the glass and he lolled unconscious.

The lights went on. Gaunt sensed there were two others behind him. He heard the whine of charging las-packs.

He spun and threw his unconscious prey at the nearest, who tumbled under the weight. The other tried to take a bead with his gun, but Gaunt dropped, slid sideways, and broke his jaw with a heavy blow. Only then, a few seconds after the whole thing had begun, did he see the man he had dropped was a security trooper dressed in the brown armour of the hexathedral. His comrade, scrambling up from under the weight of the fallen robed man, lunged forward, and Gaunt turned, catching his probing hands, breaking an elbow with a deft twist and then flooring him with a straight punch to the bridge of the nose.

Gaunt pulled out his compact and covered the room. Two hexathedral troopers and a man in long robes lay at his feet, twitching and moaning.

The door opened.

'Many would look with disfavour at such violence, commissar,' the figure who entered the room announced softly.

Gaunt kept the gun trained at the intruder's throat. 'Many look on intrusion and burglary in a similar way. Identify yourself.'

The figure moved into the light. She was tall, dressed in a simple uniform of black: boots, breeches, jacket. Her ash-fair hair was pinned tight up around her skull. Her face was calm, angular, lean, beautiful.

'I am Lilith. Inquisitor Lilith.'

Gaunt lowered the pistol and set it down on the side-table. 'You have not requested my seal of office. You believe me then?'

'I know of you. Pardon, ma'am; there are few females holding your rank and duty.'

Lilith moved forward into the room and gently kicked one of the troopers. He moaned and roused. 'Get yourself out of here. These two as well.'

The bloodied trooper clambered to his feet and dragged the others out.

'I apologise, commissar,' Lilith said. 'I had been told you were in a planning session. I would not have sent my men in if I had known you were sleeping here.'

'You'd have had my rooms searched had I been absent?'

She turned to him and laughed. It was attractive, confident – and hard. 'Of course! I'm an inquisitor, commissar. That's what I do.'

'What, precisely, is it you're doing here?'

'The boy.' She pulled out a chair and sat back, leaning against the back rest with relaxed ease. 'I need to know about the boy. Your boy, commissar.'

Gaunt stayed where he was and fixed his gaze on her. 'I don't like your tone, or your methods,' he growled. 'If I continue not to like them, I can assure you the fact you are a woman won't—'

'Are you really threatening me, commissar?'

Gaunt breathed deeply. 'I believe I am. You saw what I did to your lackeys. I won't stand for this unless you show me good reason.'

Lilith sighed and steepled her long, pale fingers. Then she pointed the compact laspistol right at Gaunt.

He started, amazed. She had not moved, but now she held a gun which had been lying right across the room from her.

'How good a reason do I need?' she asked, smiling. Gaunt stepped back.

'That little demonstration would seem good enough…'

Lilith smiled and dropped the gun into her lap. She clasped her hands together again and set her head back.

'Good. We'll begin. By the proclamation of the Most High Emperor, governed as I am by His will, in totally, till the end of all days, as a servant of the Inquisition, I require you to furnish with me with answers of complete truth and veracity to your best knowledge. The penalties for deception are manifold and without limit. Do you understand?'

'Get on with it.'

She smiled again. 'I like you, commissar. "The very devil", they said. They were right.'

'Who's "they"?'

Lilith didn't answer. She rose, holding the pistol loose in her left hand. She circled Gaunt. He was unnerved by her masculine height and her unblinking stare.

'Skipping further formalities, as you suggest, why don't you tell me about the boy?'

'What boy?'

'So coy. His name is Brin Milo, a Tanith native, part of your cadre but a civilian.'

'What do you want to know, inquisitor?'

'Oh, everything, Ibram; everything.'

Gaunt cleared his throat. 'Milo is… here by chance. The regimental piper, mascot… my aide.'

'Why?'

'He's smart, sharp, eager. The men like him. He can do the jobs I ask of him quickly and efficiently.'

Lilith held up a finger. 'Start from the beginning. Why is he here?'

'When Chaos fell on Tanith, and consumed it, I elected to withdraw all the able bodied men I could from the world. My own exit was barred and the boy intervened, clearing my way. In gratitude, I took him with me. He's too young for infantry, so I made him my aide.'

'Because of his skills?'

'Yes. And because there was nothing other to be done with him.'

Lilith came close to Gaunt and stared into his eyes. 'What are his skills?'

'Efficiency, ability, keenness to–'

'Really, commissar. You can admit it. Taking a liking to a clean-limbed young cabin mate and–'

The slap resounded in the close air of the cabin. Lilith didn't flinch. She turned away, laughing.

'Very good. Very direct. So we can cut the crap, can we? I have notice that the boy is a witch. How do you respond?'

'He is not.' Gaunt swallowed. 'The poison of the warp turns my guts. You think I would have truck with it for a second?' He paused. 'Present company excepted, naturally.'

Lilith circled him. 'But he's useful. I've done my ground work, Gaunt. He predicts things, guesses them before they happen… attacks, incidents, what files the commissar needs. What the commissar wants for breakfast–'

'That's no witchcraft. He's smart. He anticipates.'

'There was a game… a scam… in the lower decks. He was a key part of it. He knew how to win it. He was perfect in his guesses. What do you say to that?'

'I say: who put you up to this?'

'Does it matter?'

'It was Sturm, wasn't it? And his pet ox, Gilbear. They have an agenda; how can you trust their word?'

She faced him and fixed him with her eyes. 'But of course. They cannot hide it from me. Sturm and Gilbear hate you and despise your Ghosts. They tried to obliterate you on Voltemand and failed. Now they seek to bring you down by whatever means they have.'

Gaunt was almost speechless. 'You know this and still you come here?'

'I'm an inquisitor, Ibram,' she replied with a smile. 'Sturm and his men are brutes. I have no interest in their internecine hatred for you and your men. But Lord Militant General Bulledin has brought me here to assess and sanction the dangers of witchcraft during the liberation of Monthax. Enemy witchcraft... and also that which lurks within like a cancer. The boy has been brought to my attention and I am duty bound to examine the evidence. They say he's a witch. I don't care why they say it or what they hope to earn from such accusations. But if they're right... That's why I'm here. Is Milo touched? Is he a psyker? Don't protect him, Gaunt. It will be so much the worse for you if you do.'

'He isn't. This is all political nonsense. The Bluebloods have seen a potential weakness they wish to exploit.'

'We'll see. I need to speak with this Milo. Now.'

To BE SUMMONED by his commissar during night cycle was not a new experience for Brin Milo; there were often out-of-hours errands to be run. But as soon as he arrived outside Gaunt's quarters, he realised something was wrong. Gaunt was in full dress uniform, with jacket and cap, and his face was grim. A tall woman in black with an oddly malevolent air about her waited to the side.

'This servant of the Emperor has some questions for you,' Gaunt explained. He refrained from using the loaded word 'inquisitor'. 'Answer her honestly and directly.'

Wordlessly, Lilith led them down the long deck hall and into the docking ring. They crossed over into the hexathedral itself. Milo was apprehensive. He had not set foot on the great docking craft before. The air smelled different,

sacred and cool after the stuffy humidity of the troop transport, and the scale of the chambers they passed through
startled him. The only people they met were deacons in
robes, brown-armoured troopers and small groups of rank-
ing officers. It was another world.

Lilith led the way on a route that took twenty minutes to
walk and passed through several main chapels and chambers of the hexathedral, including the Orrery. Gaunt
understood her tactics. The route was overlong and unnecessary, except it would disarm and over-awe the boy and
make his psychological reserve weaker. She was clever to the
point of cruel.

They reached an iris shutter at the end of a long corridor
flanked by windows of stained glass. Lilith made a slight
gesture with her hand and the hatch spiralled open. She
waved the boy inside and turned on the threshold to speak
with Gaunt.

'You may attend, but make no interruption. Gaunt, you're
a valuable officer, and if this boy turns out to be tainted, I
can make it so you suffer nothing more than a slight reprimand for being unaware of his status.'

'A generous suggestion. What are the conditions?'

Lilith smiled. 'We are complementary instruments, commissar, you and I. My duty is to worm out corruption, yours
is to punish it. If Milo is corrupt, you will exonerate yourself
by performing summary execution yourself. It will reflect
your outrage and determination to clean house.'

Gaunt was silent. The possibility clawed at his mind.

'There would be no other way to salvage your reputation,
command or career. Indeed your very life may be forfeit if it
is thought you conspired to protect a pawn of the Darkness.
Do you hear me, Gaunt?'

'I hear your threat to my life and its future. I deal with
threats as a profession.'

'Then I'll be blunter. Sturm has initiated this process
because he sees it as a way of bringing you and the Ghosts
down. If Milo is corrupt and you do not distance yourself
from him and act like a commissar, your life will be over –
and Sturm will make sure the Ghosts are dismantled. He has

already seeded the idea in Bulledin's mind that if one Ghost
is a witch, so might others be. The Tanith First would be
taken, to a man, by the Inquisition and they would all suffer extreme investigation. Most would die. The rest would be
cast aside as no longer fit to serve the Imperial Guard. I am
bound by duty to investigate Sturm's claim. I do not wish to
be party to his vendetta against the Tanith, but I will become
so if you do not act accommodatingly, willingly and hon-
ourably.'

'I see. Thank you for your candour.'

'Chaos is the greatest threat mankind faces, Gaunt. We
cannot allow psychic power to exist within any untrained
mind. If the boy is touched, he must be destroyed.'

'Not evaluated by the Black Ships… as you were?'

She looked at him with a sharp frown. 'Not this time. The
political situation is too delicate. If Milo is a witch, he must
be put to death to appease all parties.'

'I see.'

She nodded and stepped inside. Gaunt paused and
found himself looking down at his holstered bolt pistol.
Could he do it? The life of every Ghost might depend on
the sacrifice of Milo, and to have struggled to bring them
so far, to save them and give them purpose was not something Gaunt felt he could throw aside. He owed it to the
Tanith to do all he could to safeguard them. But to execute
Brin… the boy who had selflessly saved his life, selflessly
served… it went so against his personal honour the
thought crushed his chest.

Yet if the boy really was touched, really was tainted with
the unbearable stain of Chaos…

His face grim and cold, he ducked inside, and the iris
hatch whispered shut behind him.

THE ROOM WAS wide and high, lacking windows in its walls
but sporting a great circular port in the roof. Stars gleamed
down from above and their light was almost all there was,
except for small, dim lamps set around the edges of the
floor. There was a carpet on the floor, a thick, coloured
weave that bore the Imperial eagle crest. Two seats, facing

each other, sat in the centre of the carpet – a high-backed wooden throne with knurled armrests, and a smaller wooden stool. Lilith sat on the stool and motioned Milo to occupy the huge throne. Its wooden embrace seemed to swallow him up. Gaunt stood back, watching uneasily.

'Your name?'

'Brin Milo.'

'I am Lilith. I am an inquisitor.' That word now, finally, biting the air with its menace and threat. Milo's eyes were wide and fearful.

She asked him about Tanith, his past, his life there. He answered, halting at first, but as her questions flowed – innocent, innocuous questions about his memories – he spoke more confidently.

She asked him to recount his first meeting with Gaunt, his memories of the fall of Tanith, the choice he had made to fight for Gaunt there.

'Why? You were not a soldier. You are not a soldier now. Why did you defend this off-worlder you hardly knew?'

Milo glanced at Gaunt briefly. 'The Elector of Tanith, whose household I served as musician and attendant, ordered me to stay with the commissar and see to his needs. His needs at that point were mortal. He was being attacked and had little chance of survival. I was doing as I had been ordered.'

She sat back, drumming her fingers on her knees. 'It interests me, Milo, that you have not yet asked why this interrogation is happening. Most brought before me usually express outrage and protest innocence, wondering why this should be happening to them. But you do not. In my experience, the guilty always know why they're here and seldom ask. Do you know why you're here?'

'I can guess.'

Gaunt froze. *Wrong answer, Brin, wrong answer…*

'Guess out loud,' she invited. 'I hear you're remarkably good at guessing.'

Milo seemed to tremble. 'I am considered by many to be a misfit. Some of the Tanith don't like to have me around. I am not like them.'

Feth, Milo! I said answer honestly, but there's honest and there's this! Gaunt thought darkly. His heart raced.

'What do you mean? How are you not like them?'

'I… I'm different. It makes them uneasy.'

'How are you different?' she asked, almost eager.

Here it comes, thought Gaunt.

'I'm not a soldier.'

'You're… what?'

'They're all soldiers. That's why they're here, that's why they survived the fall of Tanith. They were all new-founded Guards, mustered to leave Tanith anyway, and the commissar only evacuated them because of their worth to the Emperor. But I'm not. I'm a civilian. I shouldn't be here. I shouldn't have survived. The Tanith see me and they think "Why did that boy survive? Why is he here? If he's here, why not my brother, my daughter, my father, my wife?" I represent a possibility of survival denied to them all.'

She was silent for a moment.

It was all Gaunt could do to stop himself smiling. Milo's answer had been perfect, as had the way he had allowed it to seem she was leading him into a trap. It made his response seem all the more honest.

Lilith got to her feet and crossed to Gaunt's side. He could see the fierce annoyance in her face. She whispered, 'Have you briefed the boy? Coached him in good answers for just such an event?'

Gaunt shook his head. 'No, and if I had, don't you suppose such an admission might make it look as if I knew Milo had something to hide?'

She hissed a curse and thought for a moment.

'Why this charade of questions?' Gaunt asked. 'Why not just probe his mind? You have the gift, don't you?'

She looked and him and nodded. 'You know I do. But a good psyker, a dangerous psyker, can hide his power. The questions are an effective method of opening up his guard and winkling out the truth. And if his mind is the seething furnace we fear, I have no wish to touch it directly.'

She turned back, pacing around Milo's throne. From behind him, she said. 'Tell me about the game.'

'Game?'

'The game you and your Tanith friends play in the troop decks.'

She paced round in front of him and held out her right hand, palm down, balled in a fist. She turned it over and opened it. A grain-louse sat in the palm, twitching and alive.

'This game.'

'Oh,' Milo said. 'It's a betting game. You bet on which hole the bug will come out.'

She put the bug on his knee and it made no effort to jump away. Milo looked down at it with fascination. Lilith crossed to the side of the room and took something from a wall cupboard. The object was covered in a velvet cloth. When she unveiled it, it was like a magician about to perform a conjuring trick. But not half as much as when Varl did it.

She gave the rusty censer ball to Milo. 'Open it. Put the bug inside.'

He obeyed.

'Now, Milo. This isn't a game, is it? It's a scam. It's a trick the Tanith use to win cash from the other Guards. And if it's a scam, it needs a sting. It needs a foolproof method to make it a sure thing the Tanith will win. You're the sting, aren't you? On demand, you can guess right... because that's what you do, isn't it? Your mind does the trick and makes it a certainty.'

Milo shook his head. 'It's just a game...'

'I have it on good authority that it is not. If it's a game, why do you play it with unsuspecting troops from other regiments? By my own investigation, you and your friends have earned a small fortune from other men in these last few days. More than you would expect to win if it was just chance.'

'Lucky, I gu– I suppose.'

'You cannot run a scam on such wide odds. How do you really ensure the bug emerges from the right hole?'

Brin lifted the censer. The bug ticked inside. 'Okay... if it matters so much, I'll show you. Pick a hole.'

'Sixteen,' she said, sitting down on the stool facing him, apparently eager.

'I say nine.' He set it down. The bug emerged from hole twenty.

'You win. You were closer.'

She shrugged.

He opened the censer and put the bug back inside. 'That was round one. You're more confident now. You'll play again. Pick.'

'Seven.'

'Twenty-five,' said Milo. They waited, and then the bug wriggled out of hole six and hopped across the carpet.

'Again you win. You're feeling good now, aren't you? Two wins. On the troop deck, you might have a pile of coins now, and you might wager the lot. You put the bug in.'

She did so and handed the censer back to Milo.

'Pick?' he said.

'Nineteen. All my money and all the cash my comrades-in-arms have on nineteen.'

He smiled. 'One,' he said.

The bug squirmed out of hole one.

'And so I take my huge winnings, look you in your open-mouthed face and say good night.' Milo sat back.

'A beautiful demonstration… and one that may have just incriminated you. How could you do that, to order, at just the right moment, unless your mind knew in advance which way the bug was going?'

Milo tapped his head. 'You're so sure it's my mind, aren't you, ma'am? So sure it's the twisted workings I've got up here… You think I'm a *psyker*, don't you?'

Her expression was icy. 'Show me an alternative.'

He tapped his jacket pocket. 'It's not up there, it's down here.'

'Explain.'

'At the start of each game, we reach into our pockets for the next wager. I let you place the bug and so on, but I'm the last to handle the censer. The bugs love sugar dust. There's some in the seam of my pocket. I wipe my finger in it as I take out my money and then wipe that finger around the hole I want as I place the censer down. The dust's invisible on that rusty surface of course. But the scam is, I always

know which hole it's going to come out of. I choose every
time: the first few rounds to let you win, and then when
you're confident you've got me on the ropes and start wager-
ing everything, I play to win.'

Lilith got up smartly, crushing the bug underfoot with a
deliberate heel. It left a brown stain on one beak of the
Imperial crest. She turned to Gaunt.

'Get him out of here. I will report to Bulledin and Sturm.
This matter is closed.'

Gaunt nodded and led Milo to the doorway.

'Commissar!' she called out after them. 'He might not be
a witch, but if I were you I'd think twice about having a devious and underhand little cheat like him anywhere near me.'

'I'll take that under advisement, Inquisitor Lilith,' Gaunt
replied and they left.

THEY WALKED BACK together through the hallways of the hexathedral. Night cycle was coming to an end, and dawn
prayers and offerings were being made in the echoing
chapels and chambers around. Incense and plainsong filled
the air.

'Well done. I'm sorry you had to go through that.'

'You thought she'd get me, didn't you?' Milo asked.

'I've never doubted the goodness or honesty in you, Brin,
but I've always been uneasy about your knack of anticipating things ahead of time. I always feared that someone
would take exception to it and that you would land us all in
trouble.'

'You'd have shot me though, right?'

Gaunt stopped in his tracks. 'Shot you?'

'If I'd let you down and landed the Ghosts in trouble. If I'd
been... what she thought I was.'

'Oh.' They walked on. 'Yes, I would. I would have had to.'

Milo shrugged.

'That's what I thought you'd say,' he murmured.

# ELEVEN
# SOME DARK &
# SECRET PURPOSE

GAUNT WOKE, AND remembered that he had been dreaming of Tanith. That wasn't unusual in itself; the visions of the fall of that world stalked his dreams regularly. But this time, for the first time, it seemed to him that he had been dreaming about the world as it had been: alive, flourishing, thriving.

The dream disquieted him, and he would have dwelt on it, had there been time. But then he realised that an urgent commotion had roused him. Outside, the pre-dawn gloom of Monthax was riven with shouts and alarms and the distant, eager sounds of warfare. Someone was hammering on the door of the command centre. Gaunt could hear Milo's insistent voice.

He pulled on his boots and went outside, the cool morning air stiffening the night-sweat soaking his tight undershirt and breeches. He blinked at the cold glare, batting aside a persistent insect, as he half-listened to Milo's hasty reports, half-read the vox-caster print-outs and data-slates the boy handed him. Gaunt's eyes looked westward. Pink and amber flashes underlit the low night clouds to the west, like a false dawn, every now and then punctured by the brief, trailing white star of a flare-charge, or the brighter, whiter flashes of some powerful energy support weapon.

Gaunt didn't need Milo or the printed communiqués to know that the major offensive had begun at last. The enemy was moving, in force.

He ordered the platoon leaders to ready their men – though most had begun to do so already – and summoned the senior officers for a tactical meeting in the command centre. He sent Milo away in search of his cap and jacket, and his weapons.

In under ten minutes, Corbec brought Rawne, Lerod, Mkoll, Varl and the other seniors to the centre, to find Gaunt, now dressed, spreading out the communiqués on the camp table. There were no preliminaries.

'Orbital reconnaissance and forward scouting has shown a massed, singular column of Chaos moving through the territory to the west.'

'Objective?' Corbec asked.

Gaunt shrugged. It was a disarming gesture from one usually so confident. 'Unclear, colonel. We've been expecting a major attack for days, but this doesn't seem to focus any strength on our positions at all. Early reports show the enemy have cut through – well, destroyed, in fact – a battalion-strength force of Kaylen Lancers. But I have a hunch that's only because the Lancers were in the way. It's as if our enemy has another objective, one they're determined to achieve. One we don't know about.'

Mkoll was eyeing the charts carefully. He'd scouted and mapped the area in question thoroughly during the previous week. His sharp tactical mind saw no obvious purpose to the assault either. He said as much.

'Could their intelligence be wrong?' Varl asked. 'Maybe they've made their play at positions they think we hold.'

'I doubt that,' Mkoll answered. 'They've seemed well informed up to now. Still, it's a possibility. They've committed a huge portion of their strength to a mistake if that's true.'

'If it's a mistake, we'll use it. If they have some dark and secret purpose, well, we'll do ourselves no favours by waiting to find out what it is.' Gaunt paused and scratched his chin thoughtfully.

'Besides,' he said, 'our orders are clear. General Thoth is sending us in, as soon as we're ready, on orders from Lord Militant General Bulledin himself. The Tanith will form one arm of a counter assault. Upwards of sixty thousand men from various regiments are to be deployed against the enemy. Because of the peculiar, not to say perplexing orientation of their advance, we'll catch them side on. The Ghosts will cover a salient about nine kilometres long.' Gaunt indicated their area of the new front on the chart, marking little runic symbols on the glass plate with his wax pencil. 'I don't want to sound over-confident, but if they've presented laterally to us by mistake, or if they're driving towards something else, we should be able to do a lot of damage to their flank. Thoth has demanded a main force assault, what the beloved and devout Chapterhouses like to call a meat-grinder. Rip into them along the flank and try, if nothing else, to break their column and isolate parts of it.'

'Begging your pardon, commissar,' Rawne's sibilant tones whispered through the centre's close humidity like a cold draught. 'The Tanith aren't heavy troops. Main force, without playing to our strengths? Feth, that'll get us all killed.'

'Correct, major.' Gaunt fixed the man with a tight stare. 'Thoth has given the regimental commanders some discretion. Let's remember the depth of ground cover and jungle out there. The Ghosts can still use their stealth and cunning to get close, get in amongst them if need be. I'll not send you in en masse. The Ghosts will deploy in platoon sections, small scattered units designed to approach the foe unseen through the glades. I think that way we will give as good an account of ourselves as any massed charged of armoured infantry.'

The briefing was over, save to agree platoon order and position. The officers filed out.

Gaunt stopped Mkoll. 'This notion they've made a mistake: you don't hold with it?'

'I gave my reasons, sir,' Mkoll said. 'It's true, these jungles are dense and confusing, and we can use that. But I don't believe they've made a mistake, no, sir. I think they're after something.'

'What?'

'I wouldn't like to guess,' Mkoll said, but he gestured down at the chart. Just off centre in the middle of the area mapped out as the new front, Gaunt saw what he was pointing to. A mark on the map representing the estimated position of the pre-human ruins Mkoll had found while scouting just a few days before.

'I never did get a look at that, first hand. I... couldn't find it again.'

'What? Say that again?'

Mkoll shrugged. 'I saw it from a distance on patrol – that's when I reported it to you. But since then, I've been unable to relocate it. The men think I'm slipping.'

'But you think...' Gaunt let the silence and Mkoll's expression finish the sentence.

Gaunt began to strap on his holster belt. 'When we get in there, prioritise getting a good assessment of that ruin. Find it again, priority. Keep this between us. Report it back to me directly.'

'Understood, colonel-commissar. To be frank, it's an honour thing now. I know I saw it.'

'I believe you,' Gaunt said. 'Feth, I trust your senses more than my own. Let's move. Let's go and do what they sent us here to do.'

THE STONE WALLS were lime quartz, smooth, perfectly finished, lambent. They enclosed the Inner Place like walls of water, like a section cut through the deepest ocean. As if some sublime power had cut the waters open and set aside a dry, dark place for him to walk in, unmolested by the contained pressure of the flood.

He was old, but not so old that such an idea couldn't touch him with the feeling of older myth. It warmed his dying bones somehow. Not a thrill as such, but a powerful reassurance. To be in tune with such an ancestral legend.

The Inner Place was silent, except for the distant chiming of a prayer bell. And beyond that, a muffled clamour, far away, like an eternally restless god, or the rumble of a deep, primeval star.

With long, fragile fingers, freed from the mesh-armoured glove which swung from his wrist-guard by its leather loop and the energy coupler, the Old One traced the gold symbols inscribed on the green stone of the lower walls. He closed his real eyes, dry rheumy lids shutting tight like walnut shells, and the auto-sensitive iris shutters of his helmet optics closed in synch.

Another old tale remembered itself to him. Back, before the stars were crossed, when his kind only knew one world, and knew the star and the kindred worlds that revolved around it only through the astronomical lenses they trained at the sky. Then, as the weight of years swung by, slow and heavy as the slide of continents, and their abilities grew, they slowly learned of other stars, other worlds, a galaxy. And they realised they were not one and alone but one amongst countless others. And those other lights beckoned and, as they were able to, they fled to them.

So it seemed now, an echo. The Old One had been alone for a long while, conscious only of the few lives that orbited his in the Inner Place, the lives of his devoted kin. Then, in the outer blackness, other lights began to emerge and reveal themselves to his mind. A few at first, then dozens, thousands, legions.

The Old One's mind was a fearfully powerful apparatus. As hundreds of thousands of life-lights slowly appeared and began to congregate on this place, it seemed to him as if whole constellations were forming and becoming real. And so many of those life-lights were dark and foul.

Time was against him and his kind. He despised the urgency, because haste was one thing his long, careful life had previously been free of. But now there was precious little time left. A heartbeat by his measuring. And he would have to use every last pulse of it to achieve his purpose.

Already his mind had set things in motion. Already, he had shaken out his dreams and let his rich imagination drape across the place like a cloak. Simple deceits, such as would normally beguile the lesser brains of other races, had already been set in motion.

They would not be enough.

The Old One sighed. It had come to this. A sacrifice, one that he knew would one day punctuate his long life. Perhaps it had been the very reason for his birth.

He was ready. At least it would, in its turn, make a new legend.

UNDER THE THICK, wet trees and creeper growth, Third platoon skirted the ditches and mud-banks of the glades, moving ever nearer to the thunder-war in the west. Dawn was now on them and light lanced down through the canopy in cold, stale beams.

Third platoon; Rawne's. They'd had Larkin seconded to them from Corbec's unit because Rawne's sniper was busy heaving his fever-ridden guts into a tin bucket in the infirmary. Blood-flies, and tiny biting insects that swirled like dust, had begun to spread disease and infection through the ranks. Dorden had been braced for wounded, but what he had got, suddenly in the last day and night, were the sick.

Milo was with Rawne's platoon too. The boy wasn't sure who hated his presence there most, Rawne or Milo himself. Just before deployment, Gaunt had taken Milo to one side and instructed him to accompany the major's advance.

'If anyone's going to benefit from your rousing pipes, it's going to be the Third,' the commissar had said. 'If any section is going to break, it's going to be them. I want you there to urge them on – or at least vox me if they falter.'

Milo would have refused but for the look in Gaunt's eyes. This was a trust thing, a subtle command responsibility. Gaunt was entrusting him to watch the Third from the inside. Besides, he had his lasgun now, and his shoulder pip, and Rawne's sniper wasn't the only man in the Third to fall sick.

'Keep up!' Feygor hissed to Milo as they crept through the weeds. Milo nodded, biting back a curse. He knew he was moving more swiftly and silently than many in Rawne's platoon. He knew too that he had fastened his webbing and applied his camo-paint better than any of them. Colm Corbec had taken time to teach him well.

But he also knew he wasn't an outsider any more, a boy piper, a mascot. He was a Ghost, and as such he would obey the letter of his superiors. Even if they were dangerous, treacherous men.

With Rawne's scout Logris in the vanguard, the ten men filed through the glades and thickets of the Monthax jungle. Milo found himself behind Caffran, the only trooper in the platoon who he liked. Or trusted.

Rawne paused them in a basin of weed and silt-muck which stank of ripe vegetation while Logris and Feygor edged ahead. Tiny flies swirled like dust over the soup.

Caffran, his face striped with camo-paint, turned to Milo and gently adjusted the straps of the lad's weapon, like a big brother looking after a younger sibling.

'You've seen action, though, haven't you?' Caffran whispered. 'This is nothing new.'

Milo shrugged. 'Yes, but not like this. Not as a trooper.'

Caffran smiled. 'You'll be fine.'

Across the silky water, Larkin watched them from his position curled into the root network of a mangrove. He knew that Caffran and the piper boy had never been friends before now. He had heard Caffran talk of it. Though little more than two years separated them, Caffran felt uneasy around the lad, because he reminded him too much of home. Now that seemed to be forgotten and Larkin was glad. It seemed having Milo in his company had given Caffran purpose. A novice, a little brother, someone junior to the youngest Ghost that Caffran could take care of.

Caffran felt it too. He no longer despised Brin Milo. Trooper Milo was one of them now. It was like… it was like they were back home. Caffran couldn't understand why he had shunned the boy so. They were all in this together. All Tanith, after all. And besides, if Gaunt had seen fit to protect Milo all this time, Caffran was damned if anything would happen to the boy.

Rawne waited at the ditch edge for Logris and Feygor. His eyes were fierce diamonds of white with hard, dark centres, flashing from the band of camo-paint across his face. There was something terribly familiar about their situation. He could feel it in his marrow. Soon there would be killing.

SPOONBILLS FLAPPED BY. Mkoll turned to Domor and slung his weapon.

'Sir?' Domor asked quietly.

'Take them forward, Domor,' Mkoll said.

'Me?'

'You're up to it?'

Domor shrugged a 'yes', the focussing rings of his bionic eyes whirring as they tried to manufacture the quizzical expression his real eyes would have wanted.

'I need to move ahead. Scout. I can only do that alone. You bring the Ninth up after me.'

'But–'

'Gaunt won't mind. I've spoken to him.' Mkoll tapped the ear-piece of his micro-bead intercom twice and softly told the rest of his platoon that Domor was now in charge. 'Follow him like you would me,' he urged them.

He looked back at Domor. 'This is important. It may be the life or death of us. Okay?'

Domor nodded. 'For Tanith.'

'For Tanith, like it's still alive.'

Mkoll was gone an instant later, vanishing into the brooding, puffy, waterlogged vegetation like a rumour.

'Form on me and renew advance,' Domor whispered into his bead, and Ninth platoon formed and renewed.

UNDER THE SHADE of great, oil-sweet trees, Corbec's platoon, the Second, moved into the mire and the glades. The colonel missed Larkin, but his squad already had the crack-shot Merrt, so it would have been churlish to complain.

Feth, Corbec was thinking, all this time driven mad by Larks's babbling and scaremongering, and now I actually wish he was here.

Ahead, the glades widened into a lagoon. The still water was coated with russet weed, and black, rotten wood limbs and roots poked up out of it. Corbec motioned the Second on behind him, the thigh-deep water leaving a greasy film on his fatigues. He raised his gun higher.

'Up there!' Merrt breathed through the intercom. Along the far end of the lagoon, Corbec could see shapes: moving figures.

'Ours?' Merrt asked.

'Only Varl could be dumb enough to bring his platoon in front of ours, and he's on the eastern limit. No. Let's go.'

Corbec raised his gun to firing position, heard nine other safeties hum off. *'For Tanith! For the Emperor! For us!'* he bellowed.

Las-fire volleyed across the water of the lagoon and figures at the far end fell. Some dropped into the water, face down; others knelt for cover in the tree roots of the bank and returned fire. Laser shots echoed and returned across the water course. The lowest bolts cut furrows as they flew across the water. Others steamed as they hit the liquid or exploded sodden, decomposing bark.

Others hit flesh, or cut through armour, and figures tumbled down the far bank, sliding into the water or being arrested by root systems. Merrt made three priceless head shots before a stray return took him in the mouth and he dropped, face down and gurgling, into the ooze of the lagoon.

Corbec bellowed into his vox-bead that contact had been made and that he was engaging. Then he set his lasgun for full auto-fire and ploughed into the water, his finger clenching the trigger.

One for Merrt. Two. Three. Four. Not enough. Not even *half* enough.

'Second platoon has engaged!' Comms-Officer Raglon reported quickly to Gaunt.

'Ahead now!' Gaunt ordered, urging the men of First forward through the shin-deep water along the glade bed. His chainsword was in his hand and purring. They could hear the close shooting, harsher and more immediate than the distant thunder of the mysterious war they were approaching: Corbec's platoon, fighting and firing. But the source was unspecified, remote. Gaunt damned the thickness and false echoes of the glades. Why was this place so impossibly confused?

Las-fire spat across the glades at the First platoon. Lowen fell, cut through and smouldering. Raglon went down too, a glancing burn to his cheek. Gaunt hauled the vox-caster man to his feet and threw him into cover behind a thick root branch.

'All right?'

'I'll live,' returned the comms-officer, dabbing the bloody, scorched weal along the side of his face with a medicine swab.

The enemy fire was too heavy to charge against. Gaunt fell his platoon into cover and they began to return fire with drilled, careful precision. They loosed their las-rounds down the funnel of the glade, and the salvos that came back at them were loose and unfocused. Gaunt could see the position of the enemy from their muzzle flashes. They were badly placed and poorly spaced.

He ordered his men up, searching for a rousing command. None came but for: '*First platoon… like you're the First and Only! Kill them!*'

It would do. *It would do.*


THIRD PLATOON froze, half at a hand gesture from Rawne, half at the sudden sounds of fighting from elsewhere in the glades. They settled in low, in the dark green shadows of the canopy, white eyes staring up from dark camo-paint at every ripple of sound. Feygor wiped a trickle of sweat off his cheek. Larkin tracked around with his custom rifle, hunting the trees around them with his night-scope. Wheln chewed at his lower lip, eyes darting. Caffran was poised like a statue, gun ready.

'To the left,' Rawne hissed, indicating with a finger. 'Fighting there. No further than two hundred metres.'

Just behind him, Milo jerked a thumb off to the right. 'And to the right, sir. A little further off.' His voice was a whisper.

Feygor was about to silence the impudence with a fist, but Rawne raised a hand and nodded, listening. 'Sharp ears, boy.

He's right. The echoes are confusing, but there is a second engagement.'

'All around us, then... What about our turn?' Feygor breathed.

Rawne could feel Feygor's itching impatience. The waiting, the fething anticipation, was often harder than the fighting itself.

'We'll find our fight soon enough.' Rawne slid out his silver dagger – given to him by Gaunt, Emperor damn his soul! – the blade dulled with fire-soot, and clipped it into the lugs under his lasgun's muzzle. His men fixed their own knives as bayonets in response.

'Let's keep the quiet and the surprise as long as we have it,' Rawne told them, and raised them to move on.

THERE WAS THE sound of water, drizzling. The spitting noise almost blocked out the muffled fighting elsewhere. But not the distant heavy bombardment of the duelling armour.

Mkoll followed a lip of rocks, slick with black lichen, around the edge of a pool in deep shadow. A skein of water fell from a mossy outcrop thirty metres above, frothing the plunge pool. It was as humid and dark as a summer night in this dim place.

Mkoll heard movement, a skittering of rocks high above at the top of the falls. Cover was scant, so without hesitation he slid off the lip of stone into the water, sinking down to his neck, his lasgun held up in one hand at ear level, just above the surface. With fluid precision, he glided under the shadow of the rock, moving behind the churning froth of the cataract.

Shadows moved along the top of the rock above him. Fifteen, perhaps twenty warriors. He caught their scent: the spicy, foul reek of something barely human. He heard low, clipped voices crackle back and forth via helmet intercoms, speaking a language that he was thankful he could not understand.

Mkoll felt his guts vice involuntarily. It wasn't fear of the enemy, or of death; it was fear of what the enemy was. Their nature. Their *abomination*.

The water seemed glass-cold around him. His limbs were deadening. But hot sweat leaked down his face. Then they were gone.

Mkoll waited a full two minutes until he was sure. Then he crawled up out of the water and padded off silently in the direction from which his enemy had come.

SEVENTH PLATOON CAME out of a deep grove into sudden sunlight and even more sudden gunfire. Three of Sergeant Lerod's men were down before he had time to order form and counter. Enemy fire stripped the trees all around, pulverising bark and foliage into sap mist and splinters. The enemy had at least two stub guns and a dozen las-weapons in cover on the far side of the narrow creek.

Lerod bellowed orders in the whistling flashes of the exchange, moving backwards and firing from the hip on auto. Two of his men had made good cover and were returning hard. Others fought for places with him. Targin, the vox-operator, was hit twice in the back and fell sideways, his twitching corpse held upright, like a puppet, in a drapery of moss-creepers.

A las-round stung Lerod's thigh. He knelt helplessly, then dropped to his belly in desperation, blasting up into the trees. His wild fire hit something – a weapon power-pack, perhaps – and a seething sheet of flame rushed out of the far creek bank, stripping and felling trees and tossing out two blackened bodies which cartwheeled in the air and fell into the creek bed. Pin-pointing Lerod as the source of this little victory, the unseen stubbers traversed and sent stitching lines of firepower down the earth trail where he sprawled.

He saw them in a split second: the twin lines of ferocious tracers etching their way across the loam to slice him into the ground. There was nothing he could do... no time. He closed his eyes.

Lerod opened them again. By some miracle, both lines of fire had missed him, passing either side of his prone form.

He began to laugh at the craziness of it and rolled into the cover of trees a few metres to the left, exhorting his surviving company with renewed vigour to give back and give hard. He felt jubilant, like he had on the Founding Fields below Tanith Magna, before the Loss. He had never thought he would have that feeling again.

WITH BITTER RESENTMENT, Corbec pulled the Second back from the lagoon where they were stymied. They were outgunned and partly circled. The Tanith fell back quickly and silently into the trees, leaving tripwires and tube rounds in their wake.

A quick vox-exchange brought the Second round alongside the First platoon and Gaunt himself, holding the line of a wide creek.

'Thick as flies!' Corbec yelled to Gaunt as his men reinforced the First. 'Big numbers of them, determined too!'

Gaunt nodded, directing his men forward a metre at a time trying to out-mark and topple the enemy possession of the far bank.

Explosions crackled through the trees in the direction of Corbec's retreat as the advancing foe tripped the first of the mines. Gaunt cursed. This terrain was meant to give the Ghosts the advantage with their stealth skills, but the enemy was everywhere, as if milling and confused. And though that meant they were not working to a cohesive plan, it also meant the larger enemy force was splintered, unpredictable and all around them.

Raglon was firing from cover and Gaunt ducked in behind him, waving Corbec over. Corbec sprinted across the open ground, his tunic and face splattered with pulverised leaf flecks and sap. He looked like the Old Man of the Woods in the traditional Feast of Leaves, back home on Tanith, whe–

Gaunt froze, startled and confused. *Back home on Tanith?* What tricks was his mind playing now? He'd never heard of any Feast of the Leaves, yet it had seemed to bob up from his memory as a truth. For a moment, he could even smell the sugared nal-fruit as they roasted in their charcoal ovens.

'What's up, sir?' Corbec asked, trying to squeeze his bulk into the scant cover as las-rounds whipped around them.

Gaunt shook his head. 'Nothing.' He pulled his data-slate from the pocket of his leather coat and plugged the short lead into the socket at the base of the vox-link on Raglon's back. Then he tapped his clearance into the small board of rune-marked keys, and main battle-data began to display on his slate, direct from General Thoth's Leviathan command base. Gaunt selected an overall tactical view so he and Corbec could take in the state of the battle.

The Tanith were shown as a thin, vulnerable line, static and held along the main watercourse. To either side of them, heavier regiments and armoured units were making greater headway, but these too were slow and foundering. The Volpone were pushing from the east, with massive artillery support, but the Trynai Sixth and Sixteenth were pinned down and slowly being slaughtered.

'Feth, but it's bad…' Corbec muttered. 'This whole push is grinding to a halt.'

'We'll have to see if we can improve matters,' Gaunt returned, solemn and occupied. He wound the dial to bring up a specific display of the Ghosts' struggling advance. All of the platoons were essentially halted and most engaged in heavy fire. Lerod's unit was taking the brunt of it. Rawne's, Gaunt noticed, had so far failed to engage.

'Have they got the luck?' Corbec asked.

'Or are they not trying?' Gaunt said aloud.

THE THIRD EDGED on, passing a deep hidden pool with a glittering waterfall that fell from a crop of mossy rock. Rawne split his platoon and moved them up either side of the water.

Feygor stooped to pick up something and showed it to the major. It was a cell from a lasgun, but not Imperial issue.

'They've been through here.'

'And we've missed them!' Rawne cursed. 'Feth take this bastard jungle! We're in amongst them and we can't see them!'

On the far side of the pool, Milo paused and turned to Caffran. 'Smell that?' he whispered.

Caffran frowned. 'Mud? Filthy water? Pollen?'

'This jungle doesn't smell like it did before. I can almost smell… nal-wood.' Milo rubbed his own nose, as if he distrusted it.

*Dan Abnett*

Caffran was about to laugh, but then realised that he smelled it too. It was astonishing, almost overwhelming in its nostalgia. The air indeed smelt of the rich conifers of Tanith. Now he thought about it, the trees and foliage around them seemed darker, much more like the wet-land forests of his lost homeworld. Nothing like the stinking, seething jungle they had known since arriving on Monthax.

'This is crazy,' he said, reaching out and touching one of the familiar trees.

Milo nodded. It was crazy – and scary too.

FROM THE COVER of some low, flowering bushes, busy with insects, Mkoll could see a clearing ahead. There had been brief, heavy fighting there not more than two hours before. The earth was churned up, trees burned back and splintered. Bodies smouldered on the ground.

He crept forward to look. The dead were Chaos soldiery, heavily armed and armoured in quilted red fatigues and bare steel armoured sections. Their helmets were inscribed with such horrific symbols and figures he began to dry-heave until he looked away.

Others had fallen here too, but their bodies had been removed. No Imperial unit had got this far in. There was another force at play on Monthax. Mkoll looked at the wounds on the fallen. Here and there, a helmet or metal breast-plate had been punctured, not by an energy round or explosive shell, but by something sharp and clean which had punched right through composite metal. In a tree stump behind one corpse, Mkoll found a missile embedded, a wickedly sharp metal star with razor-edged points.

WITH A LONG, slow sigh that wheezed out of his helmet's mouthpiece, the Old One sat back on the stone seat at the centre of the Inner Place.

Like a spider at the heart of a complex web, he reached out mentally and tested the strands of his net of deceit, the cloak of confusion he had spread out around him, leagues in every direction. It was serving its purpose for now. He studied the minds caught in his net: so very many of them cruel and brutish and overflowing with the poison of Chaos. And the others, the brief human sparks. The Imperials had engaged too, he realised, coming in to try their strength against the forces of Chaos as they moved. He saw bloody fighting. He saw primitive courage.

Humans always surprised him that way. Such little life-spans, so furiously exhausted. Their valour would be almost admirable if it wasn't so futile.

Yet perhaps he could use that. To make allies was out of the question, but he could use all the time he could buy, and these determined Imperial humans, with their relentless urge to fight and win, could help him in that.

It was past time for him to play his last hand. He would work the humans, for what little good they could do, into that gambit. A final check now.

Muon Nol, Dire Avenger, master of the bodyguard, entered the Inner Place at the Old One's mental summons. He held his great white-crested helm under one arm, the red plume crest perfect and trim, and his opalescent blue armour glittered with flecks of gold, like the heart of a cooling star. The braided tassels of his cape hung down to his waist, shrouding the weapons cinched tight to his back. His noble, ancient eyes studied the Old One. There was fatigue in his long, solemn face.

'Muon Nol: how goes the work?'

'The Way is open, lord.'

'And it must be closed. How much longer?'

Muon Nol looked down at the smooth stone floor where the shimmer of his blue armoured form was reflected. 'All but the bodyguard have departed, lord. The Closing of the Way has now begun. It will be a little time yet before we are finished.'

'A little time for us, perhaps, Muon Nol. Not for the enemy. More than long enough for them, I fear. There is no time for proper closure now. We must sever.'

'Lord!'

The Old One held up his hand, the one that was bare of a glove. The sight of those ancient fingers, almost translucent with wasting age, silenced Muon Nol's protests.

'It is not the way we wished it, Muon Nol. But it is all we can do now. Dolthe must be protected. I will now do as I told you and commit my final reserves to the last delaying tactics.'

Muon Nol dropped to his knees before the seated figure and lowered his head. 'But that it should come to this, Lord Eon Kull!'

Eon Kull, the Old One, sat back with a half-smile. 'I am this Way, Muon Nol. It has been my charge and duty all these measures of time. It and I are as one. If it must be shut now forever – and it must – it is only right that the book of my life shuts with it. It is appropriate and necessary. I do not see it as a failure or a loss. Neither should you. Lord Eon Kull closes his Way for the last time, for all time. Lord Eon Kull will pass away with it.'

Muon Nol raised his head. Were those tears in his dark eyes? Eon Kull considered that perhaps tears from his most faithful warrior were not out of place.

'Leave me now. Tell your guard to brace themselves for the mind-trauma. I will call you again when it is done, so that we may say farewell.'

The master of the bodyguard rose and began to turn.

'Muon Nol?'

'Lord?'

Eon Kull, the Old One, lifted his weapon from the rim of the stone seat. The dim light shone from the long, smooth barrel of the buanna, and twinkled on the inlay at the grip and shoulder guard. Uliowye, the Kiss of Sharp Stars. The weapon of a champion, precious and celebrated. In Eon Kull's hands, it had won fabulous victories for Dolthe.

'Take this. Stand your place when the time comes and use it well.'

'Uliowye… I cannot, lord! She has always been yours!'

'Then she is mine to *give*, Muon Nol! Uliowye will not be happy to sleep through this great passing. She must kiss the foe at least once more.'

Muon Nol took the old shrieker cannon reverently. 'She will not go silently, high lord. You do me a great honour.'

Eon Kull nodded and said no more, shushing Muon Nol away and out of the Inner Place. The Old One sat for a while longer, thinking of nothing but the silence to come. Then his mind woke again to the noisy hosts outside the walls, the minds milling and fighting and killing and dying in the deep jungle of Monthax around him.

Eon Kull rose and stepped down off the throne. He knelt on the cool floor of the Inner Place and unclasped the decorated purse at his belt. The contents clacked together. Eon Kull the warlock spilled them out onto the flagstones. Slivers of bone, each inscribed with a rune of power. Though this was a dim place, they shone like ice in the noon sun and he observed their pattern. Slowly, with his bare fingers, he slid them around, forming intricate conjunctions, pairing some slivers, placing other runes alone or in small piles. The arrangement was quite precise.

Eon Kull tensed as he felt the raw moaning of the warp. The psycho-reactive runes gave him access to the unbridled power of the warp-spaces, acting as keys to open the locks of his powerful mind to the warp outside.

He started to draw and channel the force of the warp through the rune keys. They began to glow more brilliantly now, humming with energy. His mind began to struggle. He had never attempted to channel such levels of power before.

No, that wasn't true. In his youth, as he began upon the Witch Path, he had performed great feats, and then with fewer runes. He had added to his knowledge and technique over the centuries, but he was not young any more. It took more out of him now to harness the power. In sympathy, the spirit stones inset on his rune-armour flickered, as did dozens of others ranged at the side of his throne. Waking from their eternal slumber at his bidding, the souls of other seers and warlocks, long flesh-dead, conjoined with him to guide him and strengthen his power.

A few of the older and more surly spirits chided him for attempting so great a deed. Others aided him unequivocally, and soothed the complaints of their fellow spirits. The cause was simple and pure: Dolthe. Dolthe must persist, and Eon Kull was right to try the limit of his powers to make it so.

A noise from behind almost distracted him. But it was Fuehain Falchior, tasting battle, twitching in her wraithbone rack.

'Be still, witchblade,' Eon Kull murmured and turned his full attention back to the deed.

Now the runes glowed more brightly still. Some quivered on the floor, rattling as if disturbed by seismic shaking. The spirit stones flickered and pulsed. Eon Kull looked into the warp and the warp poured into him. He germinated power, a racing, fecund rhythm.

His bare hand clasped like a claw. Veins stood out on his wrist. Now the pain welled inside him. Watery blood dribbled from his nose.

Despite the pain, he laughed to himself. No matter how strange, how bittersweet, there would be victory in this. Or at least, for Dolthe and his kind, he hoped that there would.

THE SKY OVER that section of the Monthax glade-wilderness buckled and exploded. Blinding forks of lightning blinked downwards in a hundred places out of a heaven that had previously been clear and sultry blue. Stands of trees exploded under the electrical hammerblows. Several armoured vehicles in the Imperial vanguard were struck and destroyed. A Volpone Hellhound, struck by ball-lightning, went up like a torch as its huge fuel reserves were touched off. At another place, on a creek bed, fourteen Basilisk self-propelled guns, their long barrels raised to the sky ready for bombardment, became lightning conductors. Electrocuted, the gun-crews danced and jerked, or melted onto the white-hot hulls for ten seconds before the combined munitions blew a square kilometre of the jungle into the sky in a column of superheated energy and debris.

The blast shook the hulking, hundred-metre-high Imperial command Leviathan stationed sixteen kilometres back and threw the bridge crew to the deck. General Thoth leapt up as his multiple screens and main holographic display fizzled and went out. He yelled frantic orders into the darkness.

Rain sheeted down on top of the lightning, walls of cold, unseasonable downpour which demolished the ripe foliage of the upper tree cover and the moss-vines, and shredded trunks back to the heartwood. Drenched, the Imperial forces fell back blind into watercourses suddenly swollen by rich, red tides of floodwater, the battle forgotten.

Varl's platoon fell into cover under rocks, praying and gasping in the icy rain. Vox-lines were broken and no one could see more than a metre in any direction.

Fear tightened its grip on the Imperium forces. The enemy were lost in the storm all along the war-front. Chaos artillery persisted in firing, but their blasts and recoils seemed pathetic next to the elemental commotion. Guardsmen spoke of a Chaos-summoned witch-storm.

Lerod's platoon, what was left of it, ran back through the drumming rain, blind and almost grateful for the chance to break the impasse.

Half of Domor's platoon were carried away down a flash-flooding waterway. Two drowned.

Then, amidst the rain, came hail like fists. This fell on the west, breaking bones and killing nineteen men outright in the Volpone phalanx. The hail was so hard it dented tank armour.

Suddenly up to their knees in rushing, liquid mud, First and Second platoons of the Tanith backed from the breaching lagoon, Gaunt leading the way, gripping saplings and vines to stay upright. Corbec chased the stragglers, half-carrying Trooper Melk who had lost a knee.

'What in the name of Feth is this?' Gaunt screamed into the rain.

No one had an answer. Witchery, they all thought.

Typhoon-force winds surged in along the edges of the storm. Imperial air-cover was pulled out and grounded, but not before two Marauders had been torn out of the air and smashed. One, its stabilisers gone and its thrusters screaming, managed to turn its death into a pyrrhic victory by taking out a line of Chaos tanks gummed down in a clearing which had abruptly become a lake. The vast, multiple explosions were lost in the roar of the storm.

Caught in a sudden flash flood, stunned by the force of the hail and rain, Mkoll clung on to a nearly uprooted mangrove to stop himself being carried off. Blinking water from his eyes, he saw his lasgun ride away in the leaf-choked froth. He felt the loss acutely. He had been so careful and protective of that simple, standard-issue gun. There was none better kept, better cared for, or cleaner in the Tanith regiment. Now it spun away from him, ruined, swamped. But he had his life still – for as long as the roots would hold.

Rawne pushed Third platoon forward through the deluge. Their hair and uniforms were plastered to their pale skins. Some edifice rose ahead, a structure of stone raised from fashioned blocks. To Rawne, it seemed almost familiar. His urgent commands were lost in the hurricane winds.

A snapped off branch whickered through the gale and the near-horizontal downpour and struck Trooper Logris in the throat. Milo tried to help him but it was too late. His neck was broken and his head lolled around the wrong way. Already, his crumpled body was being sucked down into the swelling mud by the hideous rain.

Caffran grabbed Milo and dragged him through the storm of wind and rain and flurrying leaves into the cover of the stone ruin. Rawne yanked them in to join the other members of his platoon: Feygor, Cown, Wheln, Mkendrik, Larkin, Cheffers. But Cheffers was dead. There was no sign of injury on him until Cown spotted the blood oozing from a slit in his throat. Something protruded from it. It was a leaf. Carried point-first by the stabbing wind, the stiff leaf had punctured Cheffers's throat and cut his windpipe.

Horrified, with the wind and rain wailing against the stone block at their backs, they saw how their tunics and cloaks had been torn and sliced by other such leaf missiles.

'What kind of storm is this?' Caffran howled over the roar.

'And where the feth did it come from so suddenly?' Feygor bawled.

Rawne didn't know. Everything had been going smoothly until then. The mustering on the Founding Fields. The preparation for disembarkment. And now a storm like nothing he'd seen before had fallen on Tanith Magna.

'Bet your lives it's the work of the enemy!' he yelled to his men. 'A surprise attack to take Tanith from us! Ready your weapons!'

Every one of them responded, checking their lasguns.

Except Milo. 'Major – *what* did you just say?'

Rawne looked down at the boy. 'I know it's your first taste of battle, worm, but try to think like a trooper! You have only just mustered here, wet behind the ears from the Magna province farms, but you're in for a fight!'

Milo blinked. The roar of the storm just outside the stone blocks sheltering them seemed to have left him concussed. Rawne and the others had gone mad. *This wasn't Tanith! They were acting like it was the homeworld and–*

He stopped. The stone wall in front of him was a solid section of Tanith basalt, mined from the quarries at Pryze Junction. The crest of the Elector was inscribed into it. He knew this place... a side corridor just off the main western fortification of the capital city. But–

For a moment, Milo faltered. He could remember something. A dying world, a small brotherhood of survivors... ghosts... playing the pipes to urge them on.

Just a dream. Just a bad dream, he realised. They were mustering at the Foundation of the Tanith regiments and Chaos had attacked their homeworld. They had no choice. Stand and fight, or die. And if they died, Tanith would die with them.

THE STORM, a spinning electrical disk of clouded black fury sixty kilometres in diameter, held its position unerringly above the battle front. Its power and force were so great, even the mighty cogitators of the hexathedral *Sanctity*, high in orbit, couldn't compute its magnitude or penetrate the dome of blistering interference it created. Any Imperial forces that still had a measure of mobility, those that had not been swept away or mired, began to pull back to their lines, making what headway they could in the appalling conditions. Many units, most of them armour and heavy fighting vehicles, were cut off or swamped, helpless and detached from the main retreat.

No one, not even General Thoth's chief tacticians, could begin to guess the state, response or position of the foe they were meant to be engaging. Had they broken too? Were they just as lost, or had all of them been obliterated by the hurricane? Or was this their doing?

Many of the Imperial veterans and officers had seen psychic storms before, a favoured terror-weapon of the Chaotic foe. But this was not the same. There was no pestilential quality to it, no reek of unholy filth, no heaviness in the air that made skin crawl and bowels churn and minds spin into waking nightmares.

Just titanic fury. Almost pure, elemental power. A null. Yet, if they could read it, the warp was there. The unmistakable flavour of the warp.

Inquisitor Lilith had no doubts at all. Her attuned senses had no trouble in detecting the cold psyker power galvanising the deluge. Indeed, it was all she could do to shut it out and stop it howling and screaming through her mind. The rumours of psyker-witchery said to haunt this world were true, but this witchery had a power and clarity like none she had ever felt.

She strode through the downpour in a long cape of dripping black leather, her cowl pulled up. She stared fixedly at the storm which boiled in the sky two leagues or so from her position. Her honour guard escort marched in her train. She could feel their nervousness and unwillingness to proceed into an area all other right-minded Guard units were fleeing from. But Lord Militant General Bulledin had appointed them to serve Lilith as she prosecuted this event, and they feared the Lord Militant and the inquisitor more than any storm.

The escort was thirty troopers from the Royal Volpone 50th, the Bluebloods. They wore the grey and gold body armour and low-brimmed bowl helmets of the Volpone, with wet-weather oilskins draped lankly over their torsos. Their shoulders and arms were massive with segmented carapace armour, and they were each armed with a matt-black hellgun fresh from the weapon shops of Leipaldo. Each man had a bright indigo Imperial Eagle stud pinned into his armaplas collar section, marking them all as from the Volpone Tenth Brigade, the elite veteran force. Only the best of the best for an Imperial inquisitor. With them came a shrouded astropath, one of Lilith's own staff. He jerked and staggered at every twitch of the storm, and was given a wide berth by the Volpone soldiers.

The detail commander, Major Gilbear, fell in step with the inquisitor. His face was set grimly, but he projected a sickening sense of pompous pride at taking this duty. Lilith could barely shut that out either.

'Can you outline our purpose and approach, my lady inquisitor?' Gilbear asked, using the formal aristocratic dialect of the highest Imperial courts. It was partly to impress her, Lilith knew, and partly to establish his own self-importance. The huge Volpone clearly wanted to show he believed himself to be more than a common soldier. As if they were... equals...

'I'll let you know when I decide, major,' she replied in the blunt and crude low-Gothic of the common soldiery. An insult, she knew, but one that might make him quit his airs and graces. She hadn't time to be bothered with him right now.

He nodded curtly, and she smiled at the throb of bitten-down anger he radiated.

They crossed a foaming waterbed, shallow, but fast running, where a dozen Chimeras of the Roane Deepers were struggling to dig themselves out. Agitated, spooked troopers milled around, shouting, cursing and heaving on stripped tree trunks to lever out clogged track units. Fine drizzle from the edge of the storm whipped across them, creating a billion impact ripples in the water.

On the far side, the inquisitor's party followed the bank in towards the edge of the storm. There was debris in the spraying water here: shreds of equipment, helmets, pieces of foliage, drowned bodies, all swirling downstream in the flood.

Inquisitor Lilith called a halt in a clearing where vast decid-uous trees had been reduced to blackened columns by lightning strikes. A raft of wood pulp and leaves sloshed and ebbed over the swamped ground. She pulled out her data-slate and reviewed it. It showed the positions of all the Imperial forces, each individual unit, as last recorded before the storm came down. A complex data-mosaic of thousands of individual components, one that would take a trained tactician hours to assess. But she had already located the one element which interested her: the Third platoon of the First-and-Only Tanith.

MKOLL MADE IT to higher ground, the rain and wind pelting him. The sky was black, and it was as dark as night, but his night-vision couldn't adjust because of the frequent blinding flashes of lightning which strobed across him. He was all but deaf with the near-constant thunder. In places, mud-slides had brought parts of the high ground slope down, and more than once he was almost carried off his feet as thick, slimy folds of mud came loose and oozed away down the incline. He glimpsed something in the next lightning flash that made him stop in his tracks, and he waited for the next searing discharge to confirm what he had seen.

The ruin. The ruin he had glimpsed on patrol before and had spent so long trying to find once more. He wouldn't lose it again. Mkoll stayed put and waited through the next three or four flashes, memorising the elements of the landscape, both near and far, as it was revealed to him in split-second snapshots.

In the last flash, he saw the movement too.

Enemy warriors, higher up the slope, stumbling across him in the deluge by chance. As the world went black again, they fired his way, cracking red lines in the darkness and the rain. Mkoll slid down onto his knees in the mud, trying to use the slope to give him as much cover as possible against the killers moving down the hill from above.

Another flash. They were closer. Six or more, most holding their weapons one-handed as they clung onto sagging saplings and outcrops of rock to keep themselves upright as they came down the incline. In the darkness, more red fire-bolts.

Mkoll pulled out his laspistol. He was blind, but the red flashes were a focus in the dark. He waited for more shots, then fired directly at the source of the blasts.

Then he scrambled to his left so they couldn't use the same trick on him.

His precaution was wise. The muddy ridge which had previously sheltered him was hit by four separate bursts of enemy fire. Boiled mud spattered up in lazy splashes. The tumultuous rain washed the steam away immediately.

More lightning. This brief gift of sight revealed to Mkoll the huge shape of a Chaos soldier almost on top of him. He'd either been trying to flank Mkoll's last position or been brought down the slick, treacherous slope faster than intended. They had almost collided.

Mkoll swung up his laspistol and shot him through the chest, point blank, before he could react. The enemy, a stinking dead-weight draped in loose chains and angular, rusty armour plates, slammed into Mkoll and flattened him back into the ooze. Locked under the corpse, Mkoll began to slide back down the mud-slope. He fought to get out from under the body and freed himself. Now he and the corpse slid down the hill more gently, head first, on their backs, side to side.

Mkoll swung over onto his knees, slipping down again twice before he properly righted himself. He was coated with mud and slime, though the slap of the rain washed it out of his eyes. He felt it had poured thickly into his ears too, because he was truly deaf now. Or had the detonations of the thunder finally burst his eardrums? Gunfire chased his way, hunting his last shot. He could see the red rips in the rain, but they were silent now. There was nothing but a low, constant grumble in his ears.

He got down next to the corpse. There was no sign of its main weapon, but an antique laspistol was hooked into its waistband. He pulled it out. It was longer, heavier and far more ornate than his simple, standard-pattern Guard pistol. The pear-shaped hand-grip was wrapped in fine chain and leather cord, and grotesque symbols were inlayed along the under-barrel furniture in pearl and silver. A yellow dot of light showed it was fully charged.

Blue light, harsh and electrical, shone over him. Phosphor flares, two first, then a third, trembled up into the sheeting rain over the hillside. Mkoll's eyes adjusted to the bright, flickering twilight. He could see the trees in stark black relief, the solid, blurring veil of the rain. He could see the enemy, nine or more, scrambling down the bank onto him, the closest twenty metres away.

And they could see him.

They opened fire. It was silent still, just that rumble like grinding teeth, but plumes of mud burst up from impacts around him, and scythed through the bole of a tree to his left, bringing the fifty metre tall trunk crashing down. Mkoll slid under it where the ground dipped, pulling himself through a gully full of rushing water. Emerging on the other side, with the fallen trunk as cover, he found sound had returned. The water had sluiced the sticky mud from his ears and the sides of his head. Noise rushed in at him: the thunder, the crack of shots, the clamouring voices like a baying pack of hounds.

Digging his heels into the soft ground for purchase, he swung up and leaned across the tree trunk, firing a pistol in each hand. The laser bolts from his regular gun were stark and white. Those from the captured weapon were dirty and red. He shot at the two attackers closest to him and dropped them straight off. One fell twisted, into a tangle of foliage. The other slid on his nose, spread-eagled, right down the slope and disappeared into the rushing water of the creek bed below.

Mkoll ducked down and crept along the length of the fallen trunk as return fire cremated and split the section he had been using for cover. Digging his feet in again, he popped up once more, and shot another enemy through the side of the head.

Two more were close on him, but a thick brake of trees baffled his aim. Shots tore at him. He blasted with his twin guns again, exploding the shoulder of an attacker flanking him to the left. A las-round exploded the trunk in front of him and he reeled back into shelter, sucking at the new splinters of wood slivered into his forearms and fingers.

Mkoll fought away the sharp, superficial pain. He began to crawl along under the block of the tree trunk again, but back towards his original position of cover to wrong-foot them. The next time he rose to bring his weapons to bear, three of the enemy soldiers had reached his last position and were clambering over the fallen log to blast down into the gully beyond. Firing down the length of the tree, Mkoll killed them all before they realised they were shooting at nothing. One toppled back and slid under the trunk, another fell across it and dropped into thick mud that sucked his corpse half-under. The third fell draped across the log.

The flares were dying and the strobe lighting of the storm was beginning to reassert itself.

Mkoll saw that dozens more of the enemy were advancing down the slope from above, and there were still four or five in his immediate field of fire.

He was running out of chances and options. He began to run, back down the length of the fallen log, then across the contour of the hill towards the ruin in the incline beyond. Shots chased him. He fell once – and it saved his life, as las-rounds cut the air that had, just a second before, been occupied by his head. He rolled down the bank, only partly voluntarily, then scrambled up again and ran on. More flares lit the sky. Silver light kissed the ground, the muddy slope and the curtain of rain. The trees became black fingers with multiple shadows.

Two enemy soldiers charged at him out of the spray, head on. One fired, his shots going wild. Mkoll's guns were still in his hands and he shot each one in the head as he ran between them. Behind the dead, three more. One managed to react fast enough to pull his trigger and Mkoll felt his neck recoil as something painfully hard and hot stung across his scalp. Blood streamed down his face. He wondered if he had been shot in the head, if his thoughts and motions were simply a nervous reaction carrying him forward past the point of death, his brain cooked backwards out of the exploded cup of his skull.

Whatever the truth, he wasn't going to stop. He shot the foe who had hit him with both pistols, then leapt the corpse, extending his guns out on either side to target the other pair. The leap was brave but foolish. Treacly mud took his feet away as he landed and his shots went wild. Tracking him as he leapt between them, the two soldiers of Chaos fired simultaneously and killed each other. Mkoll struggled up, laughing out loud at this little piece of Imperial justice. Then he stopped and holstered one of his guns, feeling his scalp with his freed hand. He fully expected to find a jagged edge of skull like a broken egg, but there was a just bloody gouge across the top of his head, and a section of his hair was crisped away. His cap had vanished. It had been a glancing wound. No doubt Rawne would have remarked upon the obstinate solidity of his skull.

He stumbled on towards the rise, needles of red light sweeping his trail. Outnumbered and outgunned, he realised it was time for the most drastic action.

Mkoll reached a tough-looking stump and lashed himself to it with his webbing. He took three tube-charges out of his thigh pouch, wound them tightly in a bunch with tape and hurled them back up the slope behind him.

Lightning broke at the same second the charges went off, washing out the flash and the roar. Then the entire hill-face squealed and fell away, a vast mud-slide that brought thousands of tonnes of liquid mud, rock and plants down, sweeping the enemy away with it into a soft tomb at the creek bed.

Waves of mud and liquid filth smashed into Mkoll; timbers carried down from higher up slammed into him. He choked and vomited on the fluid rush.

Then it was over. The storm blitzed on and the air was reeking with the pungent smell of freshly exposed soil. Mkoll was hanging from the tree stump by his webbing. The slide had washed away his footing and carried off several metres of topsoil, but the stump's deep roots had been more firmly bedded. It was one of the few things still standing proud of the smooth, sagging, crescent-shaped mud-slip.

Mkoll pulled off his webbing and dropped free. Nearby, the clawing hand of a buried foe warrior jerked and clawed up from the thick mud. Mkoll fired into the mud until the hand stopped twitching.

He made it to the next rise and looked down into the deep jungle cavity where the ruin sat, solemn and mysterious on a high mound. The second volley of flares were dying away now, but he knew what he saw.

The ruin was besieged by Chaos. Hundreds of thousands of enemy warriors, glistening and churning like beetles in the downpour, assaulted the great ruin from all sides.

They were relentless, ignoring the storm as if all that mattered was the jagged crown of stones at the top of the mound.

'What is that place?' Mkoll breathed aloud. 'What is it you want?'

Still shrieking and exploding overhead, the storm didn't answer him.

THE SKY SPASMED above them, stricken with electrical convulsions. First platoon, with the remnants of Corbec's unit and the stragglers of Lerod's who had joined them by accident in the storm's chaos, struggled on as they beat the retreat.

Gaunt came upon Corbec, who was clambering in the lead through the rain and the undergrowth. Trooper Melk was now on a stretcher carried in the rear of the retreat.

'What?' Gaunt gasped to his colonel, water streaming off his lean face.

'A river!' Corbec spat, surprised. Ahead of them, a thunderous torrent roared through the trees, foamy and deep and dangerously fast. It hadn't been there when they had come in. Gaunt stood, pummelled by the rain, and tried to make sense of the landscape in the flickering dark. He ordered Trooper Mktea forward and took one of his tube-charges. Corbec watched in disbelief as Gaunt taped it to the base of a massive ginkgo trunk and primed the fuse.

'Back!' Gaunt shouted.

The explosion cut the tree above the root and dropped its sixty-metre mass across the boiling tide: a bridge of sorts.

One by one, the men crawled across. Corbec led them to prove it could be done, cursing as each handhold slipped and tore away from the sodden bark. Trooper Vowl lost his grip and dropped from the horizontal log. The flash-flood carried him away like a cork. A screaming cork.

On the far side, Corbec saw to the defence of the position, ordering each drenched man fresh from the crossing into place, lasgun aimed, creating a wide dispersal of ready soldiers in a fan to protect those still crossing the timber bridge.

Corbec moved forward himself, into the horsetail ferns and hyacinths, their fronded leaves lashed and shaken by the drumming rain. There was movement ahead. He reported it via his micro-bead but got nothing back. The storm was playing merry hell with the vox-links. Clammy, cold hands tightening on his lasgun, Corbec inched forward.

A hellgun fired to his right, wide, a piercing distinctive report. He started forward and fell into the grip of three large figures which slammed into him out of the pulsing darkness. He lost his lasgun. A fist hit him in the back of the neck and he dropped, then recovered and punched out. One of his assailants went down in the mud. Another kicked at him and Corbec kicked back, breaking something crucial.

He was wrestling with the biggest of his opponents now, blind in the rain and the mud spray. Corbec got a glimpse of gold and grey carapace armour, an Imperial Eagle stud of precious blue. Underneath his rolling foe, he punched upwards into what should have been the face twice and then rolled his stunned aggressor over so that he was straddling him.

A flash of lightning. Corbec saw he was astride a Volpone Blueblood, a big man with a battered, bloodied face. A major. Corbec had his hands around the man's throat.

'What the feth?' he gasped. Hellgun muzzles were suddenly pressing to his head.

'You stinking bastard!' the major underneath him groaned venomously, trying to rise.

Corbec raised his hands in a gesture of surrender, wary of the guns around him. The major, released, threw Corbec back off him and rose, pulling out his hellpistol and aiming at Corbec's head.

'Don't,' said a voice, quiet yet more commanding than the thunder.

Gaunt stepped into the clearing, his bolt pistol aimed squarely at Major Gilbear's cranium. The Blueblood guns swung around to point at him but he didn't flinch.

'Now,' Gaunt added. His gun was unfaltering. Corbec looked up from the mud, lying on his back, conscious that the Blueblood major's gun was still pointed his way.

'Shoot him and I can assure you, Gilbear, you will be dead before any of your men can fire.' Gaunt's voice was low and threatening. Corbec knew that tone.

'Gaunt…' Gilbear murmured, not slackening his aim.

More Ghosts moved in around the commissar, guns aimed.

'Something of a stand-off,' Corbec muttered from the ground. Gilbear kicked him, his aim not leaving Corbec's head, his gaze not leaving Gaunt.

'Lower your weapon, Major Gilbear.' Inquisitor Lilith stepped into the glade, her cowl drawn up, a staccato roll of thunder eerily punctuating her words.

Gilbear wavered and then holstered his gun.

'Help Colonel Corbec to his feet,' Lilith added in the perfect, effete tones of the courtly dialect.

Gaunt's aim had not changed.

'And you, commissar. Put up your weapon.'

Gaunt lowered his bolt pistol.

'Inquisitor Lilith.'

'We meet again,' she said, turning away, a shrouded, sinister figure in the rain.

Gilbear held his hand down to Corbec and pulled him to his feet. Their eyes locked as Gilbear brought him up. Gilbear had the advantage of a few centimetres in height, and his broad shoulders, encased in the bulky carapace segments, eclipsed Corbec's shambling form, but the Tanith colonel had the benefit of sheer mass.

'No offence,' Gilbear hissed into Colm Corbec's face.

'None taken, Blueblood… until next time.'

Gaunt passed Gilbear as he approached Lilith, and the commissar and the major exchanged looks. Neither had forgotten Voltemand.

'Inquisitor Lilith,' Gaunt began, raising his voice over the cacophony of the storm, 'is this a chance encounter or have you sniffed me out with your psyker ways?'

She turned and looked at him, clear eyed. 'What do you think, Ibram?'

'What am I supposed to think, inquisitor?'

She half-smiled, rain pattering off her white skin. 'A psyker storm lights up the battle zone, aborting our assault against the foe.'

'You're not telling me anything I hadn't already noticed.'

'Where is your Third platoon?'

Gaunt shrugged. 'You tell me. Voxing has become impossible in this hell.'

She showed him the lit dial of her data-slate.

'They're right in there, as last reported. Tell me, don't you think it's significant?'

'What?'

'Milo… Oh, he answered my questions and wriggled out, but still, I wonder.'

'What do you wonder, inquisitor?'

'A boy suspected of psyker power, given rank by you, in the depth of this when it begins.'

'This is not Brin Milo's work.'

'Isn't it? How can you be sure?'

Gaunt was silent.

'What do you know of psykers, commissar? What do you know? Have you talked with them? Have you seen the way they blossom? A boy, a girl, barely in their teens, never having shown any spark of the craft, suddenly becoming all that we fear.'

Gaunt stayed quiet. He didn't like where this was going.

'I've seen it, Ibram. The sudden development of untrained powers, the sudden eruption of activity. You can't know for sure this isn't Milo's doing.'

'It isn't. I know it isn't.'

'We'll see. After all, that's what we are here to find out.'

RAWNE STARED DOWN from a slit window in the thick stonework, night rain and high winds lashing the outside. There were fires outside, but no longer the reassuring lines of cook fires on the Founding Fields. The sky had fallen. Doom had come to Tanith. If there had been any doubt, Rawne had seen warning flares rise and fall above the tree line not three minutes past.

Rawne clutched his freshly-issued lasgun to his chest. At least he would get to use it before he died.

'What's happening, sir?' Trooper Caffran asked. Rawne bit back the urge to yell at him. The boy was a novice. First taste of battle. And Rawne was the only officer present.

'Planetary assault. The enemy have fallen on us while we were still mustering.'

Others in the squad moaned.

'We're finished,' Larkin howled and Feygor disciplined him with a blow to his kidneys.

'Enough of that talk!' Rawne snapped. 'They'll not take Tanith without a fight from us! And we can't be the only unit inside the Elector's palace! We have a duty to protect the life of the Elector.'

The rest murmured and nodded. It was a desperate course, but it seemed right. They all felt it.

Feygor checked his intercom again. 'Nothing. The lines are dead. Must be scrambling us.'

'Keep trying. We have to locate the Elector and form a cohesive defence.'

Brin Milo's head was spinning. It all seemed so unreal, but he cautioned himself that was just shock at the speed of events.

It had been stressful enough to prepare to leave Tanith for ever. All the men had been edgy these last few days. Now... this nightmare.

That was what it was like. A nightmare. A twisting of reality where some things seemed blurred and others bright and over-sharp.

There was no time to settle his nerves or soothe it away. Gunfire and a gout of flame rushed down the stone hallway from behind them. The enemy had gained access to the palace.

Rawne's squad took cover-places along the wall and returned fire.

'For Tanith!' Rawne yelled. 'While it yet lives!'

EON KULL, the Old One, awoke with a start. He cried out, an animal bark of pain. He found himself lying on the polished stone floor of the Inner Place. For a moment, he did not remember who or what he was.

Then it trickled back, like sand through the waist of an hourpiece, a grain at a time. He had lost consciousness and lain here, undiscovered, in his delirium.

He could barely rise. His hands trembled; his limbs were as weak as a fildassai. Blood was clotting in his mouth and nose. He felt his beating organs and pumping lungs rustle and wheeze inside his ribs like dying birds in a cage.

He had to take stock. Had he been successful?

The spirit stones had all gone dark. Fuehain Falchior sat silent and still in her rack. The rune slivers were scattered across the floor as if someone had kicked over the arrangement. Some glowed red hot and smouldered like iron in a smelter. Others were wisps of curled ash.

Eon Kull Warlock gasped at the sight. He clawed at the runes, gathering up the fragments and the ash, burning his fingers. In the name of Vaul the Smithy-God, what had he wrought this day? What had he done? Attempted too much, that was certain. His age and his frailty had failed him, made him pass out and lose control, but surely for only a second or two. What had he unleashed? Sacred Asuryan, what had he done?

His exhausted mind sensed Muon Nol returning to the Inner Place. The warrior should not, would not see him like this. Eon Kull found strength from somewhere and hauled himself back into his throne, clasping the purse of ash and bone-cinders to his belt. Joints cracked like bolter shots and he felt blood rise in his gorge as his head span.

'Lord Eon Kull? Are you... well?'

'Fatigued, no more. How goes it?'

'Your... storm... it is a work of greatness. More fierce than I had imagined.'

Eon Kull frowned. What did Muon Nol mean? He couldn't show his ignorance to the warrior. He would have to reach out and see for himself. But his mind was so weak and spent.

'The Way must be closed now. The storm won't last forever.'

Muon Nol knelt on both knees and made the formal gesture of petition. 'Lord, I beseech you once more, for the last time, let us not abandon the Way here. Let me send to Dolthe for reinforcements. With exarchs, with the great Avatar itself, we can hold out and—'

Eon Kull bade him rise, shaking his helmeted head slowly. He was glad Muon Nol couldn't see the blood that tracked down his septum and over his dry lips. 'And I tell you, for the last time, it cannot be. Dolthe can spare no more for us. They are beset. Have you any idea of the scale of the foe here on Monthax?' Eon Kull leaned forward and touched Muon Nol's brow with his bared hand, sending a hesitant mental pulse that conveyed the unnumbered measure of the foe-host as he had sensed it. Muon Nol stiffened and shuddered. He looked away.

'Chaos must not take us. They must be denied access to the Webway. Our Way here must be closed now, as I have wished it.'

'I understand,' the warrior nodded.

'Go see to the final provisions. When all is ready, come and escort me to the High Place. That is where I will meet my end.'

Alone again, Eon Kull the Old One flexed his mind, trying to peer out beyond the Inner Place and sense the outside world. But he had no strength. Had he expended so much? What had Muon Nol meant when he remarked upon his storm?

Shuffling, unsteady, Eon Kull crossed the Inner Place and opened the lid of a quartz box set against the wall. It was full of charred dust and some empty silk bags. A rare few still held objects and he took one out now. The wraithbone wand slipped out of its protective bag into his hand. It was warm, pulsing; one of the last he had left. He shuffled back to the throne, sank onto the seat with a sigh and clutched the wand to his chest. He prayed that there was strength enough in it to channel and focus his dissipated powers. The embers of his power lit through the wand, and the spirit stones around him and set into his armour blinked back into a semblance of life. Most of them, at least. Some remained dull and dead. Many merely flickered with a dull luminosity.

His mind blinked, two or three times, flashing images of the outside which roared and wailed. Then it coalesced and he saw.

He saw the storm, the magnitude of the storm. He cursed himself. He should have realised that he had been too weak to control such a conjuration. He had intended a storm, of course, as a diversion to cover his more subtle, complex illusions. But the stress had robbed him of consciousness, and he had lost control.

He had unleashed a warp-storm, a catastrophic force that now raged entirely beyond his ability to command. Far from covering the humans and allow them in close enough for the illusions to work them to his cause, he had all but blasted them away.

His head lolled back. His final deed had been a failure. He had exhausted his entire power, burned his runes, extinguished some of his guide spirits, and all for this. Kaela Mensha Khaine! An elemental force of destruction that fell, unselective, upon all. It roared about him, like a war-hound he had spent months training, only to see it go feral.

There were a few faint spats of light, the traces of a handful of humans who had been close enough to become wrapped in his illusions. But far from enough.

Lord Eon Kull, Old One, warlock, wept. He had tried. And he had failed.

MKOLL HAD BEEN stumbling through the torrential rain for fifteen or more minutes before he stopped dead in his tracks, shook himself in amazement, and then hurled himself into the cover of a dripping, exposed tree-root.

It was not possible. It was… some kind of madness.

He look up at the stormy sky, shuddered and hugged himself. All along, he had suspected the storm was not natural in origin. Now he knew it was playing with his mind.

This was Monthax, Monthax, he told himself, over and over. Not Tanith.

Then why had he spent the last twenty minutes making his way home to the farmstead he shared with his wife and sons in the nal-groves above Heban?

Shock pounded in his veins. It was like losing Eiloni all over again, though he knew she was dead of canth-fever these last ten, fifteen years. It was like losing Tanith again. Losing his sons.

He had been so convinced he was hurrying back through a summer storm from the high-pasturing cuchlain herds, so convinced he had a wife and a farm and a family and a livelihood to return to. But in fact he had been scrambling his way back towards the ruin and the massed forces of the enemy.

How had his mind been so robbed of truth? What witchcraft was at work?

He pulled himself to his feet and made off again, now in the opposite direction, towards what he prayed were friendly lines.

On LILITH'S ORDERS, a sizable force of men began pushing back into the storm-choked jungles. Her bodyguard formed around her, following a roughly equal number of Tanith Ghosts under Gaunt, the regrouped remnants of the First, Second and Seventh platoons. The wounded had been sent on to the lines.

Gilbear had protested, both at the advance and the co-operation of the Tanith, but Lilith had made no great efforts to disguise her contempt for him when she denied his objections. If her fears were realised, this was Gaunt's business as much as hers. Besides, the Ghosts had already been in there, and had a taste of what to expect. For all the vaunted veteran skills of the Volpone's elite Tenth Brigade, she wanted a serious fighting force, with enough numbers that losses wouldn't dent. Sixty men, or thereabouts, half dedicated heavy infantry, ordered to guard her by the general, half the best stealth fighters in the Guard, led by their own charismatic commissar.

A reasonable insurgency force, she reckoned. Still, she had had her astropath signal back for reinforcements. Thoth had been reluctant until she had pulled rank and suggested the magnitude of the threat. Now five hundred Bluebloods under Marshal Ruas and three hundred Roane Deepers under Major Alef and Commissar Jaharn were moving up in their wake, an hour or so behind them. The astropath was now dead from the effort of sending and receiving through the storm. They left his body where it lay.

It seemed bloody-minded to push a unit back into the storm zone when all other Imperials had retreated out of it, and it seemed to compound that error by sending in fresh numbers after them. But Lilith knew that, storm or no storm, Chaos host or no Chaos host, the key to victory on Monthax lay in the heart of that zone. And the focus of her own, personal inquisition too, perhaps.

Lerod led the spearhead. He had volunteered, brimming with an enthusiasm that Gaunt found faintly alarming. Yael, one of Lerod's men from the Seventh, had told of Lerod's miraculous escape from the enemy gunners on the creek bank, and explained that Lerod now thought his life charmed.

Gaunt wondered for a moment. He'd seen that sort of luck-flare before, where a man thought himself invulnerable. The consequences could be appalling. But he'd rather have Lerod laying his 'luck' at the front than cursing them lower down the file.

Besides, Lerod was a fine soldier. One of the best, the most level-headed.

And more than that… All of the Ghosts, Corbec included, seemed somehow eager to get back into the deadly storm. It was as if something called to them. Gaunt had seldom seen them so highly motivated.

And then, in a pause, he realised that he, too, was more than willing to turn back into the fatal onslaught besetting the dense jungle and creeks. He couldn't account for it. It alarmed him.

Lilith's brigade slogged in through the creek-ways and water-runs, beaten by the rain and wind. The muddy ground became steep slopes, the low rises of upland rain forests above the flooded swamps.

Lilith sent pairs of men forward to secure lines. Corbec and a couple of Ghosts and Bluebloods clambered forward with Lerod up the muddy escarpments, playing out cables that they secured to trees and stumps along the way. Lightning berated them, exploding the tallest trees round about.

The brigade moved forward, following the twin lines of cable the advance had played out.

High on a slope, Corbec nailed the end of his cable line to a stump, and then set watch with his party as the main force struggled up behind. One of the Bluebloods looked at him, smiling.

'Culcis?'

'Colonel Corbec!'

Corbec slapped the younger man on the armoured shoulder, and the other Bluebloods eyed this camaraderie with suspicion.

'Where was it – Nacedon?'

'In the farm. I owe you my life, colonel.'

Corbec guffawed. 'I remember you fought as hard as the next that night, Culcis!'

The young man grinned. Rainwater dripping down his face from his helmet lip.

'So you made the Tenth, huh?' Corbec asked, settling in next to the Blueblood and taking aim into the blistering dark.

'Your medic wrote well of me, and your leader, Gaunt, mentioned me in dispatches. Then I got a lucky break on Vandamaar and won a medal.'

'So you're veteran now? One of the Blueblood elite? Best of the best, and all that?'

Culcis chuckled. 'We're all just soldiers, sir.'

The twin lines of advance progressed slowly up the slopes along the cable lines, weaving between the heavy trees and saturated foliage.

The ground was like watered honey, loose and fluid, coming up to their shins. At least there were no insects abroad in the onslaught.

THEY MOVED ON in fire-team formation, following a deep valley into the jungle uplands and the heart of the roiling storm. Lilith called a halt, to get a fix on their position. She was just raising her data-slate when a searing light flashed and they were deafened.

Lightning had struck a tree twenty paces back, exploding it in a welter of wooden shrapnel. Two Bluebloods had been atomised by electrical arcs and another two, along with one of the Tanith, had been flayed alive by the wood chips.

Major Gilbear slammed into Lilith as he stumbled up the slope. 'We must retreat, inquisitor! This is madness!'

'This is necessary, major,' she corrected, and returned her gaze to the slate. Gaunt was by her side. They compared data, pelting rain pattering off the screens of their respective devices.

'There's your Third platoon,' she said.

'As you had it last fixed before the storm came down,' corrected Gaunt. 'They were in the eye of the storm then, but can you get a true fix on their location now? Or on ours?'

Lilith cursed silently. Gaunt was right. They were cut off from orbital locator signals, and the storm was playing merry hell with all their finders and codiciers. All they had to work on was a memory or location and terrain. And none of that seemed reliable.

Gaunt drew her to one side, out of Gilbear's earshot. 'My men are the best scouts in the Guard, but they're coming up blind. If this storm is psyker like you say, it's foxing us. I'm not sure we can find our way to the last recorded position of the Third.'

'And so you suggest?'

'I don't know,' Gaunt said, meeting her grim eyes. 'But if we move much further in, I'm not sure we'll be able to find our way back...'

'Sir! Commissar!' It was Raglon, the vox-officer. He scrambled back down the muddy slope to Gaunt and held out his headset.

'Third, sir! I've got them! Indistinct, broken, but it's Major Rawne and the others all right. I copy micro-bead traffic, trooper to trooper. Sounds like they're in a fight.'

Gaunt took the headset and listened. 'Can you get a fix?'

Raglon shook his head. 'The storm's fething everything, sir. I can't get the vox signals to jibe with anything. It's like... like they're nowhere and everywhere.'

'Nonsense!' Gilbear barked, snatching the headset from Gaunt and adjusting the dials on Raglon's caster set. After a moment, he gave up with a curse.

'Try sending to them,' Gaunt told Raglon. 'Repeat signal, wide-beam.'

'Message?' Raglon asked.

'Gaunt to Tanith Third platoon. Give status and position signal.'

Raglon dialled it in. 'Nothing sir, repeating... Wait! A response! Sir, it reads: "Position: Elector's Palace, Tanith Magna. Rearguard".'

'What?' Gaunt grabbed the headset again. 'Rawne! Rawne! Respond!'

THE THIRD WERE holed up at a bend in the hallway, las-rounds blistering back and forth from a ferocious firefight. Over his micro-bead, Rawne could hear Gaunt's signal.

'Try them again,' he urged Wheln, who was fumbling with the dials on the vox-caster backpack.

Rawne hated this Gaunt already, this new commander brought from off-world to lead them. Where was he? What did he care for Tanith?

Wheln interrupted Rawne's thoughts. 'Gaunt signals, sir! He says to withdraw and pull out. Instructs us to rally with him at the following co-ordinates.'

Rawne eyed the print out and threw it aside. It made no sense. Gaunt was ordering them to abandon the palace and Tanith Magna itself.

'Give me that!' he shouted to Wheln, taking the headset.

'SIR?' RAGLON held out his headset to Gaunt. 'I don't understand…'

Gaunt took it and listened.

'…won't give up now… won't let Tanith fall! Damn you, Gaunt, if you think we'll give up on the planet now!'

Gaunt lowered his hand, letting the headset droop.

'Crazy,' Gaunt murmured. 'He's crazy…'

MKOLL SHOULDERED on through the rain. He focussed his mind on reality and shut up the yearnings in his head. Home, the lines… he would make it…

Las-shots scorched at his heels, exploding trees. He glanced backwards and began to run.

An enemy warrior loomed ahead of him and Mkoll blasted with one of his pistols, taking the head clean off.

All around him, in the rain, Chaos warriors were closing.

He ducked into cover as laser blasts puffed up leaf-mould and weed. Two shots to the left. Two to the right. A hit, and body falling and twisting in the grime. Then Mkoll was up and running again.

A shot clipped his head and he went down, full length, into the mud. He tried to rise, but his body was slow and dazed. The mud sucked at him.

A powerful hand took him by the shoulder and yanked him over, the mud sucking as it kissed him goodbye.

Mkoll looked up into the face of Death, the raddled face of an enemy trooper. He shot him point blank and then rose, cutting the knees off the next foe who advanced with a double spit of las-fire from his guns.

Mkoll started shooting wholesale, picking off shadows that loomed between the trees through the storm, and fired on him.

Another shot kissed his flank and burned a scar that would never leave him. Mkoll dropped to one knee, firing with both pistols. He killed left and right. Maximum fire-power. Then he realised his captured laspistol was coughing inert gas. He threw it aside.

As he went to reload his issue pistol, a huge form bar-relled into him and knocked him down. The Chaos trooper had his bayonet raised to rip Mkoll's life out of his body.

They wrestled in the mud for a few moments, until Mkoll was able to use his trained skill to roll the other off him.

The sprawling warrior threw his bayonet and it impaled Mkoll's left knee with a clack of metal on bone and a ripping of tendons. Mkoll faltered and fell.

The enemy was back on him, hands outstretched and a murderous howl on his sutured lips.

They fell back, thrashing, fighting. Mkoll couldn't reach the Tanith blade in his waistband, but he found the enemy bayonet sticking out of his knee and wrenched it free.

Cursing his life and mourning Eiloni, Mkoll plunged the dagger two, three, four times into the side of his aggressor's neck, until the bestial warrior shuddered and died.

Mkoll pulled himself free of the corpse, blood jetting from his knee with a force too great for the downpour to diminish.

He stumbled on, armed only with the enemy knife now. He was getting weaker as he lost blood. The foot of his wounded leg was hot with blood, yet cool. His knee didn't work properly. More fire came his way, cutting the limbs of trees and bursting ripe fruit-flowers.

A deflecting laser round took him in the small of the back, and dropped him, face down, in the mire. Stunned, he writhed, no breath coming, mud sucking into his nose and mouth.

Something made him pull himself up. Something, some urge.

Eiloni. She stood over him, as pale and as beautiful as she had been at twenty.

'What are you doing down there? What will the boys do for supper? Husband?'

She was gone as quickly as she had appeared, but Mkoll was already on his feet when the first of the Chaos spawn closed in on him. On his feet and seared with passion.

Despite the burn, agonising, on his back, Mkoll took the first down with his hands, breaking his neck and ribs and crushing his skull.

Capturing the lasgun, he turned, setting it to full auto and cutting down a wave of Chaos infantry as they pressed in on his heels.

He was still shooting, blindly into the night, his lasgun's power cell almost exhausted and three dozen slain foe about him, when Corbec found him.

GAUNT ESTABLISHED a picket perimeter in the sloping forest to guard them as the field medics treated Mkoll. The storm continued to lacerate the sky above and sway the trees with the sheering force of wind and nearly horizontal rain.

Lilith, Gilbear and Gaunt stood by as Trooper Lesp opened his field narthecium and dressed Mkoll's many cuts and las-burns. The scout's head was bandaged and his pierced knee had been strapped.

'He's a tough old dog,' Corbec murmured to Gaunt, sidling up to the commissar.

'He never ceases to impress me,' Gaunt whispered back.

Lilith looked over at them, a question in her face. Gaunt knew what it was: how had this man survived?

'We're wasting time,' Gilbear said abruptly. 'What are we doing?'

Gaunt turned on him, angry, but Lilith stepped between them.

'Major Gilbear. Are you still my bodyguard commander?'

'Yes, lady.'

'No new duties have fallen to you since you were given that task?'

'No, lady.'

'Then shut up and leave this to the commissar and myself, if you don't mind.'

Gilbear swung around and made off to check the pickets.

Corbec poked his tongue out at the major's back and made a vulgar noise. Gaunt was about to reprimand him when he saw Lilith was laughing.

'He's a pompous ass,' Lilith said.

'Indeed,' the commissar nodded.

'I meant no disrespect, inquisitor,' Corbec said hurriedly.

'Yes, you did,' Lilith smiled.

'Well, yes, but not really,' Corbec stammered.

'Check the picket, colonel, if you please,' Gaunt said quietly.

'But the major's gone to–'

'And you trust him to do a good job?' Gaunt asked.

'Not on his current form, no,' Corbec grinned, saluting Gaunt and making an over-lavish bow to the inquisitor before hurrying off.

'You'll have to excuse my second-in-command. His style of leadership is casual and spirited.'

'But it works?' asked Lilith.

'Yes, but… yes. Corbec is the soundest officer I've ever worked with. The men love him.'

'I can see why. He has charisma, courage. Just the right amount of healthy disrespect. Colm is a very attractive man.'

Gaunt paused and looked off into the night where Corbec had vanished.

'He is?'

'Oh yes. Trust me on that.' Lilith turned her attention back to Mkoll. 'So, we have your best scout, beaten and shot to hell, come to us out of the maelstrom?'

'Yes.' Gaunt cleared his throat. 'Mkoll's the best I have, all in all. Looks like he's been through fething hell and back.'

'Feth… nice word. Good weight. I'll be using that if you don't mind.'

Gaunt was puzzled. 'Mind? I–'

'What does it mean?'

Gaunt suddenly got a very clear and vivid mental picture of what it literally meant. He and Lilith were acting it out.

'I– I'm not sure…'

'Yes you are.'

Lightning struck a tree nearby, causing Bluebloods to run yelping for cover. The detonation was like a slap in the face for Gaunt. His mind cleared, sober.

'Don't play your mind tricks with me, inquisitor,' he snarled.

'I don't know what you mean.'

'Yes, you do. Twisting a feeling of jealousy in me against Corbec. And the images you were broadcasting. Feth is one of the Tanith tree-gods. Not some barbaric euphemism. I'll work with you, but not *for* you.'

Lilith smiled solemnly and held up her hands. 'Fair point. I'm sorry, Gaunt. I'm used to making allies where I can't find them, using my powers to twist wills to my purpose. I suppose it's strange for me to have a willing comrade.'

'Such is the way of the inquisitor. And I thought the commissar's path was lonely.'

She stared into his eyes and another smile lit her pale face. Gaunt wondered if this was another of her guiles, but it seemed genuine.

'We both need to find and conquer the source of this,' Gaunt told her, gesturing up at the storm. 'We both want victory here. You'll find me a much more able ally if I am in full command of my powers, rather than spellbound by you.'

She nodded. 'We both want victory here,' she said, repeating him. 'But that's not all I want,' she added, mysteriously.

Gaunt was about to pick her up on it when she shivered, pushing back her cowl and running a hand through her fine hair. The commissar-colonel realised how strained she looked.

'This storm… it's really hard for you, isn't it?'

'I'm at my limit, Ibram. The warp is all around me, tugging at my mind. I'm sorry about before. Desperation.'

Gaunt stepped towards her, ushering her towards Mkoll. 'You said you liked to make allies where you couldn't find them. Why so hard on Gilbear?'

She grinned. 'He loves it. Are you kidding? A powerful woman ordering him around. He wants me so bad he'd die for me.'

Now Gaunt grinned. 'You're a scary woman, Inquisitor Lilith.'

'I'll take that as a compliment.'

'Just promise you won't use such base tactics on me.'

'I promise,' she said. 'I don't think I need to.'

Gaunt suddenly became aware of how long he had been looking into her eyes. He broke the gaze. 'Let's talk to Mkoll.'

'Let me.'

'No,' he corrected. 'Let *us*.'

GILBEAR WALKED THE picket in the slicing rain. Invisible amphibians croaked and rattled in the wet gloom. By a fold of trees, watching the left flank, he found two Tanith Ghosts occupied in trying to light smokes from a damp tinder box.

Gilbear pounced at them, kicking one in the gut and punching the other over onto his back.

'What is this?' he seethed. 'Are you watching the flank? No? You're too busy lighting up and joking!'

One of the men protested and Gilbear kicked him again. In the face, the ribs, the kidneys as he went down. He kept kicking.

'There's a universe of hate out there, and you can't be bothered to watch for it!'

The other Ghost had risen to defend his fallen, balled-up comrade, and Gilbear turned on him, punching him out, then laying in with the boot.

A big hand caught the Blueblood major by the shoulder.

'There's a universe of hate waiting in here too,' Corbec said.

He dropped Gilbear with a headbutt that split the Blueblood's forehead. Then Corbec whaled in with two hard punches to the mouth and chest. The latter was deflected by the carapace segments.

Gilbear sprawled in the mud, pulling Corbec down on him in a threshing frenzy.

'You want me, Ghost? You got me!' he growled.

'Not before time,' Corbec agreed, snapping Gilbear's head backwards with his fist. 'It's been a long while coming. That was for Cluggan, rest his soul.'

Gilbear folded his legs up and propelled Corbec headlong over him with a kick. The big Ghost slammed down against a tree stump, upside down, the sharp stump-ends raking his back.

Now Gilbear was on his feet, fists balled. Corbec leapt up to meet him, throwing off his cape, fury in his eyes. They edged around the muddy clearing in the slanting rain, water washing off them and sluicing the blood from their wounds. Punch and counter-punch, followed by bellow and charge. The two beaten Ghosts were up on their feet, cheering and jeering. Others, Ghosts and Bluebloods both, congregated in a ring as the two officers battled by lightning flash.

Gilbear was a boxer, a heavyweight champion back on Volpone, with a stinging right hook and a terrifying capacity to take punishment. Corbec was a wrestler, Pryze County victor three years running, at the Logging Show. Gilbear bounced on spread legs, throwing humiliating punches. Corbec came in low, soaking them up, clawing his hands around Gilbear's throat.

With a roar, Corbec drove in under the whistling fists and slammed Gilbear backwards through a break of trees. They tumbled together down a short incline into a creek bed swollen with storm water. The Ghost and Volpone audience hovered at the rim of the creek, looking down and chanting.

Gilbear rose first, black with the muddy water, and swung a punch. It kissed air. Corbec exploded up out of the flood, greased jet-black with liquid mud, and doubled Gilbear with a low punch to the gut, then sent him over in a spray of silver droplets with an upper cut to the chin.

Gilbear wasn't done. He came back out of the water like a surfacing whale, as loud and vicious as the storm which quaked the sky above, and knocked Corbec back two, three steps with blow after blow. Corbec's mouth was split open and his nose broken, flooding his beard with blood.

Corbec ducked in low, throwing punches before he shoulder-charged Gilbear off his feet. Corbec lurched the massive Blueblood backwards on his shoulder, legs dangling, then twisted and threw him over himself in a perfect wrestling move, slamming Gilbear down into the creek on his back. Corbec kicked him for good measure.

Trooper Alhac, a Blueblood, was pounding his hands together wildly until he realised his side had lost. He was about to turn his venom on the cheering Tanith beside him when the undergrowth to his left flickered.

Alhac froze. So did the Ghost he was about to strike.

Something black and abominable grew out of the jumping lights in the thicket.

Alhac died, cut into streaks of evaporating flesh. The Ghost beside him perished the same way a second later. Then another Blueblood, skinned in an instant. The other Ghosts and Bluebloods who had been cheering the fight from the creek edge fled in panic.

'Oh feth!' Corbec said, dripping with ooze, looking up.

'What?' asked Gilbear, rising beside him.

'That!'

The creature was like a dog, if a dog could be the size of a horse, if a horse could move as fast as a humming bird. A red, arched-backed quadruped with long, triple-jointed limbs and a skin-less, blistered pelt. Its skull was huge and short, blunt, with the lower jaw extending beyond the upper, and multiple rows of triangular saw-teeth in each. It had no eyes. A warp creature, loosed from the storm and hunting for Chaos.

'Oh feth!' Corbec spat.

'Great Vulpo!' barked Gilbear.

The dog-thing leapt down into the creek and began to pound towards them. Corbec and Gilbear turned and ran as fast as they could through the root-twisted waterway. It was right behind them, baying.

The thing leapt on Gilbear and dragged him down, ripping at his carapace armour with its tusks. Strips of armaplas shredded off his shoulder panels. Gilbear cried out, helpless.

Corbec leapt astride the warp-beast, pulling its head back by the mane and plunging his Tanith dagger into its throat. Foetid purple blood squirted from the wound and the thing opened its mouth to howl and squeal.

'Now, Blueblood! Now!' Corbec shouted, riding the beast, pulling its skull back.

Gilbear pulled a frag grenade from his belt and threw it straight into the beast's mouth, right down its gullet past the wincing pink larynx.

Gilbear threw himself down and Corbec propelled himself clear.

The dog-thing exploded from within, showering both them and the creek bed with stinking meat.

Corbec pulled himself up out of the fluid muck at the bottom of the watercourse. He looked across at Gilbear, sat with his back against the creek wall, eyes straining.

'You all right?' Corbec gurgled.

Gilbear nodded.

'About time we called a truce, eh?'

Gilbear nodded again. They both got up, unsteady and filmed with mud and flecks of putrid meat.

'A truce. Yes. A truce...' Gilbear was still stunned. 'For now.'

'THE RUIN, SIR, the one I glimpsed before. I found it again.' Mkoll's voice was soft and brittle, his breath laboured. He sat on a fallen log, sipping alternately from a water canteen and a sacra flask that Bragg had manifested. He was bandaged and caked in mud. Gaunt crouched by him, listening carefully. Mkoll seemed a little spooked by Lilith, but she read this response quickly and held back so Gaunt could talk to his valued scout.

'What is it?' asked Gaunt.

Mkoll shrugged. 'No idea. Big, old, fortified. It's on top of a mound that I don't think is natural. Too regular. All I know is, the enemy are surrounding it thicker than sap-flies round a glucose trap.'

Gaunt felt a tingle of alarm. Not only did he know precisely what Mkoll meant, he had a brief, vivid mental flash of the long-bodied insects themselves, swarming around a beaker of glistening fluid on a woodsman's hut-stoop. Insects native to Tanith. Insects he had never seen.

'Numbers?' he pressed on.

'I didn't take a headcount,' Mkoll muttered dryly. 'I was a little busy. Tens of thousands is my guess. Maybe more, beyond my line of sight. The terrain was hilly, thick cover. There could have been hundreds of thousands up there.'

'What are they after?' Gaunt wondered out loud.

'I think we have to find out,' Lilith said quietly.

Gaunt rose and looked round at the inquisitor, her face in shadow from her cowl. 'Before we explore the insanity of sending sixty men up against a possible force of hundreds of thousands, may I remind you that we can't even find this place? Our locators and auspex are screwed, my scouts can't tell one direction from another. Feth, Mkoll's my best, and he admits he only found it again by accident.'

Lilith nodded. 'There is a deep level of misdirection and concealment in this storm. I don't know the answer.'

'I could lead you there again,' Mkoll said darkly from behind them.

Gaunt turned to look at him. 'You could? You claimed it was elusive before.'

Mkoll rose shakily to his feet. 'That was then. I don't know... I just feel I could find it again now. Something in my bones. It would be like... like finding my way home again.'

Gaunt looked at Lilith. 'Let's try,' she said. 'Mkoll seems confident and I trust him like you do. If opposition gets too hot, we can pull out again.'

Gaunt nodded. He was about to call up Raglon and issue new orders to advance when the dull crump of a frag grenade rolled through the storm. A few moments later, las-guns and hellguns were firing, sporadic, the distinctive crack of laser fire overlapping the higher shriek of hell-shots. Gaunt scrambled down the bank, pulling out his chainsword, shouting for reports.

Sergeant Lerod was directing the men in the east flank of the picket.

'Lerod?'

'Sir! There are things coming out of the storm, sir! Brutes! Creatures!'

Gaunt peered out into the dark jungle, and saw scuttling monstrosities being born out of tendrils of lightning. There

was a sickening whiff of Chaos. Blueblood and Tanith guns
blew the things apart as they came close.

'Warp creatures,' Lilith hissed, appearing by his side. 'Manifestations of this unholy storm. Mindless, but lethal.'

Corbec staggered up, looking very much the worse for
wear. He was ordering the west flank of the picket to loop
back closer to the centre.

'What happened to you?' Gaunt asked sharply, seeing an
equally bedraggled Gilbear moving in with a fire-team of
Bluebloods.

'Bit of a fight,' Corbec said. 'Some fething thing came out
of the dark.'

Gaunt didn't want to know any more. This was no time
for fierce reprimands. He had to keep the whole unit tight
and together. He keyed his micro-bead. 'Gaunt to brigade.
We're advancing, double time. Spearhead formation. Tanith
First platoon and half the Volpone unit at the point. Take
your direction from Scout-Trooper Mkoll. Everyone else,
watch the flanks and the rear. Inquisitor Lilith instructs that
warp-spawn could appear around or among us at any time.
Don't hesitate; shoot. Sergeant Lerod, take a six-man drill
and guard the back of the formation. All commanders
acknowledge understanding of these orders and signal
readiness.'

A chatter of responses came back swiftly. Raglon, monitoring them with the vox-caster, nodded to Gaunt that all
the brigade had signalled in.

Gaunt hadn't finished. The devoted Tanith had made his
commissarial duties easy these last few years. But now they
were in thick, spooked, and the company was mixed with
troopers he didn't know or even trust. Morale, discipline –
the watchwords of the commissariat. He thought back to his
training at the Schola Progenium, to his field apprenticeship
as a cadet under Oktar. He took the speaker horn of the vox-
set from Raglon.

'I won't pretend this will be easy. But it is vital. Vital to
Imperial success on this world, vital perhaps to the entire
Crusade. The enemy and their ambitions will be denied, if it
takes every spark of our lives and every drop of our blood.

We fight for the Emperor today, fight as if we were standing at his side as his chosen bodyguard. Protect the men to your left and right as if they were the Emperor himself. Do not slacken, do not falter. Victory awaits you, and if not victory, then the glory of a brave death in service to the Golden Throne of Terra. The Emperor will provide, if you are true. His hand guides us, his eyes watch over us, and even in death he will bring us to him and we shall sit in splendour at his side beyond the Eternity Gate.

'For Lost Tanith, for Mighty Volpone, for Imperial Earth… advance!'

Like a single, lithe entity, the brigade swept up the escarpment, pushing onwards into the jagged hills as the storm shook the world around them. Blueblood and Ghost moved in perfect, trained order together, all animosities set aside. Gaunt smiled as he observed the tight drilled formation of his own, and was suitably impressed that it was matched by the bulky Volpone elite. Every now and then, las-shots sang out from the vanguard as warp-things were sighted and dispatched.

Lilith moved with him. She slid a plasma pistol out from under her cloak and charged it with a flick of her black-gloved hands. 'Good speech,' she grinned at him. 'Got them motivated. Oktar trained you well.'

'You've checked up on me. My background.'

'I'm an inquisitor, Gaunt. What do you expect? I enquire.'

'And what are you really inquiring about here on Monthax?' he asked curtly.

'What do you mean?'

'I'm no psyker, but I read people well enough. This is about more than victory here, more than the successful prosecution of psyker-deviants in our forces. You have an agenda.'

She flashed a smile at him. 'No mystery, Ibram. Back on the Sanctity, I told you. Bulledin had reported back to us because it was suspected some powerful psyker component might be at work here. We thought that it was the enemy itself, that we were in for a mind-war. But now, this ruin. The foe embark on an advance, ignoring us completely, and seem hell-bent on taking that place. You've got to wonder why. You've got to believe that there's something very valuable up there.'

'Something that caused this storm?'

She shrugged. 'Or something that made them cause this storm to cover their movement towards it. But I think your guess is probably more likely.'

'And that's what you want?'

'It's my duty, Ibram. And I don't think I need to explain that concept to one of the Imperium's best commissars.'

'Don't try distracting me with flattery. Give me some idea what you mean by "something valuable".'

'Think back to Menazoid Epsilon. I told you, I checked your background thoroughly. As an inquisitor, I got to look at some very classified reports. You know what was at stake there.'

Gaunt was wary. 'You're talking about technology? Artefacts?'

She nodded. 'It could be.'

'Ancient human? Alien?'

Lilith produced something from her pocket. 'Mkoll found this. He dug it out of a tree stump at a battle site just before the storm hit. You tell me what you think it means.'

She held up the metal star with the sharpened points. Gaunt stared at it with dark comprehension.

'Now you know as much as I do.'

The brigade moved down a deep defile into a tree sheltered vale that blocked the raging storm partially for the first time. Gaunt was becoming numb with the incessant wind and rain, and knew his men must be too. It was a blessed, temporary relief to move through the deep gorge with its almost cathedral-like arches of ancient cattails and clopeas, where rain arrested by the leaf canopy simply drooled down to the ground in long, slow, sappy streams. The storm raged, muffled, far above them.

Gaunt moved up to Mkoll at the point of the formation.

'Still on track?'

Mkoll nodded. 'Like I said, I couldn't lose the trail now if I wanted to.'

'Like coming home, you said,' Gaunt reminded him.

Mkoll closed his eyes and saw Eiloni just ahead, beckoning him back to the farmstead. She was whispering promises of a hot supper, and of rowdy boys ready for one of their father's fireside tales before bed.

'You have no idea, commissar.'

THE ADVANCING TIDE of Chaos warriors only stopped when the numbers of their dead choked the passageway.

Rawne ordered his platoon back and they hauled a set of double doors closed, barring them to seal the tunnel. Milo helped Wheln swing the doors shut, his fingers tracing the heraldic badge of the Tanith Elector inscribed on the heavy nal-wood panels. He blinked, and for a second saw taller, more slender doors of polished onyx, marked with alien runes he did not understand.

'What's up?' Wheln asked, panting.

Milo blinked again. The doors were arched nal-wood in the Tanith pattern again, the Elector's insignia clearly marked.

Feygor and Mkendrik dropped a long bar across the door loops to lock it tight. Beyond the thick barrier, they could hear muffled explosions and the rasp of flamers as the enemy tried to unblock the corpse-packed tunnel.

The eight Tanith men were exhausted. A day ago, at the Founding, none of them – with the possible exception of Rawne and Feygor – had ever fired a weapon in anger, let alone killed. Now they were truly baptised. There was no counting the dead they had piled up.

Cown sank to his heels against the wall, fighting for breath. 'Are we lost?' he asked. 'Is Tanith lost?'

Rawne turned to face him, fire in his eyes. 'Are we alive? Is Tanith living? Get up! Get up and move! Only that feckless off-worlder Gaunt seems to have given up on Tanith! Withdraw? Abandon? What kind of leadership is that? He'd make worldless ghosts of us!'

'Ghosts…' murmured Larkin, leaning slackly against the far wall, cheek and shoulder pressed against the cold stone. 'Gaunt's Ghosts…'

'What did you say?' Milo asked directly, blood racing in his ears. It was like a dream was breaking in his head.

'Ignore him!' Feygor ordered. 'Fething fool is weak in the head. But for his good eye, I'd have shot him as dead-weight before now.'

'No,' began Milo, 'This isn't right... it...'

'Of course it's not right!' Feygor snarled into Milo's face. Milo winced as spittle hit his cheek. 'The Imperium comes to Tanith when it needs men, but where is the Imperium now when Tanith needs it? They're leaving us to die!'

Caffran pulled Feygor back from Milo sharply. 'Then we'll die well, Feygor! We'll die fething well!' The young trooper's face was bright with passion. The thought of Laria burned in his mind. She was out there somewhere and he would fight and kill and kill again to save this place and be with her once more.

'Caff's right, Feygor,' Mkendrik said. Wheln and Cown both nodded in agreement. 'Let's die well so Tanith can live.'

'And feth any off-world commissar who says otherwise!' spat Cown.

Feygor, subdued, turned and nodded, deftly exchanging the power cell of his lasgun for a fresh one.

Rawne had been absent for a few moments and now strode back into view. 'I hear fighting down the hall, maybe three hundred spans away. Sounds like another group of our boys in defence. I say we move in to support.'

Mkendrik nodded. 'Bolster our numbers. Maybe they know where the Elector is sheltering.'

'If we could get him to the transport stables, we could maybe fly him to safety in a cutter,' Cown added.

Rawne nodded. 'Feygor, make the door a surprise.'

Feygor grinned and took out a brace of tube-charges from his pack. He strapped them with quick, practised diligence to the door bar. Anything that broke in here now after them would snap the trigger wire and bring the hallway down on top of them.

'Let's go!' Rawne ordered.

Milo fell into step with the others as they hurried on down the long palace hallway, boot-steps resounding from the stone flags. He wished with all his heart and soul he could work out what was wrong with... with reality. There was no other word. Reality itself seemed wrong and dream-like and it was making his stomach turn. It must be the Chaos daemons, Milo thought. Maybe Major Rawne knew wh–

Milo paused. *Major* Rawne? In the tents of the Founding Fields outside Tanith Magna, Rawne had bivouacked with the common soldiers. A trooper, nothing more. No rank, no seniority. Since when had he got the collar pins and the promotion?

Have I forgotten something? Milo wondered. Have I...

Another flicker in his mind. An image of... of a cramped cabin on a starship. Rawne, Corbec, Milo. A deputation. A tall, powerful, lean-faced man that could only have been Commissar-Colonel Ibram Gaunt, rising to meet them. How could he know what this Gaunt looked like? He'd never seen him. He could hear Gaunt speaking, making bold, confident field promotions: Colonel Corbec, Major Rawne.

*Another dream?*

There was no time to think about it. They were almost on the fighting. Gunshots. Screaming, just ahead.

That wasn't las-fire, Milo thought to himself as he and all the platoon checked stride and raised weapons. He'd heard enough lasgun exchanges in the last half an hour to know the distinctive snap. This was an eerie, singing shrill; a shrieking, a buzzing, like the saw-note of a wasp, amplified and broken into harsh, serried blasts.

What the feth was it?

'You hear that?' he gasped to Larkin beside him. Larkin was tuning the night-scope on his long gun, stabbing a slender target beam of porcelain blue light up at the roof.

'What? Lasguns on full auto? Yeah... someone's having a busy day.'

It's not a lasgun, thought Milo, it's *not*...

Third platoon rounded a corner in the hallway, moving in tight overlap formation, and broke into a wide audience hall of dark, volcanic stone. Shattered stained glass windows depicting anroth, the household and forest spirits of Tanith, lined one side of the vaulted chamber. Nal-wood pews, many shattered or overturned, filled the main body of the room. The banner of the Elector hung in smouldering tatters over an oriole window at the far end.

Three Tanith troopers, their backs to them, were in position behind the pews, blasting with lasguns down at an arched door under the oriole. Chaos spawn were battling to get in through the door, their dead sprawled all around the entrance. Five or more other Tanith troopers lay dead amid the wooden wreckage.

Without question or hesitation, the Third fell in beside their brethren and took up the fight, blasting at the doorway and cutting into the advancing enemy. The three Tanith holding the chamber glanced around in surprise at the newcomers. Milo didn't recognise any of them, though the colonel was an unforgettable giant with a mane of white hair riven with a red streak, a long noble face and the blue tattoo of a scythe on his cheek.

'For Tanith! For the Elector! For Terra!' Rawne yelled as he blasted.

The big colonel hesitated again, then returned his attention to the killing. 'As you say,' he boomed melodiously, his accent strange, 'for... Tanith!'

MUON NOL, of the Dire Avengers Aspect, had been holding the green onyx vault with a squad of his warriors, seeing them cut down one by one as Chaos forced their way into the chamber via the diamond-shaped prayer chute at the end, under the rosette of spirit stones set high in the wall beneath the wraith-silk standard of Dolthe.

The only cover was the tangled mess of psycho-plastic benches which had once lined the celebrant vault, benches that had been splintered or wilted by enemy fire. To the side of them, slender pointed windows paned with translucent wraithbone showed images of Asuryan, the Phoenix King, Khaine of the Bloody Hand, Vaul, the crippled smith-god, Morai-heg the fate-crone, and Lileath the Maiden, goddess of dream fortune, backlit by Farseer Eon Kull's warp-storm outside. It was Lileath who Muon Nol most worshipped, that beautiful diviner of futures and possibilities. He wore her rune on a thread around his neck, under his jade-blue aspect armour.

Muon Nol's white crested helmet was dinted with black las-scores, and the red plume crest was singed. Still Uliowye, Lord Eon Kull's holy buanna, spat whickering onslaughts of jagged, flickering star-rounds at the foe, slicing them to pieces, a thousand rounds in each tight burst. The stabilising gyros whirred as the great, ornate shrieker cannon bucked in his mesh-gloved hands. The accelerator field shimmered around the muzzle base. Uliowye, the Kiss of Sharp Stars. He had perhaps six rods of solid ammunition left; he would make them count. For Lileath, he would make them count. For Dolthe.

Suddenly, eight humans in drab, muddy uniforms fell in beside him, blasting their lasguns at the enemy. They were resilient and fierce, and seemed to show no shock or surprise at their surroundings or sudden, new-found comrades-in-arms.

Psychically, Muon Nol ordered his remaining men to accept them and fight on. This was undoubtedly Lord Eon Kull's work – and Lord Eon Kull's deceit.

And, Khaine, but these mon-keigh fought! Like they were fighting for their own homeworld it seemed, fighting for everything they loved!

In under five minutes the reinforcement of the human soldiers had driven the Chaos spawn back. They pushed forward together down the prayer chute and killed the last of the attackers, closing a great stone hatch shut to block the rest.

The Master of the Bodyguard turned to the slim, dark-haired human who appeared to be the newcomers' leader. He searched for his grasp of Low Gothic, as he had learned in the training symposiums of Dolthe craftworld.

'I am Muon Nol, of Dolthe, of this Way Place. Your Intervention and aid is greeted with welcome. Lord Farseer Eon Kull will thank you for it.'

* * *

'COLONEL MUNNOL, from Tanith Dale. Good to see you boys, and no mistake. The Elector needs all the men he can get right now.'

The tall Tanith officer with the mane of white hair turned to the Third as the shutter hatch closed. The exploded carcasses of Chaos troops lay all around them.

Rawne nodded. 'Glad to help. I'm Rawne, Major, commanding... well, what's left of Third platoon. Place us where you want us, colonel.'

Munnol nodded, but he seemed bewildered somehow, Milo thought. Come to that, he'd never seen a Tanith man with anything but black hair. Not only were Munnol's white locks odd, but both his men, who seemed uneasy now he noticed, were white-haired too.

Colonel Munnol nodded to a doorway to the left. It was a strange gesture. And what kind of weapon was he holding? A lasgun... but long and extended, longer and thicker than Larkin's sniper gun. Milo felt something tugging anxiously at his mind.

'If you're willing, Rawne human, the western emplacements need support desperately,' Colonel Munnol was saying.

'Lead on!' barked Rawne, changing his energy cell and dropping the spent one to the floor. Munnol shrugged and nodded, beckoning them after him.

*Rawne human?* Had he misheard? Milo followed, unnerved. Human? The nightmare refused to slip away. He hated the terrible nauseous feeling of confusion.

At a fast pace, Munnol led the Third and his own men down a black granite corridor. Ahead of them, through an archway, they could see two dozen more Tanith troopers lining a battlement, firing lasguns down into the stormy night. Except that the noise was the shrieking chatter of something odd and otherworldly, not the reassuring snap-return of las-fire.

Rawne hurried beside the tall colonel, Feygor at his heels.

'Can you believe this luck?' he laughed. 'Chaos attacking us on the very day of our Founding?'

'No... indeed,' Munnol replied.

'I'll be honest with you, Munnol... I almost didn't sign up,' Rawne went on. 'What kind of life is it, fighting your way through the stars for the love of some fething uncaring Emperor, no hope of ever going home again?'

'Not an enticing prospect, Rawne human,' Munnol agreed.

'Feth, but I had a nice life back in Tanith Attica. A nice little business, if you understand me. Nothing too illegal, but, you know, on the wrong side...'

'I understand...'

'Feygor was with me back then. Weren't you, Feygor?' Rawne said, nodding at his comrade.

'Aye, Rawne, aye,'

'Nice work, good returns, didn't want to give it up... but, Feth take me for a chulan... I'm glad I did! Feth the Golden Throne... thank the anroth I'm armed and ready to stand for Tanith at this dread hour!'

'We all thank the anroth for that, Rawne human,' Munnol replied.

They were out on the battlements now, enemy fire ripping over them. Colonel Munnol called to his Tanith soldiers, who looked around from the loopholes and crenellations where they had been firing down at the foe. White hair, streaked with red, thought Milo with a shudder. They all have white hair.

He thought he was going to be sick.

'Men of Dolthe!' Munnol exclaimed.

Dolthe? Dolthe? Where was that? Milo wondered.

'Our Kin arrive to fight with us! Major Rawne and other humans! Treat them well, they are resolute and with us to the end!'

A rousing cheer greeted Colonel Munnol's words.

Rawne ordered the Third in alongside the Tanith already in place, taking position and firing down into the stormy dark over the jagged lip of laser-chewed stonework.

Milo was about to take his place when he saw Larkin was cowering behind them all, crouched in the corner of the battlement away from the fight, clutching his sniper rifle and shaking uncontrollably.

Milo crossed to him. 'Larkin? What is it?'

'T-took a look through my scope... B-brin... they're not human!'

'What?' Milo felt his guts clench, but he wasn't going to give in.

'I know what I saw! Through my... my scope. It never lies. This big bastard Munnol and the rest! They're not... not Tanith!'

Milo snatched the sniper gun out of Larkin's wavering hands, and sighted it at Munnol, looking through the scope. The bead of the blue light beam kissed Munnol's drab camo-cloak like a tiny spotlight. Milo looked through the scope viewer, seeing Munnol as a ghost of blues and shadows.

Munnol, as if sensing the beam on him, turned to look back at Milo. Through the scope, Milo saw Munnol as he swung slowly around, his eyes hooked and slanted in his cold pale face. A second more, and those eyes became the visor slits of a great sculpted helmet of gleaming white armour, backed by a towering crest of red feathers. Munnol's grey fatigues became a tight suit of blue armour that locked majestically about his huge, powerful frame. The lasgun in his hands became a long, fluted lance weapon with a ridged, coiled pipe, silver vents and a beautiful inlay of chased pearl and gold. Munnol became quite the most frightening thing Milo had ever seen.

'Oh my Emperor...' he breathed. 'They're *eldar!*'

LILITH'S BRIGADE BROKE from the gorge into a fan of lowlands where the jungle had vanished under sculptural folds of mud which had slid in vast curls down the slopes and obliterated everything in their path. The going was slower, the troops wading waist-deep in ochre slime in some places. Above the roar of the storm, the forward scouts could now pick up the sounds of massed combat from the valley beyond. Flashes of light backlit the hilltop, and it wasn't lightning.

Gaunt ordered battle readiness via an encrypted vox-burst, marshalling the Volpone heavyweights up the flank of the hill under Gilbear's lead and funnelling the Ghosts in two detachments led by Lerod and Corbec along the edge of the mud slip below. Gaunt and Lilith moved at the front of Corbec's band.

Mkoll had led them true. Round the curve of the hill, they got their first sight of the mound and its ruin – and the massed forces of the enemy surrounding it. Even prepared by Mkoll's description, Gaunt found the scale was immense. Thousands of enemy troops, some with heavy weapons, were swarming the mound's slopes and bombarding the great, dark edifice with a force stone had no right to resist. The entire scene was a flickering mess of fire-flashes and explosions. The wet air was pungent with blood and thermite.

The Guardsmen were engaging before they realised it. Gilbear's Bluebloods had come into the rear positions of enemy heavy weapons emplacements, and the crews were turning, startled, counter-attacking with close-quarter side arms. A moment later, and both detachments of Ghosts were hemmed in by Chaos units that peeled back from the main assault to face this surprise rear contact. Las-fire and bolt rounds seared a miserable light-streak criss-cross over the smooth mud flats.

Blasting with his bolt pistol, Gaunt saw a tiny opportunity: break and fall back now, or become locked irrevocably into the fighting.

He saw Gilbear's unit spill down the rise and fall upon the enemy weapon stations with a ferocious and admirable grace, overwhelming and slaughtering them in a matter of a minute or two. The powerful hellguns, supported by two grenade launchers and a plasma rifleman, ripped into the hindquarters of the guncrews' position and cut them down.

Gilbear haughtily voxed his success as his men took over control of the enemy weapons, turning missile launchers and field artillery on the ranks of the chaos army beyond. The Volpone Tenth Elite were damn good, Gaunt had to admit. Rotation training on all combat disciplines meant that they could take a gun post and then man that gun as surely and deftly as if they were dedicated artillery troops.

Gaunt knew the moment had gone. To break now would have left the Volpone alone. His choice was made for him. Battle was truly joined and there would be no respite.

The twin prongs of the Ghosts punched into the rear of the besiegers. Gilbear, tactically astute, turned the aim of captured guns down the turn of the valley and covered the Ghost push, creating huge breaks in the enemy's makeshift flanking manoeuvre. Shells whistled down under Gilbear's direction, pin-point accurate, throwing ribbons of mud, strands of foliage and pieces of Chaos troopers into the air not twenty metres in front of the advancing Ghosts.

The fighting was close range and white hot. Incredibly, but for a few grazes and glancing burns, Gaunt found his men suffered no casualties.

Within five minutes of first contact, the Imperials had cut a wedge into the enemy rearguard, made up half a kilometre of ground and slaughtered upwards of two hundred enemy troops, at no mortal cost.

Gilbear held the line as long as he could, but there came a point, mutually agreed between him and Gaunt over the vox-link, when the separation of the two small Imperial advances would become too great.

When the signal was given, the Bluebloods mined the gun emplacements and pushed on, scything a double-time advance to swing themselves in behind the Ghosts. Timed explosions, staggered and staggering, set off the emplacement munitions and excavated a new valley where a small plateau had been.

Into the heat now, on the lower slopes of the mound, the Imperial expedition force slicing a break in the foe as a spearhead formation, Ghosts to the right, Volpone to the left, with Gaunt and Corbec at the tip.

Gaunt knew the Tanith fought well, but he had never seen them discharge themselves so determinedly, so brilliantly. In his heart, he couldn't believe that this was a simple response to his motivational speech. They were fighting for something, something deep in theirs hearts, something that would not be denied.

'For Tanith! For Tanith, bless her memory!' he heard Corbec yelling as he advanced.

The cry, as it was taken up by Ghosts all around him, prompted a deep, emotional response in Gaunt. It shocked him. They were indeed fighting for Tanith... not for some memory or for a sense of vengeance. They were fighting for the love of their homeworld, of the misty cities, the darkling woodlands, the majestic seas.

He knew this because he felt it too. He had spent all of a day on Tanith before the fall, and most of that inside the dim ante-rooms of the Elector's palace at Tanith Magna. But it felt as if it had been his home, something he had grown to love through years of upbringing, something that was still attainable...

With Corbec and two other Ghosts, he was the first to reach a defence ditch on the lower slopes of the mound where superior numbers of Chaos filth were turning from their assault of the ruin to repel the hind attack. Gaunt led with his chainsword, slicing the enemy apart. It seemed like he was las-proof. All opposing shots went wild. The joy of Tanith sang in his heart.

He dropped into the ditch, cutting the first aggressor before him open down the middle, then swung the whining blade left to decapitate another. In his other hand, his bolt pistol blasted down the ditch, blowing the legs off two charging ghouls with fixed bayonets. His bolter clacked empty. Corbec was beside him, bellowing, blasting with his lasgun at figures who fell and squirmed and fled down the narrow defile. To the other side, Troopers Yael and Mktea fought hand to hand with silver daggers, passionate, furious. Beyond them, Bragg, blasting with his autocannon over the ditch top.

Gaunt threw his bolter and his sword aside and grabbed the firing handles of an enemy storm-bolter with a belt feed set into the lip of the ditch. The massive gun was set on flakboard, with wire tie-downs to prevent the tripod from skating. Gaunt thumbed the trigger and swept the shuddering gun left and right, decimating the ranks of enemy advancing up the hill above him.

He felt a hand on his arm. Lilith was beside him, her face pale, her eyes full of tears.

'What?' he barked, continuing to fire.

'Can't you feel it? You're swept up in the storm-magic too!'

He released his hands and the drum belt rattled round on auto-feed. 'Magic?'

'The web of deceit I spoke of... it's enflamed all your men, the Bluebloods too. It's tearing at my mind! Gaunt...!'

Involuntarily, he held her. She pushed him off after a second. 'I'm all right! All right!'

'Lilith!'

'Whatever... whoever... it is up there in the ruin, they're preying on our emotions.'

'What do you mean?'

'I... I think they want all the help they can get, Gaunt! They've woven a psychic spell through the storm that makes us... makes us respond by touching our deepest desires! For your Ghosts, this is Tanith... a Tanith where it's still possible to win and save the world! For the Bluebloods, it's Ignix Majeure, where they lost after a desperate fight! But Ibram... it's *killing me*! So strong, so powerful!'

Gaunt fought to catch his breath. 'W-why me? Why Tanith?'

'What?' she asked, wiping her puffy eyes.

'I'm not Tanith, but the will inside me responded that way. Why aren't I fighting for some great cause in my own life? Why have I been living and breathing Tanith in my waking dreams all this while?'

She smiled, simply and painfully, her perfect face lit by the fire-flashes around them. 'Don't you know it, Ibram? Tanith is your cause, no matter if you were born there or not. You've devoted your service and life to these men, to the memory of their world.

'The fate of Tanith consumes you, as it does them, and though you're not a true son of the forests, this magic plays on your deepest urges! You're a Ghost, Ibram Gaunt, whether you know it or not! You're not just their master, you're one of them!'

Gaunt pulled off his cap and wiped brow-sweat back into his cropped hair. He was panting, painfully high on adrenaline. 'This is all false?' he began.

'We're being used. Manipulated. Driven to fight by something that touches our deepest causes.'

'Then... in the Emperor's name, if it helps us kill the Chaos scum, let's not deny it! Let's use it!' Gaunt cued his micro-bead and opened a channel to his force. 'Sixty men against ten thousand! The stuff of legends! Push on! Push on, for Tanith and for Ignix Majeure! Take the slope and make for the ruin!'

At the head of his wave of Bluebloods, Gilbear heard the call and screamed into the night as he emptied yet another powerpack out through the glowing muzzle of his hellgun. The Volpone took the rise, scattering enemy before them.

Lerod, who now thought himself truly immortal, led his detachment up the mound, stampeding over the panicking, splintering waves of Chaos filth.

Corbec, with Bragg firing solid lines of destruction from his heavy weapon at his side, pushed the other Ghost band up between the prongs. To either side of the Imperial advance, a hundred thousand soldiers of the foe swarmed and regrouped. But the sixty or so Imperials cut a line up through them that wouldn't be denied.

Years later, painstakingly reconstructing the details of this assault from patchy data collected at the time, Imperial tacticians on Foridon would be utterly unable to account for the success of the action. Even given the surprise nature of the assault, from the rear, there was no sense to the data. Simple statistics should have had Gaunt's expeditionary force cut down to the last man, at most a half kilometre from the ruin. The tacticians would factor in charismatic leadership, tactical insight, luck... and still there was no mistake. Gaunt's men should have been entirely slaughtered long before they reached the ruin.

But that was not the case. Gaunt drew his forces, without the loss of a single man, up to the walls of the ruin perhaps thirty minutes after they had first engaged the back of the enemy positions. They had cut through a legion of the foe who outnumbered them ten thousand to one, and attained a target area the enemy had been trying to force its way into for hours. They slew, approximately, two-point-four thousand soldiers of the enemy.

Eventually, after a prolonged analytical study, the tacticians would decide that the only explanation could be that there were no enemy units on the field that day. It was all an illusion. Gaunt had mounted an assault through open, undefended ground. Only then did the computations and the statistics and the possibilities match up.

None of them could admit that this wasn't the case. And so, perhaps the greatest and most spectacular success of Macaroth's great Crusade, out-classed and out-numbered but still successful, was deleted from the Imperial Annals as a phantom engagement. Such is the fate of true heroism.

THERE WAS A DOOR: a tall, pointed arch of stone faced with stone, in the side of the smooth flank of the ruin. Gaunt grouped his force around it as relentless firepower strafed up at them from the muddled but regrouping legions of the enemy.

Gilbear intended to mine the door in the hope of blowing it open, though, as Corbec pointed out, the scorch marks on the stone facing seemed to indicate that the enemy had tried that more than once and failed.

They were about to argue the point some more when the door opened. Brin Milo stood there, looking out at them, flanked by Caffran and a spectacularly grim eldar warrior with a red plume set behind his white helmet.

The storm flashed above, still furious and wild.

'You've come this far,' Milo said. 'Now let's finish this.'

SEALED INSIDE THE onyx walls of the Way-Place, Gaunt and his force heard the low wailing of eldar mourners, remorsefully singing the last songs of closure.

Muon Nol faced Gaunt for a long while, until Gaunt saluted and held out his hand.

'Ibram Gaunt.'

Nothing more need be said, Gaunt thought.

Muon Nol looked at the proffered hand, then slung Uliowye over his shoulder and clasped it.

He spoke, a bewildering slither of otherworldly language.

'You've just been formally worshipped as a fellow warrior,' Lilith said, stepping up. Muon Nol turned his huge gaze to look at her.

'I am Lilith, of the Imperial Inquisition,' she stated.

Muon Nol, a head taller than even Gilbear, paused and nodded slowly.

Gaunt looked round sharply at the inquisitor. 'We're not getting anywhere fast,' he hissed. 'Does anyone here speak eldar?'

'I do,' Lilith said, but Muon Nol spoke simultaneously.

'There is no need,' he said in melodiously accented Low Gothic. 'I understand. You must follow me now. The farseer-lord awaits.'

'Fine...' Gaunt began.

Muon Nol stepped back. 'No. Not you. The female.'

LORD EON KULL felt the wash and burn of the Chaos hosts as they assaulted the ruin around him. Fuehain Falchior had begun to rattle in her rack again.

The door of the Inner Place slid open and Muon Nol entered, escorting a cowled human female, a hulking stormtrooper in grey and gold, and a human male in a long coat and cap.

Muon Nol bowed. Lilith did likewise. Gilbear and Gaunt remained upright.

Eon Kull spoke, perfectly using the clumsy Low Gothic he had once wasted a brief year mastering.

'I am Eon Kull Farseer. My enchantments have brought you into this. I make no apologies. The Way must be closed to the Dark and I will use all my powers to accomplish that.'

Muon Nol took a step forward, gesturing to indicate Lilith. 'My lord... this female is called Lilith, in the human tongue. Is that not a sign?'

'Of what?'

'Of purpose... lord?'

Eon Kull seemed about to answer, as if he too recognised the symbolic coincidence. But then he slumped against the side of his throne, blood leaking from under the seal of his helmet.

'My lord!'

Gaunt reached him first, pulling off the tall helm and cradling the pale skull of the worn-out, dying Eldar farseer in his gloved hands.

'I can send for medics… healers,' he began.

'No… n-no… no time. No purpose to it. I want to die, Gaunt human. The Way must be closed before Chaos can corrupt it.'

Holding Eon Kull, Gaunt looked up hopelessly at Lilith. She came and took his place, embracing the frail eldar's head and body.

'That's what the Chaos forces are here on Monthax for, isn't it, farseer lord?'

'You speak truth. This Way has stood open for twenty-seven centuries. Now the enemy have found it and through it they will invade Dolthe craftworld. For the sake of Dolthe, for the living souls of the eldar, this Way must be closed. For this great purpose I have conjured you. For this great purpose, my aspect warriors have given their all and their last.'

'All of this… some trick of a stinking alien scumbag…' Gilbear growled.

Gaunt launched himself forward, bringing down Muon Nol before the enraged eldar could splinter Gilbear to pieces with his shrieker cannon.

Gaunt got up off the aspect warrior and strode across the onyx room to face Gilbear.

'What? What did I say that was so bad?' Gilbear asked, a second before Gaunt's fist laid him out unconscious on the flag stones.

'Ibram!' Gaunt turned as Lilith cried out. She was cradling Eon Kull in her arms. Gaunt rushed to her, with Muon Nol at his elbow, but there was no mistaking the signs.

Farseer Eon Kull, the Old One, was dead.

They placed his frail remains on the floor.

'We are lost, then,' Muon Nol said. 'Without the farseer, we can no longer conjure the pacts with the warp and close the Web. Dolthe will die as surely as Farseer Eon Kull.'

'Lilith can do it,' Gaunt said suddenly.

Muon Nol and Lilith looked at him.

'I know you can, and I know you want to. That is why you're here, Lilith.'

'What are you talking about, Ibram?' she said

'You're not the only one with pull, the only one who can chase records and dig out hushed files. I did my research on you as surely you did mine. Lilith Abfequarn... psyker, inquisitor, black notation rating.'

'God of Terra,' she smiled. 'You're good, Ibram.'

'You don't know how good. The Black Ships singled you out when they found you. Daughter of a planetary governess whose world edged the stamping grounds of the eldar. She died in one of their raids. You swore... first to destroy them and then, as you grew, to understand the strange species that had robbed you so. And that's why you wanted this mission: you craved a chance to contact your nemesis. You want this, Lilith.'

She sank and sat hard on the onyx floor beside Eon Kull's corpse.

Muon Nol lifted her up. 'You are Lileath. You can do what the farseer would have done. Close the gate, Lileath. Take us back to Dolthe forever.'

Lilith looked at Gaunt. Gaunt noticed for the last time how beautiful she was. 'Do it... That is why you came.'

She took his shoulders, hugged him briefly and then pulled away to look into his face.

'It would have been interesting, commissar.'

'Fascinating, inquisitor. Now do your job.'

THEY SAID GOODBYE. Mkoll said goodbye to Eiloni, Caffran said goodbye to Laria. The Ghosts said goodbye to Tanith and the Blueblood bade farewell to Ignix Majeure.

A cold light, hard as vacuum, bright as diamond, pierced the sky above the ruin, evaporating the storm in little more than a minute. Seventy-five per cent of the astropaths

aboard the Imperial fleet elements in orbit suffered catastrophic seizures and died. The others passed out. The
psychic backwash of the event was felt light years away.

The spell ended as the Way finally closed. The eldar left
Monthax forever, and took Lilith back to Dolthe craftworld
with them. She closed the Way, as she had, perhaps, been
born to do. Once the Way was shut, closely-targeted orbital
bombardments incinerated the massed forces of the
enemy.

The jungles of Monthax burned.

ONCE THE bombardment stopped, Gaunt led his Ghosts and
the Volpone unit back towards the line. The storm was dead
and pale sunlight fell on them. The world around them was
a wasted desert of baked mud and burned vegetation.

The only man Gaunt had lost in the final assault had been
Lerod, taken by a remarkably lucky glancing shot off the
roof of the eldar temple.

IBRAM GAUNT SLEPT for a day and half in his command cabin.
His fatigue was total. He woke when Raglon brought him
directives from Lord Militant General Bulledin, orchestrat-
ing the Imperial withdrawal from Monthax.

He put on his full dress uniform, adjusted his cap and
went out into the smoky sunlight to oversee the Tanith as
they packed up and prepared for evacuation. The vast troop
transports cast flickering shadows across the lines as they
came in, droning down from high orbit.

Gaunt could sense the feeling of the men: weariness,
aches, the joy of a great victory somehow dulled and strange.

He found Milo, sat alone on the side steps of the aban-
doned infirmary, cleaning his lasgun. Gaunt sat down next
to him.

'Odd the way things work out, isn't it?' Milo said bluntly.

Gaunt nodded.

'I think it was a good thing, though.'

'What?'

'The eldar trick. Good for us. Good for the Ghosts.'

'Explain?' Gaunt asked.

'I know how I feel. I've heard the men talking too. This was Tanith again for us, for you too, I think. Deep down I think we all hate the fact we never got a chance to fight for Tanith. Some are blatant about it. Men like... like Major Rawne. Others can understand why we had to leave, why you ordered us out. But they don't like it.'

He looked around at Gaunt.

'Just a mind trick maybe, but for a few hours there forty or so of us got to fight for Tanith, got to fight for our world, got the chance to do what we'd always been cheated out of. It felt good. Even now I know it was a lie, it still feels good. It... exorcised a few ghosts.'

Gaunt smiled. The boy's pun was awful, but he was right. The Ghosts of Tanith had laid their own ghosts to rest here. They would be stronger for it.

And so would he, he realised. They were *his* ghosts after all.

Gaunt's Ghosts.

# ABOUT THE AUTHOR

*Dan Abnett* lives and works in Maidstone, Kent, in England. Well known for his comic work, he has written everything from the *Mr Men* to the *X-Men* in the last decade, including *Legion of Superheroes* and *Superman* for DC Comics, and *Sinister Dexter* and *The VCs* for 2000 AD.

His work for the Black Library includes the popular strips *Lone Wolves*, *Titan* and *Darkblade*, the best-selling Gaunt's Ghosts novels, the acclaimed Inquisitor Eisenhorn trilogy and the novels *Ravenor* and *Riders of the Dead*. He was voted Best Writer Now at the National Comic Awards 2003.

More Warhammer 40,000 from the Black Library

# THE EISENHORN TRILOGY
## by Dan Abnett

*IN THE 41ST MILLENNIUM, the Inquisition hunts the shadows for humanity's most terrible foes – rogue psykers, xenos and daemons. Few Inquisitors can match the notoriety of Gregor Eisenhorn, whose struggle against the forces of evil stretches across the centuries.*

### XENOS

THE ELIMINATION OF the dangerous recidivist Murdon Eyclone is just the beginning of a new case for Gregor Eisenhorn. A trail of clues leads the Inquisitor and his retinue to the very edge of human-controlled space in the hunt for a lethal alien artefact – the dread Necroteuch.

### MALLEUS

A GREAT IMPERIAL triumph to celebrate the success of the Ophidian Campaign ends in disaster when thirty-three rogue psykers escape and wreak havoc. Eisenhorn's hunt for the sinister power behind this atrocity becomes a desperate race against time as he himself is declared hereticus by the Ordo Malleus.

### HERETICUS

WHEN A BATTLE with an ancient foe turns deadly, Inquisitor Eisenhorn is forced to take terrible measures to save the lives of himself and his companions. But how much can any man deal with Chaos before turning into the very thing he is sworn to destroy?

More Warhammer 40,000 from the Black Library

# THE GAUNT'S GHOSTS SERIES
## by Dan Abnett

IN THE NIGHTMARE *future of Warhammer 40,000, mankind is beset by relentless foes. Commissar Ibram Gaunt and his regiment the Tanith First-and-Only must fight as much against the inhuman enemies of mankind as survive the bitter internal rivalries of the Imperial Guard.*

## *THE FOUNDING*

### FIRST AND ONLY

GAUNT AND HIS men find themselves at the forefront of a fight to win back control of a vital Imperial forge world from the forces of Chaos, but find far more than they expected in the heart of the Chaos-infested manufactories.

### GHOSTMAKER

NICKNAMED THE GHOSTS, Commissar Gaunt's regiment of stealth troops move from world from world, playing a vital part in the crusade to liberate the Sabbat Worlds from Chaos.

### NECROPOLIS

ON THE SHATTERED world of Verghast, Gaunt and his Ghosts find themselves embroiled within a deadly civil war as a mighty hive-city is besieged by an unrelenting foe. When treachery from within brings the city's defences crashing down, rivalry and corruption threaten to bring the Ghosts to the brink of defeat.

# THE SAINT

### HONOUR GUARD

COMMISSAR GAUNT AND the Ghosts are back in action on Hagia, a vital shrine-world of the deepest tactical and spiritual importance. As a mighty Chaos fleet approaches the planet, Gaunt and his men are sent on a desperate mission to safeguard some of the Imperium's most holy relics: the remains of the ancient saint who first led humanity to these stars.

### THE GUNS OF TANITH

COLONEL-COMMISSAR GAUNT and the Tanith First-and-Only must recapture Phantine, a world rich in promethium but so ruined by pollution that the only way to attack is via a dangerous – and untried – aerial assault. Pitted against deadly opposition and a lethal environment, how can Gaunt and his men possibly survive?

### STRAIGHT SILVER

ON THE BATTLEFIELDS of Aexe Cardinal, the struggling forces of the Imperial Guard are locked in a deadly stalemate with the dark armies of Chaos. Commissar Ibram Gaunt and his regiment, the Tanith First-and-Only, are thrown headlong into this living hell of trench warfare, where death from lethal artillery is always just a moment away.

### SABBAT MARTYR

A NEW WAVE OF HOPE has been unleashed in the Chaos- infested Sabbat system when a girl claiming to be the reincarnation of Saint Sabbat is revealed. But the dark forces of Chaos are not oblivious to this new threat and when they order their most lethal assassins to kill her, it falls to Commissar Gaunt and his men to form the last line of defence!

Inferno! is the Black Library's high-octane fiction magazi
which throws you headlong into the worlds of Warhamm
From the dark, orc-infested forests of the Old World to
grim battlefields of the war-torn far future,
Inferno! magazine is packed with storming
tales of heroism and carnage.

Featuring work by awesome wri
such as:

- DAN ABNETT
- BEN COUNTER
- WILLIAM KING
- GRAHAM MCNEILL
- GAV THORPE

and lots more!

Published every two months,
Inferno! magazine brings the
grim worlds of Warhammer
to life.